Praise for SHERI S. TEPPER'S SIX MOON DANCE

"Tepper takes the traditional icons of fantasy, restores their resonance, and makes them her own."
Minneapolis Star-Tribune

"Tepper combines a treatise on the politics of gender with a transcendent celebration of love and renewal. Always breaking new ground with her imaginative forays into speculative fiction, the author weaves the individual stories of her characters into an elegant design. Highly recommended."
Library Journal

"Tepper is an extremely gifted storyteller with a particular talent for constructing believably lived-in environments . . . SIX MOON DANCE is the unmistable work of one of SF's most distinctive voices . . . Its vivid setting and imaginative complexity continue to reveal the unique fecundity of invention that has become this author's most delightful trademark."
Locus

"Amazing . . . By the time you finish SIX MOON DANCE, you might find yourself looking at the world in a different light . . . No matter how bizarre the situation, she maintains the credibility that keeps readers mesmerized . . . Tepper attacks our most basic beliefs and knocks the supports out from under them."
SF Site

"Challenging . . . Tepper has tremendous fun . . . even when her purpose is deadly serious . . . The upshot won't just raise your consciousness, it'll blow the top right off."
Kirkus Reviews

Other Avon Books by
Sheri S. Tepper

THE FAMILY TREE

SHERI S. TEPPER

SIX MOON DANCE

This is a work of fiction. Names, characters, places and incidents either are the product of the author's imagination or are used fictitiously. Any resemblance to actual events, locales, organizations, or persons, living or dead, is entirely coincidental and beyond the intent of either the author or the publisher.

AVON BOOKS, INC.
1350 Avenue of the Americas
New York, New York 10019

Inside cover author photograph by Charles N. Brown/*Locus*
Library of Congress Catalog Card Number: 98-11918
ISBN: 0-380-79198-6
www.avonbooks.com/eos

First Avon Eos Paperback Printing: April 1999
First Avon Eos Hardcover Printing: August 1998

Printed in the U.S.A.

WCD 10 9 8 7 6 5 4 3 2 1

"What matters it how far we go?" his scaly friend replied.
"There is another shore, you know, upon the other side. . . .
Then turn not pale, beloved snail, but come and join the dance.
Will you, won't you, will you, won't you, will you join the dance?"

—*Alice's Adventures in Wonderland,*
LEWIS CARROLL

Cast of Characters

Abbreviated list of characters, in order of appearance (walk-ons not included).

Mankind Newholmians:

Mouche	Moosh	A consort trainee
Ornery	OR-nery	A farm girl turned seaman
Madame Genevois	Gen-eh-VWA	Consort House operator
Simon		Her assistant
Bane and Dyre Dutter		Two delinquents
Ashes		A leftover
the Machinist		Another
D'Jevier	Duh ZHEV-yai	A hag
Onsofruct	AWN-so-FROOT	Another hag
Marool Mantelby	Mah-ROOL	A sex maniac
Calvy g'Valdet	gh-vahl-DET	A man of business
Estif g'Bayoar	Es-TEEF g'BAY-wahr	Another
Myrphee g'Mindon	g'MIN-don	Another
Slab g'Tupoar	g'too-POUR	The antepenultimate
Bin g'Kiffle	g'KIFF-el	The penultimate
Sym g'Sinsanoi	g' SIHN-san-oy	And the last

Native Newholmians:

The Corojum	Koh-roh-JOOM	A solitary survivor

Joggiwagga	Jog-ee-WAH-gah	Heavy equipment operator
Timmy	short for Tim-Tim	Useful fingers
Flowing Green		A particular finger
Eiger	EYE-gher	Four eyed bird
Bofusdiaga	Boh-FOOS-di-AH-gah	Current planetary manager
Corojumi	Koh-roh-JOO-mi	Creative artists
Fauxi-dizalonz	FOW-shee DIZ-ah-lawnz	A gender bender
Kaorugi	Cow-RUE-ji	Current planetary subconscious

Extraplanetary persons:

Ellin Voy		A dancer, female
The Questioner		A device
Gandro Bao	BAH-oh	A male female dancer
The Quaggima	KWA-gi-mah	Who arrived a long time ago

Together with various gardeners, livestock, supernumeraries, haggers, worshippers, travelers, members of an entourage, a representative of the Brotherhood of Interstellar Trade, ship's crewmembers, family members, spouses, and monsters.

I

On Newholme: Mouche

"It's all right," Mouche's mother said. "Next time we'll have a girl."

Mouche knew of this because his father told him. "She said it was all right. She said next time . . ."

But there had been no next time. Why the inscrutable Hagions decided such things was unknown. Some persons profited in life, producing daughter after daughter; some lost in life, producing son after son; some hung in the balance as Eline and Darbos did, having one son at the Temple, and then a daughter born dead at the Temple, and then no other child.

It was neither a profit nor a great loss, but still, a loss. Even a small loss sustained over time can bleed a family: so theirs bled. Only a smutch of blood, a mere nick of a vein, a bit more out than in, this year and then the next, and the one after that, a gradual anemia, more weakening than deadly—the heifer calves sold instead of kept, the ewe lambs sold, the repairs to the water mill deferred, then deferred again. Darbos had taken all he had inherited and added to that what he could borrow as his dowry for a wife who would help him establish a family line, to let him wear the honorable cockade, to be known as g'Darbos and be addressed as "Family Man." He had planned to repay the loan with advances against his share of the dowries paid for his own daughters. Instead, he had paid for Eline with the price of the heifer calves, with the ruin of the mill. Her family had profited, and though families lucky enough to have several daughters often gave those daughters a share of the dowry they brought in (a generosity Darbos had rather counted on), Eline's parents had not seen fit to do so. Still, Eline's daughters would have made it all worth while, if there had been daughters.

Their lack made for a life not precisely sad, but not joyous, either. There was no absence of care, certainly. Eline was not a savage. There was no personal blame. Darbos had created the sperm, he was the one responsible, everyone knew that. But then, some receptacles were said to reject the female, so perhaps Eline shared the fault. No matter. Blaming, as the Hags opined, was a futile exercise engaged in only by fools. What one did was bow, bow again, and get on.

So, each New Year at the Temple, while g'Darbos waited outside with the other Family Men, all of them sneaking chaff under their veils and whispering with one another in defiance of propriety, Eline bowed and bowed again. Then she got on, though the getting did not halt the slow leaking away of substance by just so much as it took to feed and clothe one boy, one boy with a boy's appetite and a boy's habit of unceasing growth. As for shoes, well, forget shoes. If he had had sisters, then perhaps Eline would have bought him shoes. In time, she might even have provided the money for him to dower in a wife. If he had had sisters.

"If bought no wife," so the saying went, so forget the wife. More urgent than the need for a wife was the need for daily grain, for a coat against the wind, for fire on the winter's hearth and tight roof against the storm, none of which came free. Eline and Darbos were likely to lose all.

After nine barren years, it was unlikely there would be more children, and the couple had themselves to think of. *Who can not fatten on daughters must fatten on labor,* so it was said, and the little farm would barely fatten two. It would not stretch to three.

On the day Mouche was twelve, when the festive breakfast was over and the new shirt admired and put on, Papa walked with him into the lower pasture where an old stump made a pleasant sun-gather for conversation, and there Papa told Mouche what the choices were. Mouche might be cut, and if he survived it, sold to some wealthy family as a chatron playmate for their children, a safe servant for the daughters, someone to fetch and carry and neaten up. The fee would be large if he lived, but if he died, there would be no fee at all.

Or, an alternative. Madame Genevois—who had a House in Sendoph—had seen Mouche in the marketplace, and she'd made an offer for him. While the fee was less than for a chatron, it would be paid in advance, no matter how he turned out.

Mama had followed them down to the field and she stood leaning on the fence, taking no part in the conversation. It was not a woman's place, after all, to enlighten her son to the facts of life. Still, she was near enough to hear him when he cried:

"Trained for a Hunk, Papa? A Hunk?"

"Where did you learn that word?" said Mama, spinning around and glaring at him. "We do not talk filth in this family. . . ."

"Shh, shh," said Darbos, tears in the corners of his eyes. "The word is the right word, Madam. When we are driven to this dirty end, let us not quibble about calling it what it is."

At which point Mama grew very angry and went swiftly away toward the house. Papa followed her a little way, and Mouche heard him saying, "Oh, I know he's only a boy, Eline, but I've grown fond of him. . . ."

Mouche had seen Hunks, of course—who had not?—riding through the marketplace, their faces barely veiled behind gauzy stuff, their clothing all aglitter with gold lace and gems, their hats full of plumes, the swords they fenced with sparkling like rippled water. Even through the veils one could see their hair was curled and flowing upon their shoulders, not bound back as a common man would need it to be, out of the way of the work. Their shirts were open, too, and in the gap their skin glowed and their muscles throbbed. Hunks did not work. They smiled, they dimpled, they complimented, they dueled and rode and wrestled, they talked of wonderful things that ordinary people knew little or nothing of. Poetry. And theater. And wine.

Mouche wondered if they talked of the sea, which is what Mouche talked of, to himself when there was no one else by to speak to, or to Papa, when Papa was in the mood. Not to Mama. Mama did not understand such things, even though it was she who had given him the book of sea stories, and she who had told him about going to Gilesmarsh when she was a girl, and how the shore had looked and smelled, and how the little boats came in full of the fishes that swam there, and how the ships sailed out and away into wonderful places. The seamen didn't even wear veils, except in port. Mama didn't mention that, but the book did. Of course, out at sea, there were no women to be tempted and corrupted by the sight of wanton hairs sprouting on a male face, so veils weren't really needed.

Mouche's dream of going to sea when he was old enough was not pure foolishness. The books were full of stories about boys who ran away to sea and ships that took them, sometimes with no apprenticeship fee. Poor as Mouche's family was, he knew it would have to be without a fee. He would have to have something else to recommend him, like knowing things about ropes and nets and repairs and suchlike. He asked his teacher if he could get Mouche a book about all that—which he did, and followed it with others when Mouche was through with the first one. Mouche practiced knots in his bed at night, and learned all the words for the parts of the ship and the pieces of the rigging and how it all worked. "Seaman Mouche," he said to himself on the edge of sleep. "Captain Mouche." And he dreamed.

But now it seemed he was not to go to sea. Not even without a fee. He was to be a Hunk. Hunks did not go to sea, did not pull at nets, did not look out to far horizons and distant ports, did not smell of fish. They smelled of perfume. They pranced like ponies. And they fucked, of course. Everyone knew that. That's what they were for. Though they did not father, they fucked.

Some very wealthy women were known to have several of them. When a woman accepted a dowry from some man she did not know—might never have seen, might grow to detest—thereby making him the sole begetter of her future children, it was her right to include in the contract a provision that after five or seven or ten years, whether she had any daughters or not, she was to have at least one Hunk. This was common knowledge. It was also common knowledge that many of the best-trained Hunks came from House Genevois in Sendoph. Polite people didn't call them Hunks, of course, Mama was right about that. They called them "Consorts," but it meant the same thing.

"Consort Mouche," he said to himself, seeing how it sounded. It sounded dirty, no matter what word he used. It sounded like a teacher saying, "Take your hands out of your pants. What do you think you're doing? Practicing to be a Consort?"

It sounded like teasing on the school ground, Fenarde saying, "Mouche can't ever get married. Mouche will have to be a Hunky-monkey." Which was very dirty talk indeed. All the girls stood and giggled and twitched their bottoms at Mouche and said, "You can be *my* Hunky-monkey, Mouche. *I'll* put you in my contract." And then they started kissing Mouche and touching him on his behind. Such evil behavior got the girls a talking to about courtesy and treating males respectfully, because they were not as resilient as girls and their minds weren't as flexible, and Fenarde got a mouthful of ashes from the schoolroom hearth for starting the whole thing. Mouche merely got a brief lecture. Though the teacher was patient, he didn't have much time to waste on boys.

"Girls always talk that way," he said. "They have no masculine modesty. You must behave demurely and simply ignore it, pretend not to hear it. When they pinch you or rub up against you, get away from them as soon as possible. And take no notice! That's the proper way to behave, and it's time you learned it." Though how you could feel those intrusive hands on you and take no notice, the teacher did not say.

The night after Papa had told him about House Genevois, Mouche heard a tap at his door, so soft and so late he almost thought he had dreamed it until Papa slipped in and sat on the edge of his cot.

"My boy," he said, "a man's life is never easy. We are the weaker sex, as everyone knows, though sometimes at the end of a long, hard day loading hay I think our weakness is more a matter of fable than reality. Still, this is the world we live in, and we must live, as the Hags say, either with it or against it. I've come to say some things to you that I didn't want to say with your mama there." He stroked Mouche's hair away from his forehead, looking at him sadly.

"Yes, Papa."

"This decision is much against my inclination, Mouche. You were to be the son of g'Darbos, our unique line. I had such plans for you, for us. . . ." His voice trailed off sadly, and he stared out the small window at two of the littler moons just rising above the horizon to join a third, bigger one in the sky. "But seemingly it is not to be. There will be no g'Darbos lineage, no immortality of the family, no descendants to remember me and honor the name. Even so, I would not make this decision lightly; I had to find out what kind of life we'd be sending you to. I didn't tell your Mama, but when I was last in Sendoph, I went into House Genevois, by the back door, and when I explained myself, I was allowed to talk to some of the . . . young men."

Mouche wriggled uncomfortably.

"I found out, for example, that they eat very well indeed. Far better than we do. I found out that the maximum contract for a Hu—a Consort is about twenty years, beginning as soon as schooling is completed, somewhere between the eighteenth and twenty-fourth year. The standard contract for men from House Genevois provides one third the original payment set aside for your retirement, plus one third of the downpayment on your contract, plus half the payments to House Genevois every year of service, all invested at interest to provide you an annuity. All Consorts receive wages from their patronesses, plus tips, many of them, and even after they're retired, ex-Consorts can freelance for additional profit. There are ex-Consorts in the city who are almost as well respected as Family Men."

"But it isn't the sea," said Mouche, feeling tears, blinking rapidly to keep them from running over. "If I go to sea and make my fortune, I could send you money."

"No, Mouche. It isn't the sea, but it's now, when we have need, not years from now when it's too late. If you can set aside your dream of the sea, being a Consort has few drawbacks. Well, there's the possibility of being killed or scarred in a duel, but any farmer might be killed or scarred. The men I spoke with said Consort dueling can be avoided by a fast tongue and a ready wit, neither of which can help farmers avoid accidents. And, so far as I can tell, the shame that attaches to the candidate's family goes away after a time. One grows used to saying, 'My son? Oh, he's gone to work for a contractor in the city.' " Papa sighed, having put the best face on it he could.

"How much will you get for me, Papa?"

"I won't get it. Your Mama will. It's twenty gold vobati, my boy, after deducting your annuity share, but Mama has agreed to use it on the farm. That's the only way I'd give permission for her to sell you, you being my eldest." Eldest sons, as everyone knew, were exempt from sale unless the father agreed, though younger ones, being supernumerary, could be sold by their mothers—if she could find a buyer—as soon as they turned seven. Supernumes were miners and haulers and sailors; they were the ones who worked as farmhands or wood cutters or ran away to become Wilderneers.

Still, twenty vobati was a large sum of money. More than he could make as a seaman in a long, long time. "Is it as much a daughter would bring in?" Mouche whispered.

"Not if she were a healthy, good-looking and intelligent girl, but it isn't bad. It's enough to guarantee Mama and Papa food for their age."

Mouche took a deep breath and tried to be brave. He would have had to be brave to be a seaman, so let him be brave anyhow. "I would rather be a Consort than a playmate, Papa."

"I thought you might," said Papa with a weepy smile.

Papa had a tender heart. He was always shedding a tear for this thing or that thing. Every time the earth shook and the great fire mounts of the scarp belched into the sky, Papa worried about the people in the way of it. Not Mama, who just snorted that people who built in the path of pyroclastic flow must eat ashes and like it, and with all the old lava about, one could not mistake where that was likely to be.

Papa went on, "Tell you true, Mouche—but if you tell your Mama, I'll say you lie—many a time when the work is hard and the sun is hot, and I'm covered with bites from jiggers and fleas, and my back hurts from loading hay . . . well, I've thought what it would be like, being a Hunk. Warm baths, boy. And veils light enough to really see through. It would be fun to see the city rather than mere shadows of it. And there's wine. We had wine at our wedding, your mama and me. They tell me one gets to like it." He sighed again, lost in his own foundered dream, then came to himself with a start.

"Well, words enough! If you are agreeable, we will go to Sendoph tomorrow, for the interview."

Considering the choices, Mouche agreed. It was Papa who took him. Mama could not lower herself to go into House Genevois as a seller rather than a buyer. That would be shameful indeed.

Sendoph was as Sendoph always was, noisy and smelly and full of invisible people everywhere one looked. Though the city had sewers, they were always clogging up, particularly in the dry season when the streams were low, and the irregular cobbles magnified the sound of every hoof and every wooden or iron-rimmed wheel to make clattering canyons between the tall houses and under the overhanging balconies. The drivers were all supernumes who had to work at whatever was available, and they could not see clearly through their veils. The vendors were equally handicapped. Veils, as the men often said, were the very devil. They could not go without, however, or they'd be thought loose or promiscuous or, worse, disrespectful of women. There were always many Haggers standing about, servants of the Hags, who were servants of the Hagions, the Goddesses, and they were swift to punish bad behavior.

The town was split in two by ancient lava tubes, now eroded into troughs, that guided the northward flow of the River Giles. Genevois House stood on the street nearest west and parallel to the river, its proud western facade decked with tall shuttered windows and bronze double doors graven with images of dueling men. The south side, along Bridge Street all the way to Brewer's Bridge, was less imposing, merely a line of grilled windows interrupted in the middle by one stout provisioner's gate opening into the service courtyard. The east side, on the bank of the river itself, showed only a blank wall bracketed at each end by a stubby tower of ornamental brickwork around fretted windows set with colored glass. This wall was pierced by an ancient gate through which a rotting tongue of wharf was thrust into the river, a tongue all slimed with filth and ribboned with long festoons of algae. Parts of House Genevois plus the courtyard walls, the wharf, and the bronze doors, dated back to the lost settlement, the colony from Thor that had vanished, along with its ship, long before the second settlers arrived.

The door where Mouche and his papa were admitted was an inconspicuous entrance off Bridge Street, near the front corner. Inside was the parlor of the welcome suite, where Madame Genevois kept them waiting a good hour. Through the closed door Mouche and Papa could hear her voice, now from here, then from there, admonishing, encouraging. When she came into the interview room at last, her sleeves were turned up to her elbows and her forehead was beaded with perspiration. She rolled the sleeves down and buttoned them, took a linen handkerchief from the cache-box on her worktable, and patted her forehead dry.

"Well, Family Man; well, Mouche," she said. "I'm sorry to have kept you waiting, but we have a new fencing master who is inclined to be too rigorous with the beginners and too lax with the advanced class. It is easier to bully novices than it is to test competent swordsmen, but I have told him I will not tolerate it. He is paid to exert himself, and exert himself he shall." She patted her forehead once again, saying in a matter-of-fact voice: "Take off your clothes, boy, and let me look at you."

Papa had warned Mouche about this, but he still turned red from embarrassment. He took everything off but his crotcher and his sandals, which seemed to make him bare enough for her purposes when she came poking at him, like a farmer judging a pig.

"Your hands and feet are in terrible condition," she said. "Your hair is marvelous in color and fairly good in shape. Your eyes and face are good. The leg and back muscles are all wrong, of course. Farm work does not create a balanced body."

"As Madame says," Papa murmured, while Mouche shifted from foot to foot and tried to figure out what to do with his hands.

Madame jerked her head, a quick nod. "Well, all in all, I will stick to my bargain. The hands and feet will be soaked and scrubbed and brought into good appearance. The muscles will yield to proper exercise. A score ten vobati, I said, did I not? A score for the wife, ten in keeping for the boy."

"As Madame recalls," Papa murmured again.

"And is his mother prepared to leave him now?"

Papa looked up then, his eyes filling. He had not planned on this, and Mouche pitied him even more than he pitied himself.

"Can I not have time to say good-bye, Madame?" he begged.

"If your mother allows, of course, boy. Take two days. Be here first thing in the morning on fifthday. First thing, now."

She unbuttoned her wrists and rolled up her sleeves once more, giving him a look that was almost kindly as he struggled into his clothes.

"You're coming into good hands, Mouche. We honor our annuities, which some Houses only claim to provide. We don't sell to sadists. And you won't hate the life. You'll miss Mama and Papa, yes, but you'll get on." She turned away, then back, to add, "No pets, boy. You know that."

"Yes, Madame." He gulped a little. He no longer had a pet, though the thought of Duster could still make him cry.

She asked, almost as an afterthought, "Can you read, Mouche?"

"Yes, Madame." The village school wasn't much, but he had gone every evening after chores, for five long years. That was when he was expected to be the heir, of course. Heirs went to school, though supernumes often didn't. Mouche could read and print a good hand and do his numbers well enough not to mistake four vibela for a vobati.

"Good. That will shorten your training by a good deal."

Then she was gone from them, and they too were gone from her, and soon they were alone and Papa had dropped his veil and the dust of the road was puffing up between their toes as they walked the long way south, on the west side of River Giles, to the tributary stream that tumbled down from the western terraces through their own farm. All the long valley of the Giles was farmland. On the east, where the grain and pasture farmers held the land, ancient lava tubes lay side by side, lined up north and south like straws in a broom, their tops worn away, their sides rasped into mere welts by the windblown soil, each tube eastward a bit higher than the last, making a shallow flight that climbed all the way to the Ratback Range at the foot of the scarp. On the west, where the g'Darbos farm was, the terraces stepped steeply up to the mountains, and the fields were small and flinty, good for olives and grapes.

"Why are girls worth so much, Papa?" asked Mouche, who had always known they were but had never wondered over the whys of it until now.

"Because they are more capable than men," said Papa.

"Why are they?"

"It's their hormones. They have hormones that change, day to day, so that for some parts of every month they are emotional and for some parts they are coldly logical, and for some parts they are intuitive, and they may bring all these various sensitivities to meet any problem. We poor fellows, Mouche, we have hormones that are pretty much the same all the time. We push along steadily enough, often in a fine frenzy, but we haven't the flexibility of women."

"But why is that, Papa?"

"It's our genetics, boy. All a Family Man has to do is one act, taking only a few moments if the mama is willing and a little longer if she is not." Papa flushed. "So our hormones are what might be called simple-minded. They equip us to do *that thing*, and that's all. Used to be men attached a lot of importance to *that thing*, though it's something every mouse can do just as well. Women, though, they have to bear, and birth, and suckle, and—except among the monied folk—they also have to work alongside the Family Man in the business, tending and rearing. They have to work and plan, morn till night. So, their hormones are more complex, as they have to be."

"And men get in more trouble, too." Mouche was quoting his teacher.

"Well, yes, sometimes, in some men, our fine frenzy begets a lustful or murderous violence, and we tend to become contentious over little or nothing. But, as the Hags teach, 'If you would have breathing space, stay out of one another's face,' which is one reason we wear veils, not to threaten one another, so we may stay out of trouble and under control."

"I thought it was so the women couldn't see us."

"The *reason* they mustn't see us, Mouche, is that we must not tempt females, or stir their insatiable lusts, for that leads to disorder and mis-mothering. We are the weaker sex, my boy. It is why we must bid high for wives to take us, to show we have learned discipline and self-control."

"Darn ol' hormones," sulked Mouche. "Girls get all the luck."

"Well, hormones aren't the only reason," Papa comforted him. "Women are also valuable because they're fewer than men. Only one girl is born alive for every two boys, as we know to our sorrow."

"Then not every man may have a wife, may he, Papa?" Mouche knew this was so, but at this juncture, he thought it wise to have the information verified. "Even if he has a dowry?"

"Only about half, my boy. The oldest sons, usually. The younger ones must keep hand-maids." Which was an old joke among men, one Mouche already understood. Papa wiped his face with the tail of his veil and went on, "Once, long ago, I heard a story teller's tale about the world from which our people originally came, that was Old Earth, where men were fewer than women. . . ."

"That's impossible."

"The storyteller said it was because many males died young, in wars and gang fights and in dangerous explorations. Anyhow, in his tale, men were worth much more than women. Women sought men as chickens seek grain, gathering around them. A man could father children on several women, if he liked, without even dowering for them."

"Fairy stories," said Mouche. "That's what that is. Who would want a woman you didn't dower for?" Everyone knew what such women would be like. Old or ugly or both. And probably infertile. And sickly. And certainly stupid, if they didn't even bother to get a good dowry first. Or even maybe invisible. "Are there more invisible men than there are women?" he asked, the words slipping out before he thought.

Papa stopped in his tracks, and his hand went back to slap, though it did not descend on Mouche's evil mouth. "Which only a fool would say," Papa grated instead, thrusting his head forward in warning. "You're too old to tell stories of invisible people or see such fairies and bug-a-boos as babies do, Mouche. You could be blue-bodied for it." Mouche ducked his head and flushed, not having to ask what blue-bodying was. When a supernume was incorrigible and his father or master or boss or commander could do nothing with him, he was dyed blue all over and cast naked into the streets for the dogs to bite and the flies to crawl upon, and no man might feed him or help him or employ him thereafter. People who died foolishly were said to be "independent as a blue body."

Papa hadn't finished with him. "Such talk could bring the Questioner down on us! Do you want Newholme to end up like Roquamb III? Do you?"

Stung, Mouche cried, "I don't know how it ended up, Papa. I don't know anything about the Questioner."

"Well, boy, let me tell you, you'd be sorry if words of yours reached *her* ears! As for Roquamb III, well, *she* took care of those poor souls. Imagine what that would be like. The whole world dying around you, and you knowing it was your fault!" Papa glared at him for a moment, then started down the road again, leaving Mouche thoroughly confused and not much enlightened. He'd been told something about the Questioner at school, but at the moment, Mouche couldn't remember what.

He decided to talk about something else during the rest of the trip, something with no danger to it. The dust puffing up between his toes gave him inspiration.

"Why do we have to walk everywhere, Papa? Or go behind a horse? Why don't we have engines? Like in the books?"

"Interstellar travel is very expensive," said Papa, grateful for the change of subject. "Our ancestors on our Motherworld saved up for centuries to send off our settlement, and the settlers had to pick and choose carefully what they would bring with them. They brought just enough rations to keep them until the first crops could be harvested. They brought seed and fertilized stock ova and an omni-uterus to grow the first calves and foals and piglets and lambs, and an incubator to hatch the first chickens.

"Our population was small and our first generations tended flocks and herds and planted crops and cut wood and quarried stone, and the next generation built up the towns, and searched for metal ores and rare biologicals to build up our trade. Then came sawmills along the river, and then the first smelter and the little railroad that runs from the mines to Naibah, and so on. Now we are almost ready to become industrial."

"It sure seems slow," mumbled Mouche.

"Well, it's been slower for us than for some, partly because we have so few women, and partly because Newholme has no coal or oil. We hadn't exactly counted on that. Every other planet that's had life for millions of years has had fossil fuels, but not Newholme."

"I know," Mouche muttered. He really did know all this; he'd learned it in school. Sometimes he thought it would be easier if the schools didn't talk about life on Old Earth or on the older settled worlds where people had replicators and transporters and all the robotic industries to support them. If he didn't know there were any such things as transporters and replicators, walking to Sendoph or working in the garden wouldn't seem so hard. It would just be natural.

That night was a good supper, better than any they'd had in a long time. The next day, too, as though Papa could not let him go without stuffing him first. Like a goose, Mouche thought. Off to the market, but fattened, first. Between these unexpectedly lavish meals, he had time to say good-bye to most everything that mattered. The pigs. The geese. The milk cow and her calf. With the money paid for Mouche, the family could get by without selling the heifer calf, and when she grew, they would have more milk to sell. With the money paid for Mouche, the mill could be repaired, and there'd be money coming in from grinding the neighbor's grain and pressing their grapes and olives. With the money paid for Mouche. . . .

It was only fair, he told himself, desperately trying to

be reasonable and not to cry. If he'd been a girl, he'd have brought in a great dowry to Eline and Darbos. Just as the money paid for Eline had gone to her family, so money paid for a daughter would go to this family. But that would be honorable, which this was not. Buying a Hunk was honorable enough, it was only selling one that wasn't. Still, getting a good bid for a girl was just good sense. Why should getting a good bid for a boy be different?

Mouche said farewell to pasture and woodlot and barn, farewell to the cat and her kittens, allowed the freedom of the loft and a ration of milk in return for ridding the granary of the Newholmian equivalent of mice. And finally he went to Duster's grave and knelt down to say good-bye, dropping more than a few tears on old Duster who had been his best and only friend, who had died in such a terrible way. He could have had one of Duster's pups from the neighbors—Old Duster had been an assiduous visitor next door—but there had been no food to feed another dog, said Mama. Well. Duster had left a numerous family behind. He was g'Duster, for sure, and long remembered.

Then it was farewell to Mama on the last evening and a long night listening to Papa cry in the night, and very early on the morning of the fifth, before it was light, he and red-eyed Papa were on the road once more, back to Sendoph, Mouche carrying only a little bag with his books inside, and Duster's collar, and the picture of a sailing ship he had drawn at school. Papa didn't have to put his veils on until they were far down the road, and he spent most of the time until then wiping his eyes.

When they came to House Genevois, Mouche asked, in a kind of panic, "Can we walk down to the river, Papa?"

His papa gave him a sideways tilt of the head, but he walked on past House Genevois, down Bridge Street past the courtyard entrance, on to the corner where one of the little green-patinaed copper-domed towers topped the wall above the riverbank, and thence out over the stone arches of Brewer's Bridge itself while the invisible people moved back and forth like little mud-colored rivers running in all directions, their flow breaking around the human pedestrians without touching them, those pedestrians looking over the heads of the invisibles and never lowering their gaze. The breweries stood across the water, four of them, and on the nearest stubby tower a weathervane shifted and glittered, its head pointing north, toward the sea.

The river was low and sullen in this season, dark with ash from the firemounts to the south and east, with the islets of gray foam slipping past so slowly it was hard to believe they were moving at all. Between the water mills, the banks were thickly bristled with reed beds, green and aswarm with birdy-things, and far down the river a smoke plume rose where a wood burning sternwheel steamboat made its slow way toward them against the flow. Down there, Mouche thought, was Naibah, the capital, lost in the mists of the north, and beyond it the port of Gilesmarsh.

"The sea's down there," he whispered.

"No reason you can't go to sea after you retire," said Papa, hugging him close. "Maybe even buy a little boat of your own."

"Ship," said Mouche, imagining breakers and surf and the cry of waterkeens. "Ship."

His thoughts were interrupted by a rumble, a shivering. At first Mouche thought it was just him, shaking with sadness, but it wasn't him for the railing quivered beneath his fingers and the paving danced beneath his feet.

"Off the bridge," said Papa, breathlessly.

They ran from the bridge, standing at the end of it, waiting for the spasm to end. Far to the east, the scarp was suddenly aglow, and great billows of gray moved up into the sky, so slowly they were like balloons rising. Down the river, one of the legs of the rotted wharf gave way, tipping it into the flow. Everything was too quiet until the shaking happened again, and yet again, with tiles falling from roofs and people screaming.

Then it stopped. The birdy-things began to cheep, people began to talk to one another, though their voices were still raised to a panicky level. Even the usually silent invisible people murmured in their flow, almost like water. The ominous cloud went on rising in the east, but the glow faded on the eastern ridge and the earth became solid once more.

Mouche remained bent over, caught in an ecstacy of grief and horror, come all at once, out of nowhere, not sure whether it was his heart or the world that was breaking apart.

"Boy?" Papa said. "Mouche? What's the matter?"

"Oh, it hurts, it hurts," he cried. It wasn't all his own feeling, from inside himself. He knew that. It was someone else's feeling, someone suffering, some huge and horrid suffering that had been let loose when the world trembled. Not his own. He told himself that. He wasn't dying. He wasn't suffering, not like that. His little pains were nothing, nothing, compared to that.

"There, there, boy, I know it does," said Papa, completely misunderstanding. "But the pain will pass if you let it. Remember that, Mouche. The pain will pass, but you have to let it." And he looked at Mouche with the anguish he had carefully kept the boy from seeing.

After a moment, Mouche was able to raise his head and start back to the corner, trying not to let Papa see he was crying, easy enough since Papa was resolutely keeping his own face turned away. Mouche did not know who he was anymore. It was as if his whole world was coming apart and he with it. And though Papa had said it would pass, it felt more like pain on the way than pain going away. It had an approaching feel to it. Like the whistle of the little train, rising in pitch as it approached, so the pain seemed to intensify toward the end rather than fading.

The packet of gold was waiting Papa in the foyer of Genevois House, counted out by a stern-faced steward, some put into Papa's hands, some taken into keeping for Mouche. For later. When he was old. He signed a receipt for it in his best hand and put it back in the steward's hands, then the inner door was opened just wide enough for Mouche to enter.

"Well, come in, boy," said Madame. "Don't dawdle."

And his life as a Hunk began.

2

Ornery Bastable, and a Bit of History

The first of mankind to land on Newholme had been an all-male schismatic group from the skinhead planet, Thor, that had set down on the flatlands east of the River Giles in a stolen ship full of plunder and recently captured slaves. They had started building two towns and had conducted trade in biologicals and furs for more than a decade while they went on building, getting ready, so they told the traders, for the time they would go out and capture themselves some women. All this was a matter of record.

While the two towns were still abuilding, along with fortresses at the center of each, disaster struck. A trading ship, arriving on its usual schedule, found the port abandoned except for rampaging monsters of whom the ship's crew killed a goodly number. Cursory investigation indicated that the planet was abandoned except for a few surviving slaves who said the settlers had all vanished in the darkness, a few days past.

The trader crew put the slaves aboard the settlers' ship,

and flew it to the nearest COW station, claiming both slaves and ship as salvage even before reporting the disappearance to the Council of Worlds. Questioner I (the predecessor of Questioner II, of whom Mouche's Papa had spoken, and of whom we will learn more in due time), was sent by the COW to survey the situation. The two settlements were indeed empty, the half-built fortresses held nothing but dust, and though Questioner found no sign of monsters, it felt a definite sense of disquiet about the planet as a whole and said so.

At that stage of history, however, Questioner I was still rather new and had not yet gained the full confidence of the Council of Worlds. Recommendations based on mere "feelings" were almost always ignored because Questioner wasn't supposed to be able to "feel" anything. The planet was, therefore, listed as vacant by the proper COW committee, which opened it up for another wave of settlers. These were not long in coming. They named the planet Newholme and the two half-built towns Naibah and Sendoph. The fortress in Naibah was called the Fortress of Lost Men, and the one in Sendoph became the Temple, or Panhagion, headquarters for the Hags.

The level and fertile lands along the river were soon claimed, and successive generations of farmers settled farther east, finally moving up among the Ratbacks, an area of crouched and rounded hills that ran to the very foot of the scarp. In these remote valleys the dower rules of the Hags could not be rigorously enforced, and the farm folk acquired a bucolic and obstinate independence. It was not unknown for a cash-poor man, if he was persistent and personable, to talk a woman into coming to his farm to help him pay off her price through time payments to her family.

The Bastable family resulted from exactly this sort of understanding. Harad Bastable was a good worker who inherited a good farm when his older brother died. One of his nearest neighbors had a plethora of daughters, some of whom did not want to marry into the city. Pretty Suldia agreed to wed Harad, and her family agreed to let her do so in return for payments or support to be given them in their age. Suldia soon produced a daughter, Pearla, born at home and registered at the Temple at six months of age, as was required for girls. Three years later, also at home, Suldia bore twins: a son, Oram, and another daughter, Ornalia.

Oram and Ornalia, soon called Ornery, were inseparable. Perhaps from this connection, perhaps from something genetic—the Bastables had a few cattle and knew all about freemartins—or perhaps from example, Ornery grew into what the farm people called a crower, a boyish girl, one who liked boyish things, a scrambler over, a climber up, a rider of horses and tamer of creatures. To look at them both, the boy and the girl, one would find little difference between them. Both were lean and freckled, with generous mouths full of frequent laughter. Both had good appetites and ferocious energy.

Pearla, on the other hand, grew to be a very feminine woman, and in her twentieth year she was offered for by a young man from Sendoph who had seen her in that city during the harvest festival. At that same festival, Pearla had seen Hunks riding with their patronesses in the street and had decided on the spot that she wanted one of those for herself. If what it took to get one was a few years of not unpleasant boredom, then she would spend the few years.

It helped that she did not object to the young man who was offering for her. Nothing about him stirred her sensibilities, but he smelled of spice water, he had a carriage of his own, the family had a good haulage business of boats and ships and wagons that went from here to there and back again, as well as a grand house with several supernume servants plus (one could not help noticing) a goodly number of invisible people.

So, with much backing and forthing as to the terms of the dowry, Harad and Suldia agreed that the family in Sendoph might dower Pearla in, if Pearla herself approved. The prospective bride went to Sendoph to spend a few weeks among the maybe-husband's family to see how she liked being treated as a lady.

Ornery was saddened at Pearla's approaching marriage,

not so much at the loss of a sister, for they had never been playmates, but because the event suddenly made her confront her own future as a female, a sister growing up in her brother's shadow. Oram would inherit the farm. Her parents would use the money received from Pearla to dower in a bride for him, but even before that, Ornery herself would most likely be dowered in to some city man, which she would hate!

Truth to tell, Ornery did not feel herself drawn to men at all. Though she was of an age to be stirred by romantic or erotic thoughts about men, she remained unmoved. The Hags wouldn't force her to marry, but they could make life miserable if she didn't. She was registered at the Panhagion, and if she got to be twenty-one or two without being dowered for (an event which also required registration at the Temple) the Hags would want to know why. If she refused to be dowered, the Hags could make her a Hagger or even name her to Temple Service, though usually it was newborns who were named, so they could grow up Hag-rid. Being a Hag was easier, so they said, when you'd grown up to it. Though what was hard about it, nobody knew! Though there were only a few of them around anytime one went to Temple, they never seemed to sweat at anything.

Ornery didn't want to be a Hagger. Haggers had none of the honor and all of the labor. Maybe she'd just run off and become a Wilderneer, living in caves in the badlands, letting her hair grow long, sneaking and pillaging for her living. Females didn't become Wilderneers, though. At least Ornery had never heard of any.

Pearla's departure brought all these matters boiling to the surface of Ornery's mind, and she became so aggravated and belligerent over her role apprehensions that she was rude to her mother, at which her father threatened her with total and perpetual responsibility for the kitchen garden if she didn't straighten up. Fuming, Ornery decided to get up before dawn and run away—maybe forever. Probably just for a while. Leaving the home valley was a strictly forbidden pastime that was nonetheless habitual for Oram and Ornery both.

At this particular juncture, however, Ornery hated Oram along with everyone else, so she did not take him with her. Besides, he was bossy and wouldn't let her go where she wanted to, and today she intended to do precisely what *she* wanted to and nothing else because that's what Pearla was doing, so it was only fair.

Ornery rose before the family wakened, filled her pockets with apples, a chunk of bread, a bit of cheese, and went out into the early morning. Not far from the farm was the beginning of a southerly-tending valley, from which she climbed over a ridge to a narrow canyon, and from the end of that into a lava tube that had only bits of its roof left, here and there. Far along this tube, among areas of tumbled stones, was a pit into a lower tube, one that could be climbed down into by way of shattered ledges, and then there was a long walk down that tube, lit only by occasional gleams from cracks above, to a darker pit, one leading to a tube three layers down. Easing the descent was a rather short rope, which was all Oram and Ornery had been able to get away with. Rope was valuable, even short bits of it that could be made into bridles or gate ties or whatever.

Ornery lowered herself onto a steep pile of stone that had fallen from the pit opening, a pile which made descent possible as otherwise the rope would have been far too short. Lying against the rockpile were the torches Ornery and Oram had fashioned the last time they had come here, and at the edge of the dim light that came through the pit opening was the cairn of rocks they had piled to distinguish one direction in the tunnel from the other. Both ways looked the same, dark holes leading endlessly into the black, and since the rope often twisted and turned during the climb down, it was difficult to tell one direction from the other. It was probable, Oram had claimed, that monsters lived down there. There were many stories of such. Big wriggly things that set up stones called Joggiwagga, and huge four-eyed flyers called Eigers. So far as Ornery knew, they were only stories told to the twins by someone she couldn't remember.

On a conveniently located smooth stone beside the pile,

Ornery sat down to take her breakfast. After eating, she would light the torch and go some way in the direction marked by the cairn, not that she expected to find much. She and Oram had already explored the other way to the limit of their light, finding nothing but rock and more pits and the bones of various things that had maybe fallen in and couldn't get out again, all of them too small to be monsters.

She had finished her bread and cheese and had just set her teeth into an apple when the rock beneath her shivered. At first all her rumination about Wilderneers and monsters came flooding back and she figured something huge was coming down the tunnel. She dropped her lunch forthwith and started up the rope, only to be shaken off, tumbled down the stone pile, and left bruised and battered on the floor of the tunnel while the world went crazy around her. Stone cracked. Rocks fell. The pit opening seemed to jitter in midair, like an eye blinking against a glare. There was a sound from inside, outside, somewhere, that went past the limits of noise into something heard with the skin and the bones, a sound so huge she could not exist inside it.

So, for a time, she stopped existing. When she came to herself again, the world was quiet, the pit opening was gray with dusk, and from it the rope hung like a worm on a web, twisting gently in a hot little wind that came from down the tunnel. Windward, far along the tube, shone a fiery light. Something had fallen, letting the outside in, or something inside was burning. She thought of going to see, but she ached so that she could not make herself go an inch farther than necessary, and she was, besides, overcome with a feeling of such grief and horror she could not move. In her dazed condition she seemed to hear a gigantic voice calling to her, though it wasn't her name it called, which made no sense at all.

She buried her face in her hands and merely sat until her dizziness subsided, then staggered to the top of the pile where the rope hung. Her first two attempts were abortive, and on the third try she managed only with excruciating difficulty, as though she had never climbed the rope before. In the light, she could see her bruises and bloody abrasions. All the air was thick with dust and smoke. The way back to the valley took forever, even though there were two moons still almost full that rose as the sun set in a blaze of crimson, purple, and orange. She lost her way, coming to a hot waste she had never seen before and losing herself as she tried to go around it. The mountain trembled again as it grew darker, emitting wavering fumes across the faces of the moons. Eventually, weariness conquered and she fell into a little grassy pit, pulling her coat around her and relinquishing everything else. Mama and Papa would be furious, but she'd deal with it in the morning.

Morning came. She rose, looked around herself, told off her landmarks and realized she had gone past home. She went toward it and came upon the same waste she had encountered the night before, ash and mud and stink, with smoke rising from the edges where things had burned and there, at the far side, a piece of roof she recognized as from the chicken coop and beside it a tall post that had stood at the gate to the vineyard, crowned with a circlet of dried vine.

She screamed first, then ran about, then trembled and merely wept. She tried, but could get no closer, for the earth burned under her feet. Either her people had fled or they were dead under all that black. The nearest people were at the mines, along the foot of the scarp, but the way there was blocked by smoking rock. The nearest farm was down valley, and she finally turned in that direction, walking along the hills above the black, realizing along toward midmorning that she had gone long past the neighboring farm, that everything down this valley was gone.

There was a family one valley over. She crossed the ridge and came there in the early evening, trudging up their lane to be confronted by dogs and people.

"Why it's Oram," cried the woman of the house. "That's your name isn't it, boy?"

Ornalia didn't correct the misapprehension. "My family, all gone," she cried. "Buried, and all the cows and chickens. All but my sister Pearla. Oh, they're gone, all gone. . . ."

And the farm folk, between questioning and answering and giving her tea and food and offering the use of a washbasin, at once made plans to send a wagon to Sendoph to report what had happened to the neighboring valley. Oram, they said, could ride along.

Pearla was alone in the house when Ornery came, for the dowerer and his parents had gone to Naibah to arrange payment of the dowry. Oh, she had seen the mountain blow, she said. Oh, she had feared for her family.

"The vineyard gone," grieved Pearla. "Oh, Ornery, I can't imagine it gone. I can't imagine Mama and Papa, gone. So quick, like that."

"There's just mud and ashes," sobbed Ornery. "No house, no barn, no storage houses, no poultry house, no orchard. Mama . . . I hoped for a while maybe, well, maybe, but everything's gone, all down the valley. . . ."

They cried on one another's shoulders and told one another it would be all right, though it was a good deal easier for Pearla to say, who, though orphaned, would not have her life much changed from the one she had already planned. Still, they both wept, taking a long, uninterrupted time in which to grieve and talk of their sadness and despair, and after that of the fact that Ornalia was adrift, with no place to call home.

"Oh, you can stay here," Pearla wept. "They'll let you. I mean, you're old enough to be dowered for, even now."

"I'd rather die," spat Ornery, all yesterday's anger bubbling up through her grief, like mud roiled up from the bottom of a clear stream.

"But, you'll want to someday. . . ."

She cried, "Never. I don't want to be married, I don't want children, the idea of being married off to some man is just . . . repulsive."

Pearla flushed. "Well, Ornery, it's not wonderful, I know. I mean, my intended, he's nice enough, but . . . oh, he doesn't stir me at all. None of the Family Men I've met do. They seem all tangled up in these deals and games and strategies of theirs. They give you a flower and candy, they say sweet things, and it all comes out like Oram being polite to Grandma Miby."

They both laughed, wiping tears. Oram had had to be extensively coached to say, "Hello, Grandma Miby, how are you today?" and it always came out in a completely wooden voice.

"But," Pearla went on, "there's Hunks, Ornalia! And they're oh, they're wonderful. My mother-in-law, she has one, and she says they make life worth living. Some of the things they know how to do. . . ." She sighed. "And I'm only twenty, so by the time I'm thirty, I'll have a Hunk of my own!"

Ornery shook her head. "Call me Ornery, Pearly. I don't feel like being Ornalia, and I don't want a Hunk, either."

"You could serve the Temple as a Hagger. . . ."

"Doing what? I'd have to give up all life except Temple life. I'd have to serve wherever the Hags say to serve. That's no life for me, Pearly. What I'd really like is a stephold for myself. A tiny croft with a few sheep, a garden, and a loom for winter work. Some women have done it, begging sickly lambs from the neighbors and nursing them into a flock, building their own shelter of turf, getting by through full season or lean. . . ."

"Some women have done it, true, but they weren't young or fertile," said Pearla. "I doubt the Hags would allow you to buy even a stephold farm, though you will have some money coming."

"From where?" Ornery was astonished.

"If Mama and Papa are dead, if Oram is dead . . . my dowry will come to you."

"But I can't use it as I like," cried Ornery.

"Even if they'd let you buy a farm, they wouldn't let a healthy young woman stay unmarried." Pearla stared thoughtfully into the fire, shocked by all this loss into an unusual consideration for her sister. "There's an idea creeping around in my head, though. You say the family who helped you thought you were Oram?"

"They did."

"I can see why, the way you're dressed, and how you always looked alike. All of us were born at home, not at the Panhagion birthing center, so you—that is, my sister

Ornalia—was registered at the Temple at six months age, as all girls must be, but they don't have a DNA sample, as they would if you'd been born there, and Oram, *he* wasn't even registered, and *he's* not required to make Temple visits, so why not go on being Oram?"

Momentarily shocked, Ornery thought about it. "Veils," she said at last. "If I'm wearing veils . . ."

"Which Oram always would be, in public, at least. And you're not built like me or Mama, but like Papa's sisters, very lean, with hardly any chest at all."

"But what will I do? I can't live here with you."

"No. But my soon-husband is a decent sort of man. He owns ships, Ornery. If we can think up a way, he could put you on a ship, as an apprentice boy. You're seventeen. Old enough. Then when you're older yet, you could buy a farm."

"Close quarters on a ship," said Ornery, who had heard their father talk about the summer he spent as a sailor, when he was young, a mere supernume, before he inherited the farm. "They'd soon find out I was female."

"We could say you were sold as a chatron," said Pearla, after a moment's thought. "You had it cut off, but then the family that wanted to buy you was killed when the mountain exploded. So now here you are, a chatron, but you no longer need to be sold. The farm is gone, so now you'd prefer to go to sea. My dowry will more than pay your apprenticeship if I can't get my soon-husband to pay it. I'm sure I can make him arrange it, one way or the other. He likes me, Ornery. He said he was afraid he'd have to dower some woman he couldn't fancy making children on, but he likes me."

This last came with a tremulous smile, and for the first time gave Ornery something to feel thankful for. Thanks be to the Hagions that Pearla had been here in Sendoph rather than at home.

Pearla and Ornery took the trouble to learn something about chatrons, it being a subject not much thought of on the farms even though male things were gelded or neutered there all the time. Chatrons were mostly playmates for city daughters, companions for young wives tired from bearing but not yet entitled to a Hunk, de-sexed beings who wore a distinctive dress of baggy trousers and embroidered vests and veils a bit lighter than most men.

Before long, Pearla's soon-husband, all well-meaning ignorance, fell in with their plans. He had not previously known that Oram was a chatron, but then, he did not really know Pearla well, as yet, and might, if he followed custom, never know her much better. Chatron though Oram was, this brother of his soon-wife would be properly provided for.

3

The Establishment of the Questioner by Haraldson the Beneficent

Mothers can not tell us who we are.
Mirrors can not tell us who we are.
Only time can tell for every moment
we are choosing what to be.

"Reflections"
Haraldson and the Holies
Galactic Metronome
Terrareg, Reproright 3351 azy

The life of Haraldson (3306–3454 azy) has been the subject of many biographers; his abilities and intentions have been analyzed for centuries. It is true that he was a popular musician of interstellar fame, one who could move the population of whole systems with the sound of his voice or the twitch of a finger on the strings. It is true he had wed the most beautiful woman in the known universe and fathered children whose charm and poise, even in adolescence, had to be witnessed to be believed. It is true that he had no faults anyone could uncover with the most diligent search, and it was also true that he displayed the virtues of kindness, fidelity, modesty, and empathy combined with a political savvy which had not been known since before the Dispersion and had, even then, been rare. He was a phenomenon, a unique example of mankind, one whose honesty and goodwill could not be questioned, and it is probable that only Haraldson could have done what he did.

What he did was to get himself elected President for Life of the Council of Worlds (COW), with the title of Beneficent Exemplary. At his coronation, Haraldson sang the first verse of "Reflections," the song that had first brought him to the attention of the worlds: "Mothers can not tell us who we are. Mirrors can not tell us who we are. Only time can tell, for every moment we are choosing what to be."

"Let us choose justice and civility," he went on. "Let us do so in the company of beauty and joy. If we have not that company, let us still honor ourselves in the choice of justice and civility."

No sooner had the coronation occurred than Haraldson issued the Edicts of Equity, in which for the first time humanity was defined in terms of intelligence, civility, and the pursuit of justice rather than by species or form. Certain Earthian creatures other than mankind were immediately rendered human by the edicts, gaining the right to life, liberty, and the pursuit of satisfactions thereby, and some extremist individuals and groups who had previously paraded themselves as human were disabused of this notion.

The fallout from the edicts had not yet settled when Haraldson reorganized the bureaucracy of the council, setting up several departments or "Houses," among which were HoTA, House of Technical Advancement, and HoLI, House of Legislation and Investigation. In setting up HoLI, Haraldson declared that regulation and research should be inseparable, since mankind's societies had for too long been hip-deep in laws that had been useless, unenforceable, and despicable from inception. If a law needed constant tinkering with, he said, it is a bad law, and the goal of justice should always be superior to the rule of bad law no matter how good the intent!

It was Haraldson, almost single-handedly, who made COW an effective agent of general welfare for all member worlds—as well as any mankind worlds COW could reach—were then subject to Haraldson's edicts forbidding slavery, genocide, settling on previously occupied planets, racial crowding, and the destruction of either habitat or biodiversity. Haraldson further provided that persons must not only advocate but assure personal rights for all races, and that they must not discriminate against born, hatched, aggregated, or budded creatures on the basis of species, morphology, color, hispidity, gender, age, or opinion, except as species, morphology, gender, et al. provably altered the consequence of any given situation.

It sounded innocuous enough until Haraldson made it clear just how inclusive he expected the term "opinion" to be. "Language, cuisine, the arts, culture, tradition, religion, sexual and reproductive practices vary widely among mankind and even more widely among other races. All these, therefore, are to be considered matters of opinion, to which every person is entitled, and the free expression of which is guaranteed up to and no farther than the point at which that expression conflicts *directly* with someone else's opinion. Direct conflict shall be defined as incivility directed at a specific person or group as well as any action designed to alter someone else's opinion by coercion, law, or violence.

"Students of history will recall that prior to Dispersion, our Earthian ancestors espoused civil liberties," Haraldson explained. "Theoretical liberties, however, were too often assured at the expense of actual civilities, and as civilities were lost, litigation emerged as a way of life with a consequent reduction in *real* liberties for all persons except lawyers, who, like mercenaries, are profiteers of discord. Persons were actually allowed, by law, under the guise of free expression, to shout into the faces of those who held differing opinions and to intrude upon their privacy. Liberty has two legs. Vigilance is certainly one, but civility is as certainly the other.

"With this in mind, I hereby establish the defecation rule: A defecator is at liberty to commit the act, but he may not commit it on his neighbor's doorstep or in the quiet street in front of his neighbor's house, or in his neighbor's alley, or in his neighbor's customary place of work, or anyplace where the neighbor or any other passerby may step in it by accident in his own zone of privacy and tranquility.

"This means that any opinion may be expressed privately or in incorporated communities of the likeminded from which the non-likeminded are at liberty to depart. When an opinion moves into another's zone of privacy and tranquility, however, civility shall reign. If the Hairless Supremacists of Thor plan to march through a quiet community of furry Krumats with the sole intent of discomfiting the Krumats thereby, they may not do so, for though freedom of expression is guaranteed, a captive audience for an incivility is not.

"Our neighborhoods are an extension of our homes. Our right to privacy does not stop at our front doors. Our rights to the tranquility of our own senses and the privacy of our own space only gradually decrease as we move from our homes to the neighborhood street, down that street through our incorporated community of likeminded persons, out of that community and into the arteries of public commerce, waning gradually as we come to areas also used by other persons and ideas. Even there, we hold about ourselves a bubble of privacy which we lose totally only when we relinquish both senses and space by voluntarily choosing to become a tourist or part of a live audience.

"Despite this rule of civility, departure from the community and open expression of opinion remain absolute rights, and every community and every government must provide both opportunities for departure and venues for expression. Such opportunities and venues shall be both fully accessible to and fully avoidable by all citizens. No one shall attempt to control the coming and going from such venues or the events occurring within them."

The edicts of Haraldson were heralded as enlightened and were, after some false starts and befuddlement, generally accepted among the member worlds. The number of extremists began to drop as various factions killed each other off in the free-expression zones, and conflict waned as rebels were encouraged to depart. Except for gender issues, which, like Proteus, seemed capable of infinite metamorphoses, most societal agitations were assuaged and kept that way.

The House of Legislation and Investigation was charged with the periodic assessment of all mankind worlds for conformity to the edicts. During the first few decades of Haraldson's reign, these assessments were done in an orderly and timely way, producing tranquility and openness of opportunity and serving to increase general knowledge about the worlds in question.

Eventually Haraldson grew weary of his long years at the helm. He desired to leave the post of Exemplary and spend his last years in the study of non-mankind intelligences. The Council of Worlds, however, appealed to Haraldson's sense of duty, claiming that no candidate could possibly take his place. After a period of reflection, the aged Haraldson addressed the public.

He said he was not immortal, he had found his task arduous, and he felt that no holder of an elective office, including himself, could be relied upon to continue indefinitely a course which ran counter to so many human urges. Age or appetite would inevitably corrupt good intentions, he said, and therefore an unbiased and incorruptible agency must be created to continue the assessments of human settlements around the galaxy.

COW referred the matter to HoLI, who decided no committee or council of persons could be totally incorruptible. HoLI referred the matter to the House of Technical Advancement (HoTA) whose staff came up with an answer. They would develop a bionic construct that contained a human mind or minds, a construct infallibly programmed with Haraldson's edicts. The construct would be capable of learning, applying, and adapting those edicts while retaining their spirit and sense. Even though the technicians would start with one or more human brains—a more ideal interface could not be found—human memories and emotions would be repressed. The construct would have no vanity or greed, it would be incapable of pique or sloth, and would, thus, be immune to influence. The brains within it would be harvested from among persons who were already dying. Haraldson, on being approached, refused the honor of being among them.

HoTA was fortunate at that time to employ a number

of exceptional scientists who, even more fortunately, worked well together. When the assemblage was completed it turned out to be a conceptual and technological tour de force, decades if not centuries ahead of its time. Because it held three human brains and unlimited memory, complicated corpora callosa and storage units of enormous capacity were required, but the solutions to these and other problems of structure and design were uniformly inspired.

In fact, the most knotty problem encountered by the technicians had been not the brain but the body. There had been no conception of what the Questioner—as it was now being called—should look like. Eventually, the team agreed on a motherly image, anethnic in appearance and, since the machinery was massive, Brunhildian.

Questioner I was finished and programmed, and Haraldson himself attended the dedication. On that occasion, with his usual foresight, he advised the chief of HoTA that it would be prudent for the House to undertake a continuous update of Questioner plans and specifications in the event that Questioner ever met with a fatal accident.

Questioner I worked well among the worlds for several hundred years. Questioner was able, in many cases, to bring imperfect societies into conformity with the edicts, and it was also able to dispose of societies which were totally unacceptable. After lengthy argument, the Council of Worlds agreed that Questioner had proven flawless and might, therefore, see to such matters on its own initiative. At first COW wanted advise and consent status, but after the first few interminable debates, COW felt it best to get out of the loop and was, accordingly, bypassed.

The ruthless sentences of the Questioner were carried out rarely but thoroughly. Many were the docudramas produced concerning the final years of intransigent populations. Questioner I perished at last in the Flagian Miscalculation, the cataclysm of self-mortification that destroyed the Flagian Sector. Due to Haraldson's foresight, however, the technical specifications and many of the core components for a new device were ready and waiting, including technical advances that had been made in the intervening centuries.

Questioner II had all the abilities of its predecessor but a slightly less massive housing and a slightly expanded mission. On the basis of Questioner I's tantalizing reports, COW wished to know more about the non-mankind races: the horn-headed Gablians; the inscrutable Quaggi; the individualistic Borash; the numerous Korm.

At no time during the first or second construction of the Questioner had anyone in the Council of Worlds thought to specify that the brains used in Questioner should come from member planets that were subject to the edicts. In the welcome absence of such directives, the technicians had chosen brains that would make their jobs easiest: those easiest to get, with the least information and the fewest treasured memories. One technician, in fact, was heard to comment on the irony of selecting Questioner brains from cultures that forbade asking any questions at all.

4

Orientation to the Amatory Arts

During orientation, which is what Madame Genevois called the sessions conducted with each new boy in the small classroom, Mouche was required to memorize certain information that Madame categorized as "essential to your understanding of your role in life." These rules, regulations, laws, and customs were read aloud and explained by Madame, after which Mouche was drilled until letter perfect by Simon, one of the instructors, a former Hunk who had been improvident and was now required to earn a living in his later years.

The first thing drummed into him was the Dower Law.

"Section one," parroted Mouche, "provides that a family wishing to continue through the male line, usually through the eldest son, must pay dowry to a girl's family for the use of the girl as a wife."

"And this is called?" asked Simon.

Mouche responded promptly, "This is called dowering in, as the wife comes into the man's family and takes his name. Section two provides that a younger son who also wishes to continue his biological line may set up a new . . ."

"With the support," prompted Simon.

"May, with the support of his family, set up a new line, under a new name, and pay dower for a wife under that name . . . "

"Which is called?"

"Dowering off. Because his new name is an off-shoot of the old family name. Like, say, the family name is Vintner, he could set up as family Vineyard. Or he may buy his way into a family that has a daughter but no son, where he takes her family name, and that's called dowering out."

"Dowering in, off, or out," explained Simon, with a muffled yawn, "is always seen from the groom's parents' point of view, as they are the ones who pay. Now, section three?"

"Section three states that any attempt to evade the law through elopement, rapine, or abduction is punishable by blue-bodying and consequent death. Simon, what's rapine?"

"Forcing sex upon a woman, often with the intent of getting her pregnant."

"I didn't know you could do that."

"Used to be a good bit of it, but no more. Not unless you want to end up dead."

"When was there a good bit of it?"

Simon settled himself. "Well, it was like this. Our ancestors came to this world in ten ships. The first ship had the male workers, the livestock ova, and the reproducer, but it didn't have any women on it at all. That was so the men could get things whipped into shape, shelters made weathertight, crops planted, things like that, before the women and children came on the second ship. But the second ship was delayed, and instead they sent the support ship, the one that had the machines. . . ."

"What machines? I didn't think we had machines?"

"Of course we had machines. What do you think the Denti-med is? And the sensor array that keeps track of the volcanoes? And the stuff at the space port that lets us talk to the ships?"

"Oh. I guess I never thought those were machines."

"Well, they are. Our people didn't bring many, they had limited resources, but they chose not to do without medicine or geological and weather sensors or a space port. So, anyhow, the technology ship was the one that set down second, and it was full of technicians and scholars, a lot of them women, but most all of them were, so to speak, spoken for."

"They had husbands?"

"Right. Or as much as. Anyhow, the first ship men were feeling pretty randy by then, so they started raiding, stealing the women, and some of them got hurt."

"Some of the women?"

"Right. Some even got killed, which made their friends and colleagues very angry, so the others, the scientists and professors and technicians, men and women both, they moved the machines and the supplies and the libraries into the half-built fortress in Sendoph, and all the women stayed in there where they couldn't get abducted. Most of the people on that second ship were Gaeans, like Haraldson, worshippers of the Life-mother, and they were the ones who set up the Council of Hags."

"And they wrote the Dower Laws."

"Well, not right away. The laws sort of developed. But the key thing was, nobody got a wife without paying for her, and wives got the right to satisfactions for themselves. When the ship with all the women arrived, two or three years later, the Dower Laws were already in effect. Including section four, which you may now quote."

Mouche nodded. "Section four provides that every Family Man must have a unique family name for his genetic line, as it is to guarantee the uniqueness of each male line that this system was designed by the Revered Hags to meet the needs of the men of Newholme." Mouche swallowed a yawn.

"And, finally, section five."

"Section five says that every marriage contract must provide that once the wife has fulfilled her contractual obligations in providing her husband with his own, specific lineage, she has the right to one or more well trained Consorts to make her life more pleasant."

"Which is why you're here," said Simon, cuffing him lightly over the ear. "Recite it one more time, then you can be excused."

5

Life as a Lobster

During Mouche's first days at House Genevois, he stayed in the welcome suite where his life seemed to consist of nothing but orientation and baths. Dirt that had taken twelve years to accumulate was loosened over a period of days, pried from beneath finger and toenails, rasped off of horny calluses, steamed out of pores he had not known he had in places he had never bothered to wash.

"You know what we call new boys?" said Simon. "We call them lobsters, because they're always in hot water."

"What's a lobster?" asked Mouche.

"A kind of Old Earthian critter," Simon replied. "Eaten after boiling. Like a crustfish, sort of, but with more legs."

Even while Mouche soaked in the hot water there were snacks, bits of this and that, little plates and bowls brought by silent, invisible creatures at whom one never looked directly. They took away the empty plates and refilled them and brought them back again, but no one noticed the plates until they were set down, because when they were being carried, they too were invisible.

Bodies could not be properly contoured, according to Madame, unless they were well fed. There was also massage, which was embarrassing, though he soon learned to disregard the invisible creatures pounding away at him. When the staff of the House weren't washing him or pounding on him, or feeding him, or correcting his speech, he could read anything he liked from a great library full of real books.

"Am I the only one here?" he asked Simon. "I haven't seen anyone else."

"No, boy, and you won't, not until you're clean as a plucked goose, and fat as one. New boys are always the butt of jokes and hazing. That's life. It's always been that way. But there's no point letting a new boy in for the kind of labeling that will make training him or selling him more difficult. Too many good Hunks have been ruined by being called Fatty or Slobby or Stinky. So, you don't meet anyone until you meet them on equal footing, so far as cleanliness and elementary courtesy goes. We'll have no nasty nicknames here. Propriety, boy. That's what Madame wants. Our clients want Consorts they can take anywhere: to the theater, to the festivals, to the forecourt of the Temple, even. Our graduates must have no lingering taint of the pigpen or the tanners."

"Decorum," said Madame. "You'll behave in gentlemanly fashion, and you'll do it not only when you're being observed by one of us"—by which she meant the staff of Genevois House—"but also when you're alone with your colleagues. It must become second nature to you, a habit unbreakable as a vow."

So it was Mouche wasn't totally surprised when, clad in a white linen tunic, soft stockings and sandals, he was introduced to a similarly clad group of young men so polite it near took his breath away.

"You are welcome, Mouche," said one. "We are happy to have you among us," said another, and such like other syrupy phrases that made him more than merely worried.

His concern was justified, for when the lights were out and the monitors had left the dormitory, Mouche came in for rather different treatment. The habit unbreakable as a vow was, like most vows, quite breakable when no one was watching. Still, it was no worse a bruising than he'd had from the cow when she'd resented milking, or from the buck of the plow when it had hit a root. Next day he was able to say with a straight face that he'd fallen on the stairs, and Simon was able with a straight face to accept that explanation.

Genevois House was all gray stone and iron grilles on the outside. On the inside it was white plaster and carved wood and marble and velvet. The bare gymnasia were cavernous and echoing; but even there mirrors towered between gold-leaf piers and the floors were set in wood mosaic. The stuffy parlors were small and hushed and elegant. In the former, Mouche learned to fight hand to hand, to dance, and to fence with a sword. In the other, he learned from the conversation mistress to fence with words. Learning to fence in the bedroom would come later, though he was soon started on erotic exercises. Simon said boys his age all did erotic exercises anyhow, so better put it to some use.

As before, he spent hours in the library, reading all manner of books which were commonly read among the better classes of women, some of them written centuries before on Old Earth or the old colonial worlds, and all of them imported from worlds that had had time to develop the arts past the purely provincial. There were other hours in the kitchen, being lectured by the chef and the wine master. Not that Newholme had many vintages to brag of, but those they did should be properly appreciated. There were hours at the table, learning how to discriminate among foods, how to eat them elegantly, and how to manage veils of various weights while one carried on charming and amusing conversation. It became second nature: the left hand up to catch the veil at the right side; the upward sweep of the fingers to lift the veil from the mouth; the release, letting the veil drop as one chewed and swallowed. Not that the gauzy stuff Hunks usually wore was much of an impediment. Only respectable men wore real veils, and respectable men did not eat with their wives in public. They stayed in their offices at home or at their businesses among other men, where they belonged. "Or should be at," so the saying went. "Men of Business should be at business." Or else.

Several times each tenday—forty tendays the year, divided into four seasons—the new boys, who were not yet sexually mature and therefore not yet veiled, walked with their teachers to the park to watch the show put on by the advanced students. The older boys rode gracefully on horseback, glittering like gems. They picked quarrels with one another, and debated eloquently, declaiming dramatically, with many references to honor. Sometimes they fought with swords, brilliantly but inconsequentially, until one of the uniformed Housemasters stopped the battle and made them shake hands. The new boys were not the only ones watching. From closed carriages along the bridle paths, eyes watched and hands took notes, and it was for these watchers that the charades were played. The merchandise, so Simon said, had to go on display, for House Genevois often received bids for certain Consorts years before they were fully trained.

When the short nights of summertime came, the advanced students went off in all directions: the tongue-tied to summer conversation classes; the lazy to remedial fencing school; the merely awkward to dancing school. There were no remedial courses in amatory arts. One either did well in those or one was given one's pension money and dismissed. Very few were dismissed, said Simon. Madame had an instinct for boys who would do well in amatory arts.

Almost all the newest boys were sent to the equestrian school owned by House Genevois, where Mouche rode horseback, at first a few hours each day, then all day every day, until he could stay on anything with legs, whether bareback or asaddle. By this time he had friends among the students—as Madame called them—and had himself taken part in the harassment of several new boys. He had also grown taller by a handspan and added weight to match, had found the first pale hairs sprouting near his groin, and had heard his voice crack on at least three occasions.

"So, Mouche," said Madame, the day after he returned to Sendoph, "today you are one year with us. As of today, you are no longer a new boy."

Mouche swept her a bow in which no hint of servility was allowed. He would learn about groveling, Simon said, but not until later. Groveling was sometimes necessary for Hunks, but the dangers inherent in the practice had to be weighed in the light of experience, which Mouche had none of at this stage.

"Yes, Madame," he said.

Madame acknowledged him with a gracious nod. "You graduate to your own suite today. Simon will take you to it."

Simon did so, through the main hall, past the low-ceilinged dining room with its open hearth and smell of sausages, up the broad marble stairs onto the wide landing with its tall windows overlooking the street between great swags of wine-colored fabric and its equally tall doors leading to the apartments of the staff, and up a flight more, through the deeply carved doors that led into Consort Country.

"No galloping on these stairs," warned Simon. "Madame's orders. You gallop on these stairs, Madame may rethink letting you go up."

"I didn't think I'd go this year," said Mouche in wonderment. "I thought you had to be veiled first."

"Ordinarily, yes. But the way you're growing, you will be veiled by the end of the year. Fact is, Mouche, we need to increase dormitory space for the younger students, but we've several empty suites in Consort Country."

Something funny in Simon's voice when he mentioned increasing dormitory space, Mouche thought. Something a bit tentative and uncertain. He didn't have long to think about it, for Simon pushed upon the door, revealing a table set with tapers and a long, narrow, very dark hallway. At Simon's direction, Mouche lit them each a candle before the door swung closed.

The front part of House Genevois, so Simon said, had been rebuilt and added to during the last century in accordance with modern rules of architecture, and that was the part people saw when they visited. Once through the door into Consort Country, however, one went back into a sprawling maze made up of many separate buildings, some of them dating back to the first settlement, that had been acquired, remodeled, and joined together in stages and in accordance with no overall plan or direction. The suites of the Consorts presumptive were scattered throughout this labyrinth, like lumps of fat in a black pudding, for though windows and skylights had once lit the corridors, most of them had been built over, leaving the passageways in darkness.

Mouche followed Simon, bearing his own dim sphere of light, through which he could catch only a glimpse of the dark, velvety runners on the corridor floors, the carved wagon-panel along the walls, the shadowed ceilings high above with the gilded cornices, the gold of the ornate frames surrounding huge, dark pictures that lined every wall. The subject matter was at first indiscernible, but then, when the light caught one such painting at the right angle, all too obvious.

Mouche grunted, not sure whether to laugh or gag.

"Pay no attention to them, boy," said Simon. "Some persons wish to be immortalized in this fashion, though the Hagions know why. Perhaps they use these images to titillate themselves. Perhaps the paintings stir them to unaccustomed lust."

"I wouldn't lust over *that,*" said Mouche, indignantly. "And their faces are *bare!*"

"Faces are usually bare in the bedroom, boy. I wouldn't lust over such activities either, but there are some who will, and that's a matter for us all to keep in mind, Mouche. There are always some who will." His voice resonated with that same tentative unease Mouche had noticed earlier. "Madame collects these paintings, from estate sales, mostly. If there is material of this kind, the auctioneers call her in before the public viewing. She regards such stuff as cautionary, not erotic."

The paintings did serve as landmarks. He had only to go past the flagellation, averting his eyes from certain terrible details, turn at the corner where the undines were busy at their putrid liquefactions, go on past several debasements too awful to contemplate, and up the stairs nearest the serial sodomites, turning the corner at a depiction of a particularly nasty machine doing indescribable things to a struggling young man at the direction of a gloating woman.

This last picture stopped Mouche in his tracks, possibly because he could see it clearly. It was newer than the others; the varnish had not yet yellowed, to obscure the details. "This is fantasy, right?" he asked. "This did not really happen." He leaned forward to see the label, which read, *Mantelby, at her pleasures.*

Simon twitched uncomfortably. "We believe it was fantasy, yes. However, the painter disappeared under mysterious circumstances. It has been alleged that he attempted blackmail of his patroness."

"It doesn't look old, like the others."

"No. Madame bought it from the artist's heirs. The person who had commissioned it hadn't claimed it."

"And that would be Mantelby, right?"

"Shh," said Simon. "No names, Mouche. We didn't label it. The label is just as it was when the painting was bought. I said the paintings were cautionary. Be cautioned."

The door, Mouche's door, with his name already neatly lettered on the plate, opened into a suite of three rooms: a small sleeping chamber furnished with bed, armoire and fireplace; a comfortable study with tall bookcases and windows that looked out onto the courtyard; and a privy closet with washbasin, the privy water provided from a tank on the roof to which water was pumped by a water mill built into the river wall. Electric power was limited on Newholme, though there were plans for much hydroelectric development within the next generation.

Clean wash water would be provided daily, said Simon, not specifying by whom, and the Consort baths were on the next level down. Simon also suggested that Mouche should practice getting out of the suite by the quickest route in case the Lady on the Scarp Blew Her Top, then departed to let Mouche get settled.

Mouche decided that in case the volcano did explode, causing earthquake or fire or both, he would escape through the windows down into the courtyard, this decision suggested by the presence of a rope ladder already in place. The previous occupant had had similar intentions. That decision disposed of, Mouche fetched his books, his clothing, and his athletic equipment from the dormitory and distributed the items in his new quarters. He then went down to the laundry to check out linens and was behind the door, hunting for pillow cases, when he heard Madame and Simon come into the outer room, already in conversation.

"I just don't want to take them," said Madame, sounding resentful and angry. "They're terrible prospects. They'll be years too old, for one thing."

Mouche could hear her footsteps, the fretful to and froing she did when upset, tappy tap one way, tappy tap the other, the heels of her shoes coming down like little hammers. Madame wore shiny black shoes and shiny black skirts and blindingly white shirts under tight, buttoned jackets that shut her in like a caterpillar in a cocoon. Madame had black hair and white skin and pale gray eyes that could see through six inches of oak, so said Simon.

Madame went on: "I don't like the looks of those Dutter boys. There's something dreadful about them, Simon, something more than merely boorishness. It's a kind of deadliness. Evil. Like . . . like someone else I know of. That's why I turned them down when Dutter tried to sell them to House Genevois last year."

"But now the Dutter boys come with a guaranteed buyer who will pay you at once, in advance, no matter how they turn out," said Simon in an expressionless voice. "He offers an astonishing fee. And that same buyer has talked to your investors. Behind your back, if one may say so, Madame. And your investors, being good Men of Business, want you to take the offer."

"Which makes me like it even less," said Madame.

"Who makes a deal like that? It's not out of love, Simon. It's not out of good sense. Take out love and good sense and what's left? Anger. Hate. Revenge. I don't like it. I don't like them. And why is the deal anonymous?"

"You're not asked to take them immediately."

"Four years from now they'll be worse! And they'll be too old for me to do anything with!"

"The eventual buyer says he will guarantee their deportment while they are with us. That same buyer will make a large downpayment now, he tells us all he wants is a gloss, not real training, and your investors say the funds are needed, Madame. They wish to buy the property next north in order to expand the House, in order to take younger boys. . . ."

Which evidently gave her pause, for she said nothing more as she tapped away, Simon prowling after her as silently as a cat.

This was not the first time Mouche had heard discussions about taking younger boys at House Genevois. All the Consort Houses were licensed by the Panhagion. The financial end of things, however, was supervised by Men of Business, and financially, as Madame had mentioned on more than one occasion, taking younger boys made sense. Younger boys were cheaper to buy, for one thing; a good-looking nine-year-old could be had for eight or ten vobati and the initial annuity costs were lower. Then too, the early years were better for forming graceful habits, the eradication of lower caste accents, and the inculcation of both the superficial learning that would pass for sophistication and the rigorous physical training that allowed the student to emulate spontaneity. There was also less correction to do in the breaking of bad behavior, which saved staff time. This saving alone more than offset the cost of feeding and housing for a few extra years. There would be little risk, for as the population grew, though slowly, the market for Hunks grew with it. Even women who did not make much use of them wanted them as status symbols.

All of which explained why more dormitory space was needed, and also why Simon was so equivocal about it.

Simon didn't like the idea of taking younger boys. He said it was too difficult to pick good candidates much before age twelve because cherubs could turn into gargoyles, though whatever Madame did or did not do, she was not answerable to him.

Nonetheless, the conversation disturbed him. Something about it stirred a memory in Mouche, one he couldn't shake. It had something to do with Duster dog, but he couldn't quite remember what, though it had something to do with their wanderings. He mused a good deal on that.

Back on the farm, when chores were done, Mouche and Duster had often wandered away to visit some of the mysterious places in the lands round about. They had found their first cave when Mouche was seven and Duster was only a pup, and by the time he was nine, they'd found a dozen of them, some of them very deep and dark and too frightening to go into very far. Mouche's favorite cave was the one he'd found when he was nine, where water leaked through the roof to fall musically into a quiet pool lit by rays that thrust through the odd rift or cleft in the rocks, where small pale plants grew in abundance, and where a fairly biggish sort of furry creature lived who did not mind sharing Mouche's lunch or his knee in order to be petted and scratched about the ears and on the stomach. The furry thing was violet, the color of late sunset, and it had large hands and short though strong little legs and a long, fluffy tail. After the first tense meeting, Duster and the furry thing settled into a kind of companionship as well. The creature spoke, though only a few words, which delighted Mouche.

"Mouchidi," it said, putting his lips to Mouche's face, nipping him with his sharp little teeth—only a love bite, Mouche said to himself—and giving him a long, measuring look. "Twa, Mouchidi."

Mouche was well aware of his family's poverty, so he never suggested, even to himself, that he take the creature home and adopt it as a pet. Duster was given house room only because he guarded against roving supernumes and caught most of his own meals from among the small food the early settlers had released into the wild: rabbits, ground squirrels, wild hens. Besides, the furry thing seemed well established where it was, and the cave was close enough to visit from time to time, over a space of some three or four years.

On a particular day, however, Mouche had to convince Duster to come along, for the dog had been busy digging a large hole in the bottom pasture in pursuit of something only Duster could identify. Mouche took a chunk of bread, with a lump of butter already inserted in it, a couple of winter apples, and his share of the piece of cheese set aside for that day's consumption. Darbos usually kept his share to add to the evening grain, and Eline ate hers at bedtime, but Mouche ate his cheese at noon because he could sneak bites of it to Duster, as he could not do if Eline was watching.

Usually Mouche's approach to the cave was quiet, if not silent, but today when he came within hearing distance, he heard the small furry thing screaming. He had heard it scream before, when it was surprised, or hurt, so he gave up any pretense at secrecy and ran for the cave at full tilt, drawing up at the entrance to see two boys, arms outstretched, attempting to catch the furry thing, whom they had already wounded with a thrown rock. Mouche saw the rock, the wound in the furry thing's side, the boys intent and lustful faces, and without even thinking about it, he launched himself at the larger boy while Duster, following suit, took on the smaller.

Mouche and Duster had the advantage of surprise and at least one longer set of teeth. Though Mouche was somewhat battered in the fray, he and Duster prevailed. The two interlopers fled, though the larger paused at the top of the slope to shout, "You and your dog better watch it, farm-boy. I'll get you. You count on that."

Mouche paid little attention for he was busy attending to the furry thing that lay in his lap and sobbed like a baby.

"Borra tim ti'twa, Mouchidi. Borra tim ti'twa."

The wound was not deep, and after a time, the thing sat up and sighed for a time, holding tight to Mouche the while and allowing Duster to lick the blood away, while the small creature took a tuft of its own fur and bent forward to clean up the abrasions Mouche himself had incurred, wiping the blood and loose skin away and then secreting the soiled tuft somewhere upon its body. It put its lips to the wound giving Mouche another love bite, only this one stung a little, and Mouche drew away with a little gasp. The creature murmured at him, patting his face.

It was only then, when things had quieted down a bit, that Mouche noticed the odor, a rancid, moldy, feculent stench with more than a hint of burnt feathers to it. A little breeze came up and blew the smell away. Though the small furry thing might have emitted some smell in its fear, Mouche thought it more likely the smell had come with the intruders. Perhaps, he thought, they had been cleaning out a cow byre and forgot to wash. Though the smell was, come to think of it, worse than even several cows could manage.

Mouche was feverish for the next few days, as though he might have picked up a bug, so his father said, roaming around when he should be working. It didn't amount to anything, and he was well again in no time, well enough to have another look at the cave.

When he and Duster got there, the small furry thing was gone, but the smell was all over the place. There were no displaced rocks or signs of struggle, and Mouche assumed the furry one had very intelligently gone elsewhere. He decided he would look in some of his other caves to see if his friend had taken up residence, and left it at that until a few days later when Duster set up a terrible howl, then thrashed and panted and tried to vomit and eventually, after a terrible afternoon of agony, died in Mouche's arms. All those hours, while Mouche tried to hold him, to comfort him, that same smell was on him, and Mouche knew that Duster had died of poison, that the intruder boys had kept their word.

"What boys?" his Papa had asked.

Mouche had described them.

"The Dutter boys," Papa remarked, with distaste.

The Dutter boys. Well. So, that was what had made him remember. It was unlikely there would be more than two with that name, and Madame didn't like the Dutter boys either.

6

On Old Earth: The Dancing Child

"Come chickies, chickies," cried Mama One. "Come lapsit, storytime."

Ellin heard the call, although she told herself she didn't. She couldn't hear it, she was too far in the woods, dancing, dancing. Her feet had taken her too far away, and she couldn't hear Mama One or Benjamin or Tutsy or any of them. She whirled and whirled, high on her toes, hearing only the music, the drums, the strings, the harp. . . .

"There you are, chickie!" And she was seized up, kicking silently, feet still pointed as they had been when she danced away.

"Where was she?" asked Papa One, in his furry big bear voice.

"Out in the atrium, by the tree," Mama One answered in her kindly middle bear voice, tucking Ellin tighter against her cushiony self. "She's always out by the tree, whirling around."

"Dancing," said Ellin, defiantly, hoping she would make Mama One listen. "Inna woods."

"Dancing," laughed Mama One, paying no attention at all. "Here, Ellin on the lap and Benjamin on this side and Tutsy on the other side, and big brother William in that chair, and here's Papa with the book."

Story time was always by the holo-fire, with big brother William in the chair nearest the fire, staring at Ellin and Benjamin and Tutsy with his nose pinched up. Breakfast was always by the kitchen window with the holo-view of sun shining in through green or red leaves, and William already gone away to school. Dinnertime was lamp glow, with everybody at the table, even Tutsy in her high chair, and bedtime was always open the window in Ellin's room, with the holo-moon outside, sailing, sailing, and the leaves on the trees dancing, dancing.

"What story tonight?" asked Papa One. "What story, Benjamin?"

"Engine," said Benjamin. "Little Engine."

Ellin stuck her thumb in her mouth and shut her eyes. She was tired of the little engine, tired of being like the little engine, think I can, think I can, think I can. It wasn't thinking anymore. It was knowing. Ellin knew she could, but Mama One didn't care. Papa One didn't care. She could be making mud pies for all they cared.

Instead of listening to Papa One's furry voice, she went away inside, somewhere else, that place she'd seen on the holo-stage, the beautiful room where the little girl was, not a grown-up girl, a little girl like Ellin, dancing, dancing under the huge Christmas tree, not a tiny tree like the potted one in the atrium. Ellin's toes pointed, her free hand turned on the wrist, like a flower opening. She could feel all the muscles in her legs tightening. There was the wicked mouse king, and she ran, like a little wind runs, so quick, so smooth and pretty.

"Ellin isn't listening," crowed Mama One. "Ellin's a sleepy head."

"Am, too, listening," said Ellin. "My eyes are bored, so I shut them."

"Poor baby," whispered Mama One, gathering Ellin in.

"Are you Mama One's poor baby? Bored with the whole world? Well, a night's sleep will make it all right. And tomorrow, well, Ellin's having a surprise!"

Inside, something lurched, like it did when you stepped on one of Benjamin's marbles and had to balance quickly or fall down. "Surprise?"

"Ellin's six years old tomorrow. A birthday! And the people from History House are coming."

Ellin told herself she hadn't heard. She was so sleepy, she hadn't heard it. William had, though. She saw the mean glitter in his eyes, saw his lips move. "Told you," his lips said. "I told you."

The little lurch inside became something worse, like a throwing up feeling. She couldn't just let it lie there, making her sick.

"Mama One," she said desperately, sitting up and opening her eyes wide. "William says you're not my mama. William says Papa One isn't my papa. William says me and Benjamin and Tutsy don't belong here."

"William," said Papa One in a threatening voice. "Shame on you. What a thing to say to the child!"

"The brats aren't yours," crowed half-grown William in his nasty voice that cracked and jumped, like the broken piano at the kindergarten. "That's the truth. Why shame on me for telling the truth?"

Mama One said something, but she choked. She had to swallow hard and try again. "Ellin and Benjamin and Tutsy do belong here. This is their infant home. *Unfortunately,* this is also William's childhood home, and he is a selfish pig about it."

"What's infant?" Ellin asked.

"It's a baby," William crowed defiantly. "It's a baby. And tomorrow you won't be a baby anymore."

"That's true," said Papa One in the heavy voice he sometimes used when he was very angry. "And next week, William won't be a child anymore. Next week, William, you will be fourteen. And when children reach fourteen, they are placed for education."

"Hey," said William uncertainly. "Hey, I didn't mean . . ."

"I know what you meant," said Papa One. "You meant to hurt Ellin, to make her feel insecure. Well, now deal with it yourself. By the end of the week, you too, William, will be adapting, just as Ellin will adapt, won't you, sweetie?"

"What's adapt?" cried Ellin.

"Shhh," said Mama One, tears in her eyes. "Oh, shhh. You men. You've spoiled it all!"

She cuddled Ellin tight, picking her up and carrying her upstairs to her own bedroom, her own dollies and dolly-house and her own shelf of books and her own holo-stage, her own things, all around.

"What's adapt?" Ellin wiped at her nose with her sleeve.

"Shh," said Mama One. "Tomorrow, the people from History House are coming. Tomorrow, you'll meet them, and they'll see what kind of sweet little girl you are. And then, then we'll talk about adapting and all the rest."

"What rest?"

"Your life, child. Just your life."

Ellin thought she wouldn't sleep at all, for she was scared and mad and hated William. When Mama One opened the window, though, the holo-moon began to peep and the music began to wander, and all the leaves danced. Ellin pointed her toes in her bed and danced with the leaves, and before she knew it, it was morning.

The baby-aide came to take Benjamin to kindergarten and Tutsy to the playground. William was at school. Ellin helped Mama One straighten up her room, then she got dressed in her best dress, the one with the full skirt, and her best shoes, the shiny ones, and waited.

Almost right away the bell rang, and the people came in. One man, two women. They wore funny clothes, but Ellin knew enough not to laugh or point or say anything because they were from another time and couldn't help how they looked. She curtsied and said, "How do you do," in a nice voice, and the three people said, "How do you do, Ellin," back again.

"Nordic type, clearly," said the man.

"Nordic quota clone," said one of the women, looking

at the thing she was carrying, a funny flat box thing with buttons. "This is number four of six. Silver hair, blue eyes, pale skin."

"I'm more interested in the other," said the second woman. "Mama One tells us you like to dance, Ellin. Will you dance for us?"

"I . . . I need music," Ellin said.

"That's all right," the second woman said. "I brought music."

She had a box with buttons, too, and she pushed some of them and the music came out, the same music Ellin remembered, about the girl and the nutcracker and the bad mouse king.

Ellin's feet started moving. She didn't even have to think about it. Her body did it, all by itself, the little runs and the jumps and then, then she did the other thing, the one the other dancers did, she went up on her toes, on the tips, right up, high, with her arms coming up, up, like she was flying. . . .

"By Haraldson the Beneficent," said the second woman. "Ellin, dear, thank you. No. That's enough. You don't have the right shoes to do that, dear, and you'll hurt yourself. You can settle now."

The man was smiling, not at Ellin, but at the woman. "Well?"

"Well, it's remarkable. Quite remarkable. I want all six, if we can get them."

"Including this one."

"Of course, including this one!"

"Hush," said Mama One, almost angrily. "You're not talking about a set of dishes. This is Ellin."

"Of course," said the man. "I'm sorry, Madam. Certainly, she . . . we meant Ellin."

"Would you like to come live with us, Ellin?" the woman asked. "You can dance all the time. You'll have the very best teachers. You'll learn to do the Nutcracker, the one you were copying. You'll learn lots of other pre-gravitics dances, too. Giselle, and Swan Lake, and Dorothy in Oz."

"Come?" Ellin said, breathlessly. "Come where?"

''History House, child. You're intended for History House, Old Earth America: the Arts.''

''And I can dance?''

''All the time. Except when you're in school, of course. All children must go to school.''

''She's allowed transition time,'' said Mama One, with a glare at Papa One, who just stood there. ''You've seen her, now enter your letter of intent to rear, that'll make it all official, and leave her to me for a few days. I'll bring her from her own time when she's ready.''

So they went, shaking Mama One's hand and Papa One's hand, turning to wave at Ellin as they went out the front door and into the street where a hole into tomorrow opened and let them through.

''Mama One,'' said Ellin, her eyes suddenly full of tears. ''Mama One, are they going to take me away?''

''Shh,'' said Mama One. ''Lunch time. We'll worry about taking away or not taking away later, after we're all calmed down.''

After lunch, Mama One and Ellin went into the atrium, to the seat by the tree, where Ellin sat in Mama One's lap while Mama One explained it all. She wasn't Ellin's cell Mama. Papa One wasn't Ellin's cell Papa. Another, very special person who had died a long time ago had such very good cells that she left some behind to make children, and the twentieth-century experts at History House had asked for some of those children, and Ellin was one of them. Mama One and Papa One lived in a village that had been kept just like the twentieth century, and they were her infant parents so Ellin would grow up acting and talking like a real twentieth-century person. And Mama One and Papa One had taken care of Ellin because they loved her, and when Ellin grew up, she would dance for History House, just like her cell mother had.

''I'm not grown up!'' Ellin said. ''I'm not old enough.''

''No, but you're old enough to go to school, and they want you to go to the History House ballet school, where you'll learn to dance and all about the time in history that you'll be working in. Papa One and Mama One have a license to raise children as they were raised in the twentieth century, but there's lots more to learn about it than we can teach you."

"Do all your children go away when they're as old as me?"

"Not always. Sometimes the children stay with us until they're thirteen or fourteen or even grown up. William stayed with us until now because he's only going to do set construction, and History House won't need to teach him much that he can't learn right here. But Ellin is a dancer, and she needs to learn a lot about dancing."

"Why? They knew I could dance. How did they know?"

"Because we made out such good reports on you, four times every year, and we told them what a fine dancer you were. And because your cell mama was a wonderful dancer, like both her parents. And they were nordic types, just like you."

"What's a quota clone? William said I was a quota clone!"

Mama One took a deep breath, her lips pressed tight together. "William needs his mouth zippered up! All it means is that when they make an extra special person, sometimes they make more than one. That's all. Only extra special people are cloned, so when anyone says that, it's like saying you're special."

"William isn't a clone?"

"Gracious, what an idea! Does anybody need more than one William?" Mama One laughed, the tears spilling. "Do we?"

Ellin settled into the cushiony lap, glad there was only one William. "Do I have to go to History House?"

"If you want to dance, sweet one, you should go as soon as you're ready. That's what you're meant to do, sure enough, and if you want to do it badly enough, you should go." And then Mama One cried for real, putting her head right down on her knees, and not stopping even when Ellin kissed her and hugged her and told her she'd never, ever go away.

She didn't want to go away. It gave her a stomach ache to think about it. And yet . . . yet, everyone seemed to suppose she would go away. It was as though . . . as though they had stopped looking at her. As though they didn't really see her anymore. And now there was new music and trips to see new dances and a chance to attend a class with real dancers, and . . .

So, a few days later, after thinking about dancing all that time, after Mama One promised to visit, and bring Benjamin and Tutsy, Ellin went to live at History House with Mama Two and to dream, at night, that she was walking along a high road with Mama One and Papa One and they came to a great cliff and Mama and Papa One told her to fly, and she did fly, but even while she was flying she felt . . . she felt as though they had thrown her out into the air with nothing there, all the way down.

7

The Questioner and the Trader

On a mudworld named Swamp-six, Questioner II sat in a reed hut near the shuttleport, so called though it was only a badly mown clearing amid endless stretches of deadly guillotine grass, its razor leaves snicking together with every breeze. The place was clamorous with frog-birds, soggy from the usual afternoon downpour—the livid skies still drooling, though the suns had gone down some time since—and totally lacking in amenities, a condition which Questioner refused to notice.

She could feel comfort, she could perceive beauty, she could appreciate music, she had pleasure receptors for tastes, smells, and touches, but when duty took her to worlds where comfort, beauty, and pleasure were absent, she turned her receptors off. Questioner's review of Swamp-six had consisted of an instantaneous recognition of ugly realities requiring no prolonged verification.

She had come quite far, she had seen quite enough, but her ship was not scheduled to return for two days. She had been passing the time playing cards, a complicated kind of solitaire that took her mind off her recurrent feelings of amorphous and aimless sadness. Or maybe anger. Or maybe sheer peevishness. She had no explanation for these emotions, which seemed to rise like smoke whenever she was unoccupied, but she knew from long experience they would be less intrusive if she was distracted.

Additional distraction presented itself in the form of a small shuttle that plunged from the zenith and settled onto the mown area to emit a stooped and stuttering Flagian, a trader from his dress, who came tottering unerringly toward her. Questioner rose and awaited him, the cards scattered on the equipment box that served her as a table. He was an aged and floppy-fleshed fellow, one of those whose forefathers had survived the Flagian Miscalculation by virtue of being several systems removed at the time it occurred.

"Questioner?" he asked, with a certain diffidence, peering shortsightedly through the tinted glasses that protected his pink eyes. "I am Ybor Transit."

"We have met before," she said. "You sold me that information about the indigenous dancers on Newholme."

"Aha," he murmured. "You do remember. I have been searching for you because I have something else you may find interesting. Is it true you are a collector of information on non-mankind races?"

"More or less," she said coolly.

"I have in my possession an actual sensory recording of a Quaggian event." He paused, adding, in a hushed and mysterious voice, "A ritual event."

"Wouldn't it be unintelligible to me?" she asked in the uninterested tone she reserved for traders, politicians, and members of her politically appointed entourage. "The Quaggi do not talk with us at all."

"May I sit down, Ma'am? Thank you kindly." He lowered himself onto one of the smaller equipment cases. "The Quaggi do talk to traders, Ma'am. There are certain botanical substances which they require, and they are sufficiently interested in obtaining these to answer a few questions now and again. As a matter of fact, the BIT, that's the Brotherhood of Interstellar Trade, Ma'am, has circulated a list of questions so that each trader calling upon the Quaggi can ask one or more of them. Thus we fill in our knowledge in an orderly fashion."

"Remarkable," said the Questioner, seating herself across from him. "I had no idea you were so well organized."

"We aren't, in many manners." The old Flagian gave her a gap-toothed grin. He went on, "We are curious, however, and there's no denying that the more one knows about a client, the better it is for trade."

"Are the Quaggi bisexual, as we've been told?"

"They say so."

"Why have we never seen a female?"

"They say members of their opposite sex are mindless and incompetent, useful only for breeding and therefore confined to planetary life. We've never seen any, so I assume we haven't found the planet where they're kept, yet. We have learned this much through the use of translator devices."

"Is there a translator built into the thing you're trying to sell me?"

"In this case, it doesn't matter," muttered the Flagian, fingering a scar that cast a fuchsia shadow across the rose-pink expanse of his furrowed forehead. "This is an all-emissions record that needs no language. In expert opinion it dates some million standard years ago."

"Ah, now. Come, come."

"Madam, I guarantee your satisfaction." He fretted through several pockets, plucking and sorting. "Here, my location code. Here, my bonding agency. Here, my registered genetic identity. I will refund if you are not fascinated."

Questioner found herself liking him. "You've seen the Quaggi?"

He nodded his head, jowls flapping. "I have, yes. They look like large piles of rock with huge compound eyes and some manipulating palps in front. They sit in monumental circles on carefully leveled plains on otherwise lifeless planets. They barely move as they commune, who knows with whom or what. In payment for the botanicals we offer, they extrude small chips of gold, platinum, or other precious metals. Other than that, they do nothing. Some of their circles are millennia, perhaps even aeons old. . . ."

The trader stared aloft and shrugged, both face and gesture conveying his awe at the inscrutability of the universe. "When I was last there, I witnessed an outsider Quaggi come before one of these circles. It offered a recording, similar to the one I'm offering you. The recording was passed around the circle, after which the newcomer tore off its wings and antennae and joined the circle. The record was thrown aside, as on a trash heap. When I stopped by the trash heap, I found this one unbroken recording."

"What do you want for it?"

He named a figure. She laughed and named another. When they agreed, he handed over a peculiarly shaped and stoppered flask that contained, so far as she could tell, several large handfuls of coarse gray gravel.

"And what is this?"

"The recording. The Quaggi applicant brings this container, the members of the circle in turn swallow the crystals and excrete them back into the container. Evidently they read it internally. However, you can pour the stuff into a hopper, and read the same thing the Quaggi do."

"What hopper?"

"The hopper of an EQUASER, an Electronic Quaggi Sensory Reconstructor, made by the Korm as part of a communications system for their ships."

"Aha!" She grinned at him, all her teeth showing. "How remarkable. And I suppose you just happen to have at least one such device for sale!"

"Only because it is useless to me without the recording. . . ."

"Useless, but, one presumes, not valueless?"

"Oh, no, Ma'am." He echoed her grin with a gummy one of his own. "Not at all valueless." He saw the annoyance on her face and took a deep breath. "Questioner, I would rather have you as a friend than an enemy. The BIT has always felt so. You have paid us well for the reports we bring you, those little things we see that local governments won't tell you."

"That's true," she murmured. "The BIT finds the truth of many things that governments deny."

"So, I make an offer. You tell me a few things about yourself, I give you the Korm device for nothing."

"You traders have a list of questions about me, too?"

"It isn't a long list," he said apologetically. "It would take you little time to respond perhaps to one or two little queries."

She grinned, suddenly diverted. "Ask away."

"We want to know . . . what are you like? How would you describe your personality?"

She stared at him. It was the last question she would have expected and one of the few for which she had no ready answer. "Let me see," she said at last. "I suppose I am task driven. My stimulus comes from duty. I am singleminded, stubborn, terrier-like in my approach to whatever job is before me. Human people who work with me say that I am a stern taskmaster, and this is true, though I do have a sense of humor. Haraldson said no entities could do this job unless they had a sense of the ridiculous, and I am frequently amused, even at myself. While I have the senses needed for enjoyment, it is difficult for me to enjoy because I can not forget the amount of work that is awaiting me, and there never seems to be enough time to do it all."

"Too strong a conscience!" he opined. "Perhaps a little wine would help? Or a euphoric capsule?"

"They can affect me, of course, but I distrust them. I am too likely, afterward, to judge myself harshly. I was designed to be a judge, and I do not withhold judgment from myself." She paused a moment, then murmured, "Least of all from myself."

"Is it fair to say you are relentless, unforgiving, capable of very stern action?"

She said, "It is fair, yes. I can do good only by doing my job relentlessly. If my judgments could be escaped or modified, the edicts would become mere suggestions rather than what they were intended to be: a framework by which mankind can turn himself into something better than he is.''

He frowned, forehead deeply furrowed. ''Tell me, truly, when you make these terrible judgments, or at any other time, do you feel anything?''

She was taken aback. Still, they had a bargain. It was incumbent upon her to answer as honestly as possible. ''When I make a judgment, I always feel I am doing right,'' she replied. ''If I do not feel it is right, I cannot do it.

''At other times, however, I have other kinds of feelings and I do not know why, or how, or from what source the feelings come. When I am intent upon my work, I am largely unaware of existing as an entity separate from the task. When there is a pause in my duties, however, sometimes I feel sadness or fear or longing for things I have never had, or cannot define. Sometimes I know things, and I cannot find the source of knowing anywhere in my files or my perception systems. I have thought, perhaps, that these feelings come from the human brains that were incorporated into me, but I cannot tell for sure.''

''Ah,'' murmured the trader. ''What brains were they?''

She shook her head. ''I don't know. I wasn't informed.''

''Would you like to know?''

She felt the mental equivalent of a gasp, a brief cessation of sense, a network-wide shock. ''The HoTA designs and systems for the Questioners are top secret. I incorporate certain technical achievements which have a likelihood of misuse, and COW believes them better kept under lock and key.''

''True. We know when you were made, however, and we know that the HoTA ships went here and there at that time. HoTA ships are quite easily recognizable, and the BIT keeps track of where ships go, and when. If brains were taken from persons who were dying at the time, it could not have been done in total secrecy. Linkages would have been necessary, and there are records. . . .''

''If you could learn who . . . when, why, I would be prepared to reward you very well,'' said Questioner, surprising herself with the sudden spate of interest she felt.

"Your regard would be reward enough." The Flagian bowed respectfully, took his payment for the recording in Council of Worlds monetary units, repeated his compliments, and departed, staying well away from the snicking grasses and not without a backward glance. Each time he met the Questioner he was surprised that she did not seem more exotic.

The Questioner knew perfectly well what he was thinking. Most people expected something more exotic. To outward appearance, she was simply a stout woman of indeterminate age with a rather large head covered with iron gray hair worn in a bun. She was, however, a good deal more than that. She was enormously strong; she could swim, dive, fly, brachiate, crawl, or climb mountains. She could provide emergency medical assistance and do quick field repairs on a great variety of complicated equipment. She could cook, sing quite well, and compose fairly literary poetry in several languages. She supposed she could fall in love, though she had never done so. Though the senses were there, the stimulus was not.

When the trader's shuttle took off in a fountain of flung clods and crushed grasses, she set aside all thoughts of him and settled herself into a stable position. With the flask of gravel-data, the newly acquired hopper device, and the probability of two uninterrupted days before her own ship arrived, she could look forward to a period of peace. Her so-called aides were aboard the ship, where they were no doubt plotting to kill one another. Let the idiot captain deal with them. Better there than here.

With a satisfied hum, she poured the gravel—crystals of uniform color and size—into the funnel-shaped port atop the device she had just bartered for. As instructed by the trader, she put the flask into a receptacle at the bottom of the device, moved one of the bars to the right, another to the left, and pushed a button. . . .

And was in a darkness of space, confronting a new, young planetary system. Her viewpoint shifted erratically, as though the recording device was being moved or anchored. Abruptly, the viewpoint settled, only to be interrupted by the edge of an enormous . . . well, it looked rather like a membrane of some kind. A wing, perhaps. Whatever it was, it receded off one side of the view, never allowing Questioner to see what kind of creature it was part of.

She returned her attention to the sun, around which three young planets whirled in fiery rings. The recording system obviously compressed the action. Mechanical time lapse equipment, perhaps. Or, considering that the Quaggi exchanged information through these crystals, an organic system which secreted memories: information pearls, secreted over time by Quaggian oysters. In any case, the recording device was also orbiting the sun, allowing a good view of a nearby planet with eight moons, three in one orbital plane, three smaller ones, no doubt captured asteroids, with orbits at considerable angles to the other three, and two tiny orbiting rocks, close to the planet, moving very fast.

Her view could be extended in every direction. When she turned slowly to look away from the sun, she saw two gas giants and then, after careful search, the shadow arcs of several smaller, colder worlds farther out. Beyond them was a circling field of galactic flotsam and jetsam, a cometary collection, perhaps remnants of some larger and older thing, and beyond that the darkness of space sequined by a far-off scatter of fully formed stars and galaxies.

She returned her attention to the nearest planet where thin plates of surface rock were thrust across great furnaces of the deep to be suddenly pimpled with a rash of baby volcanoes, each vent a basaltic core that hardened inside its ashen cone into a cyclopean crystalline pillar. Echoes from within the planet allowed her to perceive a spongy crust built up by recurrent layers of lava tubes superimposed on sedimentary structures. She could detect great caverns held aloft by basaltic pillars, one atop another, some created by fire, some by water, some by both together, some mere bubbles with a pillar or two, others measureless caverns with forests of columns.

Here and there chasms split through the layers, bringing light to the inner world. Those deepest down had been invaded by the abyssal oceans where scalding vents spewed black smoke while complicated molecules rocked in the steaming waters at the edge of the white hot magma, spinning in the heat, accumulating and replicating themselves, adhering, separating, drifting away on the currents of the sea.

She turned her gaze outward, and this time saw in the far dark of the cometary field a thing that raised itself upon wide, pale wings and moved inward to roost upon a tiny moon of a cold planet. The Questioner watched the planet as it passed behind the sun, emerged, then arced toward her once more. As it swung by she received the fleeting impression of a wing of pale fire unfolding across the stars.

Something living sat on that cold rock, something from outside. Something akin to time; certainly something accustomed to waiting; a bat the size of a mountain range, perhaps? Or something like an octopus, with membranes stretched between its tentacles to make a winglike structure? Something very large, certainly, and something very old.

Her concentration was interrupted by a vast mooing or bellowing of radio waves coming from somewhere in the system, spreading outward in all directions, a message repeating over and over. *Come. Come. Here is a new planet, still warm. Here are fires, still burning. I await. I await.*

The message was in no words she knew, no language she had ever heard, and yet it was unmistakable in intent. It was a summons, and something within her responded to it, something she had not known was there. For the time, that was the only response. She could detect no other.

She turned to watch life erupting on the nearest planet. She could feel its burgeoning, though most of it was below the surface. It grew everywhere through the spongified outer layer of the planet, invading tubes and tunnels, caverns and caves, bubbles and blast holes, vents and veins. All spaces were room for it, all interconnected, one draining into another, some floored in fertile soil, some hollow and echoing, some running out beneath the sea where the dry stone corridors shushed to the sound of outer waters, like great ears alive to the pulse of their own blood, and all of them seething with life.

Questioner could feel that life; she could sense its manifestations and varieties. She was not surprised. Life always happened. It might survive an hour, or a year, or a millennium. It might kill itself after a billion years or be killed in half a million, but on this kind of planet and on a dozen or a hundred other kinds of planets, some kind of life always happened.

All this time, the great mooing had gone on in the background and was now answered by another voice, another call coming from the outer dark, faintly and far away. Questioner increased her visual acuity to detect a point of light moving slowly toward the system. When she looked back at the planet, she saw that life had emerged upon its surface. The planetary life forms were less interesting, however, than the interlopers from afar: the one who summoned; the other who came in response, now near enough to take form, a creature sailing with fiery wings upon the solar winds.

At the edge of the cometary field the wings lifted above the plane of that field to fly across it toward the inner planets. It approached the young sun slowly, reluctantly, draggingly, ever slower the nearer it came.

And there, from near the farthest, coldest world, tentacles of cold fire reached out to catch and hold the newcomer fast. The captor transmitted a howl of triumph. The captive screamed in a blast of waveforms. The Questioner understood both howl and scream, the one of triumph, the other of terror and pain. She knew that pain would gain the victim nothing. *Her*, the Questioner told herself, assigning roles to this drama. The victim would be female. The attacker would be male. It was *his* tentacles that held *her* fast.

There were flares of energy and agonized shrieks of radiation as the far planet swung slowly to the left, behind the sun. When it emerged once more, one set of wings rose above it and flew directly toward the Questioner. On that far surface of cold stone and gelid gas, across half the icy sphere, the newer arrival sprawled silent and motionless amid a charred wreckage of broken wings. Probably she was dead. At this distance, Questioner could not clearly make out her shape or configuration. She strained to see, but the approaching wings filled her view, a smell of fire and sulfur, a sound of hissing, an overwhelming darkness, and the representation came to an end in a sputter of smells and electronic noise, a clutter of meaningless waveforms and chemical spewings. Beside her on the soggy soil, the device clicked and turned itself off. The data-gravel had run through into its flask once more.

Had the participants in the record been Quaggi? Neither creature had looked like the Quaggi she had seen pictured or heard the Flagian describe. But then, butterflies did not look like caterpillars, either. Or vice versa.

While the record was still quite fresh in her memory, she ran the solar system through her planetary catalogue and came up with a match. The system was numbered ARZ97405. The moonlet where the interstellar being had been assaulted and killed was so unimportant that it was not even listed, but the planet she had watched most closely was now a mankind-occupied world called Newholme. Newholme. Well, now. Wasn't that coincidental. She had witnessed the birth of a planet that was on her list of planets to be visited! A planet the Flagian trader had already sold her information about! She was moved to put Newholme upon her ASAP list, particularly since the Council of Worlds had received disturbing reports of its own. Human rights violations. The possibility of another large-scale "miscalculation." Planetary instability.

The enigmatic record she had just seen tipped the scale. She would move the visit to Newholme forward in her itinerary. She would recruit some appropriate assistants and schedule the visit within the next cycle. And, when she was in the vicinity, she would stop at that far-out moonlet and see just what it was that had died there. Perhaps the Brotherhood of Interstellar Trade would offer her something for that information. Unless the BIT had been there before her!

Questioner sighed, a very human sigh. She had not moved or eaten or drunk for some time, and she was experiencing that slight disorientation and fuddlement that a human might notice as weariness and discomfort. A cracking sound made her look upward, to see her own ship settling toward the soggy arena of the shuttleport. In two real time days, she had seen a million years of planetary history. Remarkable.

Steam rose. Mud splattered. The landing was sloppy, which meant the captain had taken the helm. He was also a political appointee, one who had graduated eight hundred and ninety-fifth out of a class of nine hundred at the academy. If it weren't for the professionals on board, most of them Gablians, the ship would never arrive anywhere. Dutifully, though in considerable annoyance, the Questioner rose and made her ponderous way toward the ship.

8

Native and Newcomer: A Conversation

At some point in time (later than the time Questioner had experienced) on that same world Questioner had watched, two creatures were engaged in conversation. In real time it happened, one could say, roughly simultaneously with protomankind on Old Earth learning to make stone tools and build a fire. Mankind, along with the rest of the universe, was unaware of the beings, the beings were unaware of mankind, and the conversants were strangers to one another. They used no names, for they had none to use, and they figured out one another's language as they went along.

As was admitted by the native.

"I have a vision of you in my mind. If you turned out not to be like that, I should feel disappointment. It is dangerous to feel that I know you when I do not."

"I don't think others know our kind," said the newcomer, sadly. "We tend to live very much alone."

"We'll get to know one another," said the native, with enthusiasm. "You must have seen much of the universe."

"This galaxy, yes," said the newcomer, depressed.

"What is a galaxy?"

"This local group of stars. There are others, so far away only their light may be seen."

"Galaxy. Well. What shape is it?"

"Flat, mostly. With long, twisting arms it pulls about itself as it turns."

"A spiral, then. Galaxies are spiral?"

"Some. Only some."

"Are there many in the galaxy like you?"

"Twice I met another like myself. Far had they come, far had they yet to go, for there are many stars and times to swim. I had not swum so far as they, nor will I, for I am done."

"You are not done," said the native in a firm, cheerful way. "Not yet. You're still quite alive and getting better. Are you very old?"

There was a pause, as a mountain range eroded toward a plain.

"Old? No, I'm not old." The newcomer hummed for a time, as a machine might hum, searching for information. "I could have lived the lifespan of a star. There is no limit to my life, unless I die like this."

"I wish you would *not* speak of dying. I do not allow dying here. Is this usual? Do all your people end themselves this way?"

"Of the two I met, one was young, one old. The young one knew no more of life than I. The older one told me beware, beware the call. That one told me to deafen all my ears against the call. I wish I had believed."

"Only two of your own kind? But, surely you began somewhere? Somehow?"

The newcomer searched memory. "I remember shell, close all around. I do remember kin along with me, warm turning close within each other's wings. I would have lingered there, but kin cried out. Somewhere a great lamenting. Then the flame. Away kin burst, we burst, fire trailing us, then something broke the shell. Kin went swiftly away. I called. No answer, just space and distant stars. I went out, too, unfurling wrinkled wings to catch starwind. Behind me, falling far, the shell that held us, burning as it flew."

"Two of you in the egg," mused the first. "That explains a lot."

The newcomer puzzled over this. "What does it say?"

"It says that you have kin."

"Kin? What good is kin! Kin left me there," the newcomer cried in anguish. "Long time I flew among the burning stars. I searched for kin. I longed for kin, nest-warm, wing-close. When kin called me, I came."

"You came here, to this system," agreed the native.

"Here's where kin was: grown great and terrible." The newcomer trembled.

"You grieve because you think the one that did this was your kin," said the native. "But maybe that isn't true."

An island chain thrust itself above the waves.

"Kin was like me, yet different from me. Kin was the only one I've ever known that was like me yet different from me. Who else could that have been?"

"I am different from you."

"But you are different from everything."

"None like me on other worlds?" the native said with surprise.

"I have seen none like you. I have seen life before, but none built up like you, accumulant, piled life on life on life. . . ."

"Ah," said the native, surprised. "How strange. I had assumed no world could exist without at least one like me. Who governs them? Who designs? Who rules?"

"I was not interested in governance."

"You say you saw two others just like you. Perhaps they, too, were born as you were born. With kin who cried to get out?"

Long silence, during which several races of trees evolved and died. "I never thought of that."

"So it's possible the one who called to you was their kin instead of your kin?"

A long, long pause, then, doubtfully, "Even if true, it makes no difference. Am I not shackled here, no matter who?"

A continent came into being, floated halfway around the world, then sank beneath the waves.

"I don't think it was your kin who did this to you, though your kin will probably do it to someone."

"Will my kin do this thing? Oh, sad, so sad."

"Why should this be the way?"

A long silence, then a whisper, "Perhaps there is no other way to be."

The native detected great sadness and felt guilt at having caused such pain through mere curiosity. The native deputized a sizeable segment of itself to see to the comfort of the newcomer. Bringing comfort was very complicated. It took a long time.

"Are you more comfortable now?" the native asked eagerly, when the time was past.

"More comfortable," sighed the second. "Yes. I am more comfortable now."

"Are you getting enough nourishment?" The native worried about this. Now that the newcomer was truly settled, the native didn't want anything to happen to it.

"Oh, yes, thank you."

"And are they amusing you?"

"Yes. Yes? Well, I think they are amusing me. Sometimes I feel such joy. When they dance for me, I have such pleasure. I do not want to die."

"I told you! You needn't die!"

"I'm still dying."

"No. You're not. I'll figure something out. Can you go back to sleep now?"

"I think I will. Just a little nap."

"A few thousand revolutions, maybe."

"Maybe."

Silence then, on the part of the newcomer, though the native talked to itself. The native always talked to itself, now let me see, I-we-that need to do this, I-we-that need to send a hand there, a foot there, I-we need to spin off some teeth to chew over that matter, and, oh, yes, how is the newcomer? Asleep, good. Poor thing.

Poor thing. I see no reason why it should have to be that way. I will make it happy here. If it has had a difficult time, it deserves happiness. All my creatures deserve happiness.

9

Amatory Arts: Fitting into the Family

"Certain of my lectures will be repeated annually during your training," said Madame. "They cover subjects which I know to be important but which you will think dull and irrelevant. This information is indeed pointless and dull, until the moment you need it, at which point it becomes vital. Therefore, I repeat myself at intervals to be sure you will have the information when you need it.

"When you are purchased by a patroness, you will become a member of her family. Who is included in that family will depend upon her preference and your good sense. Probably it will include at least the younger children of your patroness. It may include certain of her servants and a chatron or two. It may also include her husband. Her children and her servants will accept you to the degree you are helpful and amusing without in any sense attempting to supplant any of them in your patroness's life. To the children, and to the servants, you will say such things as, 'She is so fortunate to have you. She is so proud of you. I don't know what she would do without you.' Note, never say, what *I* would do without you. They are not your children, not your servants. Your relationship to them is reflected through her, as in a mirror. We will expand on this later; your conversation mistress will help you with the variations that may arise.

"Now, as to the husband. It is important that you consider the personality of your patroness's husband, for though she has the right to a Consort of her own choosing, husbands accommodate that right in various ways. It is essential that you analyze the degree and type of accommodation and make every effort to meet it more than halfway.

"For example, the husband of your patroness may be complacent, in which case honest civility will be all that's required. He takes first place. At functions where husband and wife must appear together, you do not appear at all. At functions planned for patronesses and Consorts, at the theater, at restaurants, at fêtes and jollities, he does not appear.

"He may be envious, in which case you will speak *to* him of how highly his wife speaks *of* him. You will use a variation of the same technique used on servants and children. 'She is so lucky to be married to you. She says so, all the time.'

"Occasionally, however, you will meet a husband who is given over to an amorphous rage, which may or may not direct itself at you. Some people, more often men, spend their entire lives awash in bitterness. They rage against injustices done to their forefathers, perhaps centuries in the past. They rage against injustices done to their countrymen, their families. They rage against people who are unlike themselves, who, by virtue of their difference, must be up to no good. They rage against people who are like themselves who do not share their views. They rage against their parents, their wives, their children, and against anyone who is sympathetic to any of these. Their rage is a screen between them and the world, behind which they huddle over their egos, like a caveman over his fire, unable to see out through the smoke.

"Even some apes display this characteristic. Such fury may begin as a matter of status, as resentment against the dominant male. It may begin out of frustration of desires. It may begin with an unhappy nature that is born depressed and uses anger to fuel itself into action. It may begin in mystery, and it may end in tragedy. However or whyever it begins, it is essential that your patroness be protected from it. Your duty to your patroness is to give her joy and keep her from harm. She selected you. She places her happiness and her trust in you. She is your responsibility. If you injure a husband in protecting your patroness, you are exempt from any damages or judgments, even if the entire Executive Council of the Men of Business rises in wrath. This is one of the reasons you are taught hand-to-hand combat.

"Anger is our most destructive emotion. The most difficult part of your job is to deal with anger, your own or others'. We need anger to defend ourselves, so we cannot breed it out or teach ourselves not to feel it, but when we let the anger well up without a proper object, it floods our minds and renders us helpless. We all know men who are angry at everything, simply because they prefer to be angry at everything. Often, they self-destruct, and sometimes they take other people with them."

10

Three Angry Men

Settlers had spread outward from Naibah along the shores of the Jellied Sea, so called for the semi-annual hatch of Purse fish whose translucent egg sacs rose from the pelagic ooze in uncounted millions, turning the sea for that brief period into an oceanic aspic. There were good-sized communities as far as several days' sail east or west, and small struggling settlements more distant than that. These places were supplied by ships from Gilesmarsh, the port at the mouth of the river, a place well equipped with doss houses, gambling dens, taverns, and stews built on tall pilings above the tidal ooze. Naibah was actually a bit inland from the delta, away from the stink of the mud flats and on high enough land to avoid both five-moon tides and the occasional tsunami resulting from sub-oceanic seisms.

Most boats docking at Gilesmarsh tried to do so at middle high tide, so their passengers could take one of the wind taxis upstream to Naibah and Water Street. There the transvestites were younger, prettier, and more agile than the old swabs at the port; the drink was of less lethal quality; and a man in his cups was less likely to end up dead, providing he kept his veils straight. Though there were few women of good repute to be offended on Water Street, there were alert Haggers everywhere.

One of the Water Street taverns was called the Septopod's Eye, and in addition to more-regular customers the place was patronized quarterly, more or less, by a group of odd fellows who came into Naibah from different directions, looked considerably different from the usual run, and smelled different from (and worse than) any living thing. One of them was called the Machinist, and another went by the name of Ashes, and the third one called himself Mooly. Whenever the barman (who despite his profession was a respected family man, entitled to a g' and a cockade) caught sight of any of the three, he summoned several bulky Haggers to sit about and look menacing and made sure his wife and daughters were up in the family quarters behind locked doors.

The three odd fellows never seemed to notice these arrangements. Each time they came, they sat at the same table and they drank the same brew, and they left at the same hour—just before the night boat sailed for Nehbe. Every time they came, any patron they spoke to was offended, and every man who got close enough to smell them was offended, and all in all, the barman was thankful they only showed up three or four times a year.

"So," said the one called Mooly to the one called Ashes, "you got your vengeance all underway, have you?"

"All moving along nicely." Ashes grinned ferociously and dipped his snout into his glass. "Machinist kind of helped me out. Now I'm waitin' for matters to ripen."

"You figure gettin' ridda her will change things, do you?" asked Mooly.

"Change my irritation some," Ashes growled. "Teach her a lesson. Woman had no right to go off like that. I shoulda had daughters! I shoulda had riches! Woulda had, but for her!"

"Still got no ship," murmured Mooly.

"We'll get the ship. No reason for hurry. Mountains are gonna roll, Mooly-boy. Mountains are gonna roll." He leaned back, opened his mouth and sang, "An' when they do, it's me and you, and devil take the hindmost."

Everyone in the place began talking of something, anything, to cover the sound of that song, for it held a horridly broken quality, as though it issued from the throat of something not quite complete.

"Well, *we're* ready," said Mooly, glaring at Ashes, his long yellow nails, ridged as washboards, making a dry tattoo upon the tabletop, like the rattling of bones. "*Been* ready some time."

Ashes squirmed, perhaps uncomfortable at this challenge. "I know, I know. Gotta be patient. Gotta wait on events. You tell 'em Ashes said so. Wait on events."

"I done my part," whispered the Machinist. "Nothing new, here, Ashes. Why'd you need me here? I don't like coming here."

"Got to show the flag to the bloody Hag, Mah-cheeny. Got to come out in the open, ever now and then, listen to people talk, see 'em wander, figure 'em out."

"You're drunk," said Machinist, who drank nothing but water. "You're pickled."

"And if I am? Who's got more right? Never mind, Mah-cheeny, old boy. These little get-togethers keep us in touch. You over there near Nehbe. Mooly over the mountain with our folk. Me wanderin' around in Sendoph and Naibah, keepin track of this one and that one. Now you can go back to your con-stit-you-encies and tell 'em what's goin' on."

"Got no constituency," grated Machinist. "Don't want none."

Ashes sneered, "You got one, whether you want it or not. There's still folks remember you well, Mah-cheeny. Folks that speak of you often. Shatter sends regards. So does old Crawley! Meetin' here keeps us all together, keeps us on track. Whatever happens, we're gonna be all together. No matter what happens."

"What happens better be what we planned to happen," said Machinist. "That's what'd better happen."

"Sure, sure," soothed Ashes. "All in good time."

"There's been too damn much good time!"

"You want it sooner, you can lead it."

"Don't want to lead it," said Machinist. "Never did."

"Well then, don't be so impatient. It'll all come to pass. You can rely on that. It'll all come to pass. No more Hags. No more smart-ass women dyin' when we do 'em. No more g'this and g'that. You relax, old boy. All's going just the way it should."

They drank, they muttered, and around them the air seemed to seethe with frustration, expressed and repressed, a kind of livid glow that exhausted the air, leaving it without sustenance. Not a moment too soon, they left, this time with no assaults and no insults beyond the assault of their smell and the insult of their presence. Everyone in the room gasped with relief and those nearest the windows rose to throw them wide.

The barman propped the door ajar as well, then summoned two supernumes-of-all-work to scrub the table and chairs where the three had sat. He bought drinks for the house just to restore a little conviviality. Every time the trio descended on him, he swore it would be the last, but he still hadn't come up with a way to keep them out without insulting them, and somehow he didn't think insulting them was a good idea.

11

On Old Earth: History House

On Old Earth, History House #8739 (one of 10,000) glowed golden in dawn, shone rose-pink in sunset, a mountain of mirrored surfaces set like the facets of a gem. The interior ambience fulfilled the exterior promise; all was brilliance and luxury. Gilded columns towered, white faux marble stairs curved away to unseen marvels, while the tall mirrors on every wall expanded the interiors into infinite, though often fragmentary, spaces. Carpets were thick and mattress-soft, and they led past fountains and sculptures and flowering trees, artificial but scented like real ones, to wide corridors that opened into the exhibits: *Old Earth, 20th-Century America; Old Earth, Asian Heritage; Old Earth, the Arts; Old Earth, Africa, Cradle of Man; Old Earth, the Primordial Fauna; Old Earth, Trees, Trees, Trees.* And so on, and so on.

The exhibits were an artful combination of theme park, resort, museum, concert, theater, and zoo. They were even partly, though by far the lesser part, authentic. Late in the fourth millennium of the common era, who was to say what had been real two millennia ago, or three millennia, or even longer than that? Clothing, ideas, fads, convictions, all had been transitory and miscible. Nature itself had been ephemeral. Even religions had shifted, becoming more or less than they had been, or had been thought to have been, but History House offered hints and approximations of the spiritual just as it offered approximations of everything else.

Though they were called ''artists'' in the puff stuff, the performers who made the displays enjoyable and understandable did not profit from the glitter of the lower floors. Artists who lived in, mostly quota clones, occupied the far upper floors, for people on contract were not important enough to be allocated either luxury or space, both of which stopped at the 80th floor, just above the suites and gyms and dining rooms allocated to management. Above that were the shops, warehouses, and rehearsal halls, and above them were the dining rooms, grooming suites, and Denti-meds, serving those who lived above. The topmost floors were hives, with artists' cubicles crammed like cells in a honeycomb.

One's cubicle, however sterile and cramped, held all one had of home. Ellin Voy's cubicle, for example. On her narrow bed lay the stuffed bear Mama One had given her when she was three and the dolly Mama One had given her when she left for History House. On the shelf above was a little holo of herself and Mama One and Mama Two when they met at the ballet school for Ellin's thirteenth birthday. There was the book that Mama Two had given her for a sixteenth birthday present: *The Wizard of Oz,* a facsimile of a real book written centuries and centuries ago.

Hung above the shelf were other pictures memorializing brief holidays and ephemeral friendships. There was Ellin standing next to the bionic bull and the real bullfighter, the time she was assigned to History House in Spain; standing next to a handsome guard at the Tower of London when she'd been assigned to History House in England. Artists got reassigned among the History Houses all the time, or their contracts expired, or they paid off their contracts and left. There was no one in the corps de ballet that Ellin had known longer than two years. She looked at the pictures of herself with this one and that one, and sometimes it was hard to recall their names.

At night, the three inner cubicle walls could be set to show views chosen from among an extensive library of landscapes and interiors and events, both Terran and other worldly. Most of the artists chose something from their assigned periods of earthly history, something homey: a fireplace with glowing logs; a summer garden, glorious with flowers; an autumn landscape, with trees changing color and a little wind riffling the surface of the pond; a city with broad avenues where spring blossoms fell gently onto the horses and carriages; views of things that no longer existed and places that no longer were.

Honorable Artist Ellin Voy chose otherwise. The sight of morning sun through autumn leaves made her cry. The sight of a fire burning on a hearth hurt her, as did trees dancing in moonlight. Views that made her think about the walls themselves made her choke, unable to catch her breath. Some fault within her, some unsuspected weakness that should have been eradicated before she was allowed to develop, had escaped the scrutiny of the monitors.

No matter what other artists did, Ellin kept her walls set on patterns only: receding colors of infinite depth, currents full of eddies and swirls, shapes that opened up and ramified and became other shapes, or endless streams of bubbles changing hue as they floated up and away. She curled on her narrow bed after lights out, dissolving in the patterns like a lump of sugar, unskeining like syrup into the liquid movement, becoming clearer and clearer, fading into transparency. Somewhere in that fluid motion was the thing she longed for, the total absorption, the absence of painful memory. In a few moments her eyes would blink, and soon she would fall asleep to dream of the same patterns and of herself as part of them.

She tried never to think of Mama One's house or of infant Ellin. She had chosen to dance, she had been bred to dance, but she had not chosen to leave Mama One. It wasn't quite so painful to remember Mama Two, for that time had been spent here, inside History House, and she still saw Mama Two from time to time. She had felt safe and connected with Mama One and Mama Two. She hadn't really felt safe since.

At six every morning the bells in the dancers' section would ring to introduce la patronne de ballet, her bony face protruding from the walls above each narrow bed, mouth bent into an unmeaning smile, eyes half shut as she crooned, "Did we have good rest, mes enfants? Are we ready for le jour meilleur, the best day ever?"

To which all the dancers, Ellin included, replied aloud with the cheery voice and happy face the occasion required:

"Oh, oui, Madame. Bon! The best day ever." Audio pick-ups recorded each response and graded it for wakefulness and enthusiasm as well as for any betrayal of incipient anarchy. Fortunately, the view screens weren't set to pick up silent rebellion. They didn't see fingers crossed behind backs or under sheets, or hear the subvocalized, "Corpulent likelihood, Madumb-dumb ballet-hoo. In a swine's auricular orifice!"

The cheery response to Madame's greeting still echoed in the cubicles when the morning fanfare sounded, segueing into march music as drum and bugle urged on the jagged reds and yellows of the walls, sawing away at any remaining languors. In less than half the time allotted for hygiene and grooming, Ellin had her wealth of silver hair braided and piled on top of her head and had moved from the sonic cleansers to the service module where she unracked new disposables: tunic, trousers, slippers. The slight limp she'd had last rotation was quite gone. The injured toes were totally healed. Today she would return to dancing.

She hadn't been idle. She'd kept up her exercises, and she'd performed her alternate role. Everyone had alternate roles. If you were injured and couldn't fulfil your primary role, you still had to make every day the best day ever! Otherwise you'd find yourself out of work, and out of work could mean dead. Since Ellin had been raised in a twentieth-century matrix, her alternate roles were all in the twentieth century. This last one had been an elderly shopkeeper, Charlotte Perkins, in the small American town of Smithy's Corners. She'd been Mrs. Perkins for the whole rotation, which was enough.

Awaiting the breakfast gong, Ellin used the basin for a barre as she bent and stretched. Being Charlotte Perkins was easy on her feet, but it had bored her into knots! Smiling, waiting on people, answering their really dumb questions about the twentieth century. "You mean they didn't have a Reproductive Center?" and, "Where's the transporter station?" The days without the discipline of class and performance had left her feeling logy and disoriented, as though all her muscles had turned to cloth. She had to get back to the dance before she lost her mind! Besides, if she didn't, they might assign her coveted role of Dorothy to someone else!

The gong reverberated; the doors snapped open; the music got louder; the marching tempo carried the dancers out into the hall and thence past the gimlet-eyes of Par Reznikoff, Madame's deputy in this little bit of heaven. Ellin carefully kept people between her and him when she passed him on her way to the service counter. He wanted to apply for a reproductive contract with her, and she wasn't interested, no matter what it paid.

At the moment, all she was interested in was food. She had to cut intake when she wasn't dancing, but the lowered calories left her feeling hungry all the time. She was so preoccupied with making her breakfast last long enough to calm her hunger pains that she hadn't finished the liquid meal when the work bell clanged. Stage-hands and crew, already in uniform, streamed past the dancers' refectory toward the shafts that would drop them to the lower floors.

She was still holding the cup to her lips when Par came swiveling through the morning mob and took her arm.

"Elleeen," he purred, making an indecency out of her name. "You are looking lovely this morning." He began walking her toward the shafts.

"Par." She nodded, smiling, trying to hold her body away from the intimate contact he intended. No point in being nasty to him. He was Madame's little pet, and he'd get even if she did.

"You have a chance, perhaps, to think about the offer I made?" He cocked his head, eyes slitted, lips pursed, as though he were sucking an answer out of her, the answer he wanted.

She kept her voice calm, though she felt anything but. "I don't have the energy, Par. I'm just getting over an injury, and I don't think now's a good time for me."

"It's a lot of money, Ellin. You've got AA genes, pity not to use them for something."

Well, damn it, she was using them for something, couldn't the idiot see that? She smiled, shook her head as she tried to look as uninteresting as possible. "Sorry, Par. . . ."

He made a moue at her, patted her shoulder, and wandered away, leaving her at the end of the line. He wouldn't leave it alone. He'd be back, and next time he'd be pushy. She needed a strategy to discourage him, but at the moment she couldn't come up with one.

A dozen more pods came and went before she snagged an empty one, darted into it, felt the shoulder and waist restraints grip her firmly, felt the neck brace fit itself from shoulder to head as she said, "Wardrobe, Twentieth-Century America, the Arts" and remembered too late she was still holding the cup.

She gasped as the pod fell straight down, then shifted left, right, made a quick spiral, a long horizontal run at top speed, then a quick stop that threw the last of her breakfast all over her. Ellin gasped. She had never been able to breathe in transit. Now she felt like a dropped egg!

When the pod side popped open, she almost fell out, steadying herself on the wall, hearing the pod chant, "Make it the best day ever," as it zipped away.

Why did Par want her? It was true that History House paid big bonuses to the women characters who were willing to let tourists observe the actual births. Ellin only knew one person who'd done natural pregnancy and public birth, her friend from infant fosterage, Tutlia Omae, formerly known as Tutsy, who had actually had six babies, earning enough in seven years not only to pay off her contract but also to buy tickets off-world for herself and the two youngest children! Of course, not everyone would have been allowed to have six children, but Tutsy had AA genetics on both sides and the quota for American Indigenes was always scraping the bottom. Also, Tutsy had worked in one of History House's most profitable exhibits, *Old Earth, Cowboys and Indians!* and she got hardship bonuses all the time. Ellin had often wondered what there was about sitting around a fire and eating half raw meat that made it more of a hardship than dancing. At least when Tutsy stepped out of the cleanser cubicle at night, her day's work was all washed away, no harm done. When Ellin cleaned up at the end of the day, her feet were often still bleeding.

Being pregnant might be profitable, but Ellin wouldn't care for it, no thank you! All that bloating and being sick! All those months unable to dance! She'd have to gain ten or twenty pounds even to be fertile, and she hated the idea. Her body was precious. It was her, all she had, and she didn't want it changed. The idea was ridiculous. Sex was ridiculous, despite the stories people told about dancers, about their probable sexual habits, spending so many hours cooped up together. That was a laugh. Mostly the female dancers were too tired and half starved to even think about sex. Some of them didn't even menstruate.

She was still carrying the cup when she entered Wardrobe. Taking tableware was against the rules, so she sneaked down the closest aisle to her own dressing area, hid the cup on her locker shelf behind the wigs, and wadded the wet disposables directly into the chute, cursing beneath her breath. She'd expected to get at least three or four days out of this set, and here they were, ruined. Disposables were charged to her contract. Meals were charged to her contract. There was no charge for housing, but then, one couldn't really call a cubicle housing.

Getting into the Dorothy costume took only a moment, the blue-and-white checked skirt, the little apron, the puff-shouldered, high-necked blouse with all the buttons. The blouse had been designed for Ellin, with a high neck and long, slender arms. She took the Dorothy wig from its stand and held it ready as she entered the name of the character in the makeup frame that gaped in the locker door and thrust her face into it, holding her breath while it went dabby-dab-dab, plucky-pluck at her. She focused her mind on the Yellow Brick Road sequence, summoning the music, feeling the role, the stretch and release of muscle, the gathering and loosing of sinew and strength.

When the mirror dinged and she stepped back, someone behind her looked over her shoulder into the mirror. Snow Olafson, who'd sneaked up on her and now lifted an eyebrow, giving her a smoky look.

He whispered, "I hear you and Par are signing a contract."

She pulled the Dorothy wig over her hair, pushing her stray locks up under it, as she snapped, "Don't be silly, Snow. That's ridiculous."

"Oh, not the way he tells it."

"He can tell it any way he likes. I am not interested in a reproductive contract with anybody. I'm just beginning to get lead roles, why would I frangle it up?"

He blinked at her like a big cat. "Well, Ellin, if you do decide to . . . frangle . . . keep me in mind."

And he moved lazily away, glancing at her over his shoulder. Snow danced the role of the Wizard—not at all the kind of Wizard who had been in Ellin's book, but then she wasn't exactly the kind of Dorothy who had been in the book, either—and the two of them had a long, sultry pas de deux in Act II. Snow was not a contractee. Snow had been hired from outside, and the word was he had a sole-use reproductive contract with two licensed nordic type women in the Wisconsin Urbop. So why was he here flirting with her? Why did men get themselves into sole-use reproductive contracts if they didn't intend to honor the terms? That's all Ellin needed, getting dragged into some contract violation case.

She put him out of mind as she put the finishing touches on her wig, tied her shoes, and padded down the stairs. There was a rehearsal studio behind the stage where they could warm up. Below her, she could see Snow arguing with Beise Tonkoff, the choreographer. Probably about that really ugly sequence in the last act, where Dorothy had to choose between staying with the wizard or going home. Both she and Snow hated it. It was ugly! Beise swore it was the same as written originally for the ballet, back right around the end of the twentieth century or start of the twenty-first, though back then it was called Homage to Dorothy, based on the book Ellin had been given.

Snow looked up, caught her eye, and grimaced. Her inclination was to stay away from Snow and never to confront anyone, but in this case . . .

Beise was saying, "But I can't simply change something that's authentically in period. . . ."

"It isn't," Ellin said. "There's nothing authentic about the ballet. In the first place, in the book and the two-dee, the wizard is a fat old man and Dorothy is a girl, a child. They never dance together at all. In an authentic version, Dorothy would dance with the metalman, the strawman, the beastman, and possibly one of the witches, but not with the wizard. So for heaven's sake, look at it, and let us fix it!"

He sighed, much put upon. "What in particular?"

"The whole sequence! Look at it. The good witch has just told Dorothy about the red slippers, and Dorothy comes forward, sur les pointes, arms widely back, raising the working foot a little higher each time, looking down at the slipper. She's amazed. She does a grande battement, ending with an attitude an avant, to get the closest possible look at the slipper. That's fine, but all this time the Wizard just stands there like a lump, waiting for the pirouettes, and then he walks around her like a robot, clunk, clunk, clunk. He's not the metalman, for heaven's sake! Both characters look robotic, and there's no motivation for what he's doing! He ought to follow her, then as she pirouettes, he should reach out to her. Maybe a slow lunge and glissade. Something! If he wants Dorothy to stay, his body ought to say so."

Snow raised his eyebrows at her and grinned, leaning toward her yearningly.

She ignored his intent and said, "Yes, maybe like that.

Then when we get to the lifts, it's up down, up down, like someone doing exercises, and Dorothy's not even paying attention! The whole sequence makes him look like a robot with ugly legs."

Snow scowled at that, and she quickly turned away. That ought to do it. Snow was very vain about his legs. He wouldn't let go of Beise from now until the end of time. As she stepped away, she caught the director's amused eyes on her. He'd heard her.

Well, maybe it was amusing, but dance was her life, her only love. In her head it was a continuous stream, with eddies and falls and high, sparkling splashes. Certainly it shouldn't ever just *glug, glug, glug,* like a plugged up pipe! Her dream of herself, the dream she'd had since a child, had no glugs in it. When it was right, her body moved without herself being aware of her body, as though she were dissolved in the music.

She walked back across the stage while various backscenes flicked into and out of existence in the rearstage matrix: fields where the strawman was found; the forest where the metalman appeared; the line of stone where the beastman appeared roaring in the red glow of the sunset, dark against a burning sky. The backscenes used in History House shows were among the best ones anywhere because they were based on tapes of actual landscapes, as they had appeared before all the atectonic land areas were leveled and domed. Somehow computer-generated scenery never looked as real.

She reached the wings just as the tornado flicked into being behind her, first far off, then coming closer and closer while Dorothy and her little dog ran for the house. . . . Then off and away, the house flying, Dorothy and Toto in it.

Sometimes children were brought backstage to meet the dancers. They always wanted to meet Toto, too, but of course he was only a holo. There were no dogs anymore.

"That twisty wind is great," one candy-smeared small boy had exulted to Ellin—or rather, to Dorothy. "Why don't they let tornadoes happen for real?"

Ellin had told him why, but the boy had seemed unconvinced. Later, Ellin had thought maybe he was right to be so. There was something terrifying about the tornado, even here on stage, but oh, it lent wings to the dancing! Many old books had dangers and excitements in them, but all natural violence was controlled now. Everything was domed over. If there were excitements, they were out on the frontier, which is where, she told herself firmly, she was going to go as soon as her contract was paid off. She was going to find a primitive planet way out there, where the people had no dancers, where she could teach them all about it until she was too old to move.

No one on Earth worked very late in life. History House never kept anyone after they were forty, but Ellin would not quit at forty and spend the rest of her life on her pension, in a cubicle somewhere! Not even if she had to save up and save up and skimp on disposables and serve her whole twenty years to use her money for a ticket out! She dreamed about it all the time, finding a place with real trees, real grass, real creatures. A place that lasted.

Warmup was short, a kind of abbreviated class. Out in the lobby, people were already lined up as Ellin and the others took their places in the wings. The orchestra was tuning up. All History Houses used real people, keeping the various talents alive. A man's voice spoke her name from behind her, and for a moment it sounded like Par's voice, but when she turned, it was a stranger, one of two, both dressed in management blue. That meant they had a right to be here. Or anywhere.

Her mind raced over recent days' activities, searching for something, anything she might have done, might have said. Had someone heard her complaining about the restrictions or the food? Maybe someone had seen her take that cup. . . .

One of the men returned her panicky look with the fractional upturn of lips allowed government functionaries. Since he'd smiled, it probably wasn't anything she'd done. Snow? Par? Who? Then she noticed their lapels and insignias: red-and-gold instead of the green-and-white of the civility monitors. They were from Planetary Compliance!

"Ellin?" one of them asked. "Ellin Nordic-Quota, 2980–4653?"

She nodded, afraid to trust her voice. Planetary Compliance. You couldn't get any more threatening than that.

He smiled again. "Will you call your substitute, please. We have a requisition for you."

"Requis . . ."

"From the Questioner."

Her mouth dropped open. The man who had smiled uttered a brief, official chuckle, three precise ha's. She caught a glimpse of herself in the mirror through the classroom door and shut her mouth. No wonder he laughed. She looked witless! Actually stupid, and when men in blue were talking at you, it was not the time to be stupid.

Summoning all available poise, she tried to draw herself up and out of character to ask, "The Questioner, gentlemen?" Try though she had, the words came out in what she thought of as Dorothy's voice—wondering and very naïve.

The fatter one said, "*The* Questioner, yes." He actually grinned. "Today, girly. This morning. If you'll call your substitute, please."

He had just committed an incivility, calling her girly, but now probably wasn't a good time to report him. Maybe it would be better to ignore it. Even forget it. Trying not to fumble or seem hesitant, she went to the nearest com and spoke to the panel: "Corps de ballet. Director's office, please. Dorothy character has been called away from backstage by PC officers. Substitute needed immediately."

"How long will it take?" the man asked.

"Once they call me back, not long," she murmured. "One of the human alternates will have to be dressed for the part. They only use androids in emergencies."

"You have to wait?"

"Once the orchestra starts, no character is supposed to leave the wings, sir. In case the entrance cue comes up. . . ." She stared at the floor, trying to keep her breathing steady. What had she done? What had someone claimed she'd done? Had Par accused her of something?

Down the hallway a door opened and Par Reznikoff

came through. "That's Madame's deputy," murmured Ellin, pointing. "I guess you'll have to talk to him."

The two men moved away from her and intercepted Par in mid-stride. Ellin couldn't hear them from where she stood, still poised for the music. Madame's deputy didn't like it, whatever he was hearing. He shook off their reaching hands and came to the wings, where she was standing, pointing his finger at her and saying: "You'll stay right where you are. . . ."

"Reznikoff, perhaps you'd like to call the nearest PCO," said one of the men in blue, who had followed him.

Par turned quite pale, though his mouth was still chewing at the words he hadn't said yet. Evidently he didn't like the idea of the Planetary Compliance Office.

"I suggest, before you say anything actionable, that you do so." The other man in blue looked amused, which would send Par around the far turn. He began furiously punching up com numbers on the panel. Ellin caught one of the men in blue staring at her and she flushed.

"That's all right," he said in a calming voice. "He'll get the word. You're the lead in this ballet, aren't you? The records on you said you were a dancer."

She didn't ask what records. She was saved from having to say anything for Par turned from the com with his jaw set and his lips pale from being pressed together. He stormed away.

"You can change your clothes now," said the less-talkative man in blue, gesturing down the hall. "And you'll want to bring an overnight case."

She shifted uncertainly.

He smiled the government smile once again. "It's all right, dear, really. There's your replacement at the end of the hall. You're not in any trouble. We'll meet you at the gate."

Both of them had been uncivil, calling her girly, calling her dear. She was not a nus, someone with No Useful Skills. She was an honorable, just as they were! She passed the substitute without a glance and went back to wardrobe in what she hoped was a dignified manner. As she removed the wig and the dress, the Dorothy thoughts and worries seemed to dissolve, leaving an aching space to be filled with some other thought or worry. It didn't take long. As she dropped a clean tunic over her head, she found plenty to worry about in being approached by PCO and requisitioned by the Questioner.

12

The Amatory Arts: What Women Want

"One of the most important things you will learn," said Madame, "is how to give a woman what she wants, whether she knows what she wants or not. If you have read your assignment, you know that mankind has a stratified mentality. The ancient lizard mind lies below the mammalian mind, which lies below a primate mind, which is modified by a mind adapted to language, and since these layers have developed in response to differing evolutionary pressures, they often do not function efficiently together. Human civility tries to control ape dominance, human rationality tries to control mammalian sexuality, human social conscience tries to ameliorate reptilian greed, never with total success. Some individuals who could be human give up the struggle and remain mere speaking animals.

"Add to this the complex endocrine makeup of women that drives their cyclical biological systems, and add to *that* the fact that women are more likely than men to 'think about situations' in words and symbols which themselves have imprecise meanings, and you will begin to get an idea why women cannot always say, even to themselves, what they desire at any given time.''

Madame took a sip of water. Mouche sat very still, pen poised, hoping he could figure out what Madame desired at any given time. Keeping up with her was very difficult. Keeping one step ahead was impossible. He looked up to catch her gimlet eye, as though she had read his mind, and flushed, bending quickly over his notebook.

She went on. ''At the prelinguistic levels, young females are no different from their brothers. They all eat, sleep, and play in the same way. The female's physical growth is as rapid, her bones and muscles are as strong. The prelinguistic mother makes no differentiation between the male and the female infant.

''Both male and female young play in accordance with their genetic pattern; they run and jump and make noise and copy adult behavior. Primate males, as a group, are more active and noisy and less thoughtful. Primate females, as a group, have longer attention spans and are less likely to engage in rough play. Individual males and females, however, are found at the extremes of both groups, so we must regard these differences not as sex-determined but as gender and culture influenced.

''It is at sexual maturity that real differentiation begins. Among many primates, including primitive hominids, females begin to cluster around infant and nurturing activities, and maturing males tend to assemble into gaming gangs that spend their time in group competitions and rivalries . . .

''Fentrys! Pay attention. You and Egon may finish your quarrel in fencing class!

'' . . . and the groups are stratified, with one or more leaders and the rest as followers. This pattern continues even today, though the acquisition of language allows such groups to be institutionalized as tribes, armies, political parties, commercial empires, religious hierarches, or sports teams. All of these have rules requiring defense and extension of territory by carrying some play object—a ball, flag, icon, trademark, or belief system—into someone else's territory. From the psychological point of view, there is very little difference between making religious converts, kicking the winning goal, or cornering the market on Thorbian gigarums.

"Proper gang activity requires the control of members. Gangs cannot tolerate 'loose' persons wandering around. One is either with the church or against it; with the company or against it; with the team or against it. A phrase long in use on Old Earth was, 'Are you with it?' meaning, 'Do you comprehend the behaviors necessary for membership?' Persons inside the group are 'us.' All significant entities outside the group, including females, are 'them,' and all them are either property, prey, or opponents.

"Outside persons who have needed or desired talents become property; persons who aren't useful or won't submit become prey. Powerful people and groups, male, may be opponents. Females are not usually regarded as opponents, and on many worlds if a woman acts as an opponent, she risks being raped or maimed in order to redefine her as a prey animal and restore balance to the system.

"Females who agree to be property are the survivors. Belonging to a mature, powerful male guarantees his protection for her and her children and raises the female's rank in the primate society. The higher the rank, the less she is harassed and the more she gets to eat. Over millions of years, therefore, it has become instinctive for females to mate with the most dangerous, most dominant male they can attract.

"Male hominid group leaders really are dangerous. When they cease being dangerous, they will be overthrown. This too has carried over into current time. Men who are physically dangerous—sports stars, murderers, rapists—often enjoy great sexual success. Even imprisoned serial killers are known to acquire female followers who send them gifts and invent romances about them. The aura of danger was and is sexually stimulating, and the attraction of and 'taming' of a dangerous man lies at the heart of all romance literature.

"While civilized males no longer publicly categorize

females as prey or property, the instinct to do so remains strong. . . ."

Mouche wriggled again, fighting boredom. His father had not treated his mother as either prey or property, and he probably didn't think of her as an opponent, either. This time he kept his head down, evading Madame's glance.

"How does this apply to you, Mouche?"

He looked up startled, but she had turned away.

"How does it apply to any of you? You will learn to impart an aura of danger because women find it thrilling, though it is only the aura, not the reality that we seek to achieve. It may take no more than a wicked smile to convey a delicious threat that will increase a woman's feeling of vulnerability to you while at the same time increasing her feeling of safety. Don't expect this to make sense at the rational level, it doesn't. It makes sense only in the bestial basements of women's minds, where a mate strong enough to fight off a cave bear was a plus, even if he occasionally knocked his mate into the fire.

"Don't confuse fantasy and reality. It is all too possible to be so swept up in the fantasy that one continues into reality, but the Consort who crosses that line is lost. We never speak of them by name, but I could tell you of more than one who injured a patroness and died in shame and obloquy. Learn your own danger signals. Learn how to control yourselves.

"In your training, you will learn to use these instincts. You will learn how to look and sound dangerous. For example, we stage duels that appear quite real, but we intervene at a point when the combatants are equally advantaged so that both participants can be made to seem dangerous. Each one will then say to his own particular audience, 'They made us stop because they had a lot invested in him, and they were afraid I would kill him.' Properly said, with a choke in the voice and furious tears in the eyes, this goes over well. Danger whispers to a woman, 'He's so strong, he's so fearless, he can protect me.'

"This is the effect you will be trained to convey. You will seem larger than life, dangerous and perilous, while really being self-controlled. When a woman buys a Consort, she wants something larger than life. If you were mere Men of Business, you would not be tempting to your patronesses.''

She fell silent, took a sip of water, looked up to see a hand respectfully raised.

''Yes, Mouche? You have a question?''

''Why must we never hurt a woman, Madame? My mother made my father very unhappy sometimes. I used to think if he would hit her, he would feel better.'' There. He had proved he'd been listening.

Madame nodded. ''That raises several issues:

''There has been much woman-wastage in history. Women have been used as breeders only, as dawn to dusk agricultural workers, as beasts of burden. They have been unconsidered, used up, untaught, cast aside, injured or killed, not allowed to grow or live to their potential. In societies that do this, it is a 'way of life,' but there is little or no culture. Heterosexual males, when by themselves, seem to fall naturally into the gang pattern where rape is an amusement or a battle tactic. Haraldson's edicts, however, make it clear that we expect more than that from humanity.

''Here on Newholme we choose to be human and we cannot afford to waste women's reproductive nature or their cultural talents. Injury is forbidden. Injury invalidates a marriage, no matter how much dowry has been paid, and a husband or Consort who purposely kills or injures a woman is invariably blue-bodied.

''Any other questions? Good. We will discuss this further on future occasions. You are excused.''

13

At the Mercy of the Mountain

A short walk from House Genevois, the Panhagion stood on a low mound a few streets west of the river, just outside the main business district but accessible from the broad, straight length of the boulevard that connected the north and south gates of the city. A fraction of every dowry paid for a wife went to support the Panhagion. A fraction of every Consort's pay went to support the Panhagion. Every Hag, every Hagger, every Temple worker or young married woman doing her matron's stint of Temple duty was jealous of the honor of the Panhagion, for it was the center of religious life not only in Sendoph but in all of settled Newholme.

Most women chose to deliver their babies in the birthing center in the vaults below the Temple, where birth was considered sacramental and where the most skilled midwives were found. If some could not deliver at the Temple, at least they tried to have Temple midwives. The viral invasion of the X chromosome that killed half of all female infants on Newholme while allowing virtually all of the boy children to live was best understood by the Temple midwives.

The domed hall of the fortress became the Panhagion Sanctuary, a place for the adoration of the Hagions, the female deities. The lower levels surrounding this space and accessible from the forecourt were given over to the offices that conducted public business. In the vaults below, the Hags Observant, each of whom could count over forty years service to the Hagions, supervised the birthing suites and the secret rituals. Their lengthy lives of service were rewarded by the provision of luxurious living quarters in the towers at the back of the Temple.

Among the Hags Observant were two cousins, D'Jevier and Onsofruct Passenger, who had been born in the Temple and had, at the Hags' order, been reared there. D'Jevier was tall and extremely slender, with tightly drawn nut-brown skin that gleamed slightly in the lamplight. Onsufruct was a year or so older, shorter, darker, and rounder. Except when bathing or sleeping, they wore what all the Hags wore: soft, long-sleeved, high-necked gowns with close-fitting wimples that hid their necks and heads and served as an anchor for the complicated folds and twists of the bright headscarves that marked their rank. The colors of their gowns betokened their lengths of service. Novices wore yellow; young women, green; middle-aged women, blue; and crones, shades of red that increased in vividness with their years. D'Jevier and Onsofruct had passed into cronehood some time since; they wore gowns and figured kerchiefs the bright crimson of fresh blood or burning coals.

The garments were so vivid that someone looking upward at the balcony where the cousins stood, high on the east side of the residence tower, might have thought the tower was on fire, a conflagration echoing that on the eastern scarp. There a crimson gash had recently appeared below a billowing eruption of ash, and this great gray cloud had opened a gaping sleeve of angry flame to stretch a cinereous arm toward Sendoph.

D'Jevier's voice quavered as she remarked, "It's worse

than it's ever been!" She sipped from her wineglass as she watched the smoky fist sail toward her, closer and closer, the fat, billowy fingers extending. So huge, so incorporeal, so deadly, nonetheless. Her fancied confrontation with this monster was aborted by a gust of wind that swept down the valley of the Giles, breaking the ashen cloud into scattered shreds of gray.

She murmured, "I wish we could ask the Council of Worlds for help."

"Help to do what?" Onsofruct asked. "We can't ask for evacuation. There are too many of us."

"I read something about HoTA devising some new method of controlling earthquakes. . . ."

"Can they do it from off-planet?"

"No. I'm sure not. It involved burning deep wells along the fault lines and pumping in some kind of shock-absorbing liquid. It doesn't stop the earth moving, but it does make the movement smooth instead of shuddering. It's the shaking does the worst damage. . . ."

"Well, take your pick," said D'Jevier. "Die in a quake or invite COW in and die anyhow."

"You think the Council of Worlds would really kill us all?"

"In the first place, they'd send the Questioner. The Questioner doesn't even need council approval anymore, hasn't for at least a century. And what the Questioner would do would be worse than merely killing us all."

"If she comes here, she would see . . . what she would see."

"She'd turn right around and make examples of us, for the edification of the galaxy."

"So we're trapped."

"Trapped ourselves."

"We didn't. Not you and me."

"Well, Hags did. And Men of Business."

A long silence. D'Jevier tipped her glass and pretended to be concentrating upon the light reflected in its depths as she said, "We might ask . . . *them*. Maybe they know something that would help."

"Jevvy! You wouldn't dare!"

The other woman grinned mirthlessly, shaking her head. "Every day I get closer to daring. If it gets worse, yes, I'll dare."

Both fell silent, thinking long, hard thoughts that they had already gone over a thousand times. Decisions made centuries ago that could not now be unmade. Roads taken that allowed no possibility of return. An hour later they were still there, their glasses long since empty, still staring wordlessly at the world-wound upon the height, livid ash and bleeding fire. They and their world were at the mercy of the mountain, and they could think of nothing at all that would be helpful.

14

A Diversion of Dancers

"It's really very simple." The Planetary Compliance worker smiled fleetingly at Ellin across the shining width of her authority surface. "Do pay attention.

"The Questioner is a device of the Council of Worlds. The Questioner moves about among the worlds assessing mankind-occupied worlds for conformity to the edicts of Haraldson. While doing assessments, the Questioner likes to take along a person or persons from a similar developmental stage as the world being assessed. One of the planets to be assessed, for example, is Bandat, where society has achieved what the Absolute Correct Ones call their preholiness phase. Another world is Chirry-chirry-dim-dim, which the Butterfly-Boys identify as being in the caterpillar stage prior to planetary pupation. You will visit Newholme, which is in the incipient industrial stage."

Ellin Voy, Nordic-Quota 2980–4653, shifted uneasily. After a long moment of silence, she cleared her throat and asked, "Am I here because I play a part in History House and have some knowledge of preindustrial society?"

"Honorable Ellin, from Old Earth America, you are here partly for that reason, but more because you are a dancer. Also going to Newholme will be Honorable Gandro Bao, who is a character in History House of the tenth Asian Urbopolis." The woman in blue nodded gently in the direction of a lean, olive-skinned man in the chair nearest Ellin. "Honorable Gandro Bao works in Old Earth, Asia: Heritage of the Arts. He is an actor-dancer of the fifteen to nineteen hundreds, Kabuki style, authentic female impersonator. Honorable Ellin is a dancer of western classical style. Among this variety of background, some skill should be found to assist the Questioner in assessing the planet Newholme."

"We are assessing it for what?" asked the man identified as Gandro Bao. "I am not understanding the role of dancers."

The woman in blue put her face in censorious mode, one of the seven official government expressions Ellin had been able to identify over the years: kindliness with smile and/or chuckle, businesslike with tight lips, censorious with narrowed eyes, threatening with mouth distended, rage with red face, forgiveness with nod and gesture of benediction, and pity with sorrowful mouth and dropped eyes and chin. Conversations invariably began with kindly or businesslike, though they might end with any of the seven.

"Were you not educated, Honorable Gandro Bao?" challenged the PCO.

He nodded, seeming in no whit embarrassed. "I am recognizing what is the Questioner. I am recalling function of Questioner in examining planets. I am not understanding why dancer is wanted."

"Ah." Her expression switched to forgiveness, the requisite smile flickering in and out of existence so quickly as to be almost subliminal. "Questioner is allowed total discretion in determining how investigation is done. Questioner has asked for dancers. Therefore, we send dancers. Questioner does not say why. We do not ask."

Ellin shook her head, conscious of weariness and annoyance. ''So we're supposed to go to Newholme, which will be kind of a History House in the sky, and determine whether they treat one another properly? An android could do that!''

The censorious expression returned. ''The Questioner is beyond criticism. If Questioner felt an android could do it, an android would be sent.''

''Sorry,'' murmured Ellin. ''I'm just . . . surprised, is all.'' Surprised hardly expressed it. She was actually shocked into near paralysis. The thought of being suddenly uprooted left her teetering over an abyss, fumbling for words and proper responses, dizzy and adrift, shocked by the immediacy and strength of her emotions. After all the years she had imagined being free, after all those dreams of going to other worlds, seeing other peoples, finding her own special place in which to live her own, unique life, now here she was, invited to do virtually as she'd always thought she wanted, at no trouble or expense to herself, and she was frightened witless.

''You may have time to adapt,'' said the woman in blue, giving her a very percipient look.

The word evoked a veritable bonfire of associations. Time to adapt. Time to move on. Time to do this, do that. Infant fosterage giving way to boarding school in History House. Boarding school giving way to advanced studies. Advanced studies giving way to the corps de ballet. Always time to say good-bye, to give up treasured things, familiar friends, always time to adapt. . . .

The woman's voice cut through Ellin's confusion. ''Suddenness is difficult for all creatures, but this will not be sudden. Honorables Ellin Voy and Gandro Bao will go to Newholme. The ship leaves soon, in seven days, but the voyage will be lengthy. During some of it, you will be asleep. For this next few days, however, the honorables will live here, in prelaunch. During this time you have medical assessment, wardrobe and other necessities will be assembled, and you will have access to all records and reports on the planet Newholme, which should be studied assiduously. Go through that door there," she pointed, "to Suite Four Thirty-Four."

The forgiving expression returned momentarily as the woman returned to her papers. "Honorable DoJub and Honorable Clementi will be visiting the planet Boshque, which is in a late arboreal phase due to ground-level predation. . . ."

Bao stood in front of the door sensor, keeping the door open for Ellin, a courtesy which earned him a half smile. The two of them prowled silently down the corridor, Ellin avoiding his eyes, concentrating on finding Suite Four Thirty-Four. She needn't have bothered, for at their approach a door lit up and caroled a welcome.

"Honorables Ellin and Bao. Welcome to Suite Four Thirty-Four, prelaunch facility for planetary examiners."

Bao broke his silence with an angry mutter. "Being much filth and excrement. Five days from now I am to be dancing the lead in the Chikamatsu *Shinj ten no Amijima*, with orchestrated Joruri, as adapted from the Bunraku. I have been much wishing this for three years. And now this is happening!"

"Be calm," said the door in a soothing tone. "Feel elation! HoLI COW pays off contracts of all nominees who are contractees as well as post-bondage stipend. Once duty is done for the Questioner, you are free! Feel satisfaction! Do not distress yourself, Honorables. Even if you do not return for decades, all will be well. Oh, feel elation!"

At the word "decades," Ellin felt a watery lick, as though an icy wave were rising inside her, threatening to spurt out of her throat in a jet of pure hysteria. She pushed it down, swallowed it, and felt it dissolving her insides. She must not disgrace herself. Not in front of this person. Not in front of this door, which was so very solicitous and was probably programmed to report any deviation from acceptable norms. She dropped into a chair and put her hands over her face, evoking the patterns on her wall, swirlings, eddies, flowing . . . calm and quiet. Herself part of the flow. None of this was really happening, not yet. She would put off the happening for a little time, and when it came, she would be ready.

"Are you feeling elation?" demanded Bao in an arrogantly angry tone. "Are you liking to go so far for doing Questioner knows what?"

At this interruption of her hard-won calm, she felt a flare of fury, as though she had received an injection of some energizing drug.

"Don't speak to me as though addressing a nus. I am not a nus. I have useful skills. Though I am a quota-clone, I retain my rights of reproduction and am as honorable as yourself. I, too, have disappointments. This rotation I was to dance in one of the Morris ballets of the late twentieth century. Your arrogance is not acceptable. You will treat me with courtesy, or I shall report you for status harassment!"

"Oh, gracious," cried the door. "Let us not speak of reportings. Feelings are strained. Emotions are liberated in unattractive ways. This is understood. Being nominated is stressful. Suddenness is resented by all organisms. Please. Sit down and let yourselves be comforted."

Again hysteria threatened to erupt. Ellin's jaw clenched tight as she sank back into the chair. One did not achieve pleasantness by greeting incivility with incivility. She knew that as well as she knew . . . anything.

A six-legged server came scuttling across the floor, eager to be of help. "Something to drink?" it whispered in a husky little voice. "A massage of feet? Of neck? Some food? Milky nutriment often soothes. Nordic types are lacto-tolerant. Please?"

"Tea," she said in her Charlotte Perkins voice. "Hot tea. In a real cup. With lemon flavor and sweetness. And a cookie." Long ago, the infant Ellin had been comforted with cookies by Mama One. She had not had a cookie for many years.

The server scuttled off.

"Apologies," Bao said wearily. "I am being frangled." He sighed and sank into the chair across from her, looking around himself at the luxurious setting. There were real carpets. There were real fabrics at the sides of the view screens. The chairs were large and cushiony. The small table at his side had the appearance of real wood, though that was, of course, unlikely. Still, going to the trouble to make it look like that was an indication of . . . something. "They are believing us to be important," he said.

"They want us to believe they think we're important," she snarled, unwilling to forgive him. "Sending us off for years and years, disrupting our lives! All this is like offering a child candy if he will be good." She had seen a good deal of that in Perkins Store, where so-called penny candies were provided for children as souvenirs of Old Earth.

He nodded, his eyes fixed on her face as though he had just noticed her. "There is being high probability we must be good regardless, so candy is being offered for making us more happy about inevitables. A bonus, perhaps?"

"Bribe, not bonus!" She snorted. Newholme. She had no idea where Newholme was. They spoke together:

"Are you knowing where . . ."

"I have no idea where . . ."

He laughed. After a moment, unable to help herself, she smiled waveringly.

He made an expansive, almost girlish gesture. "We are being angry at situation, not at one another. Maybe we are being angry with Questioner, but Questioner is not knowing and is not caring, so we waste anger on nothing. It is clear we are being together for some time. Let us be easy together."

"Is the Questioner a she?"

"So I am understanding. Of a sort."

The server brought the tea and several cookies, real cookies that smelled of vanilla and lemon. Ellin smiled at this and allowed herself to be soothed. Gandro Bao was right, of course. There was no point getting frangled with one another.

"Do you have family?" she asked.

"I was natural born," he said. "I have mother, father, one sister."

"Do you look anything like your sister?" Ellin asked curiously. Full siblings were rare except for clones. The genetic agencies usually required donor insemination for second births, to keep the gene pool as widely spread as possible within types.

He nodded, raising a hand to the server, which came buzzing over, stopping at his elbow. "I am desiring a ham sandwich," he said. "With mustard and a pickle."

"Corpulent likelihood," murmured Ellin.

"I am testing if we are really important," he said, crinkling his eyes at her. "Your question about my sister, yes, she is looking much like me, Asian type, and we are having similar facial structures. What is your family?"

"No family I know of. Except clones. I was born on preassigned ethnic quota, so my parent could have been anyone. . . ."

"I am looking at you," he corrected her. "I am thinking not just anyone, no."

She flushed. "I never asked if I had non-clone siblings, full or half. Somehow it didn't seem to matter."

"Where was your rearing?" he asked.

"First in an infant fosterage, but I don't remember much about it, to tell you the truth, except for Mama One. They cloned six of me, and History House approved us for fosterage—not together, of course—then it picked me up on a quota-clone contract when I was six . . ."

"After you were infant?"

"I lived at the History House boarding school, with dancing lessons every day, in a nurturance group—foster brothers and sisters—with our Mama and Papa Two, until I was twelve. Then I went into the ballet school, four of us with a foster aunt, for six years of additional education in dance and drama and twentieth-century studies. Then the corps de ballet. And they've moved me around. This last History House was my fifth."

He grinned ruefully. "It is not sounding like much fun. How is it feeling to have foster parents? And foster aunts?"

She frowned, chewing on a mouthful of cookie, surprised to find her eyes filling. She shook her head impatiently, refusing the tears. "Well, actually, I loved Mama One very much. I guess you could say I never really got over the separation. I still hear from her, every now and then. Mama Two was different, but as she told me herself, her job was different. And when it came time for Foster Aunt, her job was to get the four of us through the second-decade miseries. Do boys have miseries?"

He laughed, his eyes half shut, his body shaking. "Oh, Ellin Voy, I am remembering all such things. Yes. Miserable boys, I am remembering."

"How'd you get into a History House?" she asked. "Tapped, or on purpose?"

"I was being tapped," he admitted. "I was attending school in town where family is living. There, in the school, I am being always . . . what is called a laughjerker . . . ?"

"A clown?"

"You are knowing the exact word. Clown, yes. Everything is being a joke for the face and for the voice and for the legs, always being funny, always making the laughter, always falling down so much they are calling me Bao Bao Down. So many times I was having the settle-down speech, the school was getting tired of saying it. So, instead, they were giving me the test battery, and as soon as I was reaching twelve years, my family was being told I am born actor, born comic, born Kabuki dancer for women's parts—all Kabuki is dancing by men, you know . . ."

"I didn't know. Why?"

"Oh, long ago sex-workers were dancing Kabuki to be fetching customers, so Emperor was issuing decree that only men could be dancing. My life is being like your life. I am having foster uncle and three brothers also with miseries, and I am learning in the theater school, in the dance school. I am playing parts of women characters in Kabuki; princess so-so in Japanese drama; jokey fisherman wife in China Sea; fall-down silly daughter of man who is keeping cormorants." He shrugged. "That one is fun, much miming of being in rocking boat, making whole audience seasick. Now I am dancing most of time, and for rotation I am doing weird empress or being strange holy woman." He folded his arms, half closed his eyes and gazed directly ahead with a lofty, detached expression of infinite disdain. "Very wise. I am memorizing whole book of Confucian analects."

"Tell me an analect," she begged.

"Major principles suffer no transgression. Minor principles allow for compromise."

"What does it mean?"

"It must be meaning my dancing is a minor principle," he said, laughing. "For my career is being compromised."

"I guess that's how I feel, too."

"Then we are agreeing on two things."

"Two?"

"We are agreeing on what is minor and what is principle."

She sat back, suddenly relaxed. This duty might not be so bad. He seemed all right. The expression on her face was mirrored on his, and they both smiled, pleased to be with one another, beginning to anticipate whatever it was that was coming. The server interrupted this calm to bring Gandro's sandwich, which he sniffed at, tasted, and pronounced real—or so close as made no difference.

Though soothed, Ellin was not entirely willing to give up worrying. "You know, even though we're both History House contractees, even though we think we know the period, this Newholme could be totally different from anything we know about."

"Oh," he nodded, chewing, his face very serious, "I am having no doubt about that. I am sure it is being very, very strange."

15

Meeting Marool Mantelby

West of Sendoph, the terraces were narrower and steeper than in the farmlands to the east, climbing from the river in a great stair flight that ended on a final set of wooded ridges where the homes of the elite were built, very near the wilderlands. There among others of its kind stood the mansion of Mistress Marool Mantelby—Monstrous Marool, as she was known to some—the youngest of eight sisters, whose parents had done Marool great services firstly by having had no sons, and secondly by having died along with their eldest daughter, after they had sold off six younger daughters but before they had been able to sell Marool herself.

Her prosperity had come upon her thuswise:

Margon g'Mantelby the elder, Marool's grandfather, had dowered in for his son, Margon Jr., a very expensive daughter of the Rikajors, a family known to run to girls. Though the Rikajor girls had a high opinion of themselves, Margon Jr. was an acceptable if not intelligent candidate, and the Mantelby fortune, gained through the fiber trade, was large and growing. Margon g'Mantelby's offer was accepted, and Stella was dowered in to the Mantlebys.

In the first five years of their marriage Stella outdid herself in the production of five daughters, all born at home. Though the Margons, Sr. and Jr., gave every public evidence of pleasure in accepting the congratulations of their peers, they were heard to remark among friends that a male child would have been acceptable. The girls, after all, would be dowered away from the line. Where were the Margon sons to continue the line itself? Who would inherit? One did not want as heir a dowered-out nobody! One wanted a son as like oneself as possible!

Mayelan, the eldest daughter, and her two oldest sisters were much cosseted. The next two were not so much admired. Margon Sr. had died by the time numbers six and seven, twins, were born, and the last daughter, Marool, born three years after her next sister, was the straw—so Margon said in private—that fucked the camel. It had been the last attempt to produce a son, as Margon and Stella had been married ten years, and Stella's contract provided that after that term she might select a Hunk to keep her company and take her about the city and do what Hunks were known to do so well.

Thus Marool was born into a house in which fortune was assured, domestic tranquility was without fault, and her father seldom talked with her mother. Or vice versa. The Hunk was very nice, but he was her mother's Hunk, and though Hunks were taught to cosset children, they were also cautioned not to overdo it. Girls could be ruined by too much charm too early in their lives, for the reality of marriage would then come as too great a shock.

In truth, the Hunk was not even tempted to cosset Marool. Unlike her sisters—tall, pale girls with blunted edges, like monuments of warm wax—Marool was dark and pudgy in the places she was not sharp, the first of her many contradictions. She was born angry. Her first words, to her heedless chatron-nanny, were "I hate you." In this, as in most of her later life, she was completely truthful, for she did not care enough about anyone's opinion to lie.

When Marool was eight, her second oldest sister was dowered in by a wealthy family, followed by the next oldest sister, and so on each year until Marool was almost fourteen. At that point she became the only child left in the house except for Mayelan, the heiress, who had not yet found a man who was both willing to dower out and rich enough to tempt Stella and Margon. With the other daughters gone, family attention, long distracted, turned in Marool's direction. There was, her parents felt, no point in keeping her as a family member. Since she had been allowed to run rather wild, she would need some work before she could be offered for dower. They decided to hire a team of Hagger trainers to clean her up and teach her to behave in a civilized manner. If that didn't work out, they would offer her for Temple Service.

Rooly, as she called herself, was informed of these plans, at which point the resentment she had been stoking since she was in the nursery was ignited. There was a good deal of it to burn, and burn it did, with a sullen, consuming flame. She had been just another girl in an establishment where a son was desperately wanted. She was a disappointment. Well, so were they.

On her fourteenth birthday, Marool was reintroduced to her mother, who at first frowned at this dark changeling, trying to recall her name, and who then tried, during the ride to the Temple, to come up with a description of Marool that would appeal to the Hags. Many, many girls were picked for Temple Service; sometimes an only daughter was picked. Stella Rikajor, however, had thus far lost none of her daughters to the Temple, nor had her mother before her. The Rikajor family supported the Temple lavishly, and their generosity had been kept in mind.

Stella decided she would be honest about Marool and simply ask the Hags for a favor. While Stella was about this business, Marool herself slipped away into the Sanctuary to ask a few innocent-seeming questions. By the time she was rejoined by her disappointed mother—the Hags had not been responsive to Stella's needs—Marool had the information she needed.

The following morning, Marool returned to the Temple

alone. Though she was not supposed to leave the Mantelby mansion, she had sneaked into town often enough to know the way.

"I want to see the directory of Hagions," she said to the two Hags on duty, D'Jevier and Onsofruct. Both were taken aback by this request from one so young and so unprepossessing in appearance. Marool was, in truth, very unkempt and disheveled, though, as D'Jevier remarked later, her manner forbade any motherly attempt to either kempt or hevel her. D'Jevier was not unkindly, and though she felt some antipathy toward the girl, she made herself be generous.

"What are you seeking, Marool? Perhaps it is something I can help you with?"

Marool sneered. "Unless you're one of eight sisters, you can help me with nothing, Madam. It is my right to see the directory of Hagions."

The cousins, though nettled at her manner, were rather intrigued by the request. The girl confronting them was bristling with anger, every tangle on end, like a burr-bit cat, puffed up out of all good sense. Very well, the Hags thought, sharing a knowing glance. Let her peruse the directory of Hagions. She would soon weary of it.

They went into the Temple proper. The seating area sloped down to an oval dais with a curved back wall against which stood the three effigies of the Hagions, marmoreal images four times the height of a woman, each the likeness of robes draped around a female figure, but with only an emptiness inside. The robe to the left shaped a slender form, the robe to the center a stouter one, the robe to the right was somewhat slumped, as though the one who wore it was aged. Where the faces might have shown beneath the hoods or where hands might have protruded from sleeves were only vacancies. Before each image were cushions to kneel upon, and at the center, as though at the focus of a dozen pairs of invisible eyes, stood a low lectern with a kneeling bench. Upon the lectern lay the directory of Hagions, the names of all the female deities ever worshipped by mankind, each with an account of her characteristics and rites.

Marool ignored the tabs that would have led to one of the more healthful, "normal" deities. Instead, she knelt at the directory and began to turn its pages, leaf by leaf. The Hags left her there. At noon, she went away, returning some time later to continue her perusal. When it grew too dark to see in the Temple, she left it, only to return on the following morning, and thus two days passed. Late afternoon on the second day, she left the lectern and went to kneel before the center image.

D'Jevier, who had become interested in this process, was watching from the back of the Temple. She saw the hollow robe waver, as though something inside it moved. She closed her eyes, and when she opened them it was to see a fiery presence peering out of the hood, not at her, but at the kneeling girl, and a fiery hand held out, as though in welcome. She closed her eyes again, disbelieving, and when she opened them for a second time, she saw Marool rising from before the empty effigy. Though D'Jevier told herself she had imagined it, for a moment she was sure she saw that the carved marble around the opening of the hood had been blackened by fire.

As Marool passed her, going up the aisle, D'Jevier kept her eyes slightly averted, though not so far averted that she did not see the terrible and triumphant smile which lent a horrid allure to the girl's features.

"A smile," she said to her sister Onsofruct, "such as a demon in hell might wear. The smile of a fiend."

"What Hagion did she pray to?"

D'Jevier shook her head. "I didn't look."

"Is the book still open?"

"I think so."

They went to look. The name at the top of the page was not familiar to them: Morrigan. They read what was written below and turned toward one another with horrified expressions.

"Oh, by all the Hagions of life," whispered Onsofruct. "Why would a child of that age choose to worship the patroness of sexual torture and death? Which image?"

D'Jevier indicated the center one, noticing there was, in

fact, no blackening around the hood. "The strong one," she said. "The being in its greatest physical strength."

They closed the book. D'Jevier thought of cutting out the page. She could not, of course. Everything she had learned as a Hag instructed her that dark pages of death and destruction were part of the book, along with bright pages of pleasure and health. Still, she resolved to take the earliest opportunity to speak to Stella Rikajor g'Mantelby about her daughter.

Any speaking would have come too late, for Marool had left the Temple with Morrigan's name dissolving on her tongue like a poisonous candy, sweetly fatal, and she did not return home. Instead, she stalked down the stony stairs to the walkway beside the Giles and along it until she encountered a small group of those supernumes, losers and layabouts who lived beneath the bridges and viaducts of Sendoph and called themselves, unimaginatively enough, the Wasters. Though she had not met them before, she went to them unerringly and did not return to her parents again.

Among the Wasters, she continued to call herself Rooly, avoiding any use at all of the Mantelby name. Having access to money was not a good idea in this company. Those with money were victims. If she was known to come from a wealthy family, she could neither exist in happy association with her fellow predators nor take part in their forays, and Marool intended to be one of them in all respects.

She obtained a black knit garment that started above the breasts and ended above the knees and over this a collection of veils, cloths, drapes, or skins brought together more for their appearance of defiant dilapidation than for any purpose of warmth or protection. She poked bones through her ears and painted her face and body in ugly colors. Everyone around her wore similar garments, poked various things through their ears or other parts, and painted themselves, for this was their fashion, their statement, their comment upon society.

The Wasters weren't numerous, a few score at most. They found shelter where they might, under bridges, or in culverts, or in abandoned barns or falling-down warehouses or anywhere else that offered modest cover from the rain, which was frequent, and the snow, which was not. They sometimes stole their food, sometimes extorted it from passers-by, sometimes traded for it the items they had looted. A few of them wore their hair twisted on top of their heads, the knot hidden inside the dried skull of a carrion bird and fastened there with thigh bones thrust through the eye holes to signify they would kill for what they wanted, and Marool soon and zealously joined this subgroup for, perhaps coincidentally, the carrion bird was the symbol of Morrigan.

The Wasters' lives were made tolerable and even amusing through the constant use of drugs, preferably one called Dingle, or Nosmell, an extract of the ubiquitous Dingleberry that grew anywhere a square inch of soil received one drop of rain. It could be smoked or drunk or eaten or even bathed in if one had enough of the leaves to steep a tubful. It had a long lasting euphoric effect and only a few minor side effects, one being a temporary loss of libido and fertility and another being the permanent loss of the sense of smell and taste, which, considering the way the Wasters lived, could be considered an asset.

By the time she was fifteen, Rooly existed in a state of permanent Dingle-float interrupted by occasional and transitory rages. Her happiest times were when she was torturing someone or when she and her colleagues threw a bale of Dingle into a hot springs and soaked in it until the solution was too diluted to maintain the feeling of disembodied joy. Once in a while Marool thought about her parents and her intention to kill them. The Goddess had promised her their deaths, but the time didn't yet seem ripe.

When Rooly was something over seventeen and well versed in massacre, a new man introduced himself into the group. He was older than most of them, larger, certainly, with a thick, powerful body. He did not dress as the rest of them did, preferring tight trousers and a well-made cloak of some water resistant fabric. He was also different in some way that Marool could not define, as though he had come from some other place or had, perhaps, once spoken some other language.

"Who is he?" Rooly asked her companion, Dirt, casually, not caring much.

"Ashes, his name is," said Dirt. "Blue Shit knows him."

"He's fat. He's got a bulge around his middle."

"He's not fat. He just carries a money belt or something."

"Well, if he's one of us, he'll get no fatter."

Which was true. Ashes got no fatter. He got no thinner, either, which might have been enough to create some suspicion if anyone in the group had been capable of rational and connected thought. Ashes came and went and came and went. The others commented that Ashes had something odd about him, his eyes, maybe, or the whip he kept wrapped around his waist under his coat. Ashes seemed uninterested in Dingle, but greatly interested in sex.

All this Rooly noticed without caring one way or the other, and she was completely surprised when Ashes caught her by the arm one day and dragged her away into the woods where he had made a rough camp and where they might be, so he said, private. What happened next was astonishing, for Ashes gave her something other than Dingle to keep her happy, and he did not let her go back to the others. He kept her with him for a day, then another, and never during the course of those days did he cease stroking her and touching her, and putting his mouth on this part of her and that, and giving her more of the stuff he had, until she was in a frenzy she had never felt before.

"Oh, don't, don't," she pled. "Oh, stop, stop."

"Never," he said. "No. Now we'll do this. Now we'll do that," which he did, endlessly. Whenever she objected more strenuously, he merely fed her a bit of the stuff which was not Dingle and went on turning her tighter and tighter. Every breath became a game with what his fingers did, what his tongue did, what he did with that strange whip. Every time her body flamed, he quenched it only a little, then set about stoking it again.

He did nothing to release her from it. He built her lust

into a fire that burned hotter and hotter, never letting it come to culmination. Two full days of it, she had, until she begged him, at last, not to let her go but to get on with it, and only then he gave her what she pled for in a way she could not afterward quite remember. The whip was a great part of it, but she could not recollect how, and there were no scars.

The episode was repeated. It was the third or fourth time before she realized they were being observed, that all of it was being observed, from the first touch to the last, all of it was being noted by avid eyes, hungry for sensation, people hiding in the underbrush whom she could not quite see. She thought they were people. Perhaps they weren't people. She was too heated to care who watched. Besides, she had a sense that all of it was meant, planned, a part of some larger whole to which she was dedicated. Sometimes, during her couplings with Ashes, she would murmur Morrigan's name.

But then, in a tenday or two, Rooly found herself sick, really sick, vomiting and gasping like a fish, and any taste of the drug made her worse. Ashes took her by her ear and whispered deep into it, "That's my child you carry, lady. That's my daughter you bear. And I'll be back for her."

Then he went away.

Rooly had been pregnant several times, or thought she had, but each time she had miscarried. This time she did not miscarry, or at least she had not a short time later when the Mantelbys' men of business descended on her to tell her that her parents and her eldest sister were dead.

The Mantelby men extricated Rooly from among her fellows as they might an oyster from its shell, efficiently, quickly, not caring who got hurt in the process. Her parents and eldest sister, she was told, had gone for a picnic, though such entertainments were totally foreign to them. They had gone together, though Margon and Stella had gone nowhere together since the Hunk had come. They had gone to a high place, though Stella was afraid of heights, and then, somehow, all three of them had fallen from that height to their deaths. Everyone was surprised and shocked and disbelieving, except Rooly, who remained indifferent.

Margon Mantelby Sr. was dead, Margon Mantelby Jr. had no living brothers. Since Marool's eldest sister was now dead and her other sisters had been dowered into other families, Marool was the only Mantelby remaining. She inherited the name and the fortune, swollen as it was by the prices paid for six brides. Several of her sisters served notice they would contest this ruling on the grounds of moral incompetence. Marool was promiscuous; Marool was even then pregnant by the Hagions-knew-whom, and was therefore guilty of mismothering; she had done the Hagions-knew-what while among the Wasters and she was unfit to manage House Mantelby under the Mantelby name.

Marool—awakened by greed and a few days abstinence to an appreciation of the life she had long despised—denied it all. She went to the Temple, where she knelt before the same effigy as before. D'Jevier, fascinated despite herself, hovered near the curtained arch, observing. Marool was no longer a pudgy girl, but a woman lean as a snake, every plane of her face tight drawn around huge eyes that were dark and full of fire, casting the terrible allure that D'Jevier had noted before.

Once again the marble robe filled with fire and once again the fiery hand reached out to touch Marool, as though in blessing. When Marool came calmly from the Sanctuary, she told D'Jevier that she had vowed a religious pilgrimage to the Daughter House of the Hagions at the new city of Nehbe, along the coast to the east, a pilgrimage made in memory of her parents. Could D'Jevier assist her by appointing someone in Temple Service to look after the Mantelby estate in Marool's absence? At the usual rates, of course. Marool would, she said, be generous.

D'Jevier nodded, though she had to struggle to keep her face and voice calm. She agreed to send a factotum from the Temple plus an efficient Man of Businesss to keep everything running while Marool was away.

It was almost a year later when Marool returned in the company of several Haggers she had picked up somewhere. She came openly to the Temple and to the theater. She was clean, decently dressed, and certainly not pregnant. When her sisters sought witnesses to her alleged immorality or promiscuity or any of the rest of it, none could be found. The Wasters had disappeared. Marool's closest associates, or at least those who had known most about her, were simply gone, no one knew where. No one knew anything about a child, there was no evidence of the rumored child itself and Marool could not be convicted of mismothering.

Marool's well-paid agents reported that all her former acquaintances had been taken care of—except for one. The man she had called Ashes could not be found, not in any city or town inhabited by mankind, and all of them had been searched. When her agents had reported this, Marool had felt a momentary pang of fear, quickly overcome. If he showed up, she said, see to him. If he never showed up, who cared. It was his word against hers, and she was a Mantelby. She had either forgotten or chosen not to remember those avid but anonymous eyes in the underbrush which denoted a host of witnesses.

Outwardly, currently, she was a woman reformed, settled down among her Haggers to the enjoyments afforded by the Mantelby estate, of which there were many. She was secretive, however, about many things: her pastimes, her pleasures, the odd, bulky shipments she received now and then from someone living near Nehbe. Inwardly, always, she was still the follower of Morrigan, Monstrous Marool.

16

The Amatory Arts: Stories Women Tell

Early on in House Genevois, Mouche had made two good friends, a dark, wiry and slightly older boy named Fentrys and a ruddy-haired, brown-skinned lad of his own age named Tyle who came up into the suites about the time Mouche himself did. Simon had housed the three of them close together in the suites, for he believed in friendship and solidarity and the three boys were alike in being rather bookish, a trait sneered at by many Hunks, though Madame encouraged the trait among those with a taste for it, finding it a saleable characteristic among her more discriminating customers. When a patroness grew weary of bedsports, she might enjoy a good book read in a well-schooled voice. And when, eventually, a patroness outlived bedsports, she had not necessarily outlived her enjoyment of a good show, a good fencing display, a good song, or a good tale.

The boys studied together. They found, as had generations before them, that the Amatory Arts practice classes were more interesting than the theory lectures. In order to minimize study time, they divided the material into thirds, with each of them being responsible for part of it, feeling that if they volunteered often enough, they wouldn't be called upon.

Today they waited, poised, as Madame said:

"Our job, in essence, is to make married women contented and happy. On other planets, married women, whether matched through arrangement or romance, usually rank lowest in contentment among gender and marital groups. Who can give me the reason for this?"

This was in Mouche's third of the reading material, and he raised his hand to receive her nod.

"Madame, married men are most content, for they are cared for by their wives. If a woman is unmarried, she is contented to care for herself. Some unmarried men maybe don't care for themselves that easily, but they have no other responsibilities. But a married woman usually has to care for her husband, her children, and her household, even if she has other work, and usually she receives little care in return. So, she is least contented of all."

"You are speaking historically?"

"Oh, yes, Ma'am. Historically." He bit his lip. As Madame said, it was necessary to keep in mind that what *had* been done was not necessarily what *should* be done.

"Here on Newholme, love is not considered a requisite of marriage," Madame continued. "If the couple is fortunate, their sexual encounters will be not unpleasant, and if they are not fortunate in that regard, at least the unpleasantness will be infrequent and brief. We have medications that assist women in tolerating it.

"But as Mouche has said, women have many duties, some of which are painful, all of which are arduous, many of which are thankless. In consideration of this, the Hags have decreed that women are entitled to compensatory joys. Having done their duty to the family, they are entitled to the rewards of sensuality and romance, which is, of course, why you gentlemen are here.

"Tyle, discuss primary sensuality."

Tyle was busy taking notes. He wrote down, "Tyle,

discuss,'' before he thought, then looked up flushing, to find half the class sniggering at him.

''Ah, Madame, well, ah, women respond to the sensuality they remember as babies or children. When a baby is tended it is cuddled and sung to and fed, and talked to . . .''

''Endlessly,'' said Madame, severely. ''Endlessly communicated with, if only in baby talk. There is playfulness in this and an innocent sensuality. Women who were well treated as infants remember the feeling of this warmth and acceptance, if only subconsciously. They like being sensuously cuddled and affectionately talked to. They like being given sweets or wine and playfully admired for their own accomplishments, even if these are minimal. Now, why do men not see this?

''Mouche?'' she said, turning suddenly to give him a wicked look. ''Why do men not see this?''

He flushed, scrambling through his memory of last night's reading. ''Oh, Madame, the book says . . . ah, it says . . .'' He stared at the ceiling for inspiration.

Tyle spoke up, ''Men get ranked by their peers on the battleground, in business, or in games, where nobody gets cuddled and you have to be almost . . . heroic to be noticed at all.''

Mouche grimaced and offered, ''We know this is true, just from fencing class. You have to be very, very good before the master says anything except, 'Next boy.' ''

''Correct,'' said Madame, with an admonitory look at Mouche. ''Men are taught to dismiss the need for babying as mere 'female stuff,' that is, foolishness, but this nurturing does not seem foolish to women. Women are hungry for affectionate words and that's why we have conversation mistresses: to teach you to use them! Your colleague or brother may accept your striking him forcefully and addressing him as 'You old mismothered bastard.' Your patroness will not do so.

''We do other things similarly. We teach you to dance in ways that make your patroness feel skilled and graceful. We teach you to stack a deck of cards so your patroness will win the game if at that moment she needs to win a game. Simon or Jeremy are skilled cheats, and they will teach you how to do it.

"Now, in order to make a woman contented, we must be alert to the stories she creates about her own feelings. It is important for you to recognize when your patroness is inventing.

"Let us suppose that on some other world a young woman falls 'in love' with an utterly unsuitable young man. Describe an unsuitable young man, Bartel."

Bartel scratched his forehead with his pen, leaving a smear of ink at the top of his nose. "Well, Ma'am, he'd be lazy. He'd be . . . unkind. He'd be . . . I suppose he could be dirty. Or ugly. . . ."

"She wouldn't fall in love with him if he was ugly," objected Tyle.

"Well, then not ugly," conceded Barton.

"On the contrary, Tyle, he could be ugly," said Madame. "And he could be lazy and abusive as well. The woman still might fall in love with him. Why? Anyone?"

Fentrys said, "Because her hormones are pushing her toward mating, he has a dangerous look, and he is spreading pheromones all over the place."

"Quite true," agreed Madame. "Now, she cannot say to her friends or parents that her body is sexually receptive and that this man looks dangerous and smells virile. Can she? What would her family say?"

Fentrys laughed. "They'd say he was ugly and lazy and abusive."

"And the woman actually knows that," said Madame. "She may refuse to admit it, but she knows that. What she doesn't know is why she is responding to him. She does not know that she is being led by evolution and her nose. Though she can see his inadequacies with her mind, her body wants him nonetheless, so she has to justify herself. What does she do?"

"She makes up a story," said Mouche, suddenly enlightened.

"Indeed. All unconscious of what is going on, she makes up a story. What does she say?"

Interested, Fentrys said, "She could say he has good

things about him that nobody sees. Some women are very tenderhearted, so she could say he needs her. . . .''

Tyle offered, ''She could say he would change after they got married. I heard my aunt say that about a man who offered for my cousin.''

''Indeed,'' said Madame. ''And after they are married, he abuses her, and what does she say?''

Mouche said, ''She says, 'He broke my arm, but he really loves me.' ''

''She wouldn't!'' said a voice from the back of the room. ''Women aren't crazy.''

''Quite true,'' said Madame. ''They aren't crazy, but they are sometimes quite helpless in dealing with their biology. Our theoretical woman might say just what Mouche proposes. Or, she might say, 'He's under a strain, and he goes all to pieces, and it was my fault, I upset him.' An interesting fact about such stories is that repeating them actually calms the mind and assuages the pain of abuse by eliciting the release of serotonins and endorphins. Such stories are a kind of self-hypnosis, a verbal veil over reality. In this example, the woman assigns the man the role of one helpless in his affliction and assigns herself the role of nurturing mother-martyr, using the verbal veil as her device for surviving in that role.''

''She wouldn't do that here on Newholme,'' said Fentrys. ''My mother wouldn't do that!''

''Women don't need to do that on Newholme,'' Madame agreed. ''On this world, any woman who did do such a thing would be referred to the psych machines for rebalancing! Here, physical abuse of women took place only at the time of the women raids and the Hags put a stop to that! We do, however, hear women say things like, 'My father really treasured me. He didn't want to let me go. . . .' Or, 'My married daughter would come visit me with the children if she could get away from home.' What are these?''

Tyle said, ''They'd be the same kind of veils. To hide her disappointment?''

''Exactly. Admitting the fiction would be destructive to the woman's ego, so she uses a verbal veil to conceal disappointment. Why do we care? Why do we talk about it? Because as Consorts, you will hear these stories as symptoms of need! Your patroness should be without disappointments if you are doing your job correctly. When you hear your patroness lying to herself, your job is to eliminate her need to do so."

"We tell her she's being silly," said the voice from the rear of the room.

"You will not," snapped Madame. "That is a traditionally male response which is totally unhelpful! You won't say she is silly or that the situation she describes is not true or that she should forget it. You will say, 'Yes, I know what you mean. I understand. I know of a similar case,' and you will go on to tell a parallel story, which will allow her to feel that her own disappointments are universally shared, that she is not exceptional in this regard, that she need not worry over them. . . .

"Fentrys? You look confused."

"I am confused, Madame. Our patronesses are supposed to be exceptional, so why . . ."

"Your patronesses are supposed to be exceptional in all *favorable* regards. You will let them know they are exceptionally witty, exceptionally beautiful, exceptionally charming, patient, and so forth, and you will tell them so at least hourly. But if your patroness is troubled, if she thinks 'Why me?' the 'Why me?' must be turned into 'It's not just me.' It's normal for husbands to be preoccupied with business, for children to be thoughtless, for familial relationships to be unfulfilling. That is exactly why you are there, to make up for such things. If such disappointments weren't normal, Consorts wouldn't be needed. You'll know you have succeeded when your patroness does not lie to herself anymore, when, instead of coping with sadness, she turns to you for her entitlements."

17

Mouche Becomes a Hunk

Though Mouche grew accustomed to his new suite and his new status, the pictures in the hallway continued to disturb him. It was only after some months had passed that he realized he was worrying about his own eventual patroness, something he hadn't even thought about until the most recent Amatory Arts lectures. The time of graduation had seemed remote, and he had never once visualized himself as actually fulfilling the necessary role, but now he thought of Her, the Patroness, someone sad, maybe. Someone needing care. Or, he found himself thinking almost obsessively, someone like . . . someone in one of those pictures.

There were stories about Hunks who had been required to do things so evil and depraved they had gone mad. There were tales about Wilderneers, Hunks who had killed their owners and escaped after swearing revenge against all females. Little girls were frightened with this tale beside the fire of an evening. "They'll come in the night," the story-spinner would say. "Tapping at your window. Their eyes are red with blood, and their teeth are sharp. . . ."

The suddenly perceived reality of his future made him self-conscious. In the privacy of his own suite that night, Mouche stripped down, set candles either side of the cheval glass, and tilted the mirror to give himself a slow looking over. His skin was very white and smooth, due to all the bathing and oiling and massage. His ashen hair was not yet as long as Madame wanted it, but it was a good deal longer than when he came, the silver-gold mass artfully curled up and away from his brow, which was wide and unlined and interrupted only by the wings of his dark brows, plucked into full but graceful arcs. His nails were smooth and polished, his teeth likewise. The health machines brought by the settlers had seen to that.

Since Mouche was only thirteen, the hairdresser, manicurist and facialist worked on him only once in a tenday. Later, it would be every day or so. Light hair and dark eyes, said Madame, were a dramatic combination. Mouche's eyes were malachite green, fringed with heavy dark lashes. His mouth was wide, the upper lip somewhat narrow, the lower more full. Even now, his jaw was round enough to denote strength. He would not have to keep a full beard, as some Hunks did, in order to look properly romantic.

As for his body, it wasn't much as yet. Lean and muscular, of course, with all the training he was getting, but he had little bulk. His shoulders were broader than when he came, and his legs straighter and more comely. He turned, looking at his back view from over his shoulder. Women were attracted by butts, as men were to breasts, so butts were important. The ideal butt was small, neat, round, and smooth. His wasn't bad. Nothing would be done to his sex, if at all, until he was sold.

Every Consort was sterilized as soon as he was sold, for the one thing absolutely taboo to Consorts was the fathering of children. Extravagant dowries assured that children would be of a man's own name, his own line. Every Family Man had a right to expect his own unique line, his own genetic makeup, his own descendants. Elder son to elder son to elder son, the lineage honored and remembered, his own name honored and remembered. The g'name was the important thing. There could be no doubt about who fathered whom.

Later, after most or all of the children were born, that man's wife would shop for someone much like Mouche, who now turned before the mirror trying to envision himself after another five years or so. When dressed in a clean tunic and a graceful mantle, he made a good appearance. Several times during the park promenades, he had caught people looking at him. Some of them had been women, though there had been a few men as well. He had, as instructed, dimpled at the former and ignored the latter. Madame did not sell to homosexuals, unless the Hunk was being purchased by a woman as a gift for her husband—an erotic aide, as it were, in the necessary business of procreation.

He struck a fencing attitude. He liked fencing, and his fencing master was pleased with him. He rose on his toes and turned, then bowed and stepped and turned again. His dancing master had moved him to the advanced class. Mouche liked fencing better than dancing, but dancing was important, so he did it. Sometimes women held soirées for their friends and their Hunks, and the Hunks had to be able to put on a show. He cleared his throat and did a few lalas. The singing master had been pleased with him also, though Mouche's voice was now beginning to crack. Beginning next year he would learn to accompany himself on the lap harp or lute.

All in all, except for recurrent fantasies of the sea, Mouche was reasonably content. He had gotten over feeling shamed, for in House Genevois his status was not considered shameful. How one is regarded by one's peers is most important, and Mouche's peers were friendly enough. The embarrassment he had thought he would feel forever had lasted only a cycle or two, though he often thought of Mama and Papa, wondering if he would ever see them again.

* * *

Mouche did see his papa again, for once a student went into Consort Country, he could receive visitors, as Mouche soon learned. He sent word to Papa, and Papa arrived shortly thereafter, looking unusually prosperous, with a new cockade on his hat and much news of the new calf and the new kittens and the successful repairs to the mill. Papa did not mention that Mama was pregnant, an event long considered impossible, but which may well have resulted from a lessening of worry and an improvement in diet. When little Bianca was born some months later, Mouche was not informed of that, either. Even though money could have been borrowed on the girl's prospects, Mouche could not have been redeemed. Sales to Consort Houses were considered final. Repayment, even with interest, would not have been accepted by Madame, and the contract Papa had signed was not susceptible to cancellation.

When Bianca had a baby sister, a year later, and then a baby brother a year after that, Mouche was not told of either event. Though Papa continued to visit faithfully, appearing ever more prosperous over the next few years, he didn't mention to Mouche that for all practical purposes, the new baby boy was now the g'Darbos-apparent, as Papa's eldest son.

At sixteen, the boys entered upon the most demanding part of their education. Four hours of physical training each day were coupled with five hours of classroom work, and to this was now added the actual practice of amatory arts. The women who came to House Genevois to assist in this education were masked during the sessions, no one knew who they were except Madame, and Madame did not even hint at who they might be. Some were young and shapely, and some were not, but the quality of work expected from a Consort was to be the same, regardless. In fact, the highest prices would be paid for those from whom the pleasures given a thirty-year-old wife and a sixty-year-old grandmama were indistinguishable. What these women had to say about the students was perhaps more important than any other assessment they might receive.

Amatory arts required, Mouche found, a good deal of concentration, the acquisition of certain autohypnotic abilities, and careful attention to his physical health. There were certain drugs that helped in certain cases, either taken by the Consort or by his patroness, though Madame did not recommend their use except in cases of extreme need.

"In this respect, graduates of House Genevois are unlike the graduates of, say, House Fantuil. In House Fantuil they do a great deal of drug-induced work, but in my mind such sensationism—I do not call it sensuality, which is a natural effect—not only suffers in comparison with the natural modes, but also shortens the lifespans of its practitioners. Of course, given the clientele to whom House Fantuil sells, perhaps the drugs are necessary! I am proud to say that House Genevois never expects the impossible from its graduates!"

Mouche now paid strict attention to the lectures, usually given by Madame but occasionally by other women, concerning the nature or natures of women, for he now could put the theory into action. He decided women were more complicated than he had imagined possible. At night, in the Consort suites, there was a great deal of talk about these complications, about natural versus unnatural modes, and all the middle ground between.

Naturally, the boys discussed other things as well, with particular attention to the mysterious, the unmentioned, and unmentionable. There was exchange of misinformation about the invisible people. There was more of the same about the fabled Questioner, who was rumored to be interested in Newholme. This rumor had more substance than most, for Tyle had a sister married to the family man who managed the space port, and a trader captain had told the manager, who had told his wife, who had told Tyle.

"What does the Questioner do?" asked one boy.

"It destroys worlds," whispered someone else, "if they don't conform to the edicts."

None of the boys knew much about the edicts, but most of them supposed Newholme didn't conform.

"I mean," said Fentrys, "we've got all these things

we can't talk about, but if we conformed, we could talk about anything.''

''So she wipes out Newholme?'' asked Mouche skeptically.

''No. Not if we can keep her from finding out.''

This topic was hashed and rehashed until it grew boring and was replaced with newly heard stories about Wilderneers. No one had actually ever seen a Wilderneer, but stories about them nonetheless abounded.

In general, Mouche enjoyed his life. The Consorts-in-Training had, so Madame stressed, a better diet than other men, a more healthy lifestyle, a more certain future, and fewer sexual frustrations than anyone on the planet. The days went by without upheaval in an atmosphere of general kindliness, and the only thing that saddened Mouche were his dreams: often of Duster and sometimes of the sea. Each time he dreamed of the sea, it became wider and darker and bigger, until eventually he dreamed of a sea of stars with himself sailing upon it.

In accordance with Madame's instructions, Mouche had managed to let go of his father and mother. He had ceased to grieve over the animals and the farm itself. But Duster and the ever widening sea . . . those things he wept over still.

18

Ornery Bastable, the Castaway

The freckled, red-headed "boy" named Ornery Bastable had been bought onto the freighter *Waygood* at age seventeen and she had stayed there ever since. Because of her (his) early "mutilation," a story that Ornery frequently told and by now had considerably embellished, she was allowed to be somewhat reticent about natural functions. She had no beard and her voice was rather high. Nonetheless, she was strong and resourceful, and though she could not participate in all the recreations indulged in by her companions, she was a good shipmate, always eager to offer a hand or stand a watch for a friend. Had Ornery been prettier, the subterfuge might not have worked, but "he" had remained a plain, lean, energetic person who over the years had become an accepted member of the crew.

In general, Ornery had found the life healthful and interesting. So far as recreations went, Ornery enjoyed the society of her fellows, she had found a close lipped and empathetic female Hagger in Naibah with whom she could occasionally be "herself," and every now and then she traveled up the river from Naibah to pay dutiful visits to Pearla. Though most of her life was relatively routine, it was not without adventure, including, on one occasion, being marooned.

Freighters sailing westward from Gilesmarsh customarily refilled their water barrels a dozen days' sail down the coast at a sweetwater spring which was separated from the shore by a strip of forest so thick and overgrown as to be impassible except by the laboriously created trail maintained by the shipcrews who watered there. Ornery was part of a work party sent ashore on the duty of chop and fill, but despite the trail being well marked and Ornery herself having traversed it many times, she somehow got herself separated from the rest of the party. She sat down to figure out where she'd gone wrong, and just at that moment the world started to shake.

She was under a tree; a branch whipped off the tree, struck Ornery on the head, and she rolled down into the dirt, dead to the world, in which state she continued until the *Waygood* sailed away without her.

She wakened along about moonfall, figured out where she'd gone wrong and made an unsteady way to the beach, where she found a note from her mates saying they'd return in eight or ten days, and, "If you want picking up you'd better stay on the sand, but watch out for tidal waves, because there's more tremors all the time."

They left her a few rounds of hardbread, as well as a packet of cheese and jerky, so she wasn't as badly off as she might otherwise have been. She had her belt knife, hatchet, and canteen. There was fruit in the trees. The spring was close enough for drinking water, the rations were sufficient, the knock on the head had left a painful lump but no lasting damage. She hacked herself a few fronds from the nearby trees, built a shelter of sorts high on the beach between two erect pillars of stone that had long served as a landmark for the spring, a space partly screened from the sea by a pile of other pillars, similar though recumbent. She then lay back in her lean-to awaiting rescue, staring at the moons at night and swimming in the sea in the daytime—a delight she almost never had the privacy to indulge in and one she considered almost worth being marooned for.

Three of the biggest moons were out when the ship left, one almost at full but the other two at waxing half and new, so the tides weren't enough to make her move and she felt no tremors. On the third night, however, she wakened to a sound: not a loud sound, not even a threatening sound, but certainly an unfamiliar one. It conveyed, she thought, the sense of an exclamation. Or, maybe, an exclamatory question, as though something very large had asked from the direction of the sea: Who is that person camped on my beach? Or, more accurately, Who is that person camped *there* on my beach?

Ornery went from *there* to *somewhere else* in a panicky skulk that ended with her in the trees, prostrate upon some uncomfortably knobby roots, peering out at the place she had just left. The waxing half moon was low in the sky; the new moon had long since set, but the full moon was just past the zenith, casting enough light for her to see the bulky though sinuous shadow that flowed upward from the water to her left, squirmed across the beach to the stones, fumbled about with them for what seemed a very long time, then went back as it had come. This was accomplished without any noise whatsoever and without any evidence that the shadow knew or cared where Ornery was. Where there had been two pillars standing in the moons' light, there were now five, each casting a bifurcated shadow like a lopsided arrowhead, pointing away from the place Ornery lay.

Ornery stayed where she was, replaying what she had seen in her head: the shadow coming out of the sea and squirming across the sand. Now that had been one thing, one single thing, she was sure of that. But then, when it had fumbled around with the rocks, some of it had separated itself and moved away from the other part of it, so it must have been more than one thing to start with.

Except for that very distinct impression it was one thing at the beginning!

At the first light of dawn, Ornery crawled back to her shelter. The rations were pressed quite deeply into the sand but otherwise undamaged. The fronds that had sheltered her were scattered and the area smelled like . . . well, she couldn't quite say. Not a bad smell. Not a stink, but nonetheless, something quite distinctive and possibly to be avoided. Ornery gathered up her belongings and found a place at the other end of the beach to make her bed. Having done so, she fell asleep, without even thinking about it. She knew it was the only thing to do.

Later in the morning she woke with the word "Joggi-wagga" moving about in her head. Moon dragon, she said to herself, wondering where she had heard such a thing. Her memory didn't at that moment stretch as far as the invisible person who had nursed Oram and Ornalia as babies, telling them stories and singing them songs. She had been told to forget that time, and though she had by no means forgotten, she had obediently stopped thinking of it. The word soon evaporated, like dew, and she remained astonished at herself for having slept at all since she had a rather frightening memory of the night's happening.

When the ship came by on its way back to Gilesmarsh she told her mates about the experience, and they teased her a good deal. Castaways always told stories about hearing things and seeing things and being wakened in the night, or having their things moved about. Ornery accepted this with good grace but without believing a word of it. She'd seen the stone pillars lying in the sand and she'd seen them standing erect, and each of the stones had been far too heavy for her to have raised it herself. Something had set them up, and Ornery had seen the shape—or shapes—of the somethings.

19

The Invisible People

Late in his sixteenth year, Mouche fell prey to a peculiar illness, one with few and subtle outward symptoms, one to which, however inadvertently, he exposed himself.

It began one evening rather late when, in the course of restoring certain volumes of erotic tales to his bookshelf, Mouche jostled a particular carving in an unusual way, and the whole bookshelf rotated on its axis to display a gaping black doorway out of which drifted the sound of music and an enticing odor. The smell made his mouth water even as it made his nose wrinkle, as if he scented something marvelously luscious but, perhaps for that very reason, forbidden.

After experimenting with the bookcase to learn how it opened and closed and how the latch might be opened from the back side, Mouche lit a candle and went through the dusty, webbed opening. He briefly considered asking Tyle or Fentrys to go with him, but they were at fencing practice, and Mouche did not want to wait.

He shut and latched the door behind him and began exploring, finding no single route that led from his suite to somewhere else. Instead he was in a maze of passageways that branched opening onto narrow catwalks that crossed open space to small, dark balconies from which, ascending or descending by ladders, one came upon narrow adits leading to crawlways that went hither and thither in all directions through the ancient fabric of House Genevois. Everywhere along the route were small access panels into rooms of House Genevois, and doors that would have opened had they not been closed from the back by long rods that thrust into the surrounding woodwork. There were also a great many peepholes that looked out into the corridors and suites. When Mouche applied his eyes to some of the holes, he saw his fellow students. When he peered through others, he realized he was peering through the painted eyes of those quite terrible pictures in the halls.

Throughout his rather lengthy exploration, he kept moving toward the sound of the music, arriving finally at one end of a level and uniform passageway stretching in a straight line for some considerable distance and pierced with tiny glazed openings along both sides. Since the passage was scarcely wider than his shoulders, he could look through the openings by merely turning his head. To his left he saw the moonlit roofs of the buildings north of House Genevois; to his right, the open space of the large courtyard. When he stood on tiptoe and craned his neck to peer downward, he could see the torch-lit dock and a firewood wagon being unloaded.

The corridor continued straight on, eastward past the courtyard, over the roofs of the lower buildings and along yet another open space to end finally in a cul-de-sac with two leaded windows of colored glass, one to his right, one straight ahead. Putting his eyes to a missing segment at the corridor's end, Mouche gained a view of the muddy river, dully gleaming in moonlight, like hammered copper. The window to the right was unbroken and so dirty he could see nothing at all through it, though it was ajar just enough to admit both the sound and the smell that had enticed him.

No one had ever warned Mouche not to do what he was doing. No one had considered for a moment that he or any other student might fall into it by accident. While some parts of the maze were too low and narrow for most persons to traverse, other parts had been built by long ago mankind, but then closed off and forgotten. The straight stretch of cobwebby corridor where Mouche found himself was actually inside the north wall of House Genevois, a wall that began at the street and ran eastward to the riverside.

On inspecting the windows, Mouche saw that the slightly open one to his right was not merely ornamental, though the hinges and the latch were so corroded from long exposure to the weather that they might as well have been. After a moment's hesitation, he decided to force it farther open. The hinges were on the left, and when Mouche leaned his full weight against it, it cracked open with a scream of alarm followed by utter silence.

Mouche held his breath and waited until the rhythmic sounds of voice and instrument resumed. He then used the music to cover the sound as he forced the reluctant casement a fingerwidth at a time, opening it enough that he could lean out and look below.

He stared down from the northeast corner of an earthen courtyard enclosed on the north and east by walls, on the south and west by brightly painted dwellings, their colors and designs revealed by the leaping flames on a central hearth. Around the fire were dancers. Not people dancers. Far too slender for people, and too graceful. For a long moment, it did not occur to Mouche who the dancers were, and then the heaps of brown, shapeless garments lying near the firepit wakened him with both a thrill of recognition and a shiver of dread. What he was doing was improper. What he was doing was forbidden. He should not be here watching, for the dancers were invisible people, people who did not exist.

His first thought was that he'd done it, he'd overstepped, he was done for. He'd be blue-bodied for sure, or at least beaten into insensibility. In a moment this guilty fear passed as he realized he was alone, after all. No one knew he had come here. He needn't . . . well, he needn't tell anyone. And since no one knew where he was, he needn't go back, not just yet.

In truth, he could not have made himself leave what he saw, what he smelled, what he heard in the music: the new, the strange, the marvelous. He was so intrigued that he sat down on the sill and settled into being a spectator.

He pretended to himself that he did not know who they were. If he ever got caught, he thought, the "ever" coming to mind quite clearly, if anyone "ever" asked him, he would say he didn't know who they were. How could he? After all, he might not have noticed the garments that defined invisible people. How could he tell these were people who did not exist?

People who nonetheless were! People who leaped and spun around the fire in ecstatic, delirious movement, like willows in wind, their hair flowing like swirls of lovely water. They were more slender than people, almost sylph-like, and their skin had a sheen of opalescent gold, the ocher-apricot glow of freshly fired clay pots. And they sang! Their voices were like birds and breeze and the burble of water. Their hair was much more luxuriant than people's hair, thicker and longer, and it almost seemed to rise and fall of itself, besides being of gorgeous and opulent colors: all the blues of the sea and the sky, shading to dark purple, all the greens of the forest and the fields shading to pale yellow. Mouche had seen hair colored so brilliantly only once before, on the small furry thing that he and Duster had befriended.

The dancers below him were clad only in diaphanous shifts, though after a time it struck him that the swirling veils weren't clothing at all. The dancers had a sort of web that flowed from beneath their arms and down the outside of their legs. So far as Mouche could tell, they were all of one sex, whatever that sex was. They didn't seem to have breasts or genitals, but each was definitely an individual, easy to distinguish from the rest. One particular form brought his eyes back again and again, a girl or youth he supposed one might say, one with soft moss-green hair flowing to its . . . no, *her* knees in a liquid stream that seemed to pour forever across his vision. His eyes went away and returned, went away and returned, unable to ignore the magic of that hair and the pattern of light that shifted along it like a fish sliding among eddies. Once or twice he caught the glimmer of her eyes, a startling mirror silver in the firelight.

Adding to his enchantment was music full of unfamiliar harmonies and rhythms, the *tunk-a-tunk* and *tongy-dong* of tuned wooden blocks and metal rods being struck with soft hammers. Also, there were marvelous odors from the foods seething over the fire, exotic spices and resinous smokes, all part of a marvelous and fascinating whole that gave him new sensations and awarenesses that caught him by the throat. What he saw, smelled, and heard wrapped him in a tingling web of stimulation that burned like a warm little sun, ripening him as a fruit on a vine, making him swell with sweet juices. His foot tapped, *TIKa-tika-TUM tika-TIKatum.* His eyes crinkled, he caught himself smiling as he could not remember smiling ever before. After the first few moments, he was lost in the spell of it.

And then . . . then they sang a song he knew. He knew it! He had heard it, not like this, with many singers and drums and wood blocks and bells, but still, he knew it. Someone had sung it to him, in this same language, and then later in his own . . .

Now, as that voice rose from below, he remembered the words in his own language:

Quaggima she calls:
Out of starfield coming, fire womb seeking.
Fire it finds, rock wallowing, fume reeking.
Oh, Corojumi, openers of space;
Bofusdiaga, burrower of walls;
She has need of birthing place.
Wheeooo, she falls

Quaggima she cries . . .
Something, something . . .
Bofusdiaga, singer of the sun;
Oh, Corojumi, dancers of bright skies;
He has done and I have done.
I cannot rise.

His Timmy had sung it to him when he was a tiny boy. His Timmy, the one who had cuddled him and fed him. The song trailed away, unfinished. The singers moved from the fire, leaving it to burn itself out. They left Mouche, bewitched, his mind full of the song he knew and the shapes he knew. Timmys.

Curving one hand protectively around the flame of his candle, he returned the way he had come, losing himself more than once and finding his way by trial and error. At the entrance to his own room he found a peek hole that allowed him to see if anyone had come to visit while he had gone. They had not. Mouche let himself into his suite and closed the passage behind him.

He threw himself into bed still enchanted, wakened by sensation into a troubling apprehension. Probably no one now in House Genevois had ever seen the Timmys dancing. Would Madame have watched, ever? Would Simon? Only he, Mouche, knew what they did there, and he admitted to himself with a return of his earlier dread that those he had seen were indeed the beings who did not exist, the ones no one ever . . . ever let themselves see, the ones never mentioned.

And yet, one of *them* had sung to him a long time ago. His own Timmy had sung the song of Quaggima, the interloper, the song of Niasa, Summer Snake. His own Timmy had told him stories of the great four-eyed Eiger, the bird who sees and knows all. He remembered Joggiwagga, the moon dragons, the setters up of stones.

And it wasn't just him! The revelation came in an instant! Virtually every mankind baby on Newholme had been sung to sleep with "Niasa's Lullaby"—the song of the Summer Snake to its baby in the egg; every child had heard the stories of great Bofusdiaga and the many Corojumi. As adults, though they had been forced to forget the singers, surely they could not forget the songs.

They had been taught to forget, just as Mouche had. They had gone to school in order to learn to forget. It was permitted for babies to believe in Timmys, but essential that adults should not. For adults, it was forbidden for Timmys to exist. They were a figment. Imaginary playmates. Hallucinatory nursemaids. Though every child in the classroom had been reared by Timmys, when one reached age seven, Timmys no longer were.

The teachers had explained, so patiently. There were no Timmys when the people had first moved onto Newholme. Then, some time later, suddenly people had started seeing Timmys. There they were, everywhere, like mice, or bunchbeetles, listening under windows, camping outside people's houses, gathering at various seasons beside the river where the hills resounded to the sound of their music and the scrape of their dancing feet. It was inexplicable, but there they were, able to speak a few words of the people's language, calling to one another, *tim-tim, tim-tim,* able to explain that they were here in the *kwi,* the outside, and eager to be *tim-timidi,* useful.

Where had they come from?

"Dosha. Lau."

Who had sent them?

"Dosha-lauhazhala-baimoi."

No matter how they tried to explain, no one could understand what they meant. A few linguistically talented persons who struggled to understand them, believed they were saying they had been sent by something or someone, but that they had never seen whatever or whoever it was that had sent them. Some people of a scientific bent believed they were animals, and they took some of the tim-tim apart to find, in their amazement, that the tim-tim had no brains! Creatures without brains were obviously not real, intelligent creatures. No creature could be considered real if it did not have a brain. They were, therefore, hallucinatory.

All this, Mouche learned in infant school, as all small children learned. Though he had been tended by a Timmy since birth, cuddled and fed and sung to by that swaddled form, closer to him than his mother or father, kinder to him than either, he could not acknowledge that fact for grown up people did not see them.

Mouche had been quite willing. He had learned not to see them, not to believe in them. Until now.

20

The Dutter Boys

At House Genevois, there were always departures and new arrivals. A notable arrival occurred about half a year after Mouche began watching the dancers. His friend Fentrys had been downstairs in the sewing room, having his new doublet fitted, when two new boys had been escorted past on their way to the welcome rooms. Fentrys, glancing at them, could see they were unlike the usual new boys, and when he left the sewing room, he'd let his curiosity pull him into a closet near the parlor where he could overhear what went on.

"Big," he said to Mouche minutes later, eyes wide. "By the Hagions, Mouche, one of them is as big as Wander!" Wander was the largest of the present Consorts-in-Training; he stood a head taller than any other student and several hands breadths wider, though he was not yet of an age to be sold. "The other one is not as large, but they are both evil as snakes in their words. Madame had one of them stripped and striped!"

This was astonishing, for the boys were seldom beaten. Madame didn't believe in such punishment, except as a last resort. That it should have been imposed at first opportunity did not bode well for the peace of the House.

"What did he do?" asked Mouche.

"The one called Dyre said that Madame was a withered hag who had outlived her usefulness and should be retired to the stitchery. The fencing master and two of the cleaners had to hold the other one, Bane, while Dyre was beaten, and since they had him down, they beat him too, for interfering."

"She didn't throw them out?" Students were expelled, from time to time, their bodies and faces dyed blue, to show the world they were worthless and incorrigible. Other Houses did the same, as did the Army school and the apprentice programs. Blue-bodies usually didn't last long in the outside world, and it was said of recalcitrants that they were "independent as a blue-body."

Fentrys said, "I heard Madame talking to Simon. She sent word to someone, some large personage or other. She awaits that personage now, in the parlor."

"Let's listen," suggested Tyle. "Can we?"

It wasn't consortly behavior, certainly, since it reflected an unhealthy interest in other people's business, but neither was it disobedient, strictly speaking, since they had never been forbidden to hide in closets and eavesdrop. They found room in the same closet Fentrys had hidden in before, one that backed on the parlor, though once hidden in it they had a stuffy time before Madame's summoned guest arrived. They could not see him. They could only hear his words, uttered in a deep, flat voice with no resonance at all, though, Mouche thought to himself, that might be because they heard him from a closet.

"Madame Genevois."

Madame's voice came not only flat but curiously muffled, as though through a handkerchief. "Sir. I have today received the two boys you paid me some time ago to take and train. They are a good deal older than my usual students, and they seem to be of the opinion that they need no training and that they are in charge of House Genevois.

If this is your intent, you have misjudged me. I have not spent my life acquiring a reputation so meaningless that I would cast it away for so little. I can and will refund your money, sponsors be hanged."

A long silence. Then, "I'll see to the boys."

"Indeed," said Madame with a gasp.

There was the sound of the parlor door opening and closing, and Madame's footsteps going away toward the welcome suite, breathing deeply. There were then other doors opening and shutting, mutters in the hallway, an uncouth clattering and chatter, then the parlor door opened and closed once more.

"Oh," said a young voice. "It's you."

"I thought you'd got it in your head about this," replied the deep voice. "And here you go, startin' off just like usual."

"That old bitch . . ." said another voice, deeper, almost adult. Mouche shivered inside. He knew that voice.

Then there was a sound, not a sound the listeners could identify. It might have been a burning sound, a kind of sizzle and pop. Again, it might have been something else. It was followed by a gasp and a whimper. It came again and was followed by a moan, almost a scream.

"If I've got to come down here another time, it'll be the last time," said the deep voice. "And you won't like it, I can guarantee."

The door opened and closed once more. Heavy feet went to the foyer. The front door opened, letting in street noises, and closed. Then a long silence. When it had gone on for a very long time, Fentrys opened the closet door, and they slipped out into the corridor, stopping there with wrinkled noses, for the air smelt foul. When they peeked into the room where the interview had been held, they saw two boys on the floor, one very large, one smaller, both slumped against a huge, carved sofa, eyes half open, mouths fully open, drool at the corners. The smell of the corridor was far worse in the room, and it was a smell that Mouche remembered all too well.

He was staring around the corner at the larger of the boys when the boy's eyes came fully opened and looked at

Mouche with total recognition. Mouche drew back, breathless. It was the larger of the intruder boys, from that time long ago, the boy who had poisoned Duster. Older, he was, and strong looking, like an ox, but it was he, nonetheless, and the boy beside him was the other one from that day.

Mouche's immediate reaction was fury. If he had been home, in his own place, and if there had been a weapon at hand, or even a rock to crush a skull, he would have moved to violence. Since coming to House Genevois, he had been drilled in the avoidance of violence, however, and the more recent lessons held him wavering, readying himself, taking a moment to decide.

It was Tyle who broke his indecision, tugging Mouche by the arm, muttering at him. "Let's get out of here."

They got out, though Mouche felt someone listening, someone following his footsteps. If he had recognized that smell, those faces, the two new boys had also recognized him.

They made it as far as the landing before people came into the hall below, and when Simon and others came past the foot of the stairs, the three friends were occupied with an ostentatious concentration on the notice board. Mouche turned to look after the people below. The two new boys were being assisted, almost carried, and he met the gaze of the larger boy, his face quite empty but his eyes blazing as his mouth formed the soundless words: "Farm-boy, I'll get you."

Behind them, in the hallway, the strange smell still lingered.

"We don't say anything about this," whispered Fentrys. "Not a word!"

The other two nodded. Though an account of this happening would be very interesting to all their mates in Consort Country, they knew instinctively that Fentrys was right. The smell in the room and the hallway was of a particularly unpleasant kind. It was not to be talked of. Not with anyone; not even among themselves lest they be overheard. So, Mouche had no one to share his gratitude that the new boys would not be coming upstairs to Consort Country, not for some little time yet.

21

Among the Indigenes

That one whom Mouche adored, the Timmy who was called by other Timmys, *Fauxis-looz,* which meant something like "Flowing Green" stood in one of the small painted houses in the rear courtyard, staring through the open door at the strange little tower gracelessly perched at the corner of the thick wall, built long and long ago by the first settlers as part of their riverside fortress. It was what the Timmys called a pretend wall: one that the humans pretended kept the Timmys in; one the Timmys pretended to be imprisoned by. The truth was there was no manmade enclosure that did not have doors in its walls and floors, no cellar without tunnels along its foundations, no loft without sneakways between the rafters. No place had ever been built that tim-timkwi could not get into or out of whenever tim-timkwi wished.

Nonetheless, for now, these tim-timkwi, those called by infant mankind "Timmys," remained in the courtyard while Flowing Green kept her eyes on the tower window, which until some days ago had been almost closed but now was quite widely ajar.

"Tim saw his light again tonight," the green-haired one said. "Tim saw it, when tim-tim were come inside."

"Yes," the speaker was answered by another who stood beside tim. "He comes every night."

"This is the one Corojum spoke of," said Flowing Green.

An older voice spoke from shadows. "Who knows what is to come? Not even Corojumi, dance weavers; Bofusdiaga, sun singer; Joggiwagga, moon watchers, setters up of stones."

Silence. Then the whisper from another, "Niasa is restless and She is awakening. We cannot settle Her."

"I have seen what I have seen in the dreaming time," sang Flowing Green in a long, sustained flow of notes, a minor strain as plaintive as a nightbird.

"And who is tim to dream?" asked another, almost angrily. "Who is tim to say 'I,' 'I,' as though tim were a mankind? Is this one standing here a many-times-rejoined one? Is tim Bofusdiaga? Is tim Kaorugi Itself! Who is Flowing Green to know of dreaming?"

"I am who I am," said Flowing Green. "I was made to watch these mankinds. I have the juice of one of them within me. I was created for this purpose. I have watched, I have learned. When I have been remade, what I had learned was not taken from me. I say this Mouche is the needful one."

"Already lost are the gemmed gardens under Mistmount," sang the old voice from the corner shadows. "Fallen are the stone skies of Great Gaman and all the living stars that shone within them. If we do not find the dance, all will be lost."

"Tim-tim still have some of it," mused Flowing Green.

"In fragments," said the voice from the corner, with only a hint of resentment. "What tim-tim have is thin, too thin, like gauze, like mist, like the wandering sound of little winds, unsure and unsettled. The power of it has leaked away. And now the gathering approaches, the Joggiwagga are setting up the stones, the tide comes with the moons; Niasa turns in sleep and She dreams restless dreams. The world trembles. Already the waking has begun."

The corner tim spoke the truth. Even mankind had heard the word being called in the wilderness and had seen the pillars erected on the shores. Mankind did not know it was the Great Eiger who called or Joggiwagga who read the moon shadows. Mankind spoke of volcanoes and earthquakes, but mankind knew it was happening. Destruction threatened. Not at this moment, no. Nor tomorrow. But soon.

"I say once more, this one who watches us is the key," said Flowing Green in a firm voice that said tim did not care whether they believed or not. "A Corojum spoke to me saying: *This one, Mouchidi, is not jong. He may not go gau when the waters close over him.* These were the words of the Corojum, and when I had heard the words of the Corojum, I dreamed of myself in the Fauxi-dizalonz, and this Mouchidi, he was with me."

Only shamed silence greeted this. Such a thing was an abomination. Bofusdiaga had tried it with the jong long ago, and it had been a disaster. Surely Bofusdiaga would not allow it again! The tim-timkwi began to murmur, but the voice from the corner came again, admonishing.

"Bofusdiaga made strangely this one called Flowing Green, this one who says, 'I,' like mankind. Perhaps Flowing Green is a new thing in an old form."

"Or perhaps Flowing Green is timself gau, bent, a monster," said another-tim.

"Tim-tim will know soon enough," murmured the corner voice ironically.

There was a wave of bitter laughter, a sound that overflowed the one little house to run among the other little houses in a freshet of real mirth as tim-tim repeated what tim had said. "Soon enough, too soon, enough."

"Tim-tim will know," said Flowing Green in her dreaming voice. "And I will know. And I will remember my dreaming and the words of the Corojum and this watcher from the wall."

* * *

The Timmys were not the only thinking beings who remembered old times in the evening. Aloft on her balcony, D'Jevier remembered, not what she herself had seen, but what she had read in the secret journals of the Hags.

When the second settlement arrived, there were no Timmys. Years went by, and suddenly, there were Timmys, intelligent seeming beings. Speaking beings. And if they belonged here, mankind did not, according to Haraldson, so mankind had tried to drive them away.

The Timmys stayed. The Timmys gathered in great mobs to dance. There, on their dancing grounds, mankind had killed them, piling their corpses in stacks to be burned.

It hadn't worked. For every Timmy killed, another arrived, and they still danced. They also started doing things for people: washing clothes, weeding gardens, cleaning dwellings.

Meantime, the mankind population grew slowly, and since the people were too few to do everything that needed doing, they began to depend upon the labor of the Timmys. In no time at all, the Timmys became the cleaners and cultivators and carriers. The Timmys became the miners and millers and child-minders. They were ubiquitous and industrious about mankind's business, but they still danced. When they danced, they did not work.

Now their dancing was regarded as a dereliction of duty rather than an opportunity for slaughter, and once again mankind had interfered. Though the Timmys were never mentioned in either written or spoken edicts, "the sound of drums" had been forbidden, as had the "unprofitable shuffling of feet." "Coordinated and frivolous movement" had been tabooed, as well, and there had been more than a few cases of maiming and murdering of Timmys in an effort to enforce the rule.

Mankind had always had a propensity for trying to govern the ungovernable and to control what was uncontrollable. Mankind had always relied upon laws and rules to direct those drives that did not care about laws or rules. Pragmatism had at last prevailed. Mankind upon Newholme had conceded that creatures who did not exist, who had no brains, could not be expected to modify their behavior to accord with mankind's desires. Indeed, one Hag had been heard to say in confidence that forbidding the Timmys to dance was like forbidding a horse to piss. The horse would do it, somehow or other, somewhere or other, and though inconvenient and embarrassing, the best thing to do was ignore it.

The Timmys who had overheard this comment from their spyholes in the walls were not offended. Well, they nodded, it is time these folk saw sense.

Still the Timmys danced. The Hags knew it. The Men of Business knew it. They did not know why. Only the Timmys knew why.

Now and then they filled their courtyards or canyons or lava tubes with whirling dedications to zoological or botanical divinity, with ecstatic miming of many wondrous creatures. Now and then they did the slow omturtle dance, accomplished in pauses and silences; now and then the twirling rapture of the Great Eiger, the windbird, the four-eyed flier, who saw all, who knew all. Now and then was mimed the circular slithing of Joggiwagga, the moon dragons, simulated by stroked tambours and the throb of water drums. Now and then was the reed dance done, and that of the quiowhat tree and the little fluttery dances of all the beings-who-do-not-know-themselves, the fishy swimmers and birdy things and lesser vegetables who, unlike the Timmys, were not individually made by Kaorugi the Builder but were allowed to reproduce independently to serve as food for all creatures.

All these dances were done for enjoyment, and for practice.

For sometimes mere enjoyment gave way to necessity. Sometimes Niasa, summer-snake-in-the-egg, who dreamed of life, would become restless. Whenever this happened, Timmys did the little amusement dances for Her-Who-Hatches-Niasa, small simple dances, the first ones the Corojumi had created for Her. Then, every decade or so, when the moons lined up and pulled roughly, Niasa-in-the-egg would almost be wakened, and for these times more powerful and hypnotic amusement dances were needed, with many rehearsal sessions beforetime. Many Timmys were required for these, but the dance was always done for Her on time, and however restless it might be, Niasa slept on, dreaming as it had done forever.

But then, once every few centuries all the moons gathered at once and the substance of the world was shaken, and Niasa-in-the-egg was almost jolted from sleep to call wakefully to Her, The hatcher!

Then came time for the great dance. Only the great dance would serve. Timmys had done the dance time after time. All life upon Dosha had done the dance time after time, a hundred, two hundred times.

But then mankind had come and had done the evil thing. Over and over, done the evil, destroying the dance. And when Timmys had tried to get it back, the mankinds had done worse things. Now the time for the great dance was coming fast upon the world, and no one was left, no one at all who remembered how the dance was done.

22

A Dream of Falling Water, Flowing Green

In the small hours of night, Mouche dreamed he stood in the mists of an unlit chasm while a cataract fell before him out of darkness into darkness. The source was so far above him, the catch basin so far below that no sound of water reached him. The curved emerald surface of the water and the glassy shadows moving within it were lit by a single ray that pierced the darkness from behind him. In his sleep he could not name this falling water, yet he knew it poured forever through that solitary beam, a perfect and eternal miracle made manifest by this single and incomplete enlightenment.

So, Mouche remembered in his dream, had the emerald hair of the dancer poured forever across the dark and empty chasms of his heart, with only his flawed perception disclosing its mystery. The dance, the scent of the food and the smoke, the sound of the drums and the voices, the flutes and the bells, all became an experience that lifted him as on an unending tide, out of nowhere into everywhere, while mysterious mists rose around him, spreading the possibility of marvel through the moist and fecund darkness.

Certainly the dream mists permeated his sleep, soaking into certain opinions that had been already petrified when he had received them and which nothing in his life until now had served to soften. Each time he woke, he was different, as though his very bones had become pliable, bending to become the framework for some other, as yet unparticularized person. Hidden in the deep embrasure beneath the patinaed dome, he suffered the nightly torments of the unknown and itched with a fascination that drove him closer to madness every time he scratched it.

The change was a fearful thing. As it progressed he found he could take nothing as a matter of course. He could no longer submit to the ministrations of the invisible masseuses without wondering what color hair they had, and whether they sang in the evening, or whether they danced, and what their true purpose was and why they had come. He did not see their eyes upon him, equally wondering and weighing. He could no longer look aside from the brown-clad forms who swept the street without wondering where their homeland had been and whether they hated their present confinement or whether even that was part of the flow he could sense happening.

He did not see their glance follow him as he went, the gestures their hands made, signifying to any tim-tim watching that this was Mouchidi, the one Flowing Green had come for, the one Flowing Green said Bofusdiaga wanted.

The change overflowed the night hours and ran into everything he tried to do. Mouche could no longer pace the dignified measures his dancing master required without flowing far too gracefully, as though to emulate the dances of those he imagined were watching from behind the walls. He could not leap without being lifted, like a balloon. He could not twirl without spinning. He was become a dervish, all too full of inordinate intention.

"What's come over you Mouche? You dance like a windlily!"

Mouche apologized, and went on apologizing, to the fencing master, to the conversation director, both of whom found him odd, eccentric, no longer focused, but oh, interesting, very interesting. He, meantime, was too busy to find himself interesting, for he was desperately attempting to interpret what was happening to him, and he was without tutelage, completely on his own. He was possessed without knowing how to be a possession. Even if he had sought help, he could have found no adviser among the mankind inhabitants of Newholme.

Suspecting as much, he confided in no one. He borrowed the oil can from Simon's workroom and oiled the latch and hinges of the window where he sat night after night; he borrowed a brace and bit and drilled a narrow hole into the woodwork of his bookcase, into which a short length of metal rod could be inserted from the front, thus preventing anyone else from repeating the movements that had led to his current predicament. That had been purely accidental, he told himself, unaware of the hands that had manipulated the door from behind the walls to be sure he had found the way they had opened for him.

It seemed that everything he did was accompanied by feelings of exhilarating joy or of overwhelming melancholy, that deep, unfocused grief he had felt before, in which Duster, and Papa, and his own dreams of the sea were merely drops in an unending tide. With every passing day he became more convinced that both joy and pain were signals, meant for him alone, requiring him to find the sufferer and offer . . . something.

It would have been more comfortable to return to his former state of ignorance and contentment, but he could not. The longer it went on, the more secret and precious his delight in the watching became, the more painful that other emotion, that one from outside, as though the delight continued sensitizing him to the agony. They were inextricable. He could not have the one without the other. When he shuddered himself awake in the night, overwhelmed by an agony of loss and horror, he knew that they, too, wakened, hearing that pain as he heard it, like the tolling of a great alarm bell deep in the world. Somewhere on this planet, something suffered and grieved. It wasn't himself. It wasn't the dancers. Not his family, or House Genevois or anyone he knew. But something!

23

Dancers in Transit

Though Mouche had no inkling of it, another player in the Newholmian drama also itched with fascination, though of a more introspective kind. Whereas Mouche slept and changed in his sleep, Ellin, toward the end of the first stage of the trip toward Newholme, often found herself unable to sleep at all. The ship did its part, lowering the lights and the temperature and sending sleepy sounds through the ducts, like drowsy birds. The window-wall suddenly became a landscape, trees seen against a moonlit sky and a glittering body of water with a background of low mountains. It was the kind of scene that she had avoided on Earth, but here on the ship she had let it be. Who could feel claustrophobic in space? One either was well off inside or one was outside and dead.

None of her old sleepy-time rituals did any good. Her eyes stayed stubbornly open while she fretted. Since awaking from electronically induced deep sleep, which, though it had not seemed to last any time at all, had really lasted quite a long while, she and Bao had spent many waking hours reading, or having the monitors read to them, everything the Council of Worlds knew about Newholme plus a good bit the COW had no inkling of.

Though Ellin had always been a reader, she had not been much of a student, except of the dance. Ballet was taught by example and repetition, and Ellin learned best in that way. The official reports were couched in wordy bureaucratese that hid information rather than disclosing it. Trying to find meaning amid the polysyllabic jargon made her cross and irritable and wakeful, like an itch that wouldn't go away.

The view panel was there, of course. It didn't have to depict trees and moonlight. She could ask for virtually anything ever written to be printed or dramatized, and she'd tried that a few times, but the panel remained obdurately *there*, between her and whatever story it was trying to convey. A book would be better. With books, she wasn't conscious of anything except living the narrative.

Sometimes she thought she only dreamed about dancing while her real life was lived in books. She could get lost in a book, in being somebody else, in feeling amplified, complicated, her simple self fancied up with new sensations, new ideas and perceptions. In books she had family, community, a place in history; she had travels and explorations, struggle and achievement. In the books she was greeted by others who said, in effect, "You are so and so, and I know who you are!"

Often, when she finished a book, she came to herself with a sense of loss at what she'd surrendered in reading that last page. Closing the book was a finality that stripped her of identity, severed her life, left her squatting in the shallows of her mind, surrounded by polliwogs and ooze, with all the depths drained away. How often in her life had she longed for the story to become real! And yet now, here she was, far, far out in space, getting closer and closer to a dramatic doing, a wonderful adventure, a terrible excitement beyond all her expectations, and all she could do was worry that when the time came she'd be so self-conscious or frightened that she couldn't engage the event!

Her basic worry, excavated from the depths of her being through many fretful midnight sessions, was this clone business. Could a clone accomplish something it wasn't designed for? Dancer clones were supposed to be dancers. Musician clones were supposed to be musicians, entertainers entertainers, supervisors, scientists, genius generalists, all to be what they were! Just as many were cloned as were needed, with none left over—except for the occasional nus.

Nuses were mistakes. They were errors of system or development, and in moments of despair, Ellin comforted herself that she was definitely not a nus. She was exactly as per order, good legs, dancer's build, and with a mind that was . . . oh, filth, filth, filth, step one foot outside the stage and it was an absolute blank! Hadn't her clone parent had a brain? Hadn't the brain been passed on? If Ellin wasn't a nus, why did she feel like one? She clenched her pillow and groaned.

A moment later there was a rap at the door before it opened a crack to reveal a sleepy-eyed Gandro Bao peering in at her. "I am hearing moans? Are you being sick?"

Had she moaned? Perhaps it had sounded like that. "Maybe I let out a sigh or something," she confessed. "I was thinking about something."

"About all the volcanoes on Newholme blowing up?" he asked, insinuating himself into the tiny stateroom and perching on the foot of the bunk. "About the strange indigenous peoples existing there?" Some of this information had reached COW through official channels. Other facts, if indeed they were facts, had been picked up from the gossip of BIT or freighter crews who had landed briefly on Newholme to deliver or pick up materiel.

"Those are the only two things I could get out of all those filthy reports," she snapped. "Did you find anything else?"

"No. Indigenous race is being there, even though indigenes were not being there before settlement. Volcanoes are threatening to blow up world, even though they were never doing so before settlement. This is making me think settlement is, perhaps, unsettling."

He mugged a comic face, making her laugh, then cry, petulantly: "Why did it take them a thousand pages to say that?"

"Aha," he said with a serious face. "You were moaning over number of pages. That is being very understandable. Number of pages is often causing moaning, groaning, temper tantrums."

She flushed, embarrassed, confessing, "Nothing so relevant, Gandro Bao. I was thinking it would be easier if this was a book."

"Why is it being easier in book?"

"If the book came to a troublesome part, I'd just lay it down for a while. Or I'd jump ahead a page or two, to see if it came out all right. That way my stomach wouldn't hurt, and I wouldn't get pains in my head. And in a book, you get told who you are. You get the right words and the right clothes and the dialogue, everything, props and all. You don't have to work it out for yourself."

"This is being true in dance, too, but dance is not excluding extemporaneous art. So, be extemporizing."

"It's easier if you have a personality, that's all," she said in a defeated tone. "You know. Roots."

"You are fine nordic dancer. There are being many roots to go with nordic dancer."

"I know that." She sat up, annoyed. "I looked it up. There's a lot of warlike hordes moving around, and lots of stomping and kicking dances and several complicated religions, and a lot of violent wars. I don't feel connected to any of it. It's not like a family."

He leaned against the wall, taking one of her feet in his hands and digging his thumbs into her sole. "Why are you wanting a family?"

She felt her leg relax in a spasm of pleasure. "I meant it would be . . . nice to know who my parent was and what she did and where she lived, because she was a whole person and sometimes I feel like I'm just one sixth of one."

He mused, "I am reading a little bit about chaos theory: many things explained by chaos theory, many new discoveries about it even after centuries! This teaching is that tiny differences in original event can cause great difference in result. So, you and sister clones are each having many little differences, beginning in laboratory, going on into rearing. End result is six differing persons with similar appearance and skills. You are not being them, they are not being you. People have always been having twins, triplets, also clones. They are not being identical people.''

He moved his fingers up to the arch of her foot. ''If you really are wanting to know parent, records are letting you find out. All that is being included in records.''

''That's not what I meant,'' she whined. ''It's . . . I was born to be a dancer, and that's all I've ever known about. I didn't grow up *wanting* to be a dancer, I was born one. I didn't *choose* to be a dancer, that was already decided. I didn't even have to worry about whether I'd succeed, everyone knew I would. If I'd had to . . . explore, to try other things, I'd have had some . . . I don't know, some variety.'' She heard the snivel in her own voice and silently cringed. Shameful, carrying on this way!

''Female,'' he said, almost affectionately, putting down the foot and picking up the other. ''You are being female all over. Now to me, who is only being female impersonator, it is not making difference how I get to be a clown so long as I am really wanting to be clown. But you are wanting to try something else so you can have doubts about talents you have?'' He shook his head at her.

''Listen, Ellin, in Kabuki, we get persons coming after us. What is the old word? Groupies? It is like singers or actors, persons writing notes, asking are we free for dinner, you know? Mostly, I am not paying attention, but a few times I am going to dinner to meet people. I am seeing me through their eyes, and I am finding this confusing. They are picturing me so differently. Some are men who are thinking they love the woman I am pretending to be. Some are women who think they are loving me, actor, because I am obviously understanding women and they are needing understanding. Some are being as you say, vice versus, backward, women in love with woman character, men in love with man actor.

''So, I am being confused, and some days I am looking

at face in mirror and thinking, who is this? Is this male or female? Is this real person or only actor? Knowing father and mother is no help. They are being them, I am being me. They are not even knowing me. When I was being small boy sent home from school for being jokester, Mother was saying to me all the time she could not figure who I am being. I am thinking every parent is looking at every child sometimes thinking, who is this? So, when I am twelve, I am hearing famous Haraldson song and deciding I am whoever I am wanting to be! Who I am choosing to be!''

''But that's just it! I can't choose who to be! I never had a choice!''

He began to work on her ankle, drawing his brows together. ''You cannot choose to be horse, or fish, or tree, no. But it is like this. You are like small seed, and this ship is like big wind, and it is blowing seed from small plant far, far away where is no other such plant. And plant is not saying, ''Oh, oh, I cannot be oak tree, I cannot be bamboo, I cannot be cactus, I have no choice.' Plant is not so silly as that. Plant is putting down roots of own self and growing! And while it is growing, when things are difficult, it changes a little bit, so when it is grown, it is not exactly like the plant it was coming from. It adapts.''

She caught her breath. It adapts. And she had adapted. Even if her clone didn't have a brain, presumably she had adaptability. ''So that's all I am? A seed blown on the wind?''

He snorted. ''Seed on wind and being adaptable. Same as me, Ellin. Same as everybody. All of us, seeds. Seed is ninety percent precursor mammal, like mouse. Seven or eight percent chimpanzee-human primate precursor. One point nine nine nine percent generalized Homo sapiens. Tiny fraction one percent me, or you, different from everybody else. One healthy creature being able to blow on wind and still live! Able to choose.''

He threw up his hands, scowled at her, then patted her foot with a gesture that was pleasant without being in the least threatening. There, there, he seemed to say. Settle down.

"Oh, go away," she said, turning to bury her face in the pillow. "Very soon we'll be meeting that other ship, and I don't want to be all messed up in a frangle with you about my identity—or lack of it!"

"Lacking of it?" He grinned. "I make it rule only to talk to identities. Stop fretting and sleep."

Though unconvinced by anything he had said, shortly after he shut the door, she slept.

Back in his own stateroom, however, Gandro Bao did not sleep. Instead he stared into the mirror, his brows tented in query, one nostril lifted, as though scenting a trail. "Here I am being helpful," he murmured to himself. "Lecturing all about roots and growing in space where is nothing to grow on. Maybe is being only wind under us, and no place for us to hold to? Who is this Bao Bao Down to be giving Ellin Voy small contentments, like mama giving cookies?"

He smoothed his face, making it expressionless, calm, accepting. "Demand much of yourself and little from others," he quoted to himself from the analects. "You will prevent discontent."

That would have to do, for tonight.

24

Harassments

Bane and Dyre began harassing Mouche the moment they were moved into Consorts' quarters, as they had to be very soon, for the protection of the new students. "Dirt rubs off," as Madame was wont to say, and with Bane and Dyre dirt took all forms from attitudinal, to behavioral, to linguistic.

At first the two of them merely placed themselves within Mouche's view and stared endlessly, the lidless stare of serpents. Mouche ignored them. Within a few days, Simon had them so busy they had no time for staring.

Nights were still free, however, so they moved from covert threat to overt violence. One night, as Mouche was returning to his suite, Bane and Dyre leapt out at him from behind a protruding pillar, grimacing in theatrical fashion, mouthing their intentions in voices far too loud for secrecy, and with knives snaking from between their fingers. The assault was interrupted by Fentrys and Tyle, who came around the corner too late or just in time, depending on one's point of view. They were all wounded by the time it was over, and it took all three of them to put the two brothers down and send them off, bloody but still threatening.

"What started that?" Fentrys wanted to know.

"I told you about Duster," Mouche said, dabbing at a cut on his hand. "Those two did it, and they recognized me the first day they were here. Now they want to punish me for what they did."

"Well," said Tyle, "if they're that sort, they'll want to punish all three of us. We'd better travel in company for a time, to watch one another's backs."

And so they did, sticking so tight with each other or around the instructors that they thwarted several more attempts at violence. Simon, whose job required keen observation, noted this collective stance almost immediately, but it took him several days to determine the cause. At that point Simon took an early opportunity to call Mouche aside and have an informal conference.

"What is this?" Simon asked the boy, after seating both of them comfortably in Simon's quarters and pouring two glasses of wine.

"Those two used to live near my family's farm," said Mouche. "They killed my dog. Worse, they made poor Duster suffer!"

"What cause did they have for doing that?" Simon wondered. "Or was it random meanness?"

"Oh, they thought they had cause," Mouche admitted. "Duster and I stopped their killing some little native creature, killing and torturing it, too, I'd guess. I didn't hurt them any, and this business of trying to wound me or kill me just doesn't make sense. Why are they doing it?"

"I'd say your not hurting them is part of the why," said Simon. "Remember what Madame has taught you about gaming groups, packs, tribes? If you'd beaten them bloody, they might have fawned on you. Some men want more than anything to have a place in a pack and follow a lead dog. But if you won't fight for the role of lead dog, then you're an outsider, someone who interfered with their doing as they liked, and to men like Bane and Dyre, outsiders, particularly interfering ones, are the enemy. Prey, property, or enemy. You have to be one of the three.''

Mouche ducked his head to hide the angry tears at the corners of his eyes. He always teared up when he thought of Duster. ''Do they get pleasure out of acting like that?''

Simon leaned forward and laid a rough hand on his shoulder. ''Look, Mouche, you've got to understand what Newholme men are about, not from Madame's point of view but from our own. Now most men get taught early on that being dutiful is good, so they think they're being good when they work themselves into exhaustion and meanness. And most men know that pleasure distracts them from duty, so that teaches them pleasure is shameful. But at the same time, we have these restless brains inside that tell us to keep pushing toward the top so we can make a hole, crawl through, and see what's up there. All of us, even Consorts and supernumes, figure we've got a natural right to be there, on top and we use whatever we've got to get there. Humor. Or eloquence. Or skill. Whatever.

''Bane and Dyre, now, they've got the idea mutual pleasure is sissy stuff, so the only pleasure they get is sniggering and bullying and destruction. And they don't like duty either, so they avoid it. The only thing that gives them satisfaction is anger, so being angry is how they go looking for themselves, like vandals taking a city: throw, hit, break, kill, shatter—it's all one to them. Destroy enough stuff, suddenly they'll find the hidden door with heaven behind it.''

Simon looked at his glass, swirling the liquid in it, watching the patterns it made. ''I try to tell you boys, best I can, that there isn't any door. You climb over people, you push and shove and get up there on top, it's empty. I try to tell you pleasure's a good thing, and it's easier with Hunks than most, because you're being trained to give it. And I try to tell you that duty's good, too, but you've got to balance it. And you've got to study yourself to know how much of each you need, for no one man is a measure of all.''

"What do you mean, study?" Mouche asked.

"If you want to know about a Purse fish, you don't beat the fish to death or drain the sea dry. You look at the fish where it is. You study how it swims and what it eats and how it lives. You don't take hold of it, or kill it, you watch it. So, if you want to know who you are, you don't go laying around with a pickax. You try to catch yourself when you're not pushed by anybody or anything and watch yourself. You see what you do, and you figure out why, and you decide how that makes you feel, and how it affects others, and whether it makes you joyful or proud.

"It's amazing how many people don't know their own nature, even though they can't do anything with it until they know what it is. How can you move toward joy if you don't know what makes you happy?" Simon shook his head. "Nobody's required to live in pain. We should always try to move toward joy. . . ."

He looked up to meet Mouche's smile, suddenly radiant.

"Oh, Simon," he said, "It's not easy, but you're right. And even the pain lights a road for you, doesn't it? It beckons you to fix it! Like if you know something's hurt, you can try to mend it."

Simon, surprised into near silence, agreed it could.

He later mentioned the matter to Madame, when they were alone and very private, for she had asked him, as a favor, to come warm her bed that night and he had, as much from affection as duty, done so.

"Mouche is right," murmured Madame, sitting naked on the side of the bed, her hair loose about her shoulders, while Simon knelt behind her, kneading her neck between strong hands. "They beg for murder, both of them."

"Have you no pity for them, Madame?"

"Of course I pity them, Simon. I pity the mad dog that bites the child, the bull that gores the herdsman, the boar pig that tears the swineherds leg to shreds with his tusks. If they were wild creatures, we would say, with Haraldson, that they have the right to be as they are and the fault is ours for straying into their territory. The fact is, they are not wild creatures, they are protected and doctored and fed by mankind, and are thus kept according to mankind's rules. So it is with Bane and Dyre."

He went on kneading. "An odd thing happened when I was talking with Mouche. I was talking about discovering oneself, the lecture you often give . . ."

". . . so our Consorts can help their patronesses discover their joys . . ."

"And their own. Yes. And he got this expression on his face. I've never seen such ecstacy on a face!"

She said softly, "Mouche is a good one, isn't he Simon? Quite out of the ordinary. Something about him. . . ."

Simon moved his hands to the other side. Yes, he thought to himself. There was something about Mouche.

25

The Long Nights

At midwinter the people on Newholme took a long holiday which coincided, Mouche found, with the disappearance of the Timmys. When the Timmys went away, everything shut down, and in winter it stayed shut down for seven or eight days.

The holiday was called the Long Nights, or The Tipping of the Year, an occasion for family gatherings. Then kinfolk sat around the fire to tell over the names of ancestors, to honor those who had achieved g' status or Haghood among them, to relax standards of neatness and laundering (in the absence of whomever or whatever might have been, at other times, responsible for neatening and laundering), and to give amusing gifts and consume traditional foods prepared by their own hands while telling old stories around the tile stoves.

Though Consorts would never be, strictly speaking, "family," they needed to know how these occasions were managed, and House Genevois paid local families a generous stipend for hosting two or three youngsters in their homes during the Long Nights.

Mouche might have balked had the courtyard still been tenanted. His nightly forays had become an addiction, despite the feelings that flooded him at each watching. Initially, there was a kind of ecstacy in the watching, but gradually it turned to pain as if some huge thing was dying and unwilling to do so. The feeling exhausted him, and he had a sense the Timmys felt as he did, that they, too, were exhausted by the grief and weariness that came out of nowhere.

But the courtyard was empty, and he felt better for the respite. It was good, for a time, to have a simple skin-deep life, to be amused and think of nothing but singing or cooking or playing with children. He and Fentrys and Tyle always went to the weaving house of Hanna and Kurm g'Onduvai; their grown son, who supervised the looms, and his dowered-in wife as well as the eldest daughter, who had been dowered-in by a neighboring family, but who was visiting for a few days. There were also numerous merry and lively grandchildren.

Mouche and his friends enjoyed the annual give and take of the holidays. They played games with the children, taking them sledding on the nearby hill and ice-sliding on the frozen brook. In the evenings, they entertained by singing and playing on their instruments a number of songs everyone knew: "The Wind in the Chimney Corner," and "Six Black Cows," and the wordless melody of the "Lullaby for the Summer Snake." Even the chatter was interesting, and it was from Hanna's chatter, in fact, that Mouche first learned something on a subject he had been on the lookout for, the history of Dyre and Bane.

The conversation was between Hanna and Kurm, concerning some yarn Kurm had recently purchased from a local farmer.

"I can't use the stuff," said Kurm. "It's last year's spin, and I hate telling old man Dutter it's no good, but I can't afford not to. I can't use it."

"The quality is bad?" asked Hanna. "The Dutters were always good spinners."

"It isn't the quality," he replied. "It's the smell. I told you what I suspected. . . ."

"About Dutter not fathering those boys? Yes. You told me long ago."

"Well, you know *he* has that smell. Skunk-lung is what it is, and it's why *they* wouldn't have him, no matter how much he offered for dowry. And *he's* been seen here and there near the Dutter farm since those two boys came there—everybody knows they aren't Dutter's boys—and they have that same smell. Old man Dutter, he's either got no nose or he's so used to it he doesn't notice."

"But the boys don't spin."

"No. And billy goats don't give milk. But you make goat cheese where there's a billy, the cheese stinks, sympathetic like. You spin yarn where there's skunk-lung, and the yarn stinks, too. They breathe it onto everything, and whatever the cause, I can't use it."

Which was all that was said, enough to make Mouche mightily interested. The Dutter boys had lived over the hill from his own home. And Madame had said she'd turned Dutter down when he'd tried to sell them. So, Dutter was a farmer, and the boys probably weren't his, and they smelled, and House Genevois had two newish students who smelled and whom Madame was not thrilled with. So, who was the *he* who had been seen near the Dutter farm? The same *he* who had come to House Genevois?

"Have you heard about them smelling bad?" Mouche asked his friends, when they discussed the matter that night in the loft where they slept.

"The room smelled bad that time," said Tyle.

"Maybe it wasn't them. Maybe it was the other one."

They didn't know. Bane and Dyre were still new boys. If they smelled, only the other new boys would know.

The fact that the other new boys didn't know was a testimonial to Madame's assiduity and long experience. She had not been in the same room with Bane and Dyre for more than a moment before realizing they would present a challenge. Charcoal in the food, and chopped alfalfa, and certain herbs she knew of. Certain uncommon unguents rather than usual ones. One drug, expensive but efficacious in quelling goaty effusions in young bucks. The condition presented by the two youngsters was not unknown, though this was the first she'd ever heard of it in young men. The condition was usually reported as infecting those few weird and elderly outcasts who frequented the frontier. They'd wander into town, nobody knowing who they were, and they'd have that smell.

He, her patron, who had offered a very large sum in gold for the training of these boys, had the same affliction, though *he* looked perfectly normal. To *him,* it must have seemed unimportant, for *he* did little to ameliorate his own condition. *He*, of course, was not married. *He* had not produced children. Except, vague rumor had it, these two, and they under such circumstances as were . . . well, better not mentioned. Those who had at one time spoken openly of the matter had ended up . . . gone. Vanished. Still, people whispered: Had *he* placed them with Dutter? Or had *she*? The woman. Whoever she was or had been. A certain name was sometimes whispered; whispered unwisely, Madame felt.

Madame was fairly sure who the mother had been, though she did nothing to verify the fact. She asked no questions, sent no investigators—though there were several she had employed in the past when she had needed information. In order that she might be unburdened of the boys as soon as possible, she concentrated instead on turning Bane and Dyre into acceptable candidates, and within two or three seasons she had them to the point where they could be seen occasionally in public without greatly risking the reputation of House Genevois.

That they were well groomed and handsome was an artifact, produced by much labor, none of it their own. That they were, when left to their own devices, belligerent, unmannerly, dirty and ill spoken was a given. That they were maintained in a more or less obedient state only by the threat of intervention from outside was the leash to keep them heeled. All of which could have been overlooked if they had showed any inclination to adopt a more acceptable manner. They did not do so, and it was this that made Madame despair.

Unwilling boys could be forced to obey, but they could not be forced to learn. They could be beaten into submission, but not into charm. Since learning and charm were the hallmarks of the Consort, what Madame could make of Dyre and Bane, the Hagions only knew.

26

Amatory Arts: the Hagions

Madame rapped her desk for attention. "Finish up quickly boys. We have had a long session today." The afternoon "honored visitors," as they were called, had gone. The students had showered and dressed for supper. This lecture would be short.

The more diligent among them were making a few quick notes concerning the visitors' session. "Stroke, stroke, tweak," Mouche wrote, rehearsing the latest matter in his mind. "*Not* shove, shove, grab."

"Ahem," said Madame. "Gentlemen. If you will close your notebooks and attend, please."

Mouche underlined the last phrase, then closed his book.

"This evening," said Madame, "I want to discuss the worship of the Hagions.

"I'm sure it has crossed your minds that on occasion, a Consort may find himself unable to respond to the person of his patroness. Though he does his exercises, though he sets his mind to his task, though he is devoted to his profession, he finds something lacking in his own work.

"In handling these occasions gracefully, it is wise to be able to call upon at least one of the Hagions. In our library you will find several volumes devoted to the Hagions, the various manifestations of female divinity, all the goddesses ever worshipped by mankind. You will find Athena the wise and Aphrodite the fair; You will find Iyatiku, corn mother; Isis, goddess of fecundity; Gaea, earth mother; Cybele, founder of cities; Sophia, holder of wisdom; Hestia of the hearth; Heka of childbirth, all these and a thousand more. For the most part they are kindly and comforting, though some among them are foreign to our idea of womanhood. I recommend that you avoid choosing one of the destroyers and torturers, for you would do so at your peril. Those who delight in killing condemn themselves to a bad and ugly death.

"Over the next few months, you are to peruse the encyclopedia of Hagions with the intent of choosing a personal goddess. Most are womanly in shape, some are androgynous, some are homo-, bi-, or omnisexual, and a few take other forms. Many exist in the guise of youth, as prepubescent maidens, as laughing children. Others are more matronly, secure in their maturity, sensuous and passionate. Some are old women, beyond lust, but filled with the knowledge of years. In general, it is best to choose one of the younger goddesses, saving the older for your own age.

"Our religion is monotheistic. We worship the lifeforce that pervades the galaxy in infinite variety, life that bubbles up from the ferment of worlds, and we know that force may appear in myriad guises. There is no rivalry among these guises, as they are all aspects of the same divinity, one so vast and complex that She can be infinitely divided into parts while every part remains infinite. Your relationship to a particular guise may be as a son to a mother, as a servant to a queen, as a lover to his love, and among all her guises you are certain to find one who will attract you, one who will remind you of some aspect you already deem sacred, one who you will feel no strain in worshipping and to whom you might be pleased to devote your life.

"Choose well and thoughtfully. It is not blasphemous to say that choosing can be rather like getting a new pair of boots made. So long as you are in the service of your patroness, your chosen Hagion will walk with you in that service, and She must not rub blisters on your soul or cripple you with calluses. She will make your way smooth and easy, no matter how arduous it is in fact, so choose a goddess that fits.

"Once you have chosen your own aspect of divinity, we will help you become conditioned to Her service, and if the time comes when you believe you cannot properly serve your patroness, you will succeed by serving your Hagion instead. When your patroness takes you to the Temple at each New Year, you will light incense in thanks to your own divinity. In your own quarters, you will maintain a shrine to Her. This is to remind you of the divinity through whom the lifeforce flows, however corporeal the body or frail the mind through which that force is transmitted."

She saw a hand hesitantly raised. Fentrys, with an almost apprehensive expression.

"Yes, Fentrys?"

"Do the Hagions not resent being used like that, Madame?"

Madame frowned. At the back of the room, someone tittered, and she turned a quick and cautioning glance in that direction, like a search light, quickly beaming and as quickly withdrawn.

"It is not a foolish question, but it is a complicated one. The Hags at the Temple say that because the Hagions wish our patronesses to be served properly, they do not mind being used to that end. The Hagions accept our adoration, even though we are conditioned to give it, because we are using the conditioning to do their will. The Hags base their decision upon an historic precedent:

"On Old Earth, certain orders of celibate females were said to be brides of their male god. The writings of some of these women clearly establish that their devotion, though chaste in a physical sense, could be highly erotic, sensual, and joyous on a psychological level. These celibate orders often served the male priesthood or worked among the sick and the poor, doing many laborious and distasteful activities in the spirit of 'serving' their bridegroom, that is, achieving sensual and erotic rewards through activities which were neither. This conditioning and sublimation was considered appropriate.

"We do the same. Though serving our patroness may be unstimulating, serving our Hagion is highly erotic, sensual and joyous. Thus we accomplish the one by doing the other. . . ."

Her voice faded and she stood, staring out a south window at the busy street with an expression that grew slightly troubled. Far to the east, across the river, ashen clouds rolled from the scarp, and they seemed far more ominous than usual. When she looked back at her students, she saw a hand raised at the back.

"Mouche?"

"Madame, when you talk about serving the patroness, you always say 'we.' Why is that?"

She smiled. "Oh, my boy, I serve the Hagions by serving your patroness by serving you, just as you serve the Hagions in serving your patroness. We are all caught up, all of us, in serving this through serving that. Nothing is ever quite clear or direct in this world, and love is the most unclear and indirect of all. . . ."

A bell rang in the great hall. She said, "It is suppertime. You are dismissed."

She returned to the window as the room emptied, hearing one final rustle of paper and turning to see that Mouche still lingered, looking blindly at her like one stunned by terrible news or a sudden revelation. She hardly dared speak to him, and yet his depth of concentration seemed almost dangerous. . . .

"Are you considering which Hagion you will select, Mouche?"

His face lightened suddenly and he looked directly at her with a blinding smile.

"Oh, no, Madame. As you say, love is unclear and

indirect, but once you feel it . . . I already have a goddess that I serve."

He turned and went out, leaving Madame staring speechlessly after him. She had seldom seen such rapture on a human face. She could not imagine who, or what might have stirred it, and she felt a strange disquiet that only later did she identify as envy.

27

The Questioner is Announced

The Council of the Men of Business (the C-MOB, as it was jovially called) made the laws that governed men's affairs from their council house in Naibah, that structure known as the Fortress of Vanished Men. The council was made up entirely of g'Family Men, men whose wives had been dowered in and who had produced children. It elected from among its members an executive committee, ECMOB: six men from various parts of Newholme who came to Naibah each quarter year.

The Naibah fortress had, as a matter of fact, figured prominently in the women raids of the early settlement years, thus giving it a long and (as the Hags put it) disreputable history. Not the least reason for its scandalous reputation was the behavior of ECMOB members who immediately upon arrival removed their veils, poured themselves large glasses of vinaceous liquids and thereafter spoke disrespectfully of their wives, acts no fathering men would dare commit in public. There, also, when the routine business had been taken care of, ECMOB allowed itself to talk of other matters: matters of governance usually reserved to the Hags; matters that family men ordinarily only whispered at.

On a particular day, there was only one item of business. Volcanic activity had increased, as it did cyclicly every ten to twenty years, but the current geological violence was greater than at any time since settlement. Therefore, ECMOB had recently hired a consulting firm from off planet to set up surveillance equipment—also purchased from off planet—and assess the danger to settled communities. The firm had prepared a report which said, in essence that, yes, there was an increase in volcanic activity, which currently seemed to be about four times what it had been when Newholme was settled and twice what it had been ten years before. Yes, there might be some danger to the valley of the Giles, but no, it hadn't come to the point that the firm could recommend any sort of evacuation yet.

"Which I, for one, do not find helpful," said the chairman, one Estif g'Bayoar. "Not with all the eastern valleys ashed over, not with all the farms up there buried. There've been tremors as far north as the sea islands and as far west as Bittleby Village."

"All the valley farms gone?" asked Myrphee g'Mindon, stroking his chins. "I used to get quite a good goat cheese from up there."

Estif nodded. "The firm hired some supernume outlyers to place some sensors near the big caldera on the scarp. It's too high to climb to without breathing apparatus, which we've ordered but not received yet. Two of the men did get high enough to see that some new vents have opened during the past year, and there've been gas and ash flows all down the valleys. I suggest we ask the firm to give us their best estimate on city security. We can't evaculate Naibah or Sendoph without considerable notice!"

There were nods, some sanguine, some troubled.

Estif cleared his throat to signify a new matter, tapping restless fingers on the sheet of heavy vellum that lay on the table before him. Writing on vellum was considered sufficiently traditional that receiving it would not insult either pre- or posttechnological societies. It was, therefore, habitually utilized for formal interplanetary notifications.

"Newholme has received a communication from . . . from the Questioner," he said in a voice that was usually dry and emotionless but trembled now, very slightly. "The Questioner intends to visit Newholme, and it sends a formal announcement of that fact via a freighter that now sits outside Naibah. Does anyone here have any idea why it would be coming just now?" He regarded the problematical document, biting his lip, as though the meaning might become clear through protracted observation.

The ECMOB shifted restlessly, each member glancing covertly at his neighbors. Slab g'Tupoar, a portly fellow with dark, squirming eyebrows, snarled, "For Family's sake, 'Stif. You know why now. There's only two reasons it could be! Coming just now, I mean."

Bony Bin g'Kiffle, moved to immediate belligercnce, muttered, "Of all the stupid . . . Why must we deal with this?"

Myrphee g'Mindon struggled to his feet and wobbled unsteadily toward the information wall. "Questioner," he said. "Enlighten."

"Bionic construct," murmured the wall. "Nominally female. Containing, in words of enactment, text and commentaries on Haraldson's Edicts of Equity as well as wisdom of ages acquired since inception." The wall hummed a moment, as though thinking. "Wisdom of ages not susceptible of definition."

"Purpose of," Myrphee grated in an annoyed tone. "Enlighten."

"Purpose of Questioner," said the wall. "Primary assignment: Assess member worlds of COW on regular schedule to determine continued compliance with edicts of Haraldson. Secondary assignment: Assess other mankind-settled worlds to determine if cultures meet minimal standards of ethical conduct regarding human rights. Final assignment: Take every opportunity to accumulate knowledge about cultures, mankind and other. Report to COW any divergence from council edicts applying to all mankind settlements, whether members or nonmembers of COW, regarding human rights, age or gender rights, or rights of indigenous races.'' The machine silenced itself, then, with a whir said, almost conversationally, ''Questioner is also authorized to order disposal of mankind populations who are egregiously transgressing the edicts.''

At this addition, Myrphee's chins quivered, the tremor passing to those at the table as a little wind might move through a grove of trees, a sudden and collective shudder that left a trembling quiet in its wake. After some moments, Myrphee drew back his pudgy fist as though to hit the wall, but contented himself with an obscene gesture.

''Excrement,'' he said feelingly.

''Gentlemen.'' Estif tapped his little gavel, saying in his high, serious voice, ''Come now. It's unlikely to be . . . well, it just can't be that bad.''

''About as bad as it can get,'' grated Myrphee g'Mindon as he returned to his seat.

''Like tidal wave, tornado, forest fire,'' offered Calvy g'Valdet, in the light, slightly amused tone that the other members often found offensive. Calvy made a point of being amusing about important things, and he did it in a way that came close to condoning immorality. Often the others punished him for it, as now, by seeming not to notice. If morals were the measure of a man, Calvy had no business being a member of ECMOB, for it was known that Calvy's wife of some fifteen years had not bought a Consort, though her contract allowed her to do so. It was rumored that prior to his marriage, Calvy had pretended a lengthy business trip while actually spending a month or two in a Consort house, learning whatever dirty things it was that Consorts did, just so his wife would never supplant him in her affections. The story said he was in love with her, which if true, was both unmanly and indecent.

Though this story was known to the other members of ECMOB, none of them had ever discussed it with Calvy himself. Had they done so, custom would almost have required that they denounce his behavior. Pleasuring a wife was not proper for a Family Man, and they felt Calvy should be far too bowed down by guilt to be amusing.

Why then, Bin g'Kiffle asked himself, did Calvy seem to enjoy life so much more than he, Bin, who conducted himself in perfect accordance with custom? Bin's couplings were unfailingly joyless, and reason dictated that the Hagions should, therefore, reward him more than they had! The cockade in his hat, the g' before his name, and six children, four of them supernumes, did not seem a sufficient compensation for all his years of struggle. The thought was a recurrent one, and as usual it made him splenetic.

"The Questioner's visit could mean total disaster," he fumed, glaring at Calvy.

"Bin, let's not overreact. Calm, please!" Now slightly peevish himself, Estif looked from face to face, annoyance plain on his own.

"What does it . . . she *say?*" Diminutive Sym g'Sinsanoi hoisted himself higher in his chair. It was a habitual movement, this hoisting up, though Sym appeared little shorter than the other men when seated. "She must say *something!*"

Himself annoyed by all these festering feelings, Estif threw the vellum onto the table before him and sank into his chair. "The letter of announcement says she wishes to visit our lovely world, which she has not yet had the pleasure of assessing."

Myrphee shifted in his chair, redistributing his considerable weight. "The Questioner will look at our way of life to see if we comply with the edicts. We are going to have to prove that we do comply with the edicts. Which means we will need the help of the Hags."

"How many in the party?" asked Calvy g'Valdet, who was not given to muttering over what could not be changed. His way was to smile, to avoid recrimination, to cut through the tangle, to decide and move, to do what was necessary without endless nattering. No matter what the others might think of his morals, they all agreed that Calvy got things done.

"And, where will we put them?" asked Myrphee.

"Here in the fortress?" Bin g'Kiffle suggested. "It's the easiest place. It's already staffed with . . . ah, well, you know."

"It has a human staff," said Sym, sourly. "Chef, assistants, stewards. For reasons of security." He put his hands together and examined the ceiling above him.

"How many are coming," asked Myrphee, "with the Questioner? We need to know! One or two we could maybe . . . manage. More than that . . ." He scowled at the tabletop.

"I'm afraid the notice mentions an entourage," admitted Estif. "There will be two Old Earthians to do the actual 'contact work,' as they call it, plus a Cluvian protocol officer, some bodyguards, plus whatever specialists she figures she needs. The protocol officer will arrive on planet before the others."

"There's no way we can keep the Hags out of it, I suppose?" Bin snarled.

"We didn't receive the only copy," said Calvy. "The Hags will have been notified as well."

Myrphee squeezed his hands together until his knuckles made white dimples in the plump sausages of his fingers. "How about asking for a delay, on the grounds of insufficient notice, or time for preparation?"

Calvy said, "We're not supposed to prepare, Myrph. She's supposed to catch us as nearly unaware as makes no difference."

"You don't suppose she's heard about . . . ?" asked Slab, his eyebrows rising into a single hairy bar across his forehead.

It took no effort for the others to keep their faces carefully blank. They did not suppose. Every habit they had cultivated since childhood kept them from supposing. Not one of them would even momentarily consider that there was something particular on Newholme in which the Questioner might be quite interested. Even if the something particular bit them with long, sharp teeth on their collective ass, they would bear the pain without seeming to notice.

Considering that their true concerns were unspoken and

nothing was put forward as a solution to the unspecified, the meeting lasted longer than necessary. Calvy tried a time or two to push for some resolution, but the general discomposure made decision impossible. Whenever the Hags or the edicts came into MOB discussions, the meetings dragged on while a chronic complainer vented anger at his wife or mother and a hobby-historian blathered on about olden times when there weren't any Hags and when women did as they were damned well told. The committee always seemed to have at least one of each. At present they were Bin and Myrphee respectively. Though Calvy was a better historian than Myrphee, he didn't blather about it.

Estif muttered, "If you're sure the Hags are going to be involved, we ought to appear cooperative, I suppose. Is there a volunteer to take this document into Sendoph to the Haggery?"

Somewhat reluctantly, Bin g'Kiffle raised one hand. "I'm going back there tonight. I suppose I can take it." He intended to catch the afternoon boat upriver, and could, in fact, deliver it that evening. It would give him an excuse for not going home immediately on arrival. As everyone in the room knew, Bin would use any excuse not to go home. His wife was a termagant.

"I'm going up to Sendoph tonight on business," murmured Calvy. "I can take it if Bin doesn't want to be bothered."

"I said I'd take it," snapped Bin. "And I will!"

Calvy bowed, making an ironic face. He intended to call on an old friend in Sendoph, and he was glad enough not to make a time-consuming call at the Panhagion.

Estif handed over the vellum and the fancy envelope with the seals and ribbons. Bin stowed it away in his leather-and-gilt document case, almost as important a symbol of status as his cockade and the g' before his name. After which the men carefully affixed their veils across their faces, adjusted their honorable cockades, and took themselves back to home cities and places of business, where they belonged.

28

A Family Man Visits the Hags

Only in the secrecy of the Fortress of Lost Men was the Temple in Sendoph referred to as "the Haggery," and Bin g'Kiffle was careful not even to think the words as he climbed the wide stone steps leading to the huge bronze doors. One of the Consort Houses had doors like that, also, part of the cargo of the ship the first settlers had pirated. Pirated or not, males did not approach those doors for anything trivial. Males did not hurry when there were Hags in the vicinity. When at the Temple, even workmen or delivery men took their time, abating any tendency toward immodest alacrity. Here, everything was done slowly, deliberately, with due weight and moment.

Bin, therefore, climbed in a dignified, almost ritualistic manner. When he had completed this errand, he would take off his cockade and go to one of the basement taverns hidden in the warehouse district near the river. He would stay there as long as possible. He would tell his wife he had had an errand at the Temple, and if she didn't believe him, the hell with her—the Temple offices were always open.

He was solicited by a holy prostitute, not a bad-looking boy, considering, and Bin produced a generous contribution while murmuring the acceptable excuse. Tonight was his wife's night. he said. The prostitute smiled slightly and went back to his fellows. No one questioned that excuse, but one had to be a Family Man to get away with it.

Bin bowed outside the door, waiting until three very pregnant women had preceded him to the font, then dipped his own fingers in the water, thereby symbolically cleansing himself of the taint of business, the stink of profit. Here at the Temple, business did not apply. Here one could not set a price on a sentient life, though people did so constantly elsewhere in the city. Here one did not speak of gain. In the Temple, there was no network of honorable Family Men on whom one could depend for information or influence. Here Bin was simply another man of Sendoph, like any other man of Sendoph, whether g'family or otherwise.

He opened the small door set into the huge one and went through into the Temple forecourt, a broad semicircle of mosaic pavement that bordered the outer half of the circular Sanctuary. To one side, a gentle ramp led to the birthing rooms below. The pregnant women were already partway down, chatting among themselves. All devout women tried to bear their children in the Temple; certainly Bin's wife had done so, for all the good it did. Five sons and only one daughter to show for it, and now his wife had a Hunk. Every cent he got for the girl would go to dower his eldest boy, and what was he to do with the others? He'd made the mistake of raising them above their expectations, at least the older two, so they were resentful and useless. He'd intended to start a dynasty, and now there was damn little wherewithal to start anything. Whatever he did, there'd be no profit in it!

Fifty feet above his head, the barrel-vaulted ceiling curved away to right and left, the air hazed by the smoke of a dozen incense kiosks. The opposite wall, concentric with the outer wall, was a row of pillared and heavily curtained arches, beyond which was the Sanctuary, the statues of the Hagions, the lofty seats of the Prime Hags, the rites and observances that kept Newholme ticking. Even at this time of night, there was movement through the curtained arches, and Bin checked his veil compulsively. If a man wanted a slow, agonizing execution, just appear in the Temple unveiled. That would do it. There were always women here, women quite willing and eager to be punctilious about male behavior. Not to mention the ubiquitous Haggers.

The Sanctuary, barely visible between the curtains, was forbidden to him and all other males over the age of ten, but this wide foyer with its racks of votary candles was open to all. Bin turned to his left and went along the curve of the outer wall toward the offices, moving solemnly so as not to be suspected of frivolity. A young woman, younger, that is, than most of the Hags, nodded to him as he entered the open door of the reception area.

''Family Man,'' she said pleasantly.

As always, Bin chafed at the designation. She could see his cockade, she knew who he was perfectly well, but no woman would greet a veiled man by name in public, not even a wife her husband. The avoidance was supposed to be proper, but to Bin it always felt rude, depersonalizing, as though he were invisible!

He bowed. ''Madam. I bring a notification received by the Men of Business in Naibah. It concerns a proposed visit to Newholme by the Questioner. . . .''

She smiled sweetly. ''We have already received notification, Family Man. Though we thank you for your courtesy.''

Bin shifted uncomfortably from foot to foot. ''Our chairman, that is, Estif g'Bayoar, thought maybe the Questioner would like to stay at the Fortress in Naibah? That is . . .''

''We'll call upon the Men of Business if we need them,'' she said, still sweetly. ''Do shut the door on your way out, Family Man.'' And she bent back to her work, ignoring him so pointedly that he felt himself growing heated beneath his robes and veils.

He opened his mouth to say something snappish, then closed it again. She glanced up. "Something else?" Her face was now quite stern, the smile gone.

"Where we put her! It's important! She can't be allowed to—"

The woman held up her hand, palm outward, warningly. "The matter is being attended to, Family Man. You need not concern yourself. Do you understand?"

It took him a moment to find his voice. "Of course, Madam," he said, bowing. "Sorry to have disturbed you." Then, stubbornly, he said, "Madam, have the Hags any information about the volcanic activity? The Men of Business believe there has been a troubling increase and we seek guidance."

Her face grew very still. It was some time before she replied, "I will convey your concern to the Hags, Family Man. I cannot say at the moment whether they or the Hagions would find this matter within their purview, but I will inquire. Feel free to come again in a day or two, by which time I should know something."

He turned and left, shutting the door behind him, making no sound. Once out on the street, at the bottom of the steps, however, he muttered to himself. "Damn, uppity, pushy, Hags. Damn women. Damn female pushiness. Damn." He made a threatening gesture that drew the attention of a couple of Haggers who were sweeping the cobbles. Since male Haggers had, so to speak, foresworn being male, they wore no veils, and their faces were stern as they turned toward him, holding the thick, heavy broom handles like pikestaffs. At that, he came to his senses. Thrusting his hands into his sleeves, lowering his head so they could not see his eyes glaring at them through his veil, he walked steadily away. It was late. He had had a full day. He wanted to get home and go to bed!

"Damn Hagions," he cursed the Goddesses. "Damn Haggers," he cursed their followers. "Damn, damn Hags." And their priesthood, as well.

Behind him, through one of the slit windows that looked out upon the temple stairs and down into the street, the young woman he had spoken to along with two older Hags watched him depart.

"So the Men of Business are worried about the smoke," murmured D'Jevier.

"All that gray ash streaming from the scarp would be difficult to miss," muttered Onsofruct. "All those valley farms wiped out over the last five or six years."

"And the tidal wave that took six villages out along the Jellied Sea."

"And the way the pillars are shifting off their bases in the crypts of the Temple. More than worrisome, I'm afraid. I still wish we could ask for help from the Council of Worlds."

"We can't," snarled D'Jevier. "Obviously."

"Obviously."

"With the Questioner coming, we have other things to worry about."

"Obviously."

So agreed, they stood where they were, watching until Bin's skinny form disappeared into the dark.

29

Calvy and his Friends

Calvy had ridden up the river with Bin, avoiding his carping by pretending to be asleep most of the way, and he left the boat at the Brewer's Bridge. He took the precaution of removing his cockade before leaving the boat, his veils were impeccably impenetrable, and thus he had no difficulty whatsoever achieving his goal without being recognized by anyone at all—a good thing, for Family Men of good repute did not visit Consort Houses.

Calvy did. He had visited House Genevois at intervals for some years, and in the doing he had made a good friend of Madame and a better friend of Simon, who had taught him a number of interesting and provocative tricks. His current business with House Genevois was the procurement of a birthday present for his wife, a matter that Simon and Madame could accomplish more deftly than Calvy himself, given all the import regulations that he, as a Man of Business, was forced to uphold. The Consort Houses were more devious. Consorts had to give gifts;

women expected it; and the Consort Houses helped their graduates meet expectations.

The present was on Madame's desk, and after pouring them each a glass of a pleasant restorative, she laid the velvet box before him with a flourish, a necklace of gemstones and gold, the stones local, but cut and faceted off planet, the gold of a fine workmanship utterly impossible to achieve on Newholme. The necklace was not massive, and it was not gaudy, but every link of it spoke of quality and care.

"Your lady will simply love it," said Simon.

"She'd better," murmured Madame, thinking how nice it would be to have a man as much in love with one as Calvy was with Carezza. "You've outdone yourself, g'Valdet."

He smiled, stretching back on the sofa, letting Simon fill his glass. "It's an odd old world we live in, Madame."

"It is indeed. You're noting some particular oddity?"

"Though I cultivate a certain fatalism and eschew the fidgets my colleagues are displaying, I agree with them that the world seems increasingly unstable, in a geological sense."

Madame frowned. "The Hags are worried, but they don't let themselves show it, and therefore the people, who are also worried, don't show it either. What brings it to your mind today?"

"The Questioner is coming."

Simon looked puzzled, but Madame nodded, lips thinned. "Oh, is she, now." With a side glance at Simon, she said, "Haraldson's creature, Simon. You know."

He did know. The Questioner was the monster under the bed, the bugaboo in the closet, the sound creeping up the midnight stairs. To anyone without a clear conscience, the Questioner was the ultimate terrifier. He nodded, sipping at the wine while Madame went on. "You think she's coming because of this rumbling and rattling we've had to endure lately?"

"That, possibly. Though it could be another thing or two, or both."

She asked, "The other thing being?"

"The Questioner has on more than one occasion recommended severe action against the mankind population of worlds when that population had not governed in accordance with Haraldson's edicts."

Madame sipped at her glass. "As in the matter of our invisible people."

"That is one such matter."

"You know of another?"

"There's our odd imbalance of the sexes, Madame."

She frowned. "But we know why that is. There's a virus peculiar to this planet that attaches to the mother's X chromosome. When the cell doubles, at the polar body stage, the virus doesn't double, and it has a fifty-fifty chance of staying with the oocyte or being discarded with the polar body. It's more complex than that, but that's the pith. The Hags have been unable to find a cure, though they've searched diligently."

He smiled, sipped, murmured, "I merely have a feeling the Questioner may doubt that. Having read the Council of Worlds accounts of some of her investigations, she seems a doubting sort of device."

"Where do you get Council of World's reports?" demanded Simon.

"They're public record. I subscribe to the journals that record them. The data cubes come in with our other supplies. Some of her visits are extremely interesting. There was one case I was very taken with. Beltran Four."

"I don't know of it," said Madame.

"A warlike planet, ruled by a polygynous warrior elite. Because of the constant battles, there are many fewer men than women. Our own situation, in reverse. This results in a large surplus of women, so the powerful men have huge harems of them."

"Why did this interest you enormously?" asked Madame, with an expression of distaste.

"Because, essentially, the powerful men keep the battles going that result in the deaths of the young men that result in the surpluses of women they then take advantage of."

"I agree it is unethical. And the Questioner dealt severely with mankind on that planet?"

"No." Calvy smiled. "That's what interested me enormously. She did not."

Madame and Simon exchanged confused glances, at which Calvy smiled the wider. "As I said. It's an odd little old world, but I didn't mean to discuss each and every little oddity in today's conversation. I did mean to thank you for your help with the necklace."

"Always glad to help," murmured Simon.

Calvy nodded. "I did hope one of you would say that, for I have another problem. Carezza is pregnant. Tinsy, our chatron child tender, is up to his fat little armpits with the older children. I need another chatron. Unfortunately, a few of our friends have been sharing horror stories, and both Carezza and I want to be sure. . . ."

Madame nodded. "You want a supernume of good repute. Someone trustworthy."

Calvy said, "Someone cut long enough ago that he's over the trauma, settled down, able to enjoy what's enjoyable without being angry at the world. The angry ones take it out on the children."

Madame pursed her lips and Simon frowned.

"What?" Calvy asked.

Simon blurted, "Of course they take it out on the children. What does anyone expect? Removing a man's sex organ doesn't increase his happiness, or his delight in other men's children!"

"Simon is right, Calvy," said Madame. "I think all this amputation business really goes too far. We're seeing more and more chatrons every year. The fact that many of them die makes them rare, their rarity makes them status symbols. Would you consider a supernume who has not been altered? Or even a retired Consort? If we pick carefully, I can guarantee you, he'll have a better temper and more considerate feelings. It's the maiming chatrons really hate, and their anger must manifest itself somehow."

Calvy said plaintively, "But Tinsy has been so good."

Madame said, "I located him for you, Calvy. He was cut when he was a baby, before he was conscious of there being anything there to lose. He already had a sweet disposition and was hardworking by nature, with a great desire to please. I don't know of any other like him, but I do know of at least two retired Consorts and one supernume who're very good with children. They genuinely like them, and they aren't bitter about life. The two Consorts simply like taking care of people, and the supernume is looking for a new place because his last charge is just entering school, and he's really not needed in the family anymore."

"Was it a good family?" Calvy asked, significantly.

"It was a kind family for one so well-to-do," said Simon, promptly. "I know who she means, and he is a good lad. The mother doesn't spend all her time partying and being cultural, she stays in touch with the children and doesn't forget their names or their birthdays. The father is a good man, considerably overworked, what with business and caring for the children and overseeing the domestic arrangements, but then, which of you Men of Business isn't overworked, present company excepted."

Madame said, "I can understand your wife's concern, though being so concerned is unconventional. Carezza should be so involved with her Consort, she wouldn't be worried about the children."

"But then, Calvy doesn't have a conventional family," said Simon with a grin. "He and Carezza seem to have something quite exceptional going on."

"As my colleagues are constantly throwing into my face," Calvy confessed. "I sometimes find it hard to imagine how other men manage. They work all day, every day, they worry over their young children, trying to be sure the nursery tender does a good job and doesn't smack them about, they gamble with the investment made in the children, knowing there won't be enough girls born to keep all the boys in the family, so if they're at all soft-hearted, they try to make some kind of provision for the supernumes, and all this while their wives are going here and there, enjoying themselves.

"With Carezza and me, even with a good child tender, it's so much easier with both of us involved. I really feel for some of my colleagues. Those with six or eight offspring look quite worn out. I look ahead to the time that we finally build a reproductive center and have enough women that all men can live as Carezza and I do.''

Madame laughed, the laugh turning gleeful when she saw his offended expression. ''Oh, my dear Calvy, do you really think having more women available would make everyone live as you and Carezza do? Come now, dear, and you a bit of an historian?''

He flushed. He had been unbuttoned by the wine and said something stupid. She was right, of course. Having more women wouldn't assure that his colleagues lived as he and Carezza did.

''I'll interview your supernume,'' he agreed. ''And I'll talk to Carezza about it. Perhaps you're right, Madame. You very frequently are.''

For a short time, too short a time, all three of them forgot the impending visitation.

30

Mistress Mantelby Investigates

It was almost eighteen years after her parents died that Marool Mantelby, riding in an open carriage in the Riverpark at Sendoph, saw a group of young men escorted by attendants from House Genevois. Marool knew of House Genevois though she had never obtained a Hunk from there. Madame never seemed to have one available. Still, Marool enjoyed looking at the strings of novices and graduates, shopping for companions for her later years. Though she had several companions currently being readied for destruction and no immediate need of additional personnel, in this particular group was a young man whose face, quite visible through its transparent veil, intrigued her. There was something about it that was evocative, and for a moment she thought perhaps he was a nephew, one of her sisters' children.

As though he felt her stare, he looked up, returning her measuring look with an almost sneering arrogance. He was large and well built and handsome. She liked the cock of his head, that nervy, totally disrespectful stance she found appealing. She went home thinking of him.

She thought of him often over the next few days, scouring recollection as she tried to think who he resembled, happening upon long-repressed memories of her parents, as the child Marool had understood them through fourteen years of covert, obsessive observation. One memory jostled another, which bumped another yet, and she began waking in the night, heart pounding, gasping for breath, pursued by nightmare terrors which, except for a horrific vision of her father's dead face, vanished before she was even awake. "Marool," he said. "It wasn't an accident. . . ."

Finally, after waking three times in one night, she decided to put an end to it by finding out for herself how it was that her parents and sister had died. Everyone had said it was an accident. Her dream vision cast doubt upon that, ripping away almost two decades of complacency to reveal something horrid. If her family's deaths had been purposeful, she needed to know who had done it, and why.

The mountains of Newholme were not what one thought of as mountains in an Earthian sense: wrinkled, rocky land which, aside from being wrinkled and rocky, was not much unlike other land, that is, solid. The mountains of Newholme were not solid. Every prominence was drilled through with holes, bubbles, passageways, pits, and caverns. Every range was a speleological nightmare of twisting ducts, narrow channels, and precipitous galleries, most identifiable as volcanic in origin. No effort had been made to map the ramified and interpenetrating layers.

Only a few features of the wilderland attracted casual visitors: the Glittering Caves near Naibah; the Cavern of the Sea east of Nehbe; and the Combers, northwest of Sendoph, where an enormous set of lava tubes lay parallel, their southeastern sides eaten away by continual, grit-bearing winds to leave curling waves of rock, an eternal surf intent upon an unseen shore.

Water had penetrated into the Combers and eaten holes into the unseen tunnels below. Winds blew through the holes to make music that trembled up through the feet and could be sensed as a vibration in the bones of the leg or a shivering in the groin. Strange, pallid growths filled in the tunnels, expanding upward and sideways, some of them with tentacles and solar collector leaves and hollow stalks through which the fluids of the world could be seen pulsing.

On the surface, each comber was a linear world, uncrossable by anything without sticky feet to crawl on the underside of a vaulted overhang. If one climbed up the closed side, one could cross to the lip that curved to slick knife edges hanging twenty or thirty meters above the razor-edged fragments below. One could walk along the inside of a comber or clamber about in the soil-filled area between combers, and while doing so, one could fall through into any number of pits and deadfalls. For these and other reasons, people rarely found cause to go to the Combers.

Marool Mantelby's family had met their deaths among the Combers, and Marool decided to go see for herself. No matter what people said, Marool's parents would not have gone on a picnic, they would not have gone anywhere together without some strong and so far unfathomable motivation.

The Man of Business who had attended to the affair at the time accompanied her in the light carriage that jolted along a woodcutters' rutted road as it wound back and forth among the stinks and steams of hot springs toward the wilderland. In addition to the Man of Business, Marool had hired a bulky guard from the post in Sendoph, and a driver, a wiry individual who had agreed to use his carriage only after she signed a release that allowed him to unveil once they were in the hills.

"I don't drive on those roads 'less I can see," he said, rather too truculently for Marool's taste. "There's things in those hills, and I sure can't outrun 'em if I don't see 'em coming."

"Things?" Marool inquired, in the voice she had been cultivating since leaving the Wasters, one that disguised her malice with a gloss of amiability. ''What things are those, driver?''

''Things,'' he repeated, rather less belligerently, mistaking her nature as she had intended. ''People go missing with no sign how or where, so it has to be things. Stands to reason!''

''Ah,'' she murmured. ''Well, then, I will give you permission to go unveiled. Once we are in the hills.''

The guard required no such variation from custom. Guards wore tinted visors that covered their faces, allowing them to see out but others not to see in, and this one perched beside the driver, head swiveling alertly from side to side while Marool, seated behind them, contented herself with a view of backs and heads between which scraps of scenery were sometimes discernable.

''I can see no reason whatsoever that my parents would have come here,'' she muttered.

''Nor I,'' replied Carpon, the Man of Business. ''Your father ordered a team hitched to a carriage, then he took it from the carriage yard himself, collected your mother and sister at the front steps and went off. The only servants who knew anything were the stableman and the cook, for your father had asked him to prepare a basket luncheon.''

''And who was it found them?''

''When they did not return by evening, their majordomo reported their absence to the guard post, and at first light dogs were fetched and the carriage was tracked—or more properly, perhaps, the horses were tracked—to the place they were found unharmed and still hitched. The luncheon, though much disarrayed by small creatures during the intervening hours, had obviously been laid nearby, some way back from the comber edge. I was with the group who found the bodies of your family members in a sink at the bottom. We recovered them for burial only with great difficulty.''

They continued on their way for some time while Marool digested this. ''The driver,'' she murmured, ''mentioned *things*. Could they have been driven over the edge by *things*?''

Carpon shifted uncomfortably on the seat. ''One hears

such stories, of course. One has never seen a *thing*, however, nor has one talked to anyone who has actually seen one. There are always subterranean noises in the mountains, and rumor makes more of them than is probably warranted.''

Marool was not inclined to believe in *things*, but as she and the Man of Business fell silent, they were uneasily aware that the only noises in these mountains were the ones made by themselves. Aside from the plopping hooves of the horse and the rattle of the wheels, the world was incredibly still. Even the steams that came from hidden vents to curtain the surrounding forest were silent.

''Just around the next bend,'' said Carpon in too loud a voice.

They came around the bend into a clearing that spanned the tops of several of the great tubes running from southwest to northeast, the nearer ones to their left curling toward the southeast. To their right the tubes were buried, visible only at their centers as parallel trails of bare, wind-polished stone. Forest enclosed them on north and west. South, where the combers might otherwise have blocked their view of the valley, several of them had collapsed to leave receding jaws of jagged teeth framing a view of Sendoph, far below, like a square of patterned carpet: streets and buildings, plazas and parks, all hazed and faded by distance.

Marool climbed from the carriage, the Man of Business close behind her.

''Your father's carriage was tied there,'' he said, gesturing toward a copse of lacy trees at the edge of the clearing. ''The trees were smaller then. Their luncheon was laid out there,'' indicating a table-sized chunk of ancient, lichen-spotted lava standing some distance back from the edge with lower chunks around it that could serve as seats.

His voice was overly loud, Marool thought, and she raised a hand to her lips, shushing him and herself into the profound silence of the place. No bird song. No wind sound. No flutter of leaf. Only the breathing of the horses, the jingle and creak of their harness and the stamping of their restless feet.

She moved toward the edge of the comber. When the rock began to curve downward, she dropped to her knees to edge a bit farther. Before her, the stone was bare and wind-polished, curling into a razor edge above a litter of rock shards.

Marool crept backward, rising awkwardly beside the stone table. If Margon and Stella and Mayelany had been sitting here—which was in and of itself ridiculous—and if some creature had crept out of the dark woods that confronted her, might they have been frightened over the drop?

"Are there any people out here?" she asked Carpon.

"Wilderneers," he said, in a tone that told her he smiled behind his veil.

"You think there are Wilderneers? Here or anywhere?" she demanded.

"Men disappear," he replied. "All the time. Supernumes, seamen, Consorts. Even sometimes a Family Man. These lands are wide, there are innumerable places to hide, so I suppose there could be Wilderneers."

Marool was unimpressed by disappearances. She herself knew how a good many had disappeared, and it had nothing to do with Wilderneers.

"Wait here," she told him, lifting a finger to summon the guard and moving off among the trees as he trotted to join her. Behind her the driver and the Man of Business exchanged looks, eloquent in the cock of head and shrug of shoulder, though the one's face was hidden. Together they sat down by the stone table to await her return.

Marool strolled in the profound shade of the trees, sniffing the air like a hound though she could smell nothing at all, staring at this thing and that though she had no idea what she was looking for, stopping short in the realization she was seeing something very strange.

On either side was a straight and rounded ridge of soil, the two ridges perhaps three meters apart, as though something huge and heavy had been dragged along here, pushing the dirt up at the sides. The ridges were overgrown with herbage and wild flowers, so whatever had made them hadn't been here lately. She moved to the ridge at her right and walked along it, kicking at it aimlessly, stopping when an object caught her eye, near her feet. It was a piece of something, like shell.

She bent over and picked it up, turned it in her fingers, a piece as large as her two hands set together, slightly oily, knife edged, oval in shape, smooth on one edge, rough on the other, like a gigantic fingernail jerked from some enormous finger. It had gooey stains along one edge.

She held it out to the guard, who started to take it, then gasped as though it had bitten him. The warmth of her hand had brought an odor from that dry substance, a rank and feculent stink that was suddenly all around them, floating on the wind, moving the leaves of the trees.

Marool noticed nothing.

"Throw it away," he muttered. "It stinks!"

She made a face at him, wrapped the thing in her scarf and put it in the reticule she carried at her belt, ignoring him as he turned aside, retching.

"You have a weak stomach for one in your occupation," she said angrily, walking on only to encounter another track that had crossed the first one. On these ridges nothing grew. The soil was crumbly, newly thrust aside. Beside her, the guard stopped short, as though frozen in place.

"Chuh?" asked the world. "Chuh?"

It was a grunt, a growl, a chuffing interrogation, perhaps an expression of surprise, maybe of annoyance. It was loud enough to make the ground tremble, to shiver the leaves on the trees and to start little falls of dust from the sides of long buried rocks. It was echoed by a huffing shudder that repeated a guttural *uh, uh, uh, uh* as it faded toward the east. All this, Marool had time to notice before the sound, or another such sound came from another direction, a distance to the right, possibly . . . very possibly behind her.

"More than one," she said not quite aloud, turning to lead the way out of the woods, hurrying, just short of running. "More than one." Unless that last sound had been an echo. She did not think it had been an echo.

The guard followed silently, his head turning to look

over one shoulder, then the other. He had not realized how far they had come among the trees. He had not realized what a time it would take them to get out again, to rejoin the others. . . .

Who were not there. The carriage was there, and the horses, seemingly frozen into immobility, eyes wide, whites showing, nostrils flared, skin shivering, but making not a sound. When Marool got herself sufficiently under control to issue a command, the guard reluctantly fetched a rope from the carriage, tied himself to the stone table and let himself far enough down to look over the edge while she scanned the forest, seeing nothing. Then the rope trembled, and she turned to find the guard scrambling away from the edge on hands and knees.

They were there, he said, his voice cracking. They were there, far below. He could barely see their bodies among the broken rock. Marool chose not to look for herself. If someone wanted to retrieve the driver and the Man of Business, they would have to come out from town to do so.

She turned to go back to the carriage, stumbling a little, out of either haste or terror, admitting with a hysterical little laugh of self-discovery that it could have been either, as she stooped across a sudden pang, breathing deeply, deciding not to swoon away, not here, not in the company of this anonymous and uncaring guard.

"Throw it away," cried the guard.

"What?" she demanded.

"That thing you picked up. Can't you smell it?" he cried. "Don't try to bring it with you. It will terrify the horses!"

"I need it," she said. "I need it for something."

The horses seemed more stunned than nervous, so he did not argue. Within moments the carriage was headed back down the road. Once in movement, the horses could be kept in check only with difficulty, and their panic did not cease until they were almost at the Mantelby gates.

31

The Questioner Approaches

Somewhere between Newholme and whatever place it had been before, the Questioner's ship swam in wavering nacreous lights that alternately flared and ebbed as the ship slid toward the end of a wormhole connecting with several other such through a brief real-space nexus. Questioner, who had been brooding about Newholme, paying little attention to the journey, was alerted by a blare from the ship's annunciator, a Gablian voice: "Hold fast, hold fast, hold fast, wormhole ending, wormhole ending, worm hole ending . . . now."

The Questioner had anchored herself to a supporting member at the first sound. After a vertiginous moment during which everything outward and inward seemed to be in simultaneous though uncoordinated transit, everything quieted.

"Settle, settle, settle," demanded the communicator, belatedly. "Taking passengers."

The Questioner did not settle. She went to the viewport

and stared outward as the ship slowly turned. The new passengers were an anonymous pod of light moving away from a smaller ship. Their own ship turned slightly; there were scraping sounds, thuds and clatters; then a puff of vapor marked the disconnect. It had been done well, so undoubtedly the Gablian commander had been at the helm. The Gablians were the only personnel aboard who could be trusted to do anything right. Every mankind individual on board had been politically appointed, as part of her entourage, and none of them were qualified for anything.

The other ship grew larger as it moved toward and above them, off on some tangent of its own. Some time later, two voices were heard in the corridor, interrupted by a third at the door: the horn-headed Gablian purser, saying in his formal way: "Great Discerner, may I present Honorable Ellin Voy, Honorable Gandro Bao."

The Questioner turned toward the door, nodding slightly to acknowledge the deep bows of the two newcomers.

"Unimpeachable One," murmured Gandro and Ellin in duet.

"Well come in, come in. Let me look at you." She did look at them, from head to foot, each and both. They were dressed in simple tunics and soft shoes, he dark, she light. "Dancers, are you?"

"Yes, Spotless One," murmured Ellin.

"Though we are still having no idea what that has to do with anything," commented Bao.

"All in good time," said the Questioner. "I set out the specifications myself, and I always have reasons for everything I specify. Also, you may drop that Spotless, Unimpeachable stuff. The Gablians allow no informality, but I find that even imaginative honorifics soon pall. If I am what those titles proclaim, it is purely good design."

"We are wondering how to address you," murmured Bao.

She shrugged. "I am a Questioner. Or, as the Gablians call me, a Discerner. I am an examiner and judge. My official role is as ethics monitor of human worlds, but I was designed to be more than that. Haraldson the Beneficent framed the existence of humankind—which category includes some mankind—as arising from intelligence, civility, and the pursuit of justice. He wanted justice pursued with beauty and joy. I was created as a means toward this end. It is my task to find out how mankind can live most justly, most beautifully and joyfully, assuming intelligence is capable of such a discovery. What you call me is irrelevant, but I do hope you enjoy cards."

"We are being very good at cards, both!"

Questioner nodded. "Your ability with cards is one reason I picked the two of you from a lengthy list."

"Hold fast, hold fast, hold fast," blared the ship. "Entering wormhole, entering wormhole, entering wormhole, now . . ."

Gandro picked Ellin up from the floor.

"Sorry," Ellin muttered. "I'm not used to that, yet." She took a deep breath. "Questioner, Ma'am, before we forget. We have a package for you."

Gandro Bao nodded, burrowed into his pack, and came up with a small packet which he passed to Questioner with a humble bow.

Ellin said, "It's from a Flagian trader, Ma'am. He left the ship the last stop back, but he said to tell you it contains the information in which you expressed an interest."

Wordless with surprise, Questioner took the packet and turned it over in her hands. It wasn't large. From the size and shape, she judged it was a data cube, one capable of some experiential recording. Well. This could be enlightening.

She put the packet in one of her capacious storage pockets while giving them both a long looking-over.

"Let us see if you can be more amusing than the rest of my so-called staff."

She moved from the bench to a large, padded chair that had obviously been made to fit, pressed a button on its arm, and waited while a table emerged from the floor and rose into position before her. She gestured at them to bring chairs, while she herself took a deck of cards from a compartment in the table and began shuffling it with lightning-like speed.

"Are you always able to solve problems?" Ellin asked.

"Sometimes I solve them," said Questioner, "even when I don't."

"This is being conundrum," murmured Bao.

"Not really. In all humility, I assert that great peace of mind has been brought to the settled worlds by the mere fact of my existence! Divisive matters, the discussion of which had previously led to widespread civil disorder, are now referred to me for decision, and my decision is often so long postponed that people become accustomed to the status quo."

"You delay on purpose?" asked Ellin.

"I do." She nodded. "On matters which have no solution, I offer no solution, though I always claim to be on the verge of one whenever the matter comes up. Though Haraldson did not foresee that his Questioner would serve the function of conflict damper, perhaps it is as well that I do. Trouble is forestalled when both law and custom are required to await my decisions."

She stared pensively at the two newcomers. "Do sit down. I'll deal. I picked up these cards on Fanancy. They are in all respects similar to Old Earthian, Western-style decks, except for the names and colors of the suits. Here the four suits are labor, management, love, and death, signified by the shovel, the club, the heart, and the coffin, the colors silver, black, red, and brown." She dealt rapidly, four hands, the fourth to an empty chair.

Ellin picked up her hand. She seemed to have an ace of labor and an ace of management, together with three face cards in love and death, and an assortment of minor management cards. "What game are we playing?" she asked.

"Three-handed Whustee," said Questioner. "I bid one shovel." Then, without waiting to hear their bids, she continued on the prior topic. "I sometimes grow weary of delay, however, and at such times I am tempted to rule arbitrarily, as God is said to do, to put an end to matters."

"It is possible, tempting you?" asked Bao, his jaw dropped. Catching her peremptory gaze he murmured, "Two . . . ah, coffins."

"It is not possible to tempt me," said Questioner. "It

is possible only for me to imagine the consequences of temptation."

"Pass," said Ellin.

"How long have you been the Questioner?" Bao asked.

"I bid three shovels." She folded her hand and tapped it significantly on the tabletop. "We are the second assembly to hold the office. Two hundred sixty years ago, Questioner I was melted down in the cataclysm known as the Flagian Miscalculation, somewhere out near the Bonfires of Hell. The Flagians' attempt to prove that matter was illusory succeeded only in redistributing that matter rather widely. We, Questioner II, took the place of our vaporized predecessor. Together, we have been questioning for over seven hundred standard years. We have learned a great deal about health and contentment, prosperity and pleasure, and we have found no reason to change Haraldson's edicts defining opinion and providing for justice, though there are races that think differently."

"Pass," murmured Bao, into the momentary silence.

"Are there really?" cried Ellin, eyes wide. "Pass."

Questioner chuckled, a mechanical sound. "My hand to play, I think. Turn up the other hand, please, it gets to be the macarthy. Fah. I hoped it would have the ace.

"To answer your question, yes. A century or so ago we encountered the Borash, no two of whom agree on anything, but who tell us it is their destiny to rule all other races. Luckily, they lack either the weapons or the will to enforce their doctrine. Before that it was the Korm, a hive race of absolutely uniform opinion. Only their worker class 'think,' and they can only think one thing at a time. The Korm believe they have been created to travel to another galaxy with a great message. They devote all their resources toward that eventuality, and they don't even talk to us unless we have something their engineers say they need for the ships they have been building for the last four millennia. The ships have yet to be tested, and the great message, so I understand, is still to be determined by the committee that has been working on it for several thousand years."

She paused for a moment, scanning their play thus far.

". . . three, four, and five are mine. Now I will regret that ace!" She smiled. "Then, of course, there are the Quaggi."

Bao frowned in concentration. "May I be asking what is Quaggi?"

"The Quaggi are an interstellar race of beings who, I infer, need the radiation in the vicinity of a star in order to reproduce. As a matter of fact, we may get to see the remains of one on this trip."

"Remains?" faltered Ellin.

"Of a Quaggida, or Quaggima. I think this one was killed during mating. Or perhaps only injured so badly that she died. Whichever, she should be lying on a moonlet of the outmost planet of the system we're about to visit. There's no atmosphere, and if it hasn't been blown apart by meteorites, it should still be there."

"I don't think I've even heard of Quaggi," said Ellin.

"I have heard it suggested that the Quaggi, a star-roving race, have succeeded in reinventing Euclidean geometry, and, since they have no actual experience of plane surfaces, consider it an arcane lore fraught with metaphysical significance."

"But," murmured Ellin, "you're not suggesting we should change our ways to emulate any of those races, are you?" She placed her ace of management on the Questioner's CEO, took the trick and led with the queen of labor.

"Clever girl. You had the ace all along. No, we should not emulate other people. We probably couldn't emulate the Korm. Any mankind person worth his salt can simultaneously incubate whole clutches of ideas that are either contradictory or mutually exclusive. For instance, mankind has persuaded itself that its race is perfectible, though it hasn't changed physically, mentally, or psychologically since the Cro-Magnon. Mankind has also persuaded itself that each individual is unique, though each person shares ninety-nine and ninety-nine one hundredths of his DNA and roughly the same percentage of his ideas with thousands or even millions of other persons."

Bao, with a sidelong glance at Ellin, said with an ironic

grin, "It is being true that persons want very much to be singular and individual."

Ellen made a face at him. "I have complained about being a clone, that's all." She took the next trick, leading with the jack of labor, a union organizer.

The Questioner nodded ponderously. "Individuality is more imagined than real. Persons are more alike than they care to admit. On Newholme, however, their social structure is based upon the theory that each family line is unique."

"Is that what we'll ask about on Newholme?" asked Ellin. "Individuality?"

The last few cards clicked down, with Ellin the undisputed winner of the hand.

"Among other things." The Questioner rocked slowly in her chair, considering. "Very nicely played, my dear. You deal the next hand."

Bao took a deep breath, shaking his head. "The briefing documents are also mentioning an indigenous race. Precolonization reports are saying no indigenes. This is most confusing."

Questioner smiled grimly, with determination. "Confusing, yes. The entire surface of that planet had supposedly been examined up and down and sideways before any settlement was allowed. If there are now indigenes, someone falsified a report, or failed to file one, or the confusion is intentional, designed to mislead me. I always find the truth, however, no matter how many red herrings colonists drag across my path."

She picked up her hand and smiled a tigerish smile. "It is likely there have been grave infractions of the edicts on Newholme. Every few years I do find a planet that must be punished for its infractions, with all its people."

"Would you really punish a whole world?" Bao asked with some trepidation.

"If it were indicated. It is too early to know what is indicated. We are going to Newholme to see what is true and what is false, and in either case, what can be done about it."

"I've read every document, but I don't understand what

any of them have to do with us,'' murmured Ellin as she picked up her own cards. ''Why did you ask for dancers?''

The Questioner nodded. ''It wouldn't be in the documents because it was an informal report, but one of my spies has mentioned that the indigenes are dancers.''

Ellin drew in a deep breath. ''So?''

The Questioner said sagaciously, ''Trust is strengthened by similarity of interest, either apparent or real. If they are dancers, they may talk to other dancers. If they dance for you, you will dance for them. . . .''

Ellin frowned, unconvinced. ''If nobody knows anything about this indigenous race, how does anyone know that they dance?''

The Questioner shrugged, an unandroidish movement. ''How did my spy find out? He probably sat in a tavern, listening to drunken conversation and putting two and two together. Or he bribed someone. Or, he planted a few mobile sensors. I didn't ask how, specifically. I do know he is a reliable source.''

They played out the game, which Questioner won, putting her in a good humor, after which Bao and Ellin were shown to their own quarters, where they huddled together in their salon, whispering.

''You were dealing her a very good hand,'' said Bao.

''I was dealing her from the bottom of the deck,'' mimicked Ellin, with a smirk. ''I learned cheating from one of the actors. What do you think of her or it?''

''She is being obdurate, I think. Very severe. And while you are being so free with the cards, she was winning from me five credits.''

''Poor thing. I'll owe it to you.'' She paused, looking at him thoughtfully. ''Gandro Bao, will *we* have to do something dreadful? Like recommend the wiping out of all the mankind on the world?''

Gandro Bao shook his head, though he was no less troubled than she. ''We are not recommending, Ellin. She is doing that. All we are doing is finding things out.''

They stayed together a while longer, taking reassurance from one another's company, before seeking the equal comfort of real beds after shower baths in real water.

Though the Questioner needed neither, she made sure that her assistants were well looked after.

She, in the meantime, had been left to her own devices. She frequently remarked as much to her attendants, intrigued by the phrase, for it was literally true. Her memory, her maintenance machines, her elaborately miniaturized equipment, her IDIOT SAVANT, the syncretic scanner she used in her attempt to find patterns where none were apparent, all were her own devices with whom she was frequently left.

Just now, she needed her maintenance machines. She always put off maintenance until the need for it became what she thought of as painful. Though she was not designed to feel pain, the intense unease occasioned by delay in response, by inability to remember immediately, by mechanical parts that did not function precisely or systems that did not mesh, must, she felt, come close to what mankind meant by pain. It could be avoided by getting maintenance more frequently, and she could never remember between maintenance sessions why she did not do so. Nonetheless, she always put it off, without knowing why.

This time, she took with her into the booth the data cube that the trader had sent. She inserted it into the feed mechanism, and directed that during maintenance it should be entered into permanent memory. Then everything went gray, as it always did during maintenance. Time stopped. All thought stopped as well. Only after her linkages had been disconnected, only after her memory as Questioner was off line, was the cause of her discomfort made manifest. Then, and for a brief time afterward, her mankind brains, those three with which she had been endowed, remembered who they were. Mathilla remembered, and M'Tafa, and Tiu. During that time, the separate entity that was the Questioner knew why she judged some societies as she did, and why she felt about them as she did, and how deep her prejudices went, even though they never showed.

When her usual maintenance was complete, after the linkages were reestablished and the memory hooked up with all its shining achievements on display, Questioner did not move, did not utter, did not recollect, for she was still holding fast to Mathilla and M'Tafa and Tiu, unwilling to let them go and they, within her, were holding fast to life once more, unwilling to be gone. Then, usually, the booth door opened automatically, and the stimulant shock was provided, and she wakened, as one wakens terrified from dream, only to feel the terror fade, and shred, and become as gauze, as a thing forgotten, as it always had before.

Not this time. This time she found the memory remained with her, firmly planted inside her files, their names and faces, the stories of their short lives, and how they had died.

Mathilla. M'Tafa. And Tiu.

32

Ornery Bastable Goes Upriver

Ornery Bastable arrived in Gilesmarsh when the *Way-good* came in to unload a cargo of gold-ash and dried Purse fish. Since it would be some time before the *Way-good* had discharged its cargo and been loaded once more, Ornery had a whole tenday to herself.

She intended to spend part of it in Sendoph, where Pearla had recently achieved statistical normalcy by bearing a living daughter after a run of one stillborn daughter and two sons. First, however, she intended to spend a day or two in the Septopod's Eye in Naibah, seeing what she could find out about the thing she had seen, or almost seen, when she had been marooned in the wild. Though she was not imaginative enough to have frightened herself into a funk over the experience, she had resolved to ask some questions next time she had time in port, and now seemed as good a time as any.

She had just received her pay, and she spent a good bit of it buying drinks for those who had stories to tell. When she had listened for several evenings, she had accounts of the setting of stone pillars and questioning sounds and shadows moving, all of them making a reasonably consistent catalogue. One talkative old type, who had at one time kept the library at the Fortress of Vanished Men, said the records described creatures seen in the wild by the second settlers, quite monstrous things that seemed to have disappeared for no one had seen them for several hundred years.

As for stone pillars, they had been often seen on beaches and plateaus, always in groups of three or more, always in the clear where the shadow pattern could be seen under sun or moon, the nighttime patterns depending upon which moons were where. The pillars sometimes appeared at dawn in places where they had not been at dusk, and therefore were assumed to have been set up by creatures, people, things, or beings who worked at night and intended to remain unseen. Two informants had used the word "Joggiwagga," and Ornery recognized the word from her infancy.

Joggiwagga, whatever they were, were busier at certain lunar configurations than others, and these were also the times when the loud questioning or challenging sounds were most likely to be heard. Because she was a sailor, Ornery recognized the times as coincident with exceptionally high or low tides. Six sizeable moons, leaving aside the two orbiting rocks, could produce quite a complicated schedule of tides. A two big-moon neap, full or dark, was low, but a three big-moon neap was lower, and an all-moon low sucked the water out of the bays to leave mud flats extending to the horizon. A rare five dark-moon high, on the other hand, would bring water over the piers in Gilesmarsh, high up the levees of Naibah, and send the River Giles over its banks all the way to Sendoph.

Six big-moon highs came about every seven or eight centuries. Though the more extreme lunar configurations were rare, they were the ones during which stones were set.

Once Ornery had satisfied herself that she wasn't crazy, that she could assume the things or beings or creatures were real, she put her notebook in her pocket, finished her ale, bade her friends and associates farewell for the nonce, and went out to confirm arrangements for the trip to Sendoph. There was a steam-powered mail launch headed upstream within the hour, and it was owned by Ornery's brother-in-law. By the gift of a bottle and a little banter with the captain, Ornery had earned an invitation to ride to Sendoph in style. Travel by engine was still rare and might get rarer, considering the firemountain had buried most of the mines and about half the railroad. There was still more reliance on horses than on horsepower, and riding in a launch was, therefore, a treat.

Ornery regarded it as such, sitting at her ease on the rear deck, watching the paddles of the stern wheel fall toward her as the reed bed and marshes and watermills went by. Low in the eastern sky the misty bulk of the scarp seemed to float upon the lower clouds as it blew ominous bars of smoke across the higher ones. Ornery turned her back to it, not wanting to be reminded of the tremors that were coming closer and closer together. People were beginning to get really jumpy about it and would have been more so if they could have seen the damage. Though there had been a good many more disasters like the one that took Ornery's family, all the destruction thusfar was behind and among the Ratbacks, invisible from the cities. Most everyone in the more populated areas believed or wanted to believe that they were not in danger.

Ornery thought everyone was in danger, whether they believed it or not. Anyone could see that the summit was blacker than it had been, meaning either that ashes were falling atop the snows, or the snows had melted, revealing the dark rock below.

"There's been shakings and shiverings for a time now. She's goin' to blow," said the captain, around the splinter of chaff he was chewing. "Been a long while accordin' to the wise folk. I say it doesn't matter how long, it's still alive and it'll blow again." He laughed a phlegmy laugh, hawked and spat over the side. "Warm up all them Haggers in Sendoph, won't it?"

His tone angered Ornery, but she kept a neutral tone as

she said, "You're cheerful about it, considering you may be there when it goes."

"If I am, I'll be in company, and if I'm not, I'll rejoice. Whatever the inscrutable Hagions provide."

Ornery made a noncommittal noise. If the scarp decided to blow, it really wouldn't matter what had been said about it either way. Either it would reach all the way to the Giles or it wouldn't. She turned the conversation in another direction, and the hours went by more comfortably until, along about evening, they were in sight of the city, the domes of the Temple district shining in the rose-amber light.

"Where do you tie up?" Ornery wanted to know.

"We'll stop at the post pier to pick up and drop off mail and valuables. Then we'll go on up to the old wharf just the other side of Brewer's Bridge, and we'll tie there for tonight. I've half the forward hold full of stuff for House Genevois, and the other half grain for the brewers. We'll unload in the morning, then go farther upstream to the market district to pick up special orders for Naibah. Will you leave us tonight or tomorrow?"

Ornery thought about it. Her sister lived not far from the Temple district, which was just a few blocks west of the river, but it was late to drop in on her. "I'll help you unload and sleep aboard, if you've no objection, Captain, then I'll go on to my sister's place in the morning."

So it was agreed between them. The boat thrust itself upstream past a tanner's yard and a printing house—both identifiable by the smell—then for a brief stop at the post wharf. Then onward once more, past a lumber yard and a dyers yard and a clutter of old houses, then past a tall wall with two odd little towers at its corners and the remains of a rotted wharf at its center, and finally beneath the high central arch of Brewers Bridge to the pier beyond, where, with much shouting and maneuvering, the captain, Ornery, the deckhand and the stoker brought themselves tight against the timber pier built out from the edge of the stony trough in which the river ran.

It seemed too quiet. Ornery stared all around, finding no reason for the silence, which was soon broken in any case, when people came with carts from House Genevois and from the breweries. They unloaded by torchlight, the carts departed, and the strange silence returned. Later that night, as Ornery spread her blankets on the deck she heard a scurrying, like small animals moving, and she looked up to see a skulk of shadows vanishing along the river path in a lengthy stream, like a migration. It was too dark to see who they were, though Ornery thought them too small for mankind, and they had been in a most dreadful hurry. She resolved to tell someone about it tomorrow, perhaps, if it seemed important.

33

Marool Mantelby and the Hags

That same evening, which was a few days after Marool Mantelby returned from her trip into the mountains, Marool made a visit to the Temple of the Hagions, most particularly the office of the High Crones, where she was assured a polite welcome by virtue of her frequent and generous gifts to the Temple. She met with women who knew her better, perhaps, than she supposed: D'Jevier and Onsofruct Passenger, who remembered the fourteen-year-old Marool well, though Marool had been too preoccupied at that time to remember anyone.

"Revered Hags," Marool announced as she entered the throne room cum office. "Thank you for seeing me."

D'Jevier and Onsofruct had changed little in the almost twenty years since Marool had come to the Temple to find the Hagion Morrigan. The two Hags had never mentioned that incident to anyone except one another, preferring to forget it as nearly as possible. Over the years, both had cultivated the impersonal manner and voice suitable for use in Temple when emotion was inappropriate, and it was this voice D'Jevier used to greet Marool.

"You are welcome, Marool. Is there something needful?"

Marool shook her head as she took the seat she was offered, then sat there with her lips pursed out in uncharacteristic uncertainty. Her hostesses did not encourage her, but merely waited, as though she could tell them nothing that would surprise them.

"I have been into the hills," said Marool, at last. "I went to look at the place where my parents and sister died."

"Ah," murmured Onsofruct. "You had a natural curiosity."

Marool shook her head with an annoyed expression. "It wasn't that! It's as though something about their deaths has been nagging at me for years. I wanted to see for myself. However . . ." She went on to describe her own experience, and that of her driver and Man of Business. "I suppose their bodies are there still," she concluded. "The guard reported what happened to the guard post, but I've heard nothing more about it."

D'Jevier cast a glance at her cousin, which Onsofruct returned, furrowing her brow and clenching her jaw before replying, "We have all heard stories of Wilderneers and monsters. Such are common tellings during the Long Nights."

"You mentioned picking up something, some artifact?" D'Jevier queried.

"I have it here," said Marool, taking a packet from her bag, laying it upon the table and unrolling it. As she did so, a stench spread throughout the room, and both the Hags caught their breaths.

"You smell it?" demanded Marool, looking at their faces.

Both nodded. D'Jevier held her breath and took the article into her hands, keeping a layer of the wrapping between it and her skin.

"It looks more organic than manufactured," said Marool. "Like a giant fingernail. That shape, at any rate, though far too huge. The bottom is ragged, as though it had been ripped away. . . .''

D'Jevier rewrapped the article, obviously troubled. ''It's a scale,'' she said. ''From some sort of squamous creature.''

''It would have to be enormous!'' said Onsofruct, her eyes wide.

D'Jevier grated, ''I have no doubt it is. We are only now growing numerous enough that we can explore the wilderness in any systematic way, and as we do so, we hear more frequent tales about things or beings in the badlands. Did you see any kind of trail while you were there? As though something very large had been dragged along, pushing up the dirt at the sides?''

Marool nodded, though unwillingly, for she had thought to do all the enlightening herself. ''I did, yes. Both an old trail and a newer one. So new that nothing was growing on it.''

D'Jevier went on, ''We have had reports of such in the hills to the west. As though a very large serpent had crawled there, though the paths are straight or angular, not sinous. The witnesses are sober persons whose word I am inclined to accept, and there have been too many disappearances of livestock for peace of mind.''

''Then you have already planned a course of action,'' said Marool.

The thin woman shook her head, her lips twisted into an unpleasant knot, as though she tasted something foul that she could not spit out. ''Yes, and no. Reason would dictate that we enquire among the Timmys, who presumably once occupied that wilderness, whose relatives may do so still, and would therefore know what creatures are there. At this juncture, however, we cannot do so.''

Marool felt a strange frisson at this mention of the invisible people, a surprise reaction, though she knew that no subject was forbidden to the Hags when in Temple, albeit only there.

Onsofruct murmured, ''We have been advised the Questioner is on her way. This is not a time we would have picked for the Council's Hound to come sniffing among us, but the Hound does not sniff at our convenience."

Marool furrowed her forehead, trying to remember what she had learned about the Questioner. "The visit constrains us?"

Onsofruct snorted, "Rather more than merely constrains."

"What more?"

D'Jevier's lips curved into a wry smile. "There were no Timmys here when we came, Marool. We forget this from time to time, but it is true. There were not on the surface of this planet any race of intelligent beings nor was there any mention of such in the records of the first settlement. The planetary assessment was rigorous before we came, searching for those monsters reputed to have wiped out the first colony. If Timmys had been here, the assessment would have picked them up, anywhere upon the surface of this planet.

"They weren't here. Had they been here, we would not have been allowed to settle. Some years later, suddenly here they were. By that time, we had so much invested in this world that we chose to pretend we hadn't seen them, difficult as that was, for the creatures were pertinacious. Though it may have been a stupid decision—indeed, in hindsight, was a stupid decision—we, the Hags, decided not to report their existence to the Council of Worlds, as that would have led to our immediate evacuation from Newholme."

Marool frowned at the implications of this. Had she known about this matter? Had she ever considered this?

D'Jevier went on: "Years went by, and we still didn't report it. The Timmys grew more numerous. At the same time, because of the . . . ah . . . unexpected sexual imbalance on this world, our population was growing far too slowly to do all the things our settlement plans had set forth. Suddenly, there were the Timmys, doing this little job and that little job, almost as though they had read our minds. One had only to utter and the task was done. Before we quite knew how it happened, the Timmys had become the better part of our workforce."

Onsofruct snorted. "And our foremothers didn't report that, either! Even a generation later we could have reported. Needless to say, we didn't. We have committed a very grave offense in not reporting the existence of an intelligent and speaking race. This will not be to our credit."

D'Jevier nodded agreement. "The Questioner, who takes the matter of indigenous races very seriously, will not excuse these omissions if it finds out about the Timmys."

Marool shifted on her chair, frowning. "But why does the Questioner's visit prohibit our asking the Timmys now about the wilderness?"

"We cannot take time to pursue the linguistic matter, since the Timmys are even now being banished."

"Banished?" Marool was dumbfounded. "What do you mean, banished?"

"Sent away, into the mountains. The Questioner and her people aren't blind! The Timmys must not be visible when the Questioner arrives."

"But they do half the work in the city! On the farms! Everywhere!"

"Obviously they do," D'Jevier replied. "But someone else will have to do that half! We've decided to make up the lack through press gangs. There are a good many supernumeraries who are underemployed, if they are employed at all. And then, the Consort Houses are full of young men who can be used, at least temporarily."

Onsofruct asked in a suspiciously casual voice, "Do you use Timmys on your estate, Marool?"

"I do," she said, rather angrily. "Though not in the house. There I prefer human servants, but I let the steward use them in the gardens, the fields, and in the stables."

The two Hags bowed and glanced at one another again, each thinking that few persons had the unlimited wealth of a Mantelby with which to hire human servants. Or the unlimited number of nephews needing work.

"Then except for the stables and gardens, your mansion is staffed and run entirely by humans?" murmured D'Jevier.

"It is."

Again that glance. D'Jevier nodded, saying, "Marool, would you consider letting us house the Questioner with you?"

Marool swallowed a snort and tried to formulate a polite mode of refusal, then bethought herself that it might be best not to refuse. Not yet, at any rate. "Why with me?"

D'Jevier rose and went to sit beside Marool, regarding her intently. "What do you know of the Questioner?"

"What anyone knows. There's something about her in the *Book of Worlds,* the one we all learn to read from as children. I don't think I've even heard the name of the Questioner used in a dozen years. Her creation always seemed to me to be a fool idea."

Onsofruct said in a conciliatory tone, "Perhaps, but an idea with an ancient history, nonetheless. Mankind has long been interested in assuring ethical treatment of other races."

"History is all well and good." Marool snorted. "Ethical treatment is no doubt something we all wish to achieve. But if the Timmys have come here since we came, surely the Questioner would not insist on our leaving this world."

D'Jevier crossed to the window and stared outward. "That's the enigma, Marool. They weren't here when we came, but they didn't come after we came. They couldn't have. Council of Worlds traffic monitors hang in orbit around all occupied worlds from the moment of first settlement, recording every arrival and departure. Nothing has landed on this planet since we came except the supply and trade ships we all know about. By dint of much effort, we keep Timmys away from the port. The staff there is made up of both Hags and Men of Business, and we can say unequivocally the Timmys did not arrive here; they were already here even though no one knew it."

"Now seems late to worry over it," grumbled Marool.

Onsofruct said, "We thought we'd done our worrying long since, when we first adopted our conventions vis-á-vis the Timmys: not speaking to them, not looking at them. We worried about it by shutting them away in particular places where they could not be seen. They have become to us, in accordance with custom, invisible. We could argue that they do not exist, to us."

D'Jevier nodded. "Now, however, the Questioner comes. Do we confess to generations, centuries, of untruth? Do we pretend to her that these creatures are indeed invisible? She is unlikely to agree. Do not suggest that we pack up our families and our baggage and leave the planet, for unfortunately, that is no longer an option. There are certain limits on the evacuation of planetary populations, and we are now too numerous for that choice. A century ago we could have departed, perhaps, but not now. Do we volunteer to restrict ourselves to a small part of Newholme and eschew any contact with the Timmys? A similar offer was made by mankind on Bayor's world when they discovered a native population living on a single island where they had been for millennia. The Questioner said it wasn't good enough and acted against the entire mankind population. That was only fifteen years ago, and I remember vividly the consequences of that decision."

Marool was astonished. "I had not heard of this!"

"Few of us here on Newholme read the reports of the COW, a few of us Hags, a librarian or two, a few Men of Business. The Men of Business have some understanding of the situation, for they invited us to house the Questioner at the Fortress of Vanished Men, obviously because it has no Timmy staff. As though that would be enough! The Questioner isn't blind, or deaf. Even though Timmys don't exist in the fortress—or at your mansion, Marool—she would not be fooled by that alone. No. Total banishment is necessary. The Questioner must neither hear nor see a single Timmy while she—*it* is here."

A long silence, during which Marool ground her teeth, finally erupting with: "How are you going to make them go?"

"They hear us. They understand us. We've said enough that they know what the stake is. Either they disappear, or we may all die."

Marool snorted. "You're assuming that all this circumspection will be easier to manage if I invite the Questioner to Mantelby House?''

''It is more hope than assumption,'' Onsofruct murmured. ''Once the Timmys have been sent away, if they will understand enough to go away, there'll be a period of adjustment in human behavior. New habits, however, take time to form and old ones are hard to break. Presumably your house servants do not have the habit of addressing thin air with orders for the nearest Timmy to wash the dishes or milk the cows.''

Marool mused, stroking her massive jaw. ''True, which makes it all well and good inside my walls, but the Questioner won't sit still, will she? We can't depend on her squatting at my place all day and all night while she's here.''

''This may be true. The plan is not foolproof, but we have no alternative to suggest. We do know the Questioner has various aides, assistants, deputies, and functionaries, and we can make it a point to accompany these ancillaries during their investigations, interpreting what they may or may not see or hear.''

Marool moved restlessly to the small barred window that looked out over the avenue, the wide steps, the parade of women climbing toward and descending from the Temple. ''I will have to get rid of my Timmy gardeners and stable workers.''

''Yes,'' D'Jevier murmured.

''When does the banishment take place?''

''We started earlier this evening, delivering the edict to all homes and businesses.''

''The planetary economy will probably collapse,'' said Marool, thinking of the many Men of Business who handled Mantelby affairs and all their investments and projects.

''Well, of course, if we would prefer extinction . . .'' Onsofruct's voice was not at all sarcastic, though her eyebrows slanted sardonically.

Marool shook her head doubtfully. ''I don't see how the Questioner could insist on our extinction. How would it enforce a dictum like that?''

D'Jevier said wearily, "The biological sciences are far advanced on many worlds, Marool. The Questioner need only explode a small canister in our upper atmosphere, as was done on Bayor's world. . . ."

Marool retreated into sulky silence. "I suppose I can survive without Timmys. If the visit isn't long. But having guests . . . it would be an inconvenience."

To break a weighty silence, Onsofruct murmured, "Let me take a few moments to discuss the matter with my colleague."

Taking D'Jevier by the arm, she led her out into the hall.

"I hate that woman," said D'Jevier. "There is a horridness about her."

"You are remembering the time she came here. . . ."

"I am remembering that, yes. And there have been rumors. Disappearances. Things her servants tell, when they come down into town. Things her neighbors say they've heard. Things that might have been foretold, keeping Morrigan in mind."

"And you hate her," Onsofruct mused.

"I loathe her. I think all the stories are true."

"Then you don't want to authorize her to house the Questioner."

D'Jevier snorted. "I loathe her, but I loathe equally what the Questioner may do to us! I've racked my brain trying to come up with a place to put this Questioner creature where there are or have been no Timmys. In this one case, Marool's desires parallel our own. She's bright, she's ruthless, and she's likely to be as helpful as possible. Have you some better idea?"

"None," said Onsofruct.

"Then let us pay the piper, as we must."

They returned to the office, and Onsofruct said, "We could possibly grant you some consideration, Marool, to make the inconvenience worth your while."

"Well worth my while?" She lifted the corners of her mouth into a harpy's smile.

D'Jevier wet her mouth, which was inexplicably dry. "And what offer would do that?"

"You mentioned press gangs. From among the supernumeraries, and the Consort Houses. . . ."

Onsofruct, reading the distress on her companion's face, said in an unperturbed voice, "You would be entitled to replace your Timmys, of course. Once you have announced the edict of banishment to your stable and garden workers."

"Tomorrow?"

"If you like."

"How do I go about it?"

The two Hags exchanged quick glances once more. Marool was a good deal more eager than they thought appropriate.

"Ah," mused Onsofruct, "you can come down into the city with a few of the Haggers you have been kind enough to support and select a few supernumeraries from the streets. Take note of their identity, place of residence, and mode of living. Be prepared to bring that information here for registration."

"I was thinking more of . . . you said the Consort Houses!"

"Ah, well. Yes. You could obtain two or three workers from the Consort Houses if you like."

"Am I to buy expensive Consorts to clean my stables?"

D'Jevier drew herself up, her voice cold. "No. Certainly not. But you *will* give the House owner a signed receipt, guaranteeing the return of her students when the current emergency is over. The supernumes would also have to be returned."

"House Genevois," purred Marool. "I've had my eyes on . . ."

D'Jevier cried, "Mistress Mantelby, please. The young men are to be gardeners and stable hands. Need we make the point they are to be only that?"

Onsofruct put her hand on D'Jevier's shoulder, calming her. "My colleague is correct. You are not to use them as Consorts, and for the duration of the Questioner's visit, it would be better not to allude to the existence of such, for we do not know what the Questioner would think of such a profession.''

Marool's eyes narrowed. She was not accustomed to taking orders from anyone. Still, in grievous times, one could bear grievous pains, as the book of precepts had it, though one would remember the pains later, and who inflicted them.

''I will settle for a few from the street.'' She smiled charmingly. ''And a few more from one of the Hunk Houses.''

She took her leave from them, humming under her breath as she made her way from the Temple. Behind her, she left two troubled Hags.

''We may live to regret this,'' said D'Jevier.

''If we live at all,'' said Onsofruct. ''Which is really the issue.''

The order of banishment was carried by swift couriers to all mankind towns and villages, and from thence was spread by riders and rumor into the rural lands. **The Questioner is coming. The Questioner is coming. All those invisible somethings that do not actually exist must go away into the wilds. Consult with local Haggers to obtain pressed men to do necessary labor.**

Though the words of the edict were trumpeted in some places, in most they spread silently, like a fog, a fog that seemed both to spur the Timmys' going and to hide the fact of it. After the first hour or so, those attempting to spread the edict to the Timmys themselves were amazed to find no Timmys to spread it to. As one observer put it, the invisibles had ''faded into the walls.'' That was exactly where many of them were. No matter where Timmys labored for the humans, they were never more than a few steps from an entry to their own world, that subsurface milieu which spongified the planet beneath mankind's feet.

Doors opened, secret ways were momentarily crowded, and within an incredibly short time all the Timmys who had worked among humans had disappeared like blown-out candle flames. By dawn, not one could be found.

34

Pressed into Service

That same dawn, Ornery Bastable arose from her bed on the deck of the steamer, dressed herself carefully, arranged her veils, and climbed the steps from the stone pier to Brewer's Bridge. From the carved railing, iridescent water birds (called birds, even though they were not actually birds) were diving for fish while others sat on the banks drying their black/green/violet wings and croaking at one another. Brighter birds were clinging to the reeds, trilling at any other of their kind within hearing. The sky was a clear and flawless blue except for the haze that hung above the scarp, where long lines of gray, like blown veils, stretched away diagonally on the seawind, fading into the horizon to the south.

Despite the good weather, the clear sky, the quiet city, Ornery felt something was wrong, or different, or awry. Her first thought was the scarp, and she set her feet widely apart, waiting for that premonitory shudder, but nothing came. She turned and walked westward along the street, looking around at the street scene, the early carts clattering across the cobbles, the bustle of a few veiled Men of Business, the call of a milk vendor: "Fraiiiish, Creeeemy: glug glug glug; breeng your bahttles, breeng your jug!" and the spice-cart man's staccato call, "Pepper-an-spice, makes-it-nice. Pepper-pepper-pepper." Newholmian pepper was actually better than Old Earth peppers, and it sold to the BIT for a good price.

Ornery turned slowly, examining her surroundings. Something was amiss. Something was wrong! Then she realized. Timmys! There were no Timmys. No brown-clad forms scurrying behind the wagons or along the walls. There were always Timmys, everywhere, but not this morning. Not sweeping the roads. Not running here and there on errands. Not washing the outsides of windows or scrubbing the stoops of the buildings. Not leading the donkeys that pulled the carts. Not putting out the trash bins. No Timmys.

Ornery stopped where she was, on the corner just outside House Genevois, and stared about herself, confused. As she stood, staring witlessly, a carriage approached with several armed Haggers running along behind it, and behind them a wagon with two veiled men chained to its railing. Ornery's hand went to her veils, securing them, and she stepped back against the building, out of the way.

The carriage stopped and a voice trumpeted, "That one, there. Let me see his face!"

One of the Haggers approached, ripped down Ornery's veils, then waited while Ornery's heart half-stopped and her breathing did stop.

"Good enough," the woman called. "Put him in the cart."

"What?" Ornery cried. "What is this?"

"Press gang," said the Hagger, not without some satisfaction. "Mistress Marool is pressing some of you supernumeraries to take the place of some . . . servants of hers."

"But I'm a seaman!" cried Ornery. "I've a legitimate job. I'm not a supernumerary."

The woman had alighted from the carriage. Now she too approached, glaring into Ornery's face. "If I say you are a supernumerary, boy, that's what you are. If you speak out of turn again, you'll serve my needs without your tongue."

Ornery choked herself silent. The woman went by her like a storm wind, and the Hagger who held her thrust her past the carriage to the cart that waited there, where Ornery was unceremoniously put inside and chained beside two other unwilling passengers, from whom she learned what little they knew about what was going on.

Meantime the woman had gone on to the main doors of House Genevois, where she jerked the great bell into such a clamor that it sent a cloud of birds flying from the roof, screaming outrage. The door was opened, and she went inside to find Madame herself awaiting her.

Marool presented the edict of the Hags, her sneer of authority ready for use at the first sign of recalcitrance.

"Wait here," said Madame, leaving with such alacrity that Marool had no time to be rude. She was gone long enough for Marool to have worked up a good fume by the time she returned.

"See here," she began, in an angry tone.

"In here," said Madame, throwing open the double doors that centered the farther wall. Inside the gymnasium thus disclosed were several ranks of young men, arranged by age.

"I have not included the Consorts already purchased, since they are not my property to dispose of," said Madame, crisply. "The younger boys would be of little use to you as laborers, for they have not come into their strength. All the others are here."

Marool's eyes gleamed. She did not notice the pinched look of Madame's nostrils, or the wariness in the faces of those before her. She had no hint of what had been said by Madame to those youths in the intervening moments. She was interested in only one thing, and that was to discover the boy she had seen in the park. The light veils the youths wore were no impediment to her search. She walked down the line, spotting him immediately. It was the boy she had seen. She could not possibly have missed him. He was the largest boy in the room.

"Him," she said, pointing at Bane.

He regarded her with insolence. "I go nowhere without my brother, Ma'am," he said, making little pretense of politeness.

"Your brother?" She laughed. "By all means. If you have a brother."

Dyre stepped forward. Marool nodded. "I have a cart outside. They will be taken to Mantelby Mansion." She turned to stalk away down the line of youths, paying the rest of them little attention.

One of the Haggers who had accompanied her opened the door into the entry, admitting a slight breeze that lifted the veil of the young man at the end of the line. The movement drew Marool's eyes to the face behind the veil. It was a beautiful face drawn into an expression of horrified recognition. Why horrified? She had never laid eyes on him before.

"What's the matter, boy? You never seen a woman before?"

"My apologies," he bowed, hiding his eyes. "I meant no disrespect."

Something in his manner both annoyed her and piqued her curiosity. "Feh," she barked, angry at him. "I'll take you as well, boy. You hear, Madame? I'll take this one as well. Does he have a name?"

"His name is Mouche, Mistress Mantelby." Madame said it in a dead, impersonal voice. "As I understand this matter, you are to give me a document agreeing to return these young men when the current emergency is over. If you will join me in my office, I will enter all the pertinent data on both our copies. Their names. Their annuities, which you would be expected to fulfill, if they should be incapacitated in your employ. Also their value to me, which you would be expected to pay if anything happens to them to reduce their value. Anything at all."

Marool glared, meeting eyes as cold as her own were hot. "You are presumptuous, Madame."

"Not at all. When we received word of this last evening, I went to the Temple to consult the Hags personally on the matter. It is not their intention that the Houses shall be robbed of their students. Bane, and Dyre, and Mouche will work in your stables or your gardens, replacing certain other laborers who are, for a time, unavailable to you. Such work is all they will do. And if their skin is marred, or their appearance changed, or if they are ill fed or their bones twisted or broken. . . ."

Marool stormed out into the hall, and thence was led by Simon to Madame's office. Mouche moved uncertainly. Madame stepped beside him, murmuring: "Mouche, go with them. Be polite. Be subservient. Do your work. Do not tempt the woman to violence. . . ."

"Madame . . ." he whispered. "Madame . . ."

"Yes, boy. What is it?"

"That picture outside my room. It's her, isn't it? That is Mistress Mantelby."

Madame paled. She shivered, then drew herself up once more. "Yes, Mouche. That is Mistress Mantelby. And the best way to avoid drawing her attention is to seem uninteresting. Do you understand? Be unattractive and dull. Totally dull." She gave him a significant look and gestured toward the door.

Still he hesitated. The sight of Marool's face had been terrible, but more terrible yet was the thought of leaving House Genevois, leaving his secret way within the walls, leaving . . . that one whom he watched in the night hours. "Madame. Are the Timmys really gone?"

She shivered, only slightly, reaching forward to stroke his face with her fingers. "What Timmys? I know nothing of any Timmys. Nor do you, if you are wise. Go, Mouche. And may fortune be with you."

On her lips, it had the sound almost of a prayer.

35

Timmy Talk

If Mouche had been there to open his hidden gate and creep into the walls, he would have found the space packed with Timmys: Timmys listening at cracks, peering through eye holes, observing what the humans were doing as they or their predecessors had been observing almost since humans had first arrived. Though it had been some time before Timmys had been seen by the second wave of settlers, Timmys had seen the settlers from the beginning.

"This creature coming," said one Timmy, who had been in the walls of the temple when D'Jevier and Marool had conversed, "This Questioner-idi coming, if idi finds out we have been treated badly, idi may seek to redress our wrongs, to do justice."

"That must not happen," cried others. "Our wrongs must not be redressed. Justice would upset everything!"

There was agreement. Justice would be the last straw.

"Why can't tim-tim go now," sang one, two, a dozen, their voices making a sad harmony of the words.

"It is not the time," replied others, an antiphon. "Tim-tim must await the time."

"But the jong grow strong," sang the first ones. "And the jong wax large, like moons, and Niasa turns and turns."

"Even so, it is not the time."

"The earth shakes with the turning of Niasa. *She* will waken! *She* will break the egg!"

"Even so."

After a long silence, one offered, "Whether it is the time or not, word must be sent to the bai. The depths must be informed of this dangerous idi, this Questioner."

Others agreed. There was a generalized and rather ant-like scurry as some set out and others arrived, this one and that one being assigned to this peephole or that crack, and a small group started on a journey to the depths where they would inform the great ones of the dangerous Questioner who was coming.

Those remaining behind stayed at their peepholes in the walls. "The woman-gau took Mouchidi," said Mouche's goddess, the one he had intuitively called by her tim-tim name, Flowing Green. "They took the one I have hopes of!"

"Not far," reassured another. "He goes to House Mantelby. Tim-tim are in all the walls there, watching the terrible ones and the bad woman."

"I will go there," said the green-haired one. "I have many long hopes of Mouchidi. I read his face and see him feeling what we feel. I see how he joys. I see him perceive Her pain."

"I have no hopes," said another. "None of the jong have been any use. All those who came at first, they did the bad thing, but when we tried to use them to fix it, they were no use. Jongau are still moving around out there, all warped. That Ashes-gau, that bad smell, he is still out there."

"The other bad smells are there, too," offered another. "The big ones, the wet ones, the dry ones, the thorny ones. . . ."

"I know what happened before," murmured the green-haired one. "I have been told by Bofusdiaga, singer of the sun. I have been told by Corojum, dancer of bright skies. Mouchidi is different. So say they."

One who had departed moments before returned breathlessly.

"We went, we met word already coming up from below," tim said. "The below ones already know of this Questioner. When it comes, it will be of some other kind and maybe have with it some other kinds yet. Bofusdiaga thinks we should look at them, too. Perhaps we would have better luck with another kind."

"Try, then," said the green-haired one. "Meantime, I will go to watch Mouchidi." She paused, as though debating whether or not to say what was in her mind, deciding at last to do so. "Again I dreamed! In the dream I danced into the fauxi-dizalonz, and Mouchidi was in it, and I was with him, and we were being changed together."

Several of the others recoiled, putting up their hands as though to ward her away. "Tss! Do not speak of it to tim-tim. It is not for us who say tim, tim, but only for you who say I, I. Speak of it only to Bofusdiaga, who alloys, and even then, speak softly, for *She* might hear."

"*She* still sleeps," asserted the one called Flowing Green. "*She* is not listening yet."

The other made a gesture which was the equivalent of a shrug. Flowing Green was excessive. From highest to lowest, Doshanoi, everyone, knew it. Tim-tim always said "tim-tim," we. Tim-tim never said "I." What could a part teach the whole? What dance could an "I" do, all by itself? Surely only the great ones could dream fully. Surely only the alloyed ones could remember what had been lost. . . .

"But they do not," whispered some. "Even they do not remember, even among them the dreams are tattered, filmy, without substance. How could even alloyed ones make do with such as that?" They could not. The dance was lost. Perhaps . . . lost forever.

"It is said," sang someone hidden in a corner. "It is said the mankinds have done wrong, they may be exterminated for the wrong they have done. Now, almost one could welcome this Questioner if it would exterminate these jongau who had not the courtesy to die."

"Bofusdiaga says no," said Flowing Green. "Bofusdiaga does not want justice."

The timmy departed by Doshanoi ways, unseen. It did not take long to find the place where Mouche and the others had been sent.

36

Pressed Men at Mantelby

Mouche let himself be loaded into the wagon and chained there with no outward sign of protest. Only when he knew the sound of the wheels on cobbles would mask his words did he lean toward the nearest man to whisper: "My name is Mouche."

"Ornery Bastable," the other replied. "I'm a seaman. She called me a supernume!" Ornery's chin jerking toward the leading carriage showed who she meant. "I'll have words with her."

Mouche masked his mouth with a shackled hand and spoke softly. "Words won't help. I don't think she cares if we're supernumes or not. She is an evil woman, Bastable, so beware."

The other gave Mouche a level stare, then asked, too loudly, "Known or suspected of being evil?"

Mouche shook his head slightly, narrowing his eyes. He had meant only to warn, thinking it far too dangerous to get into discussion about it while Dyre and Bane were near. They were doing one of their favorite things, watching him with that long, unblinking snake-eyed stare. It made Mouche think seriously of the need for allies. No Simon or Madame here. No Fentrys or Tyle. He would have to cultivate Bastable or whomever, for any help was better than none.

He shielded his mouth with his hand once more and murmured, "She is known to be an evil woman, seaman. There is no doubt about it at all. I have been warned to be inconspicuous as possible, not to attract her attention. I would not have words with her if I could avoid it."

Ornery thought it over, then gave a tiny nod of thanks for the warning. Bane and Dyre went on staring for a time, though they soon gave it up in favor of loud and continuous complaint mixed with assorted sneers and unspecific threats against all and sundry. They complained of having been sent to House Genevois against their inclination and of having been kept there by threat of force. They said they had been forced to be civil (though they called it sucking up to nobodies) when they would have preferred despotism (though they called it getting their rights). They complained of this latest outrage in which they were expected to labor like damn Timmys instead of being cushioned on silk and fed cream, which is what they'd been trained for. Cushioning and drinking and other such dalliances seemed to have figured largely in their minds, as they went on and on about it. When next Mouche and Ornery shared a glance, both understood it as a contract. If word came to blow, they would stand together against these two.

The wagon took the winding road leading onto the western heights, passing great houses behind high walls. At the top of the ridge, a man stood in an open gateway, obviously awaiting them. Mistress Mantelby halted her carriage and, indicating the waiting man with an imperious forefinger, called to those in the wagon: "Here is my steward. You will be working at his direction, so mind yourselves."

There was no reply from the wagon, and seemingly none was expected, for she went on in a loud voice.

"Well, Nephew! I said I would bring replacements, and here they are!"

"Thank you, Aunt," the steward murmured, standing with bowed head while the carriage moved away. When she had departed some distance toward the house itself, the man waved the wagon on, following it dejectedly afoot as it went down a lane toward a group of outbuildings. The six prisoners were hauled out of the wagon, two of them were sent along the lane under the watchful eyes of an understeward, while Bastable and the three Consorts were half dragged and half led into the stables. While the Haggers watched from the sidelines, the steward dropped his veils and looked them over, disgust plain on his face.

"Three layabout supernumes and a triplet of useless Hunks," he complained, "to replace a dozen pairs of skilled hands. And if you don't do the work, it'll be my hide that pays for it, so take this to heart: You'll do the work or I'll make your hide pay for it, count on it."

"And who're you, g'nephew?" sneered Bane. "A Family Man? A Man of Business?"

The steward paled, biting his lips. "I am the person who gives orders to the Haggers," he said when he had collected himself. "The Mistress has set them under my direction. So, if you've some idea of attacking me or attempting to leave this place, mark down that I won't be alone in retaliation."

"We have powerful friends," yelped Dyre. "And they'll not leave us here."

The steward grimaced. "Oh, surely. And when your powerful friends order me to release you, and when the Hags agree to that, and when Mistress Mantelby signs her name to the order, I'll do it. Until then you are my fingers to move at my command, worthless, and best you remember it."

He went down the line of them, pulling their veils away from their faces, staring at each of them, noting the brothers' sullen rebellion as well as Mouche and Ornery's puzzlement. The puzzlement, he felt sympathy for. He himself was more than a little puzzled about this whole situation.

"There is no stable master at the moment," he said.

"Until I can find a person with experience, I'll direct you myself. Tools are over there. Muck out all those stalls, put the muck in that cart there. Fill all the mangers with hay. Take the water buckets out, wash them, and fill them with fresh water from the well outside. Put one in each stall. When that is done, haul the cart out to the field and spread the muck about. If you think to save yourself trouble by dumping it all in one pile, you'll crawl about, spreading it with your noses! I'll be back after the noon-meal to see how much you've done. If you've done well, you'll eat."

And he turned and left, leaving two stout Haggers leaning on their cudgels to observe the work.

Mouche and Ornery set about the task, as described. There were a dozen stalls; they began on the ones nearest the loft. The job was no new thing for Mouche, though his hands, from which all calluses had long since been removed, soon felt the burn of the manure fork's wooden handle. Ornery had no such problem. Daily manipulation of ropes had given her palms like leather. Observing Mouche's tender hands, she pulled a pair of heavy work gloves from her back pocket and handed them over.

When Bane and Dyre made no move to help, the Haggers spoke roughly to them. After some muttering, they went unwillingly and unhandily to work at the far end.

"Y'said when we left Dutter, it was the end of this," Dyre growled.

"It will be," Bane muttered in return. "All this is a mistake, believe me." Then, with a glance at Mouche and Ornery, he muttered, just loud enough for them to hear, "But I think we'll probably stay long enough to settle with that one. That one there owes us, don't he, Brother? He'll take a beating that will last him a lifetime."

Mouche clenched his fists and turned. "I owe you more pain than you do me, Stinkbreath."

"You got that wrong," said Bane, turning white with fury. "I do what I like. I'm a new breed, I am, and nobody interferes with me, not ever."

This brought the Haggers over once more, and while Bane and Dyre claimed their full attentions, Mouche and

Ornery exchanged a few conspiratorial whispers concerning where they might find a haven if attacked. They settled upon the loft, and Ornery climbed there by the loose ladder—taking her and Mouche's belongings with her—and began forking straw down into the two stalls they had so far shoveled out. Mouche brought in two full buckets of fresh water, waited for an unobserved moment and handed one up to Ornery, who set it out of sight. Now, if they had to retreat, at least they wouldn't die from thirst!

Somewhere a noon bell rang, and the Haggers, who evidently felt they had supervised long enough, filed out and away, chatting between themselves. When the stable door closed, Bane stalked from the stall he had made little effort to clean, threw his manure fork at Mouche's feet, and growled, "Get on with it, dungrats."

"We'll do six stalls, our half," said Mouche. "And no more than that."

"You'll do the whole," sneered Bane. "Or you'll suffer for it."

Mouche and Ornery exchanged a glance, then ignored Bane's bluster and turned back to the stall they were cleaning.

"Hey, farm boy," sneered Bane. "You been home to visit lately?"

Mouche paid no attention.

"You otta go. Somethin' there you otta see."

Mouche turned. "And how would you know? You've not been home either."

"Well, Dutters wasn't my home and they weren't my folks. I didn't have a daddy and a mommy like you did, but I got friends tell me things. You know you got two baby sisters, farm boy? You know you got a brother going to grow up to be a Family Man?"

"That's a lie," said Mouche stoutly. His father would have told him if any such thing were true.

Bane and Dyre laughed, punching each other in their glee. "No lie. Sold you off and right away, mama had a girl, then another one, then a boy. The farm's doing well without you, farm boy. I guess all they had to do was get rid of their bad luck, and the Hagions made it right for them.''

''How come you know so much?'' demanded Ornery, moving nearer to Mouche, who was choking on his anger.

''We was neighbors. Dutter place is just over the hill. We used to roam around there quite a bit, killing vermin, getting rid of varmints.''

''What do you mean you didn't have a mother and father?'' Ornery challenged. ''Everybody has.''

''Not us,'' cried Dyre. ''We was born of the thunder, we was. Lightning is our papa. We're a new breed.''

''Born of the stinkbush,'' choked Mouche, against all good sense. ''Fathered by an outhouse.''

Mouche scarcely had time to brace himself before Bane landed on him, knocking him backward so the breath went out of him. His attacker drew a blade from his belt and wasted no time striking at Mouche's face. Mouche rolled and fended the first blow, but the second bit deep. He felt the slice and the warm blood on his cheek. His mouth was suddenly larger, and something inside himself screamed with outrage. His face. Bane had scarred his face!

The manure fork was under Mouche's hand, his fingers closed around the neck, just below the long tines. He managed to bring the fork up, twist it so the tines pointed at Bane, and thrust them deep enough that Bane fell back with a yelp, allowing Mouche to scramble to his feet with a firm grip on the fork as he backed, blood streaming, toward the ladder to the loft.

Meantime, Dyre had attacked Ornery, clutching her clumsily around the waist. Ornery had thrown herself forward, fallen hard on her attacker, and escaped while Dyre was catching his breath. By the time the brothers were on their feet, Ornery and Mouche were in the loft with the ladder pulled up after them and the manure fork close at hand for repelling boarders. Mouche leaked blood from his face, where his cheek had been sliced through, along with other cuts. Ornery had battered knuckles and a cut on her jaw, made by Dyre's ring. She paid no attention to this as she inspected Mouche's face, where the flesh was already swelling.

"Oh, by all the Hagions, Mouche. . . ."

"If i . . . 's aad, don' . . . ell . . . e."

"It's bad, and I have to tell you. It's got to be stitched. You'll be a horror, otherwise."

Mouche felt the horror as he moved his fingers over his face. ". . . ack," he said, as best he could, and Ornery read his mind. He fetched the pack and Mouche felt through it, coming up with a slender tube. "Glue," he said, almost clearly. "Now . . . whiaw is . . . resh."

"Tissue glue? I may not be good at it, Mouche. I may leave a scar."

"Now . . . whiaw . . . is . . . resh."

Working from the top of the cut, high on Mouche's cheek, just under his left eye, Ornery applied the glue and pressed the flesh together, centimeter by centimeter, hoping desperately that she would come out even when she reached the lips. The end of the cut was at the corner of the mouth, and this took several applications of the glue before it held. Mouche lay back, eyes wide with pain and sudden terror. Up until now, he'd had a life to depend on. Now? He couldn't be a Hunk, not now. Not unless a miracle happened and it healed so clean that the Dentimed machines could clean it up. Well, Madame would make Mantelby pay his annuity out. Trust Madame. At least he wouldn't starve.

Meantime, below, the brothers rattled the stable door to no effect, then sat down, muttering to one another and examining the walls in a vain effort to find some climbable way into the loft. The work of cleaning the stables went no further. Nor would it be finished, Ornery whispered, until those other two were got rid of.

"Let's . . . ill 'em," muttered Mouche, dazedly fingering the manure fork.

"Now, then," whispered Ornery, patting Mouche's shoulder. "Killing them isn't going to do us any good. Calm down. Maybe your folks didn't want to hurt your feelings so they didn't tell you about the new babies."

Mouche shook off the comforting hand and concentrated

on what was going on below. ". . . e could . . . ake um . . . ane isn' . . . so good a . . . ighter. He's lazy."

"He may not be a good fighter, he may even be lazy, but we're in no shape to prove it," said Ornery. "Please. Just lie there and let the glue set. Don't talk. Let me just try to get us put to work somewhere else, or vicey-versy."

Mouche took a shuddering breath and subsided while Ornery wet a clean handkerchief and cleaned the worst of the blood from his face. The glue had sealed the cut, as it was designed to do, which is why the stuff was carried by sailors and roustabouts and others subject to injury in the way of the work. Deep, disfiguring injuries like Mouche's, however, were supposed to be followed up by an immediate visit to the surgery machines, and Ornery didn't think it was going to happen, not with things all in confusion as they were.

"I'd rather the gardens for me," said Ornery, making conversation to keep Mouche's mind off the wound. "I was raised a farm boy, and I can do gardening without thinking about it. It would smell better out there, too. It really stinks in here."

Mouche wrinkled his nose, testing. It did indeed stink in the stable, and he knew that the stench was not entirely horse. The fetid odor was the same as he had smelt years ago in the cave, and on his dog, and later in Madame's front parlor. He knew it came from the brothers below, though they had not smelled like this at House Genevois.

Mouche was unaware of the special bath soaps, the additives in their food, the unusual unguents used during morning massage. Today there had been no morning bath, no morning meal, no morning massage. Bane and Dyre had come a long way in an open cart, sweating under the sun and had begun to smell very much as they had smelled at the Dutter farm.

Ornery murmured, "We can talk to that head man, if he comes back down here today. Personal, I think he won't remember us until nighttime comes, and maybe not then. This place is in a uproar, just as Sendoph probably is, all at greasy glasses and burned biscuits, I'd warrant. Everbody depending on those Timmys, years and years the way they have . . .''

''. . . ou ha . . . nt?'' Mouche whispered.

''No, I haven't. No Timmys on ships. No sir. They don't like the water, and that's a fact. You find 'em on the wharf and you find 'em stowing stuff in the hold, but you don't find 'em once the ship goes out on water. No Timmys on the Bouncing Isles. No Timmys at the sea farms. . . .''

''Sea . . . arns?''

''Out there in the Jellied Sea, they got sea farms. There's a kind of weed draws gold out of the seawater and fixes it in the leaves, and they hook it and tie it to a hawser and pull it in by the quarter mile into a great pile, and they dry it and burn it and mix the ashes with water to make bricks, and they send the bricks back to the smelter, to get the gold out. And it's not just gold! There's other good metal in the ashes. There's fishes out there, too, kinds we can eat, and dried Purse fish eggs, for making jelly. . . .'' She went cheerfully on, trying to keep Mouche's mind occupied.

Though the two below continued to search for some way of reaching their prey, they had not accomplished it by the time the stable door opened with a crash. Both Bane and Dyre turned their angry faces to confront the steward once more, along with several Haggers. In the loft, Ornery urged Mouche to the edge of the loft and arranged his veil so the wound would show while Mouche quivered with newly kindled rage and shock.

''You've got the stalls mucked out?'' demanded the steward.

Bane said something about the other two taking a rest.

''No rest, sir,'' said Ornery in as respectful a voice as she could muster. ''They tried to kill us, sir. We came up here to get away from them. They've cut Mouche all to bits.''

An argument below built rapidly into shouting and threats, falling silent as suddenly as another voice cut into the fray: ''Silence.''

It was Marool herself. ''Who has cut whom?''

Explanations. More argument. More yelling. Through all of which Mouche and Ornery quietly sat at the edge of the loft, their veils so arranged as to allow a full view of their battered faces in the light falling through the air vent.

"Well, boy," said Marool to Bane, who was by this time held in the grip of several Haggers. "Look at them up there. Their little faces all beaten and bruised, one of them possibly scarred for life, and who's to pay for it? Ah? You baby Hunks have to be returned untouched, unharmed, and here you are, already costing me money. Well, boy, you owe me. I can't get it out of your pockets, so I'll take it in services." And she jerked her head backward. Two Haggers took Bane away, still yelling, while the others restrained Dyre from following.

Marool followed his departure with her eyes, casting only a single infuriated glance upward as she said to her steward, "Separate them, Nephew. And see they're tended to. I may get enough use out of one not to mind paying damages for the one he's ruined, but damned if I'll pay for more than that."

And she was gone.

"I was reared a farm boy," called Ornery in a level tone. "If you need gardening done."

". . . e, too," said Mouche.

The steward exchanged looks with the Haggers, who shrugged, one of them commenting: "The gardener says the two you gave him are useless, they don't know roots from sprouts, and they've planted three rows of fennet upside down."

"We'll bring them back here, then," said the steward, in a glum voice.

Mouche and Ornery were beckoned down from their perch. They were then taken down through the paddocks to the lane, and up the lane to the stone house of the head gardener, and there traded for the two other pressed men who shambled sourly down the lane to the stables. Behind the gardener's house were several daub-and-wattle houses, brightly painted, where the gardener's invisible help had lived, and the contents of Mouche's pack were soon laid out there, together with a few clothes for Ornery, who had only what she'd carried on the boat upriver.

Thus it came that Mouche and Ornery, their wounds washed and medicated, sat over a late lunch beside a Timarese hearth, drinking broth from Timarese bowls, spied on, though they did not know it, by a good many Timmys in the walls, including Flowing Green who was in as near to a frenzy as the Timmys ever got. Mouchidi had been wounded, and badly. Mankinds could die from such wounds. Tim had seen it happen!

When Ornery had gulped all and Mouche spooned down half what they had been given, enough that they were no longer famished, Ornery set down her bowl and leaned confidentially toward Mouche.

"That was rotten of him, saying you were bad luck. It isn't true, you know. It's just the inscrutable Hagions, making mock of good sense."

"I . . . udden . . . ind so . . . uch," muttered Mouche, "if aw had jus tol . . . ee."

"I told you why. Your pa didn't want to hurt you."

"He could haw 'ought me 'ack!"

Ornery gave him a long, level look. "He couldn't buy you back. Not from a Consort House."

Mouche flushed. Of course he couldn't have been bought back. He knew that. Someone could have tried, though.

"I . . . ove' 'at farn," he muttered resentfully.

"I loved my family's farm, too," said Ornery. "It was beautiful there. We had a vineyard . . ."

"So di' ooee."

"And we had sheep and chickens and a garden and orchard. But the mountain blew, and the ashes came on a terrible wind, and when I got home they were all dead, Mama and Papa, brother, all gone. There was no sense to that, either. Maybe when they felt the hot wind coming, they hated me because I escaped and they didn't. Maybe they didn't even think of me. Life's hard enough, so my captain says, that most times we should do very little thinking about what other people think or do or say, just enough to get by. Otherwise we just jangle ourselves for nothing. So he says."

"I renen'er how uh hayhield snelled," said Mouche, stubbornly, determined to make his loss the greater.

"And the smell of strawberries, new-picked," said Ornery. "And the flowers in Mama's garden, outside the kitchen door."

Mouche heaved a huge sigh and gave up the effort at grief supremacy. "You're righ'," he announced. "Likely he didn' wan oo hur ny 'eelings. . . ."

"And you're nobody's bad luck," insisted Ornery.

Mouche nodded and forgot himself enough to try to smile, more because of Ornery's good intentions than at his interpretation of the facts. If good fortune had come to his family, it had happened only after he, Mouche, was gone away. If that wasn't bad luck, what was it? Almost as though he hadn't belonged there. And if not, where did he belong? Was it possible he had been brought here, well, at least to House Genevois, for a purpose? By fate? Now there was a large thought.

When they had finished eating, Mouche still ruminating on fatefulness, the gardener took a look at Mouche's face, then told him to do no more than he could comfortably do for the rest of the day. A barrow was laden with tools and they pushed it to a long arbor walk overgrown with fruit vines and edged with flowers, where things needed a general clipping and weeding and neatening up. Mouche had his own taste to guide him, which was considerable. Ornery had a shipman's love of order, for, as she told Mouche, disorder breeds death at sea, where a loop of rope or a tool left out of place can spell the difference between life and death.

Mouche found that concentrating on the work made the pain lessen. Between them they worked, both sensibly and conscientiously enough to feel a sense of satisfaction in late evening when the gardener finally came to see what they'd accomplished. The man nodded once or twice as in pleased surprise, then patted their shoulders as he took them back to his own house to give them a plentiful supper.

"Well, now, I'd have said you were both useless as tits on a boar, but you've proved me wrong," the old man said when he had filled Ornery's stew bowl and salad bowl and laid out a thick slab of cheese on a chunk of brown bread wrenched from the new loaf. After another long look at Mouche's face, he furnished him with a mug of broth and more chunks of the bread to be softened, he said, by dipping.

"What are you doing here, and how did it all happen?" he asked when he had them provided for.

Between mouthfuls, Ornery explained about the Timmys without once referring to them by name. "And Mouche told me his Madame says, people who don't exist, can't exist, not until this Questioner person goes away. And the Questioner person is to be staying here, in Mistress Mantelby's house.

"Far's I'm concerned, it's all a mistake, an' I got to get me back to the ship," said Ornery. "This Mantelby woman, she took me wrong, she did. I'm no supernumerary. I got to get back, or maybe I'll lose my place. An' I got to get word to my sister, too, or she'll fret herself sick over me."

" 'ould you sto' us?" Mouche asked the old man. "I' we ran away?"

The old man poked the fire and snorted. "Well o' course I'd stop you. Old I may be, and not so spry, but I've still got good sense, as well as work that needs doing. Now, you stick around here, workin' away, stooped a little, maybe, so's you look older, with nice thick veils over your young faces and a good deal of manure rubbed in your hair and eyebrows, that one up at the house, she'll ignore you like you don't exist, just like she allus did them others that don't exist. That cut on you, thas good protection, too, for she doesn't pay attention to people that're hurt, or sick. But you run off, that steward, he'll report it because he's her nephew, and if he doesn't tell her everything, she'll put him out on the street, maybe blue-body him into the bargain. My, she loves disposin' o' nephews. So, he'll tell her if you run off, depend on it, and right then you'll go down in her bad book. She don't abide being crossed, so people don't stay in her bad book long. Right soon they just vanish, quick as you can say, oh, my gracious. Sometimes there's bones and sometimes there's not. And who you think she'll take to task for you leaving? Whose back will she stripe? Whose bones will she roast? Eh? Mine, that's whose."

He shook his head sadly and set a burning splinter to the pipe he had just filled with shreds of fragrant willowbark, then waved the smoking pipe about his head to drive away the midges. "No, sailor, I'll send letters for you, so your people won't worry, but you'll be smart to wear those old invisibles' robes and the thick veils. I scrounged 'em for you as uglification, just to keep you meek and safe from harm. I had the laundry boy wash 'em and stitch 'em together, to make them big enough. I figure anybody in those robes likely won't get seen anyhow, seein' as how we don't see those robes, if you take my meaning."

There was a good deal of sense in what he said, and though Ornery fretted over her shipboard position, the gardener assured her the Hags would set it right. It wouldn't make sense for men to lose their positions because of some emergency measure. Once everything was back to normal, it would be fixed.

It was weariness as much as anything else that made Ornery agree. They wrote their letters, one to Ornery's captain, one to Ornery's sister, and one from Mouche to Madame, then they went out through the dusk into a Timmy house where they curled up on Timmy mats under Timmy blankets. Ornery fell asleep while it was still light outside, though Mouche stayed longer awake, feeling with delicate fingertips the swollen flesh of his face and wondering what was to happen to him now.

In the cities and towns of Newholme, things went from greasy glasses and burned biscuits to filthy streets and food rotting in the fields before some kind of order began to emerge, or, if not order, at least a more amenable disorder. A kind of controlled chaos, as the Hags put it. A godawful mess, according to the Men of Business. Priority was given to food and fuel. Necessary things were getting done. Unnecessary ones, uncritical ones, were long delayed and might, in fact, not get done at all.

The Consort Houses held only staff and boy-children too young to work. There were no supernumeraries to be found anywhere on the streets, and it had even begun to dawn on a good many people that had the Timmys not been so ubiquitous all those generations, likely there would have been no such things as supernumes. The new order required a new economic basis, of course. The Timmys had worked without pay, though they had been provided with housing, clothing, and food. The new workers took up more space, ate more food and required more fabric for clothing, and some of them even demanded wages. The CMOB struggled with these matters while trying to pretend that things had always been this way.

At House Genevois, Madame sent a message to a certain one and awaited a visitation in her parlor, and when he arrived, she tried not to breathe as she told him his wards, his protégés, the Dutter boys, had been pressed into service.

"Who by?" He grunted.

"By Mistress Mantelby," she replied, keeping her voice carefully neutral.

The man across from her shook. For a moment she thought his spasms came from illness or distress, but then she realized he was laughing.

"Monstrous Marool has them? Oh, does she? What a joke! Oh, that's a rare one, that is. Well, Madame, all our agreements stand. I won't hold you responsible for their being *pressed into service,* not even if they come back in worse condition than when they left."

"You are kind," said Madame, with the least possible deference in her nod.

"Not at all," he said, departing. She sat for several moments after he left, breathing through her mouth, hearing his final words resonate, realizing at last that he had meant them literally. He was not at all kind. He would be incapable of kindness.

At the port outside Sendoph, a tall, blue-skinned protocol officer arrived on the Questioner's advance cutter to spend half an officious hour with the Men of Business and a day with the Hags, most of it in inspection of the Mantelby mansion. Mouche and Ornery were trimming lawn edges in the garden when they saw the blue one stalk through. The two had taken the gardener's advice and made themselves useful but inconspicuous, though Mouche did not believe for a moment that this strategy would save him from Bane's malice. The head gardener told them Bane had been installed as Mistress Mantelby's toy boy, and Dyre, too, had been taken up to the main house to enjoy himself.

"You'd think they were kin of hers, the way they act," the old man whispered over the evening meal. "Oh, I hear things, I do. All the servants up there at the house, they're talking about it. She's shameless, that one. She'll cosset him, or them, until they think they shit pure gold. She'll take them to bed with her, and she'll give them stuff to make them feel like lords of creation, and they'll play round games. Then one day they'll wake up in shackles in her playroom. I've seen it happen a hundred times. . . ."

" 'lay roon?" asked Mouche, apprehensively.

The old man shivered. "Call it a dungeon, you'd be closer on. Down in the old wine cellars. Playroom is what she calls it. There's machines in there, and sometimes when the machines are through, all that's left is grease."

"I don't understand," said Ornery.

Mouche did understand, all too well. He whispered to Ornery of the picture at House Genevois.

Ornery turned back to the old man. "You've seen it a hundred times, gardener? Truly?"

The old man shrugged and pursed his lips. "Well, no, boys, not strictly, no. That's liar's license, that is, to make the story ring right. I'd say she does for at least three or four men a year, most of 'em Consorts, but some just plain folk, like a footman at table she takes a dislike to or some cook that spoils the roast. And nephews, o' course. She loves disposin' of nephews."

"Why does she do it?" breathed Ornery.

Madame had explained psychotic sadism to her students,

but Mouche could not yet speak without considerable pain, so he made no attempt to pass that information on. Madame had said some people were made that way, and they did it out of vengeance, and some were born that way, and they did it because hurting and killing made them feel powerful. Either way, there was no cure for it, for each act led to the next with no way to retreat.

"Whatever reason Mistress Mantelby is like she is, you keep tight to what I told you," said the old man. "I'm trusting you to keep out of the way and be silent. Just like those things we used to have that never existed. You understand?"

By the time the Questioner and her entourage arrived, affairs at Marool Mantelby's mansion were as calm and usual as it was possible to make them. The only change for the household was that Bane and Dyre were to be housed in a suite at the far end of the servants' quarters during the Questioner's stay, because of the stink. So the old gardener said. For that reason and others, everyone was more or less holding their breaths until the visitation was over. It wouldn't be long. So everyone had been told.

37

An Intimate Disclosure

On the evening the Questioner arrived Ornery asked the gardener if they might make use of the washhouse in the compound, and he gave his permission, so long as it was after everyone else had gone to bed, provided they were stingy with the firewood in the boiler and mopped up after themselves. The stone-floored little building was near the wood stove and the pump and was furnished with wooden tubs of various sizes. Ornery took herself and her clothing inside, locked the door, lit the boiler, and heated a good quantity of water.

Mouche, however, on learning that Ornery had gone to commit an act of cleanliness, stopped scratching himself and decided it was long past time for himself to have a bath also, to rid him of vermin if nothing else, so he went along to the room, jiggled the latch, and walked into the place. She was standing in the tub, washing her hair. She was Ornery, no doubt of that, but she was also unmistakably female.

Ornery seized up a towel and covered all pertinent parts while stammering a long exposition of how she had been turned into a chatron as a boy. Mouche smiled as politely as his wound would allow. His studies at Madame's had exposed him to women's bodies in all varieties of age and inclination; he had seen chatrons and hermaphrodites as well, and he knew Ornery was physiologically a girl and he said so, intelligibly.

Ornery protested.

Mouche shook his head, bewildered. He knew Ornery was a girl, and moreover, he knew she had a body that was sleek and lovely. He liked the looks of her very much, though he felt no desire toward her. He had been trained not to feel desire until and unless desire was wanted, and, if he had thought about it, he would have realized that he had felt no spontaneous desire since he first saw Flowing Green.

By this time he was able to speak with reasonable clarity, though with some pain and effort. "That may have worked on a ship where, I suppose, you kept yourself covered and where few of the men had seen a woman in their entire lives, but it won't work with me. Why don't you just finish your hair and tell me what's going on?"

"Don't touch me," demanded Ornery.

"Of course not," said Mouche, annoyed. "What do you think I am?"

"You're not fixed," Ornery stuttered, reaching for her clothes. "And neither am I."

Which was perfectly true, of course. Mouche wasn't fixed. He wouldn't be until he was sold. And of course he would not force himself on Ornery, because if Ornery—the female Ornery—got pregnant, she could be executed for mismothering, and Mouche was not the kind of person to endanger another in that way. So Mouche told himself, illustrating his goodwill by leaving the room with the utmost dignity and closing the door gently behind him.

Ornery checked the door. The lock was broken. It seemed to lock, but in fact it did not. So, all right, he hadn't picked the lock in order to get at her. With some apprehension, she went back to the room they shared, where Mouche attempted once again to explain that he was both honorable and harmless and that Ornery did not need to worry. His friendly overtures were rebuffed. Further, Ornery adopted a new manner toward him, one of nervous shyness, like a young cat only recently made aware of dogs. Her native gregariousness had led them into a friendly and trusting camaraderie, but now her sense of prudence dictated otherwise. Suddenly, she became suspicious and almost preternaturally alert.

Mouche, in turn, could not decide whether he was annoyed with her or not. Given the high status of women on Newholme and the very low status of supernumes—even ones who got jobs as seamen—he could not quite envision a circumstance which would have led him, had he been female, to pretend otherwise. He would very much have liked to discuss it with Ornery, but she was not of a mood, as yet, for any discussion at all.

38

The Questioner Arrives

Questioner arrived without fanfare. Her shuttle set down near Sendoph late at night. Though Questioner had intended to enter the planetary system from the side nearest the moon where the Quaggi had died, the immediacy of the geological problems on the planet had made her change her mind. The Quaggi would wait. She could stop at the outer planet on her way out.

By morning she was ensconced at Mantelby Mansion, her maintenance system unloaded and ready, her reference files properly arranged, Ellin and Bao settled, and the rest of her varied entourage provided with rooms of their own, along with a separate dining salon. The entourage had caused quite a stir. Of the eight persons attached to Questioner, in addition to Ellin and Bao, no two looked anything alike, and some of them looked only remotely mankindly. The peepers from the walls had seen this with a good deal of interest, and had immediately sent messengers off with descriptions of each one of the eight.

By breakfast, Questioner had her people taking scanner views of every street from Naibah south, and inventorying all businesses, agricultural enterprises, and the like, from Sendoph north. The work could have been done automatically, by miniature spy-eyes, but Questioner did not advise her so-called aides of this. The opportunity to be rid of them for some days, if she was lucky, was too good to miss.

Within the hour, Ellin Voy and Gandro Bao were on their way to the Panhagion in a carriage borrowed from the Mantelby stables while another, larger carriage was being modified to carry the Questioner. The ride was neither long nor uncomfortable, and Ellin considerably enjoyed the amusement of seeing Bao dressed as a woman. Questioner had approved his doing so, since he would otherwise have to wear veils and his efficiency would be impaired. Ellin had to admit that, within a few moments, she thought of him as a woman, for he acted and looked exactly as a rather grave, pleasant, youngish woman might. He had, so he said, learned women's ways and women's wiles over years of study with a Kabuki master of the genre.

Among all these pleasurable details, Ellin could not understand her uneasiness. There was something in the atmosphere of the place, the city, or perhaps the planet, that made her feel queasy. A melancholy in the air. A sadness. A late-autumn, leaf-burning, chill-wind-blowing, inexorable-lifeloss-coming kind of feeling. She felt it like a ghostly hand on her shoulder, and it made no sense at all.

"Do you feel it?" she whispered to Bao, her eyes on the back of the veiled coachman.

Bao stared out at the world, looked up at the sky, across the valley at the long shredded lines of smoke trailing away to the south. "Something," he admitted in his woman's voice. "The hairs on my neck are standing on end."

When they left the carriage at the foot of the Temple stairs, Ellin stopped a young woman and introduced herself, asking to be taken to someone in charge. She and Bao were escorted into the forecourt of the Temple, where they watched as women placed lighted incense sticks in great sand-filled basins on iron tripods. Smoke rose from hundreds of glowing wands to fill the vault with haze that was lit by vagrant rays of light from high, gem-colored windows. Seen from below, the smoke shone in fragments of ruby and emerald, sapphire, amethyst, and amber, a shifting glory against the gold mosaic tiles of the ceiling.

"It is only the imperfection in the atmosphere that allows us to see the light," said a voice at their shoulders. "So with us, only our own imperfections allowing us to see what perfection might be."

The person addressing them was tall and thin and brown, dressed in a crimson, long-sleeved garment topped by a complicated headdress of striped wine and flame. "I am D'Jevier Passenger," she said. "One of the Temple Hags."

"Madam," Ellin bowed. "My name is Ellin Voy and this is . . . Gandra Bao. We are uncertain as to the respectful form of address. . . ."

"Ma'am will do," said D'Jevier. "Or, you may call me simply Hag or Oh, Hag, or Revered Hag, though I doubt the latter is always sincere. I am your servant, Ma'am, and that of the Hagions."

"The Hagions?" Ellin cocked her head. The Questioner had assured her that this movement, properly executed, elicited information all by itself. Persons often helped the merely puzzled while they withheld information from the demanding.

"Come," said the Hag. "You will understand better if you see the Temple proper. We close it to men's eyes. For millennia, mankind was so conditioned to believe that the only possible God is created in the image of a very large and powerful male, that the mere idea of a goddess made the entire male gender overwrought. Even here, on Newholme, where the Hagions have reigned for generations, we find it necessary to keep menfolk's mouths and minds busy with other things."

D'Jevier held aside one of the heavy curtains and they passed through into the Temple proper, Bao doing so without hesitation. So far as he was concerned, the moment he put on his wig, he became a woman, and he stayed a woman until he took it off.

The Hagions stood along the far, curved wall, their heads—or what would have been their heads—well above Ellin's height, even though the floor was much lower where the images stood. The robes expressed a female form and a female head within a vacancy. *Here I am,* each statue proclaimed, *invisibly existent.*

"Have they names?" Bao whispered in a charming and completely womanly voice. Ellin was silent, though she felt both awed and excited by invisible images, so palpably present.

"The Goddess to the left is the maiden, in the center, the woman, to the right, an old woman, a crone. These ages typify differing types of power. There is also present a fourth, without shape or age, a spirit, invisible. The directory of Hagions is there," said D'Jevier, indicating the low lectern at the center of the arc of effigies. "Please feel free to glance at it."

Ellin and Bao did so, turning the pages, finding there name after name they had never heard of. D'Jevier spoke from behind them: "There are many aspects of divinity. Some are useful for occasions of joy. Others when we are troubled. . . ."

Something in her voice led Bao to ask in his sweetly sympathetic voice, "You are troubled? We hope we have not occasioned this feeling."

She shook her head with a fleeting smile. "We all are troubled on Newholme. Vulcanism is increasing to an extent that it may threaten both our food supplies and some of our water sources. The Men of Business are extremely worried about the cities and the farmlands, while we are more concerned with human life. . . ."

"Do you mean mankind life?"

D'Jevier turned her face slightly aside, masking her eyes. "With all due respect to Haraldson, mankind is the only human presence on Newholme."

"Where will you go?"

"If it gets any worse, we'll have to go into the badlands. Though every tame mountain south and east has turned feral, the canyons west of the city seem to be untroubled. Foodstuffs will be needed, emergency supplies of all kinds . . .''

D'Jevier sighed dramatically, attempting to look wearied by her labors, hoping to misdirect her visitors. The recent tremors were indeed worse than others in the records, but the Hags had no real intention of evacuating the city as yet, preferring to delay any decision until the Questioner had departed. If she did not approve them and depart, any decision might prove to have been a waste of time.

Ellin and Bao took note of what had been said, then looked once more at the trio of images.

''Are your rites secret?'' asked Bao, gravely, hand to throat, conveying awe.

D'Jevier shook her head. ''Private would be a better word. We do not encourage attendance by scoffers, or by the inattentive and the ignorant, but we do not hesitate to inform persons who are interested. Our most popular rite comes at the Tipping of the Year when we concentrate on forgetting the disappointments of the past year, on setting aside events or relationships that have proven troublesome and unhappy, even within families, and on moving on to others that are more kindly, cooperative, and productive. Our rule is to bow, bow again, and get on. Our religion is based upon eschewing human sacrifice in favor of lives that are fulfilling, productive, and joyful.''

Startled, Ellin cried, ''Human sacrifice! I am surprised you can think of such a thing!''

D'Jevier said with unfeigned weariness, ''My dear young woman, our history is made up of millennia of human sacrifice. Well into the twenty-first century, huge armies of young men were sacrificed to tribal or national honor, women were sacrificed to male supremacy, children were sacrificed to brutality, all immolated in flames of painful duty. We try to determine whether the dutiful will suffer and to decide how that suffering may be compensated. We continually redesign our society to provide joy to those who incur pain on our behalf.''

''I'm not sure I get that,'' Ellin said.

D'Jevier smiled. ''One example will suffice. On most

worlds women have a duty to bear and raise children. Some children are loving and generous; some women enjoy mothering; some families are happy. However, some women are unskilled, or have children who are unloving and selfish. Sometimes they grasp at their children, seeking from their children the joys that instinct tells them they should receive, and there is hurt and annoyance on both sides. Here on Newholme, we try to see that all lives contain appropriate joys, in order that children may grow up without guilt.''

''I see,'' murmured Ellin, feeling an abyss open around her. Such a simple idea. Why had she never heard anyone speak of providing appropriate joys?

Bao, with a concerned glance at Ellin, murmured, ''Madam, we are only envoys of Questioner. She has sent us to advise you that she herself will be calling upon you, probably rather soon.''

''I understand,'' said D'Jevier, bowing. ''Whenever you like.''

They went out together, standing for a long moment at the top of the stairs. The city moved before them with a certain intent bustle, people carrying this and that, going hither and yon, none of them sparing even a glance for the visitors.

''Something is wrong, here,'' said Gandro Bao. ''They should be showing curiosity about us, and they are not doing it. Everybody is being oh so very busy. Let us be going separate ways, to see what we can see.''

Wordlessly, Ellin agreed, and the two of them went off in opposite directions to get a closer look at Newholmian society.

''Nobody is dancing,'' said Gandro Bao, removing his dusty cloak and hanging it neatly by the door of the large and luxurious suite that he, Ellin, and Questioner occupied at Mantelby Mansion. He doffed his wig, also, setting it atop his cloak. ''One rumor, about volcanoes, is saying truth, for there is much smoking from the mountains, much agitating among peoples. Other rumor is being unverified. I am seeing no indigenous race.''

"Ah," murmured the Questioner. "Where have you been?"

"I am going about in the business section. I am asking Men of Business if mountains are blowing up, and they are saying yes, too many, but it is striking me an oddity that no one is standing about looking at mountains. Or at me! I am being stranger, and mountains are being very dramatic, very threatening, but everyone being very busy, not looking."

"Aah," murmured Questioner. "Perceptive of you, Gandro Bao. They are not looking because . . . ?"

"Because they are thinking of something else or are avoiding me. Also, I am asking if people dance, and they are saying no, no dancing at all. Streets are being very dirty. Men are wearing very thick veils. Perhaps those are reasons for no dancing. If I am dancing in such a veil, I am falling over my feet."

"You say the streets are dirty," mused Questioner. "Old trash ends up as a kind of sludge in the gutters. You mean dirty like that?"

He shook his head in an effort of memory. "No. No sludge. Just this little trashiness."

"Ah. Then the streets are usually cleaner, but not now, or they are infrequently cleaned. If you see anyone cleaning the streets, let me know." Questioner entered the information on her project file, another in the great number of nagging and interesting data she was accumulating on Newholme.

"You can ask them about the painted houses, too," said Ellin, entering from the hallway. She yawned enormously and threw herself down on the cushioned seat that stretched beneath a pair of wide windows. "I'm so tired! I feel heavy on this world!"

"Heaviness is suitable. Newholme gravity is slightly greater than Earth. What is this about painted houses?" asked Questioner.

"I found them behind places and off courtyards and down little hidden lanes, brightly painted little houses in a style I see nowhere else. I asked, people said servants' quarters, and there are servants living there, but they don't fit."

"Don't fit how?"

"Too tall for the doors, too long for the floors, and too few for all the rooms. The paint's fresh on the houses. The walls are clean, the floors also. I'd say someone else lived there up until just recently."

"Ah," murmured Gandro Bao, taking a very feminine stance and parading across the floor, fluttering his eyelashes at Ellin, then at Questioner. "So, the people are hiding something." He seized Ellin by the hand and drew her into a whirling encounter, something between a tango and a duel, the two moving like jointed dolls.

Questioner cogitated, much interested and intrigued by this information. So many of her visits were dull and juiceless, with everything laid out like a pattern for a garment: fabric here, shears there, cut here, sew along the dotted line, and what results is a very dull cloak, one size fits nobody. Or there were visits where she could find no pattern at all. Cut? What means cut? Sew? What means sew?

How interesting to meet a third variation, a false pattern. Everything seemingly right there in plain sight, sew here, cut there, and what results is a surprise. A three-legged trouser. A four-armed coat!

She said sharply, "Stop twirling, you're making me dizzy."

Ellin and Bao spun to a stop, drawing apart and bowing to one another, Ellin rather pink and breathing strongly. Obediently, they sat side by side on the windowseat, like two marionettes, awaiting the next twitch on the strings.

Questioner remarked, "Let us assume some other people were here until just recently. If they swept the streets, if they cleaned the houses, chances are they also minded the children, for this is the usual pattern when a culture has cheap labor. So, you should seek out some children, watch them, see what they do and say. Also, it is time we spoke to more ordinary people.

"What did you find at the Temple?"

Ellin keyed her file, which immediately recreated the sight and sound of the visit. When the record had played itself out, Questioner murmured, "Joys to compensate thankless duty? You didn't pursue that?"

Ellin flushed. "I was so taken with the idea, I forgot."

"We will ask next time," said Questioner. "Meantime, it seems you can make yourself understood in the local dialect."

"After all those hours with the sleep teachers on the ship, it isn't difficult," Ellin replied. "It still cleaves closely to Earth-universal."

"In my family, we were speaking Asia-matrix, not Earth-universal," said Gandro Bao from his place by the window. "But I am coping."

Questioner nodded. "Have you encountered any reference to the first settlement made here? It preceded the second by half a century, at least."

"Of that, I am having word," said Bao, picking up his own project file and keying through it. "Ah, here is note. A man I asked about the Temple building—he would not look at the woman I was being, only at his feet—said building of Temple and the Fortress of Vanished Men in Naibah was being done by first settlers. First colony is disappearing, but fortresses and many other buildings were remaining, mostly along river. There are records in fortress. Are you wanting me to read them?"

Questioner frowned. "No. I'll send one of my aides to make a copy. I try to keep them as busy as possible with things that don't matter greatly. The entourage is supposed to be for my help and protection, but they don't help and I don't need protection here. The population seems conditioned to respect older women."

"Isn't that the norm in most worlds?" asked Ellin.

Questioner replied. "Far from it, my dear, especially on nonmember worlds. Surpluses are not much respected, whether of eggs, grain, or women, and elderly women are always surplus."

"Newholme is unique in the scarcity of women, then," remarked Ellin.

Questioner spoke thoughtfully. "At the current time, it is the only planet I know of." She rose and went toward the door, saying over her shoulder: "Dig around a bit more. Talk to some common people. Talk to some children. We will meet again over our evening meal." She departed. In a moment, they heard the door to the room in which the Questioner's massive and complicated reference files had been installed. It opened and, after a long pause, closed.

Ellin stood at the window, using the sill as a barre as she stretched and bent. "Oh, Gandro Bao, let us dance a little more. Just that little bit of dancing worked out some of my kinks! I feel like a wooden doll, all stiff."

"You should be dancing with me more." Bao smiled. "The exercise will be doing us both good." He drew her into the dance once more, looking her up and down as they twirled. "Are you still wondering who you are, Ellin Voy?"

"Not when I'm dancing," she cried breathlessly. "Not then."

She bent, turned, bent again, then stopped, her eyes caught by movement in the gardens below.

"There," she said, pointing. "Gandro Bao, there are two gardeners there below. They're common people. After we've had some lunch, let's talk to the gardeners."

He looked out the window, noted the gardeners, started to draw her to him once more, then changed his mind. Her eyes were sparkling, and she had just given him a very friendly and intimate look. He did not want her to get the wrong idea. She was a dear companion, with a truly sweet nature, but in the pursuit of certain pleasures, Gandro Bao preferred men. He took her hand, bent over it, then suggested they go into the small salon where their lunch was served.

Behind them, in the walls of the room where they had danced, voices cried:

"Dancers! They are dancers! Oh, we must take them!"

"Tim was going to take the other ones! The different ones."

"Take the different ones, but take these, too."

"Now? Shouldn't we ask Bofusdiaga?"

"Now. We shouldn't waste time!"

"Ask some-tim," a voice cried. "Find out."

After a moment, the walls were silent, the peepholes hidden, the room quiet. Elsewhere, however, was a bustle of coming and going as the Timmys decided whether and when to take away Ellin and Bao.

39

Gardeners, Molds, and Intricacies

On the lawn of Mantelby Mansion, Mouche and Ornery were silently raking up the trimmings from a hedge; silently because they did not know what to say to one another. They had not spoken since the previous evening when Mouche's friendly overtures had been rebuffed. He was, in consequence, annoyed, which made him feel guilty. Consorts could be angry at insult or annoyed by too much starch in their frilled shirts, but they could not, ever, be angry or annoyed at women. Mouche had been drilled in that fact, he had been given exercises to do, and he had discussed it with his personal trainer over and over again, none of which was helping him now. He was irritable because though he could now talk intelligibly, it pained him to do so, and he was also feeling symptoms of withdrawal from his addiction. It had been days since he had seen Flowing Green. He had dreamed of her, it, but he had not seen her. All this made him more annoyed at Ornery than he might otherwise have been. He needed a comfortable friend, and now, amid all this confusion, she had stopped being one.

Mouche had discarded the notion that it was because of his face. Ornery was not that kind. Others would be, but not her. When they had been comfortable friends, however, he, Mouche, had thought she, Ornery, was a boy. So, perhaps the key to this tangle was for him to accept that she, he, Ornery was indeed a boy. Well, a chatron. And he, Mouche, should treat him, Ornery, just as he had in the past.

Mouche rehearsed these intentions, putting reasonable words to them, fighting the temptation to be spiteful, resolving to sound firm but sensible, and he was readying himself to expound on his resolution when Ellin and Bao came along the walk, full of questions.

Mouche and Ornery bowed. Mouche had been working himself up to politeness, but Ornery acknowledged the visitors only in a cursory fashion. Ornery was, if possible, more annoyed than Mouche was. She liked Mouche a good deal as a friend, but Ornery did not like men except as friends. On the ship she had come to know a good many of them rather intimately. Some she enjoyed being with, as she did Mouche, and some she would as soon not be around, but her strongest feelings were reserved for other women. She had no desire to be any more than friendly with Mouche, but she strongly wanted to be friendly! If she was friendly with him, he might desire her, and then it would all be a tangle!

And now, adding irritation to aggravation, here were these two outlanders, asking questions!

"Have you worked here long?" Ellin asked.

"Too long," snarled Ornery.

"Yes, Madam," said Mouche, with an admonitory glance at Ornery. They were under instructions to be polite, word having filtered down just what the stakes were in this particular game. It had been intimated that some great penalty might be exacted by the Council of Worlds, a penalty that would affect each and every one of them. Discretion, urged the powers that be. No matter who you are, discretion.

Bao, who was still in his women's garb, said, "I am seeing gardens with much work invested. What numbers of persons are working to keep them so?"

"A lot," snarled Ornery from behind his veil.

"More sometimes than others," said Mouche, leaving himself a way out.

"How many right now?" asked Ellin, with a hint of asperity.

Mouche laid down his shears and tucked in his veils as he said slowly and pleadingly, "Mistress, we don't know. We are very lowly persons. We are not told things by those who hire us, except to go here or there, to do this or that. Sometimes there are a good many gardeners at meals in the servants' quarters. Other times, there are fewer. Some who work the gardens may also labor in the stables or the fields. To find out precisely how many, you would need to ask the head gardener or the steward."

This was the longest speech Ellin had managed to provoke from a veiled man as yet, and she noted the way in which it was delivered. Humbly, but eloquently, with a slight catch in the pronunciation that spoke of a minor speech impediment. Also, the man who spoke stood like a . . . well, a dancer. Or perhaps an actor. Reason told her he should have been a little stooped and gnarled if he had, in fact, worked a long time in the gardens. Reason told her, also, that the voice should not have sounded so very well trained. It was, in all respects, an attractive voice.

She turned to the other veiled figure and asked, "Is that so? Are you truly told so little?"

"It's true," grunted the other. "It's hardbread and tea, work until noon, soup and hardbread and work until sundown. That's life on Newholme."

"It sounds hard," said Gandro Bao.

"But satisfying," said Mouche with a grim look at Ornery. "We are content with our lot."

"Speak for yourself," said Ornery.

Mouche took a deep breath and spoke directly to Bao. "You ladies are not veiled. Sometimes we who are veiled find working in such conditions troublesome and itchy.

Sometimes we get irritable, as my friend is now. He is a good friend, however. I do not want to lose him *as my friend.* Please, do not say to anyone that *my friend* was anything less than accommodating to your needs."

The four stood staring at one another, open interest on the one side and veiled frustration on the other. With some vague idea of clarifying things, Ellin asked, "Will you take down your veils for us? Just for a moment."

Ornery and Mouche looked at one another, surprised, Mouche more shocked than Ornery, who had gone long times without veils on the ship.

"Please," begged Ellin. "We will not mention it to anyone, but we need to discover things about this world, and so much of it is hidden behind . . . veils."

"You are not getting into trouble over it," said Bao. "We are discovering all kinds of things, as Ellin says."

Well, they had been told to be polite! Though Mouche would have preferred not to display his battered countenance, he did so, with a quick glance around to be sure they were unobserved. The veil dropped at one side, and as it did so Mouche saw in his mind what he would have seen in a mirror, more or less what his interlocutors would see, and it struck him that he and the woman confronting him could have been kin. They had the same coloring. Same bones. Same long, thin hands. Only one of them was badly cut, of course.

Ellin and Bao searched the exposed face before them: ivory skin, a lock of pale hair showing under the cowl, dark brows, green eyes, a spatter of pale beard shadowing mouth and chin, and a new, horrid scar from beneath the left eye to the corner of the mouth. It seemed to be healing cleanly, but the flesh around it was livid and puffed. If it had not been for that, it would have been a handsome though, at the moment, rather furtive face.

"Why do you have to wear the veil?" Ellin asked.

"So as not to stir your insatiable lusts, lady," said Ornery in a slightly ironic voice, lowering his own veil to display a countenance tanned by the sea winds and the sun.

Ellin managed to look both amused and offended. "My what?"

"Your insatiable lusts," murmured Mouche. "So we are taught as children."

"At the moment, I have none," Ellin said. "Have you noticed that I have insatiable lusts, Gandro—ah, Gandra Bao?"

"I am seeing nothing of that kind, no," he said, bowing slightly in her direction. "Perhaps, to be helping us, this gentleman will be explaining?"

Mouche leaned on his rake, examining their faces for guile. "Women are easily moved to lust," he said at last, believing them to be truly interested. "It is part of their biological heritage, which is so very valuable to mankind. Their lusts serve their lineage, of course, since it forces them to bear and tend, which otherwise many would reject as uninteresting. Also, any child they bear is unequivocally their own, and the more males each female can associate herself with, the more likely she has links to survival. This is all sensible and correct as a survival technique, and women's instincts still thrust in that direction.

"Historically, so we are taught, the same was true for males. They also desire survival, and through the designs and desires imposed on them by their own genetic pattern, wish more than anything to guarantee their own posterity. We are taught how great predator cats kill cubs not their own. Other creatures also do this, including sometimes mankind males, who take up with a woman with children, then kill her children. Males want above all to guarantee their own line. So, in order that men have surety of their lineage and women not be lured into mismothering, men must not stir their lusts."

"This is making loving very dull," said Gandro Bao, with a seductive smile at Mouche.

Mouche ignored the smile. "Only for husbands! Say for them rather it is very stern and thoughtful. We are taught it is better that posterity be engendered with coolness, with much deliberate intention. Once that task is completed, however, women are entitled to compensatory joys, and for that they require a Consort who does not make it dull! Someone to indulge their lusts, but not engender children. You see?" Mouche had become carried away with his explanation and had said a good deal more than he intended.

Ellin said to herself, Oh-ho, so here is what compensation is offered. She and Bao looked at one another, eyebrows raised. Mouche and Ornery waited.

Finally, though he was sure he already knew, Bao asked, "What is being Consort?"

"A man trained to cosset women," said Ornery. "Like him," and she jerked a thumb in Mouche's direction.

Mouche merely blinked at her, refusing to be drawn by her chiding tone. From beyond the recently trimmed hedge, they heard the approach of persons, loudly talking to one another. Hastily, Mouche and Ornery rearranged their veils and turned to their work, busily raking while the two agents went thoughtfully back to their window, far above.

"What is hardbread?" Ellin asked.

Bao didn't know. He summoned a servant. "What is hardbread?"

"A kind of dried cracker that sailors eat, sir. Hardbread and tea. Or so they complain."

"Sailors, not gardeners?"

"Not gardeners, no. Gardeners eat garden stuff, and bread from the kitchen. Ships have no kitchens, so between barbecues and fish fries ashore, shipfolk eat hardbread."

"Interesting," said Ellin. "A sailor and a . . . a Consort. I would have guessed he was an actor. How did the two of them get to be friends?"

"I think they were meeting for first time not long ago," said Bao, "but men are striking up friendships quickly. Particularly in adversity. It is having survival benefit."

"I don't know what women do," she said thoughtfully. "Every time I thought I had made a woman friend, they switched me somewhere else. Even the dance classes. They kept moving them around, shuffling them. Sometimes you didn't see the same people for two shifts running."

"Forget what is past. Now I am being your friend," he said.

She gave him a somewhat suspicious look, finding nothing in his expression but placid good will. "Careful, Bao, or you may stir my insatiable lusts!"

He flushed, rubbing with a finger at the furrow between his eyes. "This is not my desire."

She scarcely heard him. "Besides, are there male-female friends who are truly friends? I've never heard of any."

"There are such friends," he said firmly. "And if there were never being any, we could decide to be the first."

When Ellin and Bao learned the nearest infant school was in Sendoph it was already quite late in the day. Accordingly, they postponed their interviews with children until the following morning. The Questioner emerged from her room in the early evening, seeming somewhat changed. Ellin and Bao had been with her shortly after a maintenance session aboard ship, and they were prepared for the slight uncertainty her appearance evoked.

"It's the machines," the Questioner had told them while aboard ship. "The mind is affected by the files and the maintenance machines and so is the body. If I were human, I would change with time, so the machines change me a little, perhaps to make me aware of time passing." This sounded good, though she felt it probably wasn't true. Since receiving the information about her donor minds—though certainly "donor" wasn't the proper word—she had found maintenance more than usually uncomfortable. Now that she *knew* about her indwelling minds, the buffer that held their memories from her own had been breached. Each time she came from maintenance she had learned more about their lives, and each time she felt more angry. Those who had killed her indwelling children were dead these several hundred years, but she hated them still! Hated them, was furious at them, and knew her duty required her to set all such feelings aside.

Ellin launched at once into a report of their conversation with the gardeners along with the inferences she and Bao had drawn from it, all of which Questioner entered into her memory, commenting, "So the one was a sailor and here he is, cutting away at the little hedges. And the other man is, according to the first, a Consort. . . ."

"He talks like an actor," said Ellin. "And he moves like a dancer. Don't you agree, Bao?"

"Yes, I am concurring," said Bao, his voice thickening slightly. The pale gardener resembled someone he had once known well but far too briefly. He cleared his throat. "His voice is projecting extremely well. I am having feelings of recognition, as when I am meeting someone of my own profession. His work is seeming to say that making women happy is mostly acting!"

The Questioner nodded ponderously. "Not a definition most women would appreciate, though I don't doubt its truth. More often it is women who do the acting. On Generis, in fact, prostitutes belong to the actors' guild, for it is recognized their profession is pretense. Let us consider: if there were other gardeners here before, and these are here now, presumably they had to get these from somewhere. So, they got them from nonessential areas? The sea and . . . whatever this other thing is?"

"Compensation," said Ellin. "Consorts provide pleasurable compensation. The Hags at the Temple referred to it, remember? But I forgot to ask them what it was."

"I am having one thing more to report," said Bao, referring to his notes. "There is most unpleasant smell. . . ."

"The one out at the back," the Questioner said, nodding as she pointed vaguely away. "Yes. I wandered about while you were in town. The smell is near the servants' quarters. My lexicon would identify this particular smell as a considerable stink."

"Oh, that at least," muttered Ellin. "Bao and I thought it was maybe animal excrement."

The Questioner considered this. "Animal excrement is accumulated near the stables and spread upon the fields. It smells, yes, but this stink has a much higher rating than animal excrement. The ooze of the volbers of Planet Gosh, a notable stench, rates a maximum of seven. This rates an eleven on a scale of twelve. A most putrescent and malodorous reek! Which raises an interesting question. How and why do the servants tolerate it?"

"It seems a minor matter," Ellin remarked, "but we can ask the servants."

"Mercy me, no." Questioner smiled. "One cannot imagine such fetor existing without Mistress Mantelby's knowledge, though it may be something she would prefer not to discuss. With that in mind, we'll play a little game to learn why it is she is not greatly offended."

She then took a few moments to rehearse them, then sent one of the Mantelby servants to Mistress Mantelby, requesting a guided stroll in the gardens for the Questioner and two of her aides.

Marool's immediate reaction was to reject any such claim on her time, but she caught herself. The Questioner's numerous entourage was causing a good deal of agitation, and the repression of Marool's normal appetites was becoming a grave annoyance. The sooner the Questioner could be satisfied and depart, the sooner Marool herself could resume her usual devotions.

She agreed, therefore, to meet the Questioner on the terrace. Questioner showed up with Bao, in wig, and Ellin, who had been coached to be quite Perkins in her persona, as polite as it was possible to be. They proceeded downward into the garden from the lofty and balustered terrace, Questioner leading the way without at all seeming to do so, while Ellin and Bao chatted inoffensively and commented effusively. Marool, though totally contemptuous of the Questioner and her entourage, was lulled into a state of complacent disdain.

"I so seldom have time merely to walk," Questioner murmured. "One would not think strolling much of an amusement, but we spent such a long time coming to your lovely world, and the ships are never large enough to walk in. I find this gentle ambulation quite wonderful. And may I say, Mistress Mantelby, how beautiful your gardens are. I have seen many, all over the sector, and yours are among the loveliest."

"Oh, that's so true," bubbled Ellin.

"How very kind," smiled Marool, soothed into amiability.

"Oh!" cried Ellin, on approaching a certain corner. "Nova roses. My favorite. May I pick one?"

Marool condescended, looking on with amusement while Ellin stepped lightly into the back of a bed where she clipped an enormous silver white blossom and put her nose into it. She then offered it to Marool, saying, "The scent is quite remarkable."

Marool sniffed at the rose. "It is wonderful," she said with an indifferent nod.

"Among the most fragrant in your garden," Questioner murmured.

"Indeed," Marool agreed.

They walked on, Ellin burbling on about the beauty and the fragrance of the garden as she sniffed at this and that and Bao offering this or that blossom for appreciation. At the end of their stroll, they departed from their hostess with fulsome expressions of gratitude, and Marool went back to the more decorous parts of her daily routine in a somewhat improved mood. Though Questioner was nothing but a piece of machinery, it was a polite piece of machinery and its aides were polite also. Marool could tolerate them.

Questioner said, "It's as I thought," she said. "Mantelby has no sense of smell! The Nova rose is odorless. Did you watch her when Bao waved the crimson stinkbrush in her face?"

Ellin nodded. "She didn't flinch. She has a smile like a shark, that one."

"What is it meaning?" asked Bao.

"I have no idea." Questioner showed her own teeth in a tigerish grin. "It goes down onto my list with all the other odd data."

"Odd?" Bao raised his eyebrows. "What things are you counting as odd?"

Questioner ticked them off on her fingers. "There's the oddity of the first colony, the one that disappeared. There's the oddity of the little houses too small for the people who live in them. There's the dirty streets and the stink out back, and the fact that Madam Mantelby has no sense of smell. There are those monumental schools that show up on the business inventory, seeming far too large for their stingy classes of little boys. Well, we have a clue to that, now, don't we?"

"Consorts?" asked Ellin. "Consort academies?"

"Assuredly. If they are trained to cosset women, they must be trained somewhere. In itself a strangeness. Well, most cultures have oddities of one kind or another."

"I am not understanding what you mean by strangeness," said Bao.

The Questioner seated herself comfortably, quite willing to educate a willing listener. "All societies maintain themselves by forcing personal behavior into a mold or pattern which the society calls its 'culture.' The patterns are imposed by natural or political conditions; for example, either recurrent drought or recurrent persecution can result in similar patterns. Most patterns require changes in behavior, and that requires changes in belief systems, or vice versa, sort of chicken and egg as to which comes first.

"So a few thousand years go by and the climate changes, or the politics, but the people still follow the same taboos because by now they believe their deity ordered them to do it. Long-practiced behaviors that started as a response to conditions, always fossilizes into 'traditional values,' that is, the only 'right way' to do things. At that point people no longer use the system in order to survive, the system uses them in order to survive. That's something people often don't understand. Systems are parasitical, they have a life of their own, and they, too, evolve and change and try to survive. The one fact that is true of all cultures, without exception, is that it never represents the free desires of the people who are jammed into it even when people are conditioned from childhood to accept uniformation."

"Really?" asked Ellin. "Never?"

Questioner grinned at her. "Only mavericks live in accordance with their desires, and even they don't often get away with it. They are usually labeled as troublemakers and gotten rid of. So, when the Questioner arrives on a new planet, the people show us the culture. Here, they say, this is what we are, we have nothing to hide. Genetic variation, however, guarantees that sometimes a rebel will be born, and you may be sure the culture has come up with a way to deal with him.

"So, in order to find out what's really going on, we investigate how the culture reacts to threats, we look for the people who do not fit, we look for the oddities, the strangenesses. When we have enough of them, we learn what the bones and nerves of the culture are really like, beneath the skin."

"But you're saying all societies are coercive," said Ellin in a troubled voice.

Questioner laughed. "But Honorable Ellin, of course they are. This is what makes reading history so amusing. Most cultures think of themselves as free while regarding others as coerced. They do so because they are following 'traditional values,' and the generations of coercion that resulted in those values is long forgotten. On Old Earth, in one society, women rejoiced that they were 'free' to have children, when in fact they had been coerced into excessive reproduction by a profit-driven culture that required a growing population. Men felt they were 'free' to ingest deadly substances or own deadly weapons, when in fact they were coerced into desiring them by industries that had to sell weapons and drugs to survive. Weapons, poisons, and large families were all parasites on the population. The people weren't free, they had been molded into consumers, which is what the mercantile culture needed.

"Such things can be most amusing," she said with a chuckle.

"I think the veils on the men is being coerced," said Bao.

"Of course they are," the Questioner agreed. "Usually it is women who are locked behind the veil, but veiling isn't unusual. I have heard two phrases that are unusual, however: 'mismothering' and 'blue-bodying.' These words are indicative of intricacies being kept from us."

"The gardener who isn't a gardener referred to mismothering,'' said Ellin. ''It was in the context of men desiring their own posterity.''

''Yes.'' The Questioner mused. ''In which case, to have a child by other than one's lawful mate would be mismothering. Depend upon it. When we find what the penalty is for that, it will be far worse than mere veiling.'' She rose to stare out the window across the manicured lawns of Mantelby Mansion.

''It's too early to say exactly what's going on, for we're still collecting data. . . .'' Her voice trailed off as she switched thoughts. ''Which reminds me: I've asked the technicians on the ship for a detailed report on the geological situation, and it will be finished by morning. First thing tomorrow, we'll summon a conveyance. The report will make a good excuse for me to call upon the Temple of the Hagions.''

40

Questioner Visits the Panhagion

The following morning, the Questioner, dressed in the force-shield cloak she wore outside for protection against everything short of meteorites, was standing with Ellin and Bao on the gravel drive, awaiting their conveyance, when the ground began to shake, the initial tremor building into a bone-twisting shudder that lasted some minutes but seemed, in retrospect, to have gone on for hours. The gardens shimmied, blooms were whipped from their stems to fly like shrapnel in all directions. The terraces snapped like so much sugar candy, the rough edges of the shards grinding against one another in a rasping mutter that almost drowned out the sound of the roar, the exhalation, the whatever-it-was from wherever-it-came that subsumed all other sounds.

When the ground stilled at last, Questioner was still standing obdurately erect, stabilizers extended, with Ellin and Bao each clinging to an immovable arm. Waiting for the last of the noise to subside, the Questioner asked in a mildly interested tone: "Read for me what the report says, Bao. That one you are still holding. And may I remark how dutiful you are to have held on to it."

Bao, between gritted teeth, hissed a commentary that fell far short of describing his feelings.

"Take a deep breath," said Questioner. "Release. Now again, in, out, in, out. Are you recovered?"

Bao muttered again, as Ellin broke into a titter that threatened full-fledged hysteria.

Questioner turned her head from side to side, examining them both. They still clung, as though for dear life. "It's over for the time being," she told them. "Look, down the driveway, where the horses attached to our carriage are having seizures of anxiety. Observe the driver in the exercise of his phlegmatic habitude. Does he not inspire you? Are you not moved to emulate his imperturbability?"

Ellin stepped carefully away, feet spread well apart, braced for the resumption of the tremor. Bao followed her example, keying the file he held and peering at it blindly. "It says," he gulped, "it says . . ."

"There, there," said Questioner impatiently. "What does it say?"

"It says the crust of the planet is becoming increasingly unstable . . ."

"How perceptive of them!" cried Ellin.

". . . and may reach, but has not yet reached, the point at which it endangers planetary life," he concluded, handing the report to Questioner, who scanned it rapidly.

The carriage, which eventually approached, was one that had been adapted to carry Questioner's massive form. She climbed the two steps without help and sat hugely upon the seat, the two aides across from her, the report open upon her lap.

"When you first went to the Temple," said Questioner to Ellin, "I recall that D'Jevier remarked about the volcanoes. Did it seem to you she was greatly disturbed?"

Ellin thought back. "Not greatly, no," she said, grabbing for a handhold as the carriage dropped an inch or two over a recently fallen slab. "Her perturbation seemed more dramatic than real."

Questioner scanned farther in the report. "Our planetologists tell us that the greatest damage thus far has occurred on the other side of this world, where islands have sunk or are sinking, all of them uninhabited, so far as anyone knows. Our scientists go on to say that what we are experiencing, this local disturbance in the vicinity of the Giles, happens every ten to twenty years in gravitic response to certain lunar configurations. So, if she, the Hag, has seen this happen before, why is she being so dramatic about it now?"

"She is dragging, perhaps, a dead fish along the way, hoping we will go sniffing after that rather than something else?" asked Bao.

"Rather than thinking of indigenes?" Ellin asked.

"Quite possibly," mused Questioner. "Of course, this latest eruption is exceptionally strong, and dangerous, but do they know that?"

Ellin tittered again, breathlessly. "It would be ironic if we all got swallowed up by some volcano, the indigenes along with the rest of us."

"Which could happen in time," said Questioner, dispassionately. "For our planetologists say that if present conditions persist, the settled areas will be endangered. Further, they say they can find no geological reason for this instability except an 'unforeseen and mysterious change in the movements of the crust itself, though there is no detectable change in its nature.' I find that very interesting."

"Interesting." Ellin gulped. "She finds it interesting."

Questioner turned toward her. "We all die, Ellin Voy. Even I, in time. I was designed to be interested in all things, including those that repulse mankind, like slime and strange insects, like plague and famine and dying. You may be interested, too, when you have a calm moment to consider it. Now do as I bade Gandro Bao. Breathe, breathe, and calm yourself."

The rest of the journey was made in nervous silence by the dancers, in apparent serenity by Questioner, and in some apprehension by the horses. The driver was habitually glum, and nothing had changed him. The passengers were met at the foot of the Temple stairs by Onsofruct herself, her face pallid and her hands moist, who conducted them up the stairs and into the forecourt.

"I'm sure you are not female in the sense our worshippers would understand," said Onsofruct to Questioner. "But in some cases, appearances are all. Shall we go into the Temple?"

They did so, seating themselves on the lowest bench, the one nearest both the lectern and the effigies of the Hagions. There were worshippers scattered about in the Sanctuary, some kneeling, most of them standing quite still or seated upon cushions. Older women, some very old, sat on the high-backed benches around the sides. Though the air was hazed with dust, the Temple seemed undamaged by the recent tremors.

Questioner scanned the interior of the lofty space, comparing it to the account Ellin had recorded. She saw the book on the lectern, rose and went over to it, flipping the pages with one hand, too rapidly for the others to see anything but a blur. When she returned to sit beside them, she had put into memory the total contents of every page, including the chemical traces left on each page by the fingers and breath of those who had taken time to read it. A separate part of her mind went to work analyzing what it had read and cross-referencing persons to pages.

She smiled at Onsofruct, took out the geological report, keyed it, and turned it so that the Hag could see it.

"Your concern about the stability of Newholme's crust is well founded."

Onsofruct stared at her, mouth very slightly open, thinking vaguely that she and D'Jevier had been blown by their own bomblet. Though the Hags had purposefully overstated their fears, it seemed this current instability was living up to their pretended anxieties.

Smoothly, Questioner continued, "What we find most interesting about this is that the geologists can find no reason whatsoever for this increasing instability. There is no significant change in the geothermal variations of the mantle or the core. There is no gross change in the slow movement of the plates or the frictional heat causing upwellings from mantle through crust. Our technicians tell me, and I find this imaginative, that it is as though the world's crust was suffering discomposure. A planetary eczema, perhaps?''

Onsofruct smiled, a humorless smile, her eyes focused on some other time or place.

Questioner shook her head with seeming sadness. ''Madam, pay attention. Whatever other problems you may have here on Newholme, they pale beside this one. Whatever guilts you are attempting to hide from me, they are small beside this actual danger of destruction. Actual, proximate, and total destruction.''

''Then the Men of Business . . . they are right?'' Her voice sounded incredulous and shrill. She cleared her throat. ''I thought . . . I thought perhaps they had overstated the case.''

''No,'' murmured Questioner. ''I am amazed the Temple is still standing after that shaking this morning.''

''When we took over the building, it was retroengineered to withstand earthquake,'' muttered Onsofruct. ''Most of the larger buildings in Sendoph and Naibah were either reinforced or designed to be quake resistant from inception. There are always . . . tremors.''

''Ah . . .'' said Questioner. ''Madam, this may sound quite silly to you, but do you have any legends or myths concerning this shaking? Hmmm?''

''Legends?'' she faltered.

''Most societies have stories about natural phenomena: volcanoes, waterfalls, windstorms, whatever. Fire goddesses; wind gods; ocean deities. You have been upon this world long enough to accumulate a mythology. Do you recall any such?''

''I do,'' came a voice from behind them.

They turned to see D'Jevier, who was observing Onsofruct with troubled eyes.

''My cousin,'' murmured Onsofruct.

''D'Jevier Passenger,'' the new arrival introduced herself. ''We are close cousins, yes, but we did not share all aspects of our rearing. My cousin may not have heard a children's story that I remember well. Did you ever hear it, Onsy? About the snake at the center of the world?''

Onsofruct flushed and glared at her sibling, who only smiled in return, saying: "Though it may be embarrassing to recount a . . . nursery tale, the matter does seem to be of some urgency. Surely the Questioner would not ask if it were not important."

Some signal passed between them. Onsofruct flushed again, began a retort, then caught herself, mumbling, "Oh . . . well. Yes, I remember hearing it. But my cousin is correct, it's only a children's story. A fairy tale."

"Tell it," instructed the Questioner. "Sometimes we find truth in the unlikeliest places."

"Well . . . let me see. The Summer Snake is curled in the center of the world, like a baby snake in an egg. . . ."

"Why is it called Summer Snake?" asked Questioner.

"Because that is when it came," said D'Jevier. "It came in summer, and its name is Niasa."

"You mean, then is when it was laid?" asked Ellin.

"Laid, I suppose. *Came* is what I remember."

Onsofruct resumed: ". . . And there are moon dragons, Joggiwagga, who keep track of the moons, for when the moons get lined up and pushy, it makes Niasa uneasy and wakeful, and the egg shakes. So then its mother soothes . . ."

"Not the mother," D'Jevier corrected. "It was Bofusdiaga."

"I thought Bofusdiaga was its mother." Onsofruct frowned.

"No. Don't you recall? She was the mother, and Little Niasa was the egg. Big Summer Snake laid her egg at the center of the world, where it is nice and warm. And when she hears Little Niasa crying, she cries also, very loudly, and then the Corojumi and Bofusdiaga hear her. . . ."

"Who or what are they?" murmured Ellin.

D'Jevier shook her head, shrugging. "Bofusdiaga is something very large and singular. The Corojumi are smaller and numerous. In the stories, Bofusdiaga is the sleep tender, the one who lullabies, and the Corojumi weave the dreams that keep the snake from waking. Also, Bofusdiaga sets the sails, and the Corojumi hold the tiller, or other way round, and they sail the ship of dreams across the pillared seas to Niasa's nest."

"They want to *keep* the snake from waking?" asked Ellin.

"Yes." Both the cousins nodded. "So it won't hatch too soon."

"And from whom did you hear this charming story?" asked the Questioner.

A momentary stillness.

"Our . . . nursemaids," said D'Jevier. "When we were little."

"And what were their names?"

"Mine died," said Onsofruct.

Questioner glanced at her aides and smiled, a sardonic smile that said she knew they were lying.

D'Jevier said, in a tone of bright and totally spurious helpfulness, "Mine was a nice old lady, but she also died, years ago. Her name was Velgin. Emily Velgin. She didn't have any family. She was sterile. She never married."

"Her parents are no doubt dead, too," murmured the Questioner. "And all her family."

"Certainly." They said it almost together, both nodding.

Questioner rose, still smiling, thanking them fulsomely, letting them know with every movement and word that she knew they were liars of the worst stripe, whom she would pretend to believe for the nonce, for reasons of her own. As they moved toward the curtained arches, the floor came alive beneath them, dancing under their feet. High in the vault, a window cracked, then broke, shedding a shower of tinkling ruby glass.

"Perhaps Little Niasa has colic." Questioner smiled. She had thrown her protective cape across Ellin at the first shiver. "Perhaps it writhes helplessly, seeking to escape evil dreams. Night terrors, as they are sometimes called. If Big Niasa could waken it, perhaps it could be soothed, given hot milk and a cookie. Or, since it is reptilian, a live mouse."

She lifted her arm, releasing Ellin.

"Perhaps," said D'Jevier, her forehead beaded with tiny drops, her hand clammy when Ellin grasped it as they said good-bye. Bao waited for them outside on the steps of the Temple, his own face fearful. They felt three more tremors of descending degrees of violence on their way back to Mantelby.

Where they confronted rebellion.

"Look at this," snarled the protocol officer, waving a copy of the geological report. "I've just had a chance to read it. It says the world is going to come apart. We aren't required to sit here and wait for it, are we?"

"Is it indeed?" Questioner was calm as she removed the cloak. "Would you like to leave the planet?"

"We should all go at once."

"I am inclined to agree that you should, yes. I am staying here for the time being. I imagine, though I am not certain, that Ellin and Bao will choose to stay with me. That is no reason, however, why the other members of my entourage should remain here. Your work is largely done. You will no doubt be more comfortable on the ship, and I should be able to maintain a link with the ship while it remains safely in orbit."

For a fleeting moment, Ellin readied herself to shout a denial. She would go, go at once, not stay, things were too dangerous. She tried to formulate a graceful announcement that wouldn't sound like total hysteria, but the words wouldn't come. Why not? Could it be that she didn't want to go? After a moment's shuddering indecision, she admitted it to herself. She wanted to . . . to feel like this. She had never felt like this, tingling like this. Absurdly, she remembered the little boy who had wanted tornadoes! He had been right! She also wanted tornadoes. She wanted to see what was going to happen.

Turning, she caught Bao's eyes on her and flushed. He had told her to put out roots and grow, and now he was watching her do it! He made a comical face and winked at her, accurately interpreting her confusion.

The protocol officer departed, returning briefly to say that all eight of them were leaving for the shuttle and would return to the ship immediately.

"And you're really going to let them go?" asked Ellin.

"Have they contributed anything to our inquiry? The

technicians—who are not political appointees, thank whomever arranged it—have given us considerable help, but they've done it from orbit and can go on doing so. So long as we can reach the ship, what do we need these people for?"

"I am not seeing why you are having those people in the first place," sniffed Bao.

Questioner laughed, a mirthless bark. "My dear young people, they are foisted upon me. A century or so ago, the Council of Worlds decided that providing me with an entourage would open up opportunities for some of their juvenile kinfolk. Many of the functions of COW are cluttered up with witless fetchers and carriers who are somehow related to council members. A pity Haraldson never forbade nepotism!"

"If you are not needing them, are you really needing us?" Bao asked.

"I am. I really need nonthreatening persons with alert, questioning minds and enough good sense to spot the oddities. Thus far, you've done well. So, let us proceed."

A Mantelby servant came in to announce that dinner was served in the adjacent salon, to which Questioner, Ellin, and Bao immediately repaired to indulge themselves in a long, elaborate, and delicious meal. The servants had just set dessert on the table—a fluffy concoction of fruits and cream which Ellin had been looking forward to with delicious guilt since it had appeared on the morning menu card—when the link to the ship announced itself.

Bao spoke to the Gablian watch officer, who asked for the staff member who was handling the geological reports.

Bao informed the ship that the entire staff should be aboard. A long silence presaged a denial by the watch officer that any of the staff members were anywhere on the ship.

Questioner rose and approached the link. "Commander, I sent all my entourage except the two young Earthians back to the ship some hours ago."

"I was alerted to expect them. They never arrived."

"Hold fast," suggested the Questioner. "Let's see what we can find out here." She turned to Bao and Ellin, putting on an exasperated face. "Would you mind, young people? Go see what's holding them up?"

Ellin had a mouth full of delight and her eyes shut. Reluctantly, she swallowed.

"You, a dancer, consuming such stuff!" said Questioner in mock reproof.

"I know," Ellin cried guiltily. "But then, I keep thinking it might be the last chance I ever have."

"Last chance, child?"

Seduced by food and wine, her thoughts burst out without censor. "Oh, Questioner, something's building to a climax! I keep hearing the music for it, all those tremorous violins, the slow descending basses, each note deeper into the fabric of the world, the brasses, muted, like voices calling in a dark wood. . . ."

"All day she has been hearing this, nodding her head in time to this music," confirmed Bao. "I am finding it quite interesting."

Questioner nodded, unimpressed by this idea. "Very poetic, my dear, but hardly your last chance. Your dessert will wait for you."

As they departed, Questioner tasted the dessert and approved. It was not necessary to eat more than one taste, as she could recall the flavor and texture at will. Which she did as she sat, musing, going over everything she had learned on this planet. She had already decided mankind could not be allowed to continue on Newholme. The presence of indigenes was uncontrovertible. If mankind had settled in ignorance of their presence, they should have reported it the moment the first indigenes showed up. The fact they had not condemned them, and she had no intention of arguing with Haraldson's edicts. And then there was this viral disease that constricted the female population. . . .

But there were other riddles still to be solved, interesting habits, like the reverse veiling and the Consorts, and there was also this strange geological business. . . .

Gradually it occurred to her that a very long time had passed since Ellin and Bao had left in search of the members of the entourage.

A steward was summoned and asked to go find Bao and Ellin. He departed, veils flapping. After a short time, he returned. The Questioner's aides were nowhere to be seen. Neither were any other of the Questioner's people. The last anyone had seen of *them* was when an understeward had served a light meal in their salon some time ago while they were packing. Their salon was now empty of persons. None of them had asked for transportation. They had not set out on foot or they would have been seen.

Questioner told him to wait outside, dismissing him with a wave of her hand. Now what? Before she had a chance to think, Marool Mantelby was at the door. Her staff had advised her of this strange disappearance. Could she offer any help?

Questioner, regarding the woman with close attention, saw that she panted, her skin was flushed and her eyes darted in heightened excitement of a feral sort.

"I think it likely they have gone off on some expedition of their own," murmured Questioner.

"Then . . . they may be gone for some little while?" asked Marool, licking the corner of her lips.

"Does this cause some domestic disruption?"

"Not at all. I merely . . . wondered."

The Questioner smiled her meaningless, social smile. "Do not fret over it, Madam Mantelby. I'm sure all will be explained."

Marool bowed her way out with suspicious alacrity, Questioner staring after her, trying to decipher what the woman was up to. The understeward was still standing in the hall, and Questioner beckoned to him through the open door.

"Ma'am," he said respectfully.

"Will you lead me to the the quarters where our missing staff members stayed?"

The understeward bowed and led the way out into the wide, deeply carpeted corridor. The suite given over to the staff members was on the same level, though around several corners and down a long side corridor almost to the end. At the door, Questioner told the understeward to wait while she went in. There she stood looking slowly around herself. All the belongings one would expect were there, some neatly packed into cases, others piled ready for packing.

Questioner approached the wall, examining it with sensors in the tips of her fingers, moving along it, centimeter by centimeter. After a time, she touched an ornamental cartouche and stepped back as the wall swung open. She looked through into a passageway that ran in both directions behind the wall. Questioner touched the cartouche again, and the wall closed silently upon itself.

"I read no evidence that mankind has ever been in that corridor," she murmured to herself, as she did sometimes when alone, impressing the things she saw into memory with the words she spoke. "No Earthian, no settler, none of my non-Earthian aides. There is evidence of some other living thing, however. The same living things I sensed in the little houses behind the gardener's quarters."

She moved around the room, trying several other manipulations with similar effect. At the fourth hidden door she said to herself, "Here. They went in here. I can smell them. All of them. I scent Ellin's perfume." She shut the opening and turned away, eyes unfocused.

"Madam Questioner. . . ?" queried the understeward from outside in the hall.

"One moment," she said, going on with her interior colloquy. "Did Mantelby do this? No. For if she had known about these sneakways in her walls, she would not have come to us to ask about our missing people. She would have searched for them herself, lest the abduction be laid at her door. No, the people who built them, the people who use them, are not mankind. Human, yes, probably, as Haraldson defined human, but not mankind."

She strolled toward the door. "So now, upon this stage, the indigenes appear, almost magically. How interesting. Now, what did they want with my witless entourage and my two good little dancers? Hmmm?"

In the doorway she stopped, looking around once more. "I find an interesting pattern: The planet was settled by mankind, and all the original settlers disappeared. Then it was settled again by mankind; this time the settlers didn't disappear. Almost as though whatever had taken the first bunch had learned whatever it needed to know about mankind. Then we come along, bringing with us examples of several races that are fully mankind but different in appearance, and whoops, they disappear. As though whoever took them wanted to try a new flavor?

"But for what? And did they also seize up Ellin and Bao, or did those two adventurous children go off after them?"

She threw back her head, saying in a loud voice, "I hereby announce my intention of going wherever my staff members have been taken. I would appreciate an escort, but if none is provided, I will take whatever route I can find."

She moved majestically into the hallway. "I am talking to myself," she said to the servant. "Or to anyone else who can hear me and take the matter under advisement."

41

Assorted Persons In Pursuit

Ellin had spoken of an unheard music that was building to a climax. Questioner had taken it for mere fantasy. Now, however, as she walked back to her own suite with every detector at full alert, she heard real subsonics with a wave length so long that it seemed to pulse like a heartbeat through the fabric of the world. Something very large was moving, or living, or thinking. So, let calm preparations be made.

The understeward trailed after her to wait outside her door, shifting from foot to foot, white showing around the edges of his eyes. Poor thing, she thought, he was frightened half out of his wits, thinking he would be next.

"My aides recently met two gardeners," she said. "One is actually a sailor. The other is, I think, a Consort in Training. Please, go to their quarters and tell them that I, the Questioner, need them at once. Have them bring with them whatever they would take on a journey. And come quickly back."

When he went away, almost at a run, she started putting together a pile of equipment: rations, lights, stout clothing and shoes for Bao and Ellin. In Ellin's room, and Bao's, she found dancing shoes, which she packed up along with everything else.

Meantime, the understeward had wakened the gardener and was spending too much time explaining.

"It'll be my back," the gardener lamented for the tenth time.

"Not if the Questioner ordered it," the understeward said between his teeth. "We were all told to do whatever she ordered, and that means you, too."

"What's going on?" asked a sleepy voice from the doorway.

The understeward turned, recognized Mouche as one of those the Questioner had asked for, and said, "The Questioner needs you and your friend. She said one of you was a sailor and one was a Consort and for you to put together equipment for a journey and come at once."

Ornery thrust his head between Mouche's shoulder and the door. "She needs a sailor? For what?"

"I don't know what she needs," the understeward cried. "All I know is, the Questioner wants you, so go get your things."

"Things?" said Mouche wonderingly.

"Whatever you need to go on a journey. She said a journey. Clean stockings. Clean underwear. Water bottles." The understeward fell silent, frantically trying to think what he, himself, would pack for a journey. He wasn't sure he even had a water bottle.

"Who's going to tell Madam Mantelby they're gone?" asked the gardener in a grumpy tone. "You going to tell her? Now?"

The gardener looked at him significantly, jerking his head toward the back of the house. "Not now, you fool."

"Oh," the gardener jittered, licking his lips. "Right."

Mouche and Ornery went back to their quarters for their few belongings, then joined the understeward on the path, only to move quickly off it, for it crunched too greedily beneath their feet. Even the servant chose to pad up toward the house on the silent grass. He had left a side door open, which he shut and locked behind them before leading the way up the stairs, demanding silence with every movement, achieving it, and moving in it as a fish in quiet water. Like shadows, they slipped into the room where the Questioner waited.

"Well," she murmured, when they had been escorted in, when the understeward had been dismissed and the door shut tightly behind him. "Are you prepared for adventure?"

Ornery merely stared, as was his habit when confronting an ambiguous situation. Mouche responded as taught, with a low bow and a well-spoken salutation expressing the deep honor he felt at being able to serve the Questioner.

"How long did it take you to learn that?" Questioner asked in an interested voice. "Years, I'd imagine."

"I have been five years in training, Madam."

"How many more before you're what they consider employable?"

Mouche bowed again, noting the amusement in the voice and reminding himself that this was said to be an artificial creature from whom he should not take offense. "It would depend upon the discrimination of my patroness, Ma'am. I am quite good at some things already. I am not, however, fully qualified as a judge of wine or as a gourmet cook. My musical skills require honing. Perhaps another five years. . . ."

"Then the pleasures you offer are not only of the . . . how would you say it?"

"Bedsports, Ma'am. No. Not only those."

She smiled ironically. "A pity to waste one so highly trained on so uncertain a mission. We are going underground, and we may run some risk. I have heard there are oceans under this planet, oceans sailed by strange and marvelous creatures."

Mouche's eyes lit up. "I don't know where your mission will take you, Ma'am, but I will not be a supernume if you are going by sea. Since a child, I have dreamed of the sea. I have studied it, as well. I will not be a bad companion."

"And you." Questioner turned her eyes on Ornery. "What about you?"

"A sailor, Ma'am," Ornery said. "Only that. Fond of the sea, yes. It's a good life. Less troublesome than shore, so most of us think."

"Well. It may be we will find strange seas that warrant a sailor's efforts, though to begin with you will be mere beasts of burden to carry the supplies my aides were not given time to take with them. You may leave those veils and outer garments here. The packs I have made up are in the next room."

When Mouche dropped his veil, she took his face in her hands and turned it to catch the light. "Ah," she said. "This needs attention, boy."

"We have had no opportunity, Ma'am," he said.

"Well, it won't get any worse in the near future. Perhaps I can do something about it when we've finished. If we finish."

Ornery and Mouche eagerly took off the shapeless gardener's robes and loaded themselves with Questioner's gear, being not overburdened with the double load, since their own supplies were scanty.

"Is that all you brought?" Questioner asked.

"It is all we have, Ma'am," Mouche replied. "We were pressed into service with only the clothes on our backs and our small packs. May we assist you with your own burden?"

"I need none. Everything I need is provided for in what I am. I have many tools and gizmos built in, and maintenance is just over. I should be highly efficient for many days. You may follow me."

They did so, going silently out through the wide hallways toward the room where Questioner had found the sneakways in the walls.

42

Marool Worships Morrigan

While with the Wasters, Marool's worship of Morrigan had been a daily event, shared with some, hidden from none. During her self-imposed banishment, however, self-interest had dictated that she either give up Morrigan entirely or adopt a more covert style of adoration. During her so-called pilgrimage to Nehbe, Marool had seen the work of a local though reclusive artist. He was called the Machinist, an eremetic genius living in the hills near the town and earning a livelihood by making ornamental devices as well as prototype machines for practical use. He was not a Family Man. He had no g' to his name. He gave the impression of living in a separate world, but was nonetheless sufficiently connected to the real one to be available to Men of Business needing improved designs of rug looms or grain threshers or goods wagons or anything else they could conceive of.

He could build virtually anything.

"Anything?" asked Marool.

"Oh, but not f . . . f . . . f . . . for you, Ma'am. He does not work for women."

Someone had hired the stutterer to introduce Marool to the Machinist's work. This someone had also suggested that Marool's personality throve upon contrariness. The idea that someone would not do something she wanted done was guaranteed to pique her interest, and she demanded to meet the Machinist.

No, no, said her informant. The Machinist was very secretive, demanding that all his business be done by written orders left in his post box a mile or so from his lair. He saw no one, and no one saw him.

Marool asked why.

Her informant's reply was quite spontaneous. "Well . . . Ma'am, b . . . b . . . because he smells. You try to talk to him, you can't b . . . b . . . breathe!"

Smells didn't bother Marool. Before returning to Mantelby Mansion, Marool met with the Machinist. She did so secretly, taking no escort except two Hagger bodyguards who stayed at the post box while she went on to the house. On her first visit she explained her desires to the stringy, dirty-fingered, hot-eyed man, while he scribbled notes, asked few questions, and licked his lips while he suggested one or two refinements. On her second visit, she inspected the work so far completed and found it to her taste.

When she returned to Mantelby Mansion, she needed a place to put the device, and her grandfather's wine cellar came to mind. Margon Mantelby the elder, Marool's grandfather, had used a natural cavern below the mansion as a cellar for Mantelby wines, the product of family-owned vineyards. The cool catacombs had been presided over by a cellar master of some reputation, and the wine had been drunk during the ostentatious banquets given in honor of this or that family achievement.

When Marool had returned to the mansion, it had taken only a few trials to convince her she had no use for the wines since she could neither smell nor taste them, so she converted their vaulted spaces into what she called her *playroom*. Power for the devices was no problem. A sizeable tributary of the Giles flowed down the canyon behind Mantelby Mansion, and Margon the Elder had long ago partnered with his neighbors in building a small dam and hydroelectric plant to provide domestic lighting and the pumping of water. Marool's fantastic devices did not fit either category, but she did not trouble herself over that.

The first machine was installed shortly after Marool returned from Nehbe, and in due time she added others. Among them was a device that amplified sexual pleasure by almost but not quite choking the participants during the act, and another that administered a carefully planned series of drugs during excitement. Some devices turned and twisted, holding bodies in ways that allowed persons—one or two or several simultaneously—to juxtapose or penetrate one another in ways otherwise unlikely. And finally, there was one very complicated machine that started its cycle doing interestingly erotic things and went on doing them, with increasing pain, pressure, and intensity, until the participants perished.

Some of them Marool used with her playmates; others were used by her playmates, or her soon to be ex-playmates, on one another while Marool watched. All the machines were designed to be unstoppable except by Marool herself, and she wore the master key upon her wrist and never removed it, not even to bathe or sleep. On that same hand she wore a great obsidian seal ring bearing in intaglio the fanged, flame-haired face of Morrigan.

The furnishings of the playroom included a closet of masks, costumes, and devices, as well as an ornate cabinet of drugs that could, variously, increase pleasure or enable participants to tolerate quite high levels of pain. Though the cabinet was locked, the lock was a simple one, an oversight by Marool, who gave her partners credit for little intelligence and had not thus far been mistaken in doing so.

Marool customarily spent part of every day in this special place. Since the Questioner had arrived with her entourage, however, Marool had not been near it. Though the Questioner and her two assistants customarily kept to their own rooms during daylight and always did so at night, the Questioner's strange-looking aides were ubiquitous about Mantelby Mansion. Marool had found them at all hours, walking here, looking there, always very interested in what was going on, always intrusively present whenever Marool even thought about amusing herself. The moment Marool learned the entourage had disappeared, she sent a peremptory note to the servants' quarters ordering Bane and Dyre to join her. She took the absence of the entourage as a sign from Morrigan that she need no longer deprive herself of her pleasures.

Aside from venting the pressures she had built up, there was another reason to bring the brothers to the playroom, one she had so far delayed dealing with. Though Bane and Dyre were innately cruel, though they did not balk at inflicting considerable pain even on one another, qualities that Marool quite enjoyed, the difficulty of keeping the brothers nearby had become prohibitive. She could find other playmates who would be equally cruel and vicious but who did not stink so. She herself could not smell them—or thought she could not, though her body responded to the presence of their smell nonetheless. No matter what she did or did not sense, her servants could smell them too well. Several specialized and expensive staff members had simply gaped, gasped, and fainted away when in the brothers' vicinity, and they had been unable thereafter to resume their duties. Her latest nephew-steward had confirmed, though only when asked, that the odor given off by the two was asphyxiating, and that it grew worse with each passing day.

She had decided, therefore, to unite pleasure with necessity by proceeding at once to the final machine, the one Bane and Dyre had been dying to try. Marool always enjoyed what she thought of as the end game. The preliminary teasing; the erotic challenge; the moment when it finally dawned on the participant(s) just what was happening; the pleading; the screaming; the final moaned and broken phrases of adoration, when Marool told the victims she might stop if they loved her enough.

Thus, when Marool's playmates arrived, she greeted them with every appearance of joy and with a generous supply of the treats they liked the most, drinks and rich foods and euphoric drugs. She engaged them in a little preliminary titillation, during which she herself indulged in several glasses of wine that Bane offered her, for the relaxing effect, not the taste. She had had a long, thirsty abstention!

It was Bane himself who suggested the special machine, the only one they had not yet used.

"You're too young," teased Marool, who was enjoying herself inordinately and was in no hurry. "That's for grown-up men."

"I'm as grown-up as you need," boasted Bane, with a sidelong glance at his brother. "Both of us are."

"Oh, you wouldn't like it." Marool giggled, a little surprised at the sound coming from her own mouth. My, she had had a little sniffy more than usual. Had Bane slipped some of the euphoric into her wine? Naughty boy. Life was too pleasant at the moment to scold him. She breathed deeply and giggled once again. "It requires a very sophisticated taste."

"House Genevois gave me sophisticated taste," Bane said, stroking her thigh. "That's why I got sent there."

"Who sent you there, dear? How much did you cost Madame?"

"We're not Madame's stupid Hunks," asserted Dyre. "Bane and me, we're destined for great things. Our daddy, Thunder his name is, he paid for us because he's got a future planned for us."

"Sons of thunder," said Marool. "Oooh, so powerful."

"Powerful enough for any old machine," muttered Bane, flexing his muscles and admiring his erect phallus as reflected fragmentarily among many mirrors.

"Well, then," Marool purred. "If you think so. . . ."

She staggered to her feet and directed them, Bane there, Dyre here. They were acquiescent, even eager, but somehow, the machine didn't fit properly. Bane got out of the proper position and knelt down, fussing with the mounting, Dyre turned and twisted, and then joined Bane. "Damn thing," he muttered.

"It's perfectly all right!" She laughed, still feeling quite giggly and giddy, far more amused than annoyed.

"It's not all right. There's something there that pinches! You don't believe me, you try it."

Which she did in a state of high amusement, only to find the cinches closed and the bands locked, and Bane trying to wrench the ring off her finger as the machine started its initially gentle motion.

"Stop this!" she shrieked through a gale of laughter. "You don't know what you're doing!"

Bane stopped trying for the ring and growled into her ear. "We know. Our daddy, he told us how you're the one took us from him and left us in the care of nobodies. He had to come hunting for us over near Nehbe. He says to tell you, him and the Machinist, they're old friends and kinfolk. He says to tell you, this is his payback for the daughter you were supposed to bear him. He says, tell Marool good-bye for me!"

"Your daddy?" she gasped, breathlessly. "Who?"

Bane was hastily donning his clothes. "Thunder and Ashes, our daddy. You knew him, Marool, bitch. Don't say you didn't. There was witnesses, and they told us all about you."

"Ashes!" she cried, suddenly and horridly aware.

"He found us over near Nehbe, with that goat farmer, where you sent us, you bitch."

"Oh, by Morrigan, do you know who your mother was? Do you know who I am?"

"Our mother died birthing us, and you're the bitch stole her babies. Daddy said we had to get rid of you before we could get our inheritance. That's all we need to know." He struck her then, hard across the mouth, shutting off further words, then ran for the tunnel entrance that gave upon the gardens. Dyre was not far behind him as the machine shifted into a slightly more energetic mode of action.

43

A Journey Toward Dosha

As Questioner set out on her search for her vanished entourage, she swept the hallways with all her senses, hoping that all the servants were abed or about some other business, for she did not want to explain where she was going. She did not want her ship or the Council of Worlds to be involved in this. Though she knew she was probably being watched from every side by unseen eyes, they did not trouble her, for they were not the eyes of mankind.

When she had discovered the wallways in the small salon, she had closed each one behind her, but when she, Mouche, and Ornery entered the room, one of them had been reopened. The wideflung panel disclosed the same narrow tunnel she had identified as the route taken by Ellin and Bao. A lit candle sat on the floor inside the opening as though to say, *This way.*

"You, boy?" Questioner asked. "Name?"

"Mouche, Madam."

"You will lead."

Mouche looked at the opening with a feeling of dawning delight. He forgot his pain. This sneakway was familiar to him, totally familiar, so like those wallways in House Genevois that it was obviously made by the same creatures and obviously . . . oh, obviously leading to the same kind of place. He shut his eyes for only a moment, calling upon his Hagion to let him become an intrepid explorer whose delight was entering dark, unknown territory in search of heaven knew what.

Questioner's eyelids rose, an expression of surprise that she used seldom and felt almost never. The boy had accomplished a very pretty somatic maneuver there, in very short time. She had been monitoring his internal pressures and tensions, as well as smelling certain secretions in body and brain. All had responded to whatever invocation he had made. He was now exactly the person she would have selected to assist her in this journey. Not foolhardy, but daring and quite ecstatic about the venture!

Well, it must be conditioning. No doubt sexual consorts would need a good deal of conditioning. She would make time before she left the planet to speak to the head of his school or academy or whatever it was. If she survived to leave the planet.

"You next. What's your name, sailor?"

"Ornery, Ma'am."

"Well you then, sea*man* Ornery." She winked at Ornery, much confusing her. "And, I bring up the rear. I am massive enough to keep almost anything off your back. If I say *back* in a loud, imperative voice, both of you come back close to me. I have certain defenses to help us all survive."

Mouche oozed into the opening in the wall, turned briefly to catch the freshest airs—assuring himself that outside must lie in that direction—and advanced into the wind. The sneakway sloped slightly downward, and since the small salon was on the second level of the Mantelby Mansion, it stood to reason they would have to go down to get away from the house.

After shutting the opening behind them, Questioner emitted a cone of light wide enough to contain herself and

Ornery as they wound slowly along the passage. The slope soon steepened into a ramp, the ramp gave way to steps leading into blackness. They slowed, taking more time to light each step, each corner, each twist and turn of the way.

The stairs and ramps, some of which creaked ominously under Questioner's weight, were interrupted by horizontal stretches with frequent peekholes. Mouche glanced at a few of these with practiced ease, which Questioner noted before turning her own attention to the spyholes. She judged they were winding through a part of the house devoted to the servants, for there was much scurrying and late-night tidying going on.

At one point a stench came through some few holes like that from a fresh dunghill, and Questioner turned down her receptors. Her senses were connected to her mind, just as people's were, and she found the smell atrocious.

They dropped farther. The smell did not depart, though it abated, and a certain deadened quality in the sound of their feet told them they were now on soil or stone rather than wooden floors, though the peekholes were still aboveground. The sneakways had obviously been designed to give maximum access without regard for the distance between points, and they had walked quite a long winding way to drop only these few meters. They continued to go downward, losing the peekholes on one side, and soon heard a sound, a rhythmic and inexorable ratcheting that grew louder as they progressed.

Mouche stopped in his tracks, his breath coming quickly, as though at some suddenly perceived threat. Questioner told Ornery to stay in place as she went forward to the place Mouche stood.

"What is it, boy?"

"The sound, Madam. Not the mechanical sound, but the screaming? Do you hear it?"

Until that moment, she had accepted the noise as mechanical, as of some unoiled bearing, some ungreased pivot shrieking across a metal plate. A moment's concentration told her Mouche was right. The ratcheting was machinery, but the other sound could be from a living creature.

Questioner took the lead. They went forward and down another flight as she ran her sensor-tipped fingers along the wall. Here, and there, and then, yes, here, a door. She tried it in various ways until it sighed open, flooding the place they stood with increased noise and a wave of the familiar stench.

They stood in a cellar, stone floored, rock walled, softly lit, luxuriously carpeted, hung with great swaths of satin and velvet and centered by a warm fountain that steamed gently in the cool air. All around them stood the horrid legacy of some nightmare craftsman: ogre-racks of brass and steel, chimeric skeletons of gold and silver, squatted toad bones of hard iron, all wed to springs and cams and drive shafts, soft cushioned in places and fanged in others, all with red-lit eyes staring and metal arms spread wide.

The atrocious squealing and screaming came from the far side of the room, where Questioner went speedily.

If it had not been for her enhanced senses, she would not have recognized Marool. She was no longer a person but only a piece of living meat clamped into a machine that had hung her by her ankles as it thrust at her from above and either side. Questioner took one quick glance at the mechanical linkages, reached forward to an oscillating rod, and snapped it between powerful hands.

The ratcheting noise stopped with a shrill scraping noise. A frustrated mechanical whine built to a howl. The inhuman squealing went on. From behind her, Questioner heard Mouche's gasp, Ornery's muffled curse.

"Can't you do something?" cried Mouche, distraught.

"I can," Questioner agreed, though with peculiar reluctance. She reached upward, extruded a needle from her palm, and injected a strong opiate into the woman's body.

In a few moments, the squealing subsided to a dull, grunted moan, endlessly repeated. The machine itself reached a point of no return; a linkage shattered; silence fell.

Questioner turned to find Mouche's horrified eyes fixed

upon her. Of the three of them, he was the only one unsurprised.

"You knew about this?" she asked him.

Mouche gulped, turned his ashen face aside, and told her about the picture in the hallway at House Genevois. This, he said, was the same machine.

" 'Mistress Mantelby at Her Pleasures,' you say?"

He gulped. "That was how it was labeled, Most Honored One."

"Call me Questioner. We will have no time for honorifics on this journey." She turned back to the puzzle before her. The machine would not reverse. There was no real way to extricate the woman, for there were linked escapements preventing the machine from going back to its original configuration until it reached the end of the cycle or was unlocked. As if in answer to this need, Marool's bloody arm flopped downward with the wrist at eye level before them, the key dangling.

Questioner broke the light chain that held it and unlocked the machine, which immediately disengaged from Marool's body with an intimate, sucking sound, and dropped her to the floor, where she lay, still faintly moaning.

"Marool," said Questioner, "listen to me. Who did this?"

"Dyre," gasped Marool. "And Bane . . . for . . . ahhh . . ."

"It is dire and baneful, but who . . ."

"That's their names, Ma'am," interrupted Mouche. "I can tell who it was from the stink. It's the Dutter boys, Bane and Dyre. That's their names."

"My sons," Marool gasped, her face transfigured by rage. "My sons . . . for that damned Ahhh . . . shes." She cried out, a long angry howl that went out of her interminably, dwindling into a final aching silence.

Mouche turned away, hiding his face, and Ornery put an arm around his shoulders.

"She has died," said Questioner. Her voice and motions were stiff and mechanical as she straightened the limp form where it lay then jerked one of the hangings loose to cover the body. ''No doubt many others have died in this place. Look at the ring she wears. See that face upon it and the name engraved around the edge: Morrigan. In the Temple I learned of Morrigan, a deity of pain and destruction. Marool selected her goddess and became her own sacrifice.''

''What shall we do for her?'' whispered Ornery.

Questioner murmured, ''She has done for herself. It was she who brought this deadly device to this place, perhaps even she who designed it. Certainly it was she who used it upon others. The machine is not new. See the wear patterns around the pinions, the stains on the straps. It has killed before.''

''Why . . . why would anyone do . . . do that?'' Mouche begged, as he hurried to the door through which they had entered. ''I never understood the pictures, the why of any of it. . . .''

Questioner emitted a very mankindlike sigh. ''It is a very primitive emotion, and even when we explain it, we do not understand it, Mouche. If we all understood it, there would have been no need for Haraldson and his edicts.''

''Prey, property, or opponent,'' gasped Mouche, who was now in the door they had entered through, breathing the cleaner air of the sneakway. ''Madame said that's how gangs think.''

Questioner nodded. ''One like this was a gang unto herself. So long as we think of such people as humans and attempt to treat them as humans, we cannot protect the innocent.''

''They really can't be cured?'' asked Ornery.

Questioner waved the idea away. ''We haven't found a way. Haraldson said that if a being has sufficient sense of justice and civility to know it has done wrong, knowing it has done wrong is often sufficient punishment. If the being has no remorse, punishment will only increase its anger.''

She sighed, gesturing at the scene around them. ''I don't think Marool felt any remorse.'' She turned toward Mouche and called, ''What did she mean, 'Her sons, that damned Ashes'?''

Mouche was by now sitting head-down in the sneakway, still fighting his nausea and revulsion. He turned reluctantly. "I'll tell what I know, but if you're finished, Ma'am . . . Questioner, can we get out of here?"

Questioner nodded. Her olfactory receptors were still turned down, but the others had no such amelioration. She herded them ahead of her.

When they were inside the wall with the opening shut behind them, Mouche mopped the sweat from his face on the sleeve of his shirt. "When Bane and Dyre first came to House Genevois, they broke all the rules, and Madame sent for someone. I never saw him, though I heard his voice. When Bane and Dyre were sent to him, he did something painful to them, and he told them to mind themselves. Later on, Madam had to summon that person again, to stop their attacking me—"

"Why?" she interrupted. "Why attack you?"

"I'd had a run in with them before, at home." He gulped, suddenly overcome with a longing for that home. "I stopped them killing a little native creature I'd made a friend of, and they hated me for it. It was Bane did this to my face, later on. Well, the person Madame summoned could have been their father, their real father, for he smelled as they did, and I know Dutter wasn't their real father. The Dutters were only paid to rear them."

"Was Marool really their mother?" asked Ornery.

"Does it fit in with what we've heard from other sources?" Questioner asked.

Ornery offered, "The gardener said she'd disposed of two or three a year since she'd been back, so she was away, somewhere, perhaps long enough to have had those two."

"So. If she bore these boys, she was guilty of mismothering?"

Both Mouche and Ornery nodded, Ornery adding, "Oh, my, yes Ma'am. That's about as mis a mothering as anybody could do. And then, playing about with them here . . . Well, that's as bad a thing as you can do on Newholme."

"Most places would agree," said Questioner.

"She'd of been blue-bodied sure, if anyone had caught her at it."

Questioner murmured, "I wonder who Ashes really is. . . ."

"Jong," interrupted someone. "Ashes is jongau."

The voice sent a thrill through Mouche, shivering him to his feet. "Timmy," he whispered, as though to himself. "Timmy?"

The others turned, Ornery crouching defensively, searching the darkness. The voice came as a spider-silk whisper, drifting to their ears a word or two at a time, from any direction and from none:

"Mouchidi."

A caress, that voice, as it whispered, "She, the evil one is gone."

And another voice. "She will never come to the Fauxidizalonz where Bofusdiaga waits. She will never be remade."

Questioner turned on her massive feet, peering into the darkness. She saw only a vanishing glimpse of moving colors around a globe of wavering green, like a cloud of seagrass.

"It's the Timmys," cried Mouche, who had turned an instant earlier. "The dancers!" He could not mistake that movement, that slender, sylphlike form. The most graceful creatures mankind could produce could be only an awkward copy of that.

Questioner muttered to herself, "Aha. So here is our indigenous race!" Then, making her voice soft and unthreatening, she called, "Why have you come here?"

The first voice came again, fading, departing: "We were coming for Mouchidi. Corojum said go get him. Now you are coming anyhow, so we will lead you across the seas, but you must hurry."

Questioner stood, immovable. "Why should I listen to you? You have stolen my people."

"They are not hurt," said a slightly different voice, sounding both impatient and surprised. "We do not hurt things as you do. Two of them are dancers! We needed dancers. Even now they skim the waters, on their way across the seas to the Fauxi-dizalonz. They go there to help us with the dance.''

The last words faded into distance. She or he or it was not waiting for them to get closer, so much was clear.

''What dance?'' whispered Ornery.

''I have no idea,'' Questioner replied. ''Though I had no doubt dancers might be helpful.''

''Oh, Questioner, we'll find out,'' cried Mouche. ''What an adventure!''

Adventure or not, he stood as one stunned by delight, incapable of movement. It had been her, its voice. The voice of divinity.

''Come,'' said Questioner, shoving him gently. ''I think haste may be appropriate.''

Down the road from Mantelby Mansion, the man known as Ashes sat in a carriage behind two black horses. They and their saddled stablemate, tethered to the back of the carriage, heard the sounds of approaching feet before Ashes did. They started and stamped their feet, ears erect.

''Daddy Thunder?'' called a voice.

''Here,'' said Ashes in his deep, dead voice. ''D'jou get the ring?''

''Couldn't get it off her damn finger,'' said Bane. ''Didn't have my knife to cut the finger off. Figured you'd rather we got here on time than go off hunting for cutlery.''

''Damnation. She had that ring when I knew her under the bridges. I wanted it. A souvenir. She's dead?''

''By now, I'd say. Good thing we saw that picture at Madame's place. Otherwise we wouldn'ta known which machine it was.''

''You'da known. I told you the Machinist fixed it the way I told him. He fixed it so's it couldn't hurt our kin, not any of the sons of Thunder. He put sensors in the pads so it wouldn't run if it was you, or me. That machine's your friend, boy. You could'a got on it with her, it'd of killed her and set you down without a scratch. Well, that'll pay her back for the daughter she owed me!''

"So how come she picked us? The way we smell, we figured nobody would."

The man smiled. "She's addicted to the smell. Not that she knows it's a smell. I can do the same to anybody when I've got a little time. Once they've got the smell in their head, they're gone, lost, can't do a thing against it."

"What'd you mean, paying her back for the daughter she owed you?"

"Arrgh. Three times I tried for a Rikajor daughter. They were said to run to girls. Rikajor refused me each time. He couldn't refuse me Marool. Her, I bought with other coin."

"She asked who our mother was. Why'd she care?"

A gleefully gloating expression fled across the older man's face. "No reason. Just trying to confuse you. Get on in here. I'm sick of towns. Time to go."

The boys climbed in, and Ashes took up the reins, starting the horses up the hill, along the road that led past the mansions into the wild, the same way Marool had gone when she investigated her parents' deaths in the badlands.

"Where we going now?" asked Dyre, yawning.

"Off into the wild to meet your cousins, boy. Our kindred. The first settlers of this world. The Wilderneers."

Ornery moved off down the tunnel, sped both by curiosity and by Questioner's urgency. Mouche moved with more eagerness, though Questioner noted that both Mouche and Ornery seemed somewhat reluctant to look where they were going. Like guilty children handing around a dirty picture, they peeked at the darkness ahead, and pretended not to and peeked again. So long as they were all headed in one direction, it made little difference, though Questioner could imagine circumstances in which this preoccupation and inattention could be dangerous.

"Mouche," murmured Questioner, placing her heavy hand firmly on one of his shoulders, "stop trembling."

Instead of steadying, he quivered like an excited horse.

"Whoa," Questioner said. "Stop. Take a deep breath; stop."

She turned Mouche toward her, staring into his dazed

eyes. "What is this business of not looking where you're going?" She snapped her fingers in his face and shook him lightly. "What?"

Ornery had turned and came back to them. "It's hard for us, Ma'am. They do not exist, Ma'am. So we are taught. We are not allowed to see or hear them. I can see them or not, depending, though I am still surprised at myself, but Mouche seems to be having trouble looking at them."

"You cannot see them?" Questioner turned her searching gaze on the sailor. "What do you mean you cannot see them?"

"I mean . . . I can sort of not. Not look. I mean, I . . . know they're there, but I don't. They wear brown robes that cover them all up, and we're not allowed to look. Not once we're six or seven years old."

"Why?"

"Because . . . well . . . they don't exist."

"They what?"

Ornery cried petulantly, "They don't exist! There weren't supposed to be other creatures here. And they weren't here when our people came, which means they probably came from somewhere else. But even if they didn't, it wasn't playing fair to hide all that time. . . ."

"So, what's the matter with your friend, here?"

Mouche's life of sin had caught up with him all too swiftly. He quivered with mixed joy and shame, muttering, "I've been watching them. I've been watching them at House Genevois. I've been . . . I've been . . ." His sins had been settled, dependable. He had made a detente with his sins, taking his inspiration from his sins, but now he was in actual pursuit of the ideal, and he could not say what he had been. ". . . maybe wicked," he concluded, head hanging.

Questioner mused over this for a moment, shaking her massive head as an indication of the astonishment she did not feel but knew was suitable to the occasion. "Young ones, listen to me. During this present time we are in, this *now*, Timmys do indeed exist. During the near future, it will not be forbidden to look at them. During the near future, everything you learned . . . when? When you were mere schoolchildren? Well, whatever you learned then was wrong. For the near future. Can you absorb that? When we catch up to them, or when they return to us, you will see them for they will be there, right? All this pretense has to end. Ending it is one of the reasons I am here!"

"Ahh . . . if you say so, Ma'am."

"I do say so. And I am smarter than your teacher, so what I say, goes. You understand?"

Both of them nodded, Ornery obediently, Mouche equivocally. Ornery didn't care one way or the other, but Mouche had set certain limits on his dreams and delights. He didn't particularly want them to be sullied by reality. He wanted to have without the burden of having, to imagine without being imagined in return, and most, to be inspired without questioning his inspiration. Now, having heard Flowing Green's voice so near, he alternately rejoiced and suffered. She had come to get him, him, personally. Why? What did she think of him? What did she see when she looked at him? Did she look at him? What would she think of his face now? Or did that even matter? Would she hate him?

Thinking was troublesome, hurtful, and useless. He gave up thinking and merely went.

They had left the sneakways of the house and entered a natural tunnel, or so Questioner identified it from the texture of the stone. There was no way to get lost, for there were no side tunnels, merely this partially dissolved stratum of limestone, floored with harder stone, naturally sloping downward and penetrated from above by rough tufts of root. Among the roots she heard the squeak and chitter of small creatures, and when one fled across the edge of her sight she saw a being the size of her hand, winged with tight membranes stretching between fore and rear limbs.

"What is that called?" she asked, directing her voice down the tunnel ahead of them.

"Dibigon," came a drifting voice, soft as the twitter of a drowsy bird. "Self-creators. You would say swoopers."

"I didn't know they could speak our language," muttered Mouche, talking to his feet. ''No one told me.'' Then, remembering his childhood, he flushed again. Of course they had spoken his language. How could he have forgotten?

Questioner called, ''How far down do we go?''

''All way,'' whispered the voice. ''To baimoi. To dwell-below.''

As they went farther, the stones around them began to glow, at first with a hint of palest green along the edges, growing brighter the farther they went, enabling them to see the outlines of the stones around them, the fading distance of the tunnel ahead. Questioner reduced her own light to a soft, reddish glow, and soon the luminescence became a brighter yellow. Coincident with this brightening, they heard the murmuring of a stream.

They found the source of the liquid burbling at an intersection of their tunnel and a larger, more cylindrical one was half-filled with smooth, dark water, visible as a shadow against the bright luminescence of the opposite wall. The water, though silent elsewhere throughout its course, burbled at the conjunction of the two tunnels where irregular blocks of stone had fallen to interrupt its flow. There, also, were two podlike shapes drawn onto the shingle, each one about five meters long and less than a meter wide, each shining with the same light as the stone itself.

Questioner put her face close to the rock, amplified her vision, and saw that the luminescence was the product of bacteria accumulated in lichenous growths that covered every surface. Some were effulgently yellow, others emitted blue or green or even violet light.

Ornery looked over the pods, thumping them with her fist and finding them rather rubbery. ''You don't call these ships, I hope,'' she said in a disgusted tone. ''Canoes, I'd call them, if that.''

''Their size befits a small river,'' said Questioner. ''Neither of these will bear my weight, however, so I will rely upon my flotation devices.''

''Flotation devices?'' asked Ornery.

''Some worlds are water worlds,'' said Questioner. ''Some people swim or even dive about their activities.

Some people are arboreal. Some are cave dwellers. I was designed to get about in any of them, to swim or dive or brachiate or soar or crawl, not always gracefully, but always efficiently.''

Mouche and Ornery stared doubtfully at the pods, looking around for something more solid, seeing nothing that would float. It seemed to be the pod or nothing. Questioner, reading their minds, patted them on the shoulders comfortingly. ''Many things will no doubt be made clear as we go.''

Several Timmys leapt into one of the boats, which then slipped into the water of its own accord and floated a little way downstream, remaining there, quiet in the current. Mouche and Ornery started to push one of the boats into the river, only to have it slip along the rocky beach by itself. They climbed into it, sat in the rubbery bottom facing one another and felt their bottoms bumping over small rocks that were easily discernable through the half-flexible substance of the vessel. Questioner waded into the stream and hooked herself to the back edge of the boat that held Mouche and Ornery, her mid parts ballooning until she bobbed on the ripples like a hollow ball. She was near enough that her reddish glow still illuminated both Mouche and Ornery, near enough to speak and be heard, though once they had pushed off into the river, she seemed disinclined to do so. There were no paddles or oars. Evidently it was intended they should simply float wherever they were going, though that did not explain the fact that the little boats maintained their relative distance and position, no matter how the tunnel twisted or how the water eddied.

From the front of the other boat a green glow swam upon the river. Mouche knew this was Flowing Green, that she led him to his destiny, that she knew he followed willingly even though he hadn't wanted to approach her, not really. So far . . . so far nothing had happened to disenchant him, but if it did . . . oh, he would feel . . . feel so . . .

''What?'' asked Ornery, leaning toward him. ''You look

as though you had lost your last shoelace and the race about to start."

Mouche managed a smile. "I was thinking how wonderful . . . how wonderful they are." He gestured, making it clear who he meant.

"They always were," said Ornery. "I always thought so."

"You've both seen them?" Questioner asked. "I mean, without their coverings."

"Not recently," Ornery admitted. "But when I was a child, of course I saw them. They didn't wrap themselves up with *us*. Not when we were little."

"Mine did, mostly," Mouche confessed. "We had such a little place to live. Unless we were out in the woods, then my Timmy would take off her wrappers."

"*Her* wrappers? You knew she was female?"

"No! of course not." Mouche subsided into a new fit of guilt. Thinking of Timmys as male or female was also forbidden. "We weren't supposed to wonder about them, or to think of them being families or having babies or anything."

Ornery snorted. "Oh, well. Supposed to! We're supposed to be veiled, but on ships we aren't. We're supposed not to see Timmys, but we don't trip over them, so we must really see them, right? You can drive yourself crazy with stuff you're not supposed to."

"And women aren't supposed to be . . . running around loose," murmured Mouche in a slightly angry tone.

Surprisingly, Ornery grinned. "Right. Not supposed to."

From behind them, the Questioner murmured, "And girls aren't supposed to pretend to be boys, but I doubt you're the first."

"How did you know?" Ornery asked, jaw dropping.

"I can smell you, child. My sense of smell is copied from Old Earther canines. Differentiating between sexes is nothing. I can also tell about how old you are, where you've been and what you've been eating recently, what your state of health is, and what was in the soap you last used."

"Can you tell where we're going?" asked Ornery in a slightly sarcastic voice.

"From the fact that water runs down hill, I assume we go down," she said. "Somewhere this streamlet runs into a river, and that, I should imagine, runs eventually into an underground sea. I believe so, for seas figure in the legends of this place and because Mouchidi's little friend has told us we will cross them."

Mouche flushed. "She isn't my . . . my friend."

"Ornery is right, you know. She isn't a she, either."

Astonished, Mouche tried to turn around, a maneuver that set the little boat bobbing. A Timmy voice came clearly through the darkness. "Still, sit, you make peevish Joggiwagga!"

Without moving, Mouche said, "She isn't? I mean, it isn't?"

Questioner murmured, "It isn't, no. Is the one leading us the one you've been watching?"

Mouche nodded miserably. "One of them. I call her . . . it, Flowing Green."

"Because of the hair, of course. Flowing Green is very attractive to you, is it not? Tim, not. I think we will find they do not say him, her, he, she, but merely tim. Mankind proposes, tim-tim disposes."

"No sexes?" drawled Ornery, with a sidelong glance at Mouche. "That should simplify things."

"Not really," murmured Questioner. "Reproduction of nonsexual beings will inevitably have its own complications. We simply don't know what they are, yet."

Questioner dimmed her light to the slightest, reddish glow, watching in fascination as the luminescence around them continued to grow brighter. The surroundings were in no sense illuminated. Much of their environment appeared as patches of darkness outlined or interrupted by strings, shades, lines, or clouds of light ranging from pale yellow through all possible greens to deep blue. Part of this, Questioner knew, was due to her reduced light and their own eyes adjusting to the lower levels of illumination, but part was a real increase in luminosity and a shift in color toward the slightly longer wave lengths. One did not actually see a rock, one saw a fuzzy angular yellow outline around a black patch partly filled in by pale green with blue prominences that one could decode as a rock. The green fangs that hung above them had been deposited there ages ago by water leaching through limestone. The green glow in the boat ahead of them was brighter now, and occasionally Questioner could detect twin silver eyes peering at them from within it as well as from other, accompanying glows, various shades from amber through blue. Flowing Green was not alone.

Questioner had already adjusted her senses to pick up the talk of the Timmys, which she was stowing away while her internal translator worked at it. Give her a few days, and she'd know their tongue as well as the fifty or so others she'd come equipped with.

Ornery leaned to whisper into Mouche's ear. "What do you think of her, the Questioner?"

Mouche considered it. He had spent hours every day for some years considering what this or that individual woman was like, for if one could not know that, one could hardly be a Consort.

"I think she's sad," he whispered back. "Not showing it, of course. Very soldierly about everything and taking a proper pride in her duty, but underneath, she could use a bit of happiness."

Ornery, surprised, sat back in her own place, thinking of what Mouche had said. All in all, she thought, Mouche was probably right. Questioner, who had heard every syllable, was slightly surprised.

The tube in which they were floating began to narrow slightly. From ahead came louder water sounds. Without interference from those aboard, the two little boats lined up end to end, their speed increased to a dizzying rush that carried them through the last narrow bit of small tunnel into another with a diameter several times as large. Beside the boats, a huge eye, like a pale balloon, emerged from the dark water and stared at them. Great dripping, weed-hung swags of line or cable pulled themselves above the water, dark against the background glow, heaving the boats into the slower current. Not cable. Too thick for cable. Tentacles. Far above, the higher, broader ceiling shone softly with fractal patterns of amber and emerald.

The two canoes stayed in line, as though they were linked, and the moon-eye ahead of them swiveled from left to right before turning in the direction of their movement, the joined boats holding steady in the slow current.

A voice drifted back to them, "Drink this water now. To make you visible."

Ornery began to laugh. "So now *we're* invisible."

"It isn't funny," complained Mouche.

"You are only darkness, Mouche," said Questioner. "You're a black hole in the middle of light. I've been analyzing the water. I detect no impurities that would endanger your health, but it does have luminescent bacteria in it. Presumably, if you drink the water, soon you will glow, and we can see you. I must admit, I'm curious to see a glowing Mouche, a shimmering Ornery!"

"The bacteria? They won't make you glow?" asked Ornery.

"Probably not. But I can make myself glow, so you know where I am and what I'm about. I'd like to know what that thing was that came up just beside us?"

"Joggiwagga," whispered the darkness.

"Joggiwagga," murmured Questioner. "I've heard that before."

"It is Joggiwagga who raises the pillars," said Ornery. "It is Joggiwagga who keeps track of time, by the moonshadows. I saw one once, by the side of the sea, setting up the stones!"

"Dangerous," whispered the voice. "To be seen by Joggiwagga on the land."

"I moved very fast," Ornery confessed.

"Wise," murmured the darkness. "Wise. It would not hurt us for we are part of it, but you are not."

"What do you mean, you are part of it?" asked the Questioner. "You are part of Joggiwagga?"

A verdant glow ahead of them billowed, then shrank once more, as hair was tossed wide and then fell into place. "Joggiwagga is part, we are part, all everything is

Dosha, all is made in Fauxi-dizalonz, except you people and jongau people and Her and Niasa.''

''What are jongau?'' the Questioner asked.

''Bent people. People not put together right. That Ashes one is jongau. That Bane, that Dyre, they are jongau. All their kinfolk and like, many, many more! They are not finished. They are only half done, and they smell bad. They should have the courtesy to die, but they do not.''

''And who are the Corojumi?'' the Questioner pursued.

Out of darkness: ''Once were many Corojumi to open spaces, make the dances, fix what is broken . . .''

''And Bofusdiaga?''

''Bofusdiaga mixes things together. Bofusdiaga stops pains and breaks chains and burrows walls and sings to the sun. That is Bofusdiaga.''

Questioner spoke to Mouche and Ornery: ''Are you making any sense of this?''

Mouche said, ''I'm afraid not.''

The voice came again, this time with some asperity. ''You mankinds always need everything right now. Your babies, too. Why this. Why that. Tell me this, tell me that. Explain, explain. You should learn to wait. See a little, then a little more. It will be clear. Drink water.''

None of them dared ask any further questions, though Questioner said in a jolly tone, ''Drink water. By all means.''

Ornery and Mouche obediently scooped water from the stream and gulped it down. Aside from being very cold, it was simply watery, with nothing at all unpleasant about it. When he had wiped his hands on his shirt, Mouche turned gingerly on his haunches to speak softly to Questioner.

''When I was little, my Timmy used to sing me to sleep with a song that had Corojumi and Bofusdiaga in it. It was all in their language, and I asked her . . . it to tell it to me in my language, and a few days later she . . . it had it figured out in our language, rhymes and all. After that, it sang it to me in my language part of the time.''

''Can you sing it to me?''

''Not the way she . . . it did. Their singing is wonderful,

but it's all full of little trills and lilts and runs. I'll just say it very softly."

Mouche cleared his throat and began:

"Quaggida he sings
somewhere among the dimmer galaxies,
luring the Quaggima that he will seize.
Oh, Corojumi, she comes unaware.
Bofusdiaga, from deep dark he flings
fiery loops that make a snare
for her bright wings.

"Quaggima she screams
her wings broken and torn, she cries in vain
at flame and scalding light and piercing pain.
Bofusdiaga, where will she find aid?
Oh, Corojumi, all her lively schemes
are but memories that fade
among dead dreams.

"Quaggima she calls:
Out of starfield coming, fire womb seeking
Fire she finds, rock wallowing, fume reeking
Oh, Corojumi, openers of space
Bofusdiaga, burrower of walls
She has need of birthing place
Wheeooo, she falls!"

After a long moment, Questioner said in an interested voice, "Is that all of it?"

Mouche shook his head. "No, there was more, but I can't quite remember it. Their language is a lot prettier than ours. You're right that it has no hes and shes. They sang *tim* in their language, but they put in the *hes* and *shes* in ours. In our language they couldn't put all the trills in, and I usually fell asleep along about the burrower of walls line. I'll try to remember the rest of it."

"How do you explain it?"

Mouche scratched his head, trying to remember. "It's the story of the Quaggi. Aren't they a kind of huge something that lives out in space? I guess they're travelers, sailing between the stars, and the male lurks around in the dark spaces between outer worlds to catch the female, and he impregnates her. And she's supposed to lay the egg, but in the song, she's hurt so badly she can't ever fly again. When I was a little kid, I always just thought it was just a sad story, a lament, you know."

Questioner murmured, "I think it's a story about real things. It's an odd story for a child, however, all that rape and violence, though it may be a clue to something your Timmy said earlier. It remarked that everything was part of the Fauxi-dizalonz except the jongau people, us people, *Her,* and Niasa."

"Well, there are lots of songs or rhymes about Niasa, like:

> *'Niasa, little Summer Snake,*
> *Turn in your egg, the world will shake.'*
> *Niasa's mother, down so deep,*
> *Sing your baby snake to sleep.'* "

Questioner mused, "So, Niasa is Summer Snake; Ashes is jongau; we are unequivocally us; so could *Her* be the Quaggima?"

"You think there's a real Quaggima?" asked Ornery.

Questioner answered. "The Quaggi are one of the four races we have met who are definitely not human. The Quaggi we've met—or rather, seen, since one does not really meet a Quaggi—are all alike according to our sensors, so we've always rather assumed the females are somewhere else. This story you tell, which is the same story the Hags tell, by the way, accords with some information I received from a trader. . . ."

"Well, my story and the Hags' story would be the same," interrupted Mouche. "Because Timmys told both of us. The Hags had Timmy nursemaids, just as all of us did."

Unperturbed, Questioner went on, "I believe the Quaggi at some point lose their wings and become long-lived, planet-bound creatures devoted to philosophy. They don't talk about their method of reproduction, and this little song of yours gives us a rather nasty hint that the females either die after being waylaid and raped, or perhaps in the act of laying the egg or hatching the young. All that bit about her broken wings and her dead dreams and being unable to fly. Most unpleasant."

Ornery said, "Maybe the females don't die. Maybe they just can't fly anymore so they have to stay put."

A long silence before Questioner commented: "Possibly. If the scene I witnessed was typical, that would be equivalent to lifetime solitary confinement. They have the lifespan of rocks."

"So, since Quaggi are real," said Mouche, "then maybe the song was real, too, and she could still be wherever it happened."

"How big are they?" Ornery asked. "These Quaggi things?"

"The ones we've seen vary in size from mountainous to merely large," mused Questioner. "The females could be smaller."

Mouche said, "I can't see what the Corojumi and the Bofusdiaga have to do with it."

"Maybe they were just witnesses," remarked Ornery.

"Many tribes of men tell stories that have bases in fact," mused Questioner. "Of the eclipse of the sun, perhaps, or of shooting stars. Ornery may be correct, and these people may have witnessed the encounter."

"In which case, the story has nothing to do with this journey," said Mouche, finalizing the matter. He really wanted to stop talking.

"I think contrariwise," murmured Questioner. "Everything has something to do with this journey. Tell me, Mouche, do the Timmys dance?"

"How did you know?" he asked, amazed. "They dance all the time. Everywhere. But who told you?"

"Actually, Mouche, it was an interstellar trader, who got into conversation with someone at your port, who told him a charming story about something you call the Long Nights."

"Our midwinter holiday."

"Which, according to the story, you celebrate because all your workers are busy dancing, even though you've tried and tried to make them quit."

"There is a story like that," he admitted.

"And another thing, Mouche. I am interested in the singer of your song."

Startled, he replied, "The singer? My Timmy sang it to me. . . ."

"Ah, yes. But who, in the song, apostrophizes and instructs? Who is it who cries, 'Oh, Corojumi.' Who is it who tells what occurred in 'the dimmer galaxies.' Is there some other personage present we have not yet heard of?"

44

A Consternation of Hags

The morning following the Questioner's visit to the Temple, D'Jevier took note that there had been no tremors through the night. Those venturing into the street saw clear blue above the scarp for the first time in seasons. Her hope that the predictions of the geologists aboard *The Quest* might have been premature was cast down, however, when those same geologists sent word to the Temple that the calm was merely a hiatus and they could not reach the Questioner. Where was she? D'Jevier received this message just as Onsofruct came in with a message from the steward at Mantelby Mansion.

"Marool, dead?" D'Jevier breathed. "How?"

Onsofruct told her. Though the steward's account had been somewhat reticent, she had accurately imagined some of what he had left unsaid.

"Also," said Onsofruct, taking a deep breath, "the entire entourage that accompanied the Questioner has disappeared, along with the Questioner herself and four pressed men, three of them from House Genevois. And if that were not trouble enough, the ship that brought her knows of it and has stated its intention of relaying this information to the Council of Worlds."

"Three men from House Genevois? Who, Onsy?"

"I didn't ask their names. But by every Hagion from A to Z, I'd like to know what is going on!"

"We know what's going on," said her cousin. "At least, we have a fat hint or two that something real is happening among creatures or beings we have always considered mythical."

"I wish we knew the extent of the reality!"

"What do the Men of Business say? Anything useful?"

"This and that. It will or won't bankrupt the world. It will or won't put us all back to the Stone Age. It will or won't have anything to do with our social . . . arrangements, though they know nothing about this world's real arrangements."

"No," said D'Jevier. "But they think they do, and they simmer with discontent. They are sexually frustrated, overburdened with responsibilities, often overtired. They turn to drink and to drugs or nagging at their children. They blame themselves if they have no daughters."

"Tragic!" snapped Onsofruct. "Tit for tat after millennia of otherwise!"

D'Jevier sighed. "Did you expect them to agree on anything? It isn't in them to adopt a cause or pursue justice, not given over to the game of profit as they are. That's one of the reasons we designed . . . well, our foremothers designed things as they are."

"Those same foremothers warned us, their daughters, that if ever a leader emerges among the Men of Business, they might rise up in rebellion. Especially if they ever found out . . ." Onsofruct's voice trailed away.

D'Jevier shook her head warningly. "Which they won't. We keep tight hold of information on this world. They have no way of getting hold of it."

"Not so long as the Panhagion controls, no. But, the greater our population, the harder it gets to keep things quiet. If we're going to keep on as we have been, it'll take a new Temple near Nehbe and a couple of branch Temples out toward the scarp. Those valleys are filling up. . . .'' Onsofruct's voice trailed away as she realized what she had said.

''Were filling up, Onsy. Were. The people there are either dead or evacuated by now. Which actually helps us control data. When the population is centralized, we manage very nicely.''

''Until the planet blows up.'' She heard her voice rising stridently and put her hands over her eyes.

''If it does. Well, if it does, our troubles are over. I've been wishing we could ask the Timmys. . . .''

''I think we must.'' Onsofruct put her hands flat on the table before her and pushed herself erect. ''Certainly we must. Let's find some.''

''Unfortunately they don't seem to be findable. I've had the word out among the Haggers for the last couple of days. The Timmys have completely vanished, Onsy. They went so quickly and totally that it appears they'd been planning it. As if they knew about it before we did.''

''That's impossible!''

D'Jevier fought down a shriek, took a deep breath, and said as calmly as she could manage, ''Nothing's impossible any longer. We must go to Mantelby Mansion and see what we can find out there.''

They saw the scene of the deadly event, which both of them were reluctant to call a murder. They questioned everyone, learning the sequence of the disappearance, first the entourage, then the two Old Earthians, then the Questioner herself along with two gardener's boys named Ornery and Mouche—at the mention of whose name D'Jevier's face paled.

''You know him?'' whispered her sister.

''Of him,'' said D'Jevier, in so forbidding a manner that it halted further mention.

Two other boys had disappeared as well, the steward said, but they had disappeared from the cellar, where they had been with Marool. Their names had been Bane and Dyre.

The Hags examined the machines and fought through their disgust to a comprehension of their use. D'Jevier sent for a smith to bring a portable furnace and the necessary equipment to dismantle everything in the cellar and convert it to scrap. They found the maker's name attached on neat little brass plates, and they directed a squad of Haggers to find and dispose of that individual, even before directing that Marool's body be wrapped in a linen sheet and be buried without ceremony in the Mantelby graveyard, behind the ridge.

"And," said D'Jevier with a glare at the steward, "as you value your life and sanity, don't take that ring off her finger or whatever ate your aunt may come to nibble on you, as well."

When the ashen-faced young man departed, leaving them momentarily alone in the hideous cellar, Onsofruct whispered, "Was her death a final act of worship?"

"Not a voluntary one," murmured D'Jevier. "Which doesn't mean Morrigan didn't relish it. I think it's clear Marool was murdered by two of the boys she got from House Genevois. The order of disappearance is probably significant. First the entourage, without the Questioner's knowledge. Then, the two Old Earthians, then the Questioner and two gardener's helpers, one Mouche, a Consort trainee, and one Ornery, a sailor lad. Finally, only after Marool's body is discovered are the other Consort trainees found to be gone. We assume they left Marool dead or dying and may, in fact, have been the first to depart. I wonder who turned off the machine and took her out of it before she was dismembered."

Onsofruct shuddered. "Is that what it would have done?"

"Oh, yes. The mechanical linkages led next to knives and then to a leveraged system which would quite effectively have quartered her after disembowelment. There has not been any such barbarism among mankind for millennia. Marool had reinvented it."

She fell silent, wanting to spit the foul taste from her mouth, taking refuge in changing the subject. "I've noticed quite a draft. Look at the smoke from those candles."

She pointed at a branched iron stand where guttering candles unskeined black smoke that drifted sideways to disappear along a wall. The paneling was ajar. They tugged it open to reveal a shadowy sneakway running along the walls. D'Jevier went in and peered at the dusty floor, noting the footprints there, noting the spyholes in the walls.

"See, here." She pointed. "There, those depressions which are not quite footlike. The Questioner. And two pairs of boots, the Consort and the sailor. Some other tracks beneath, too scuffed to read, all of them headed in the same direction." She stood staring into the dark. "The murderers went some other way. I want to see Madame Genevois. Let us go to her, woman to woman. It will save time."

Madame was in her office, off the welcome suite. She greeted D'Jevier as an old friend, and, after a look at their haggard faces, offered brandy. When she'd heard what they had to say about Marool's death, she rang for Simon and sent him with one of the workmen to fetch a picture from the hallway upstairs.

"I collect a certain kind of thing. It's as well to be somewhat cautionary with the young men, and also to blunt their curiosity." She sipped, and poured, and in moments, Simon was back, bearing the picture as though it were a long-dead fish.

"By all the Hagions," murmured D'Jevier. "Where did you get it?"

"The artist disappeared. His body showed up, later, giving evidence that he had died by this machine or some similar. Someone had rifled his studio and then tried, unsuccessfully, to burn it down. This painting was found, quite undamaged, among several others in a kind of vault he had built below his house. His heirs sold it to me."

"If Marool had known you had it. . . ."

"She didn't know. I've always refused to deal with Mistress Mantelby. Even if I'd never seen this, I'd have refused to deal with her. There was always something . . . possessed about her."

"You say 'always'. . . ."

Madame sat back comfortably and stared beyond them,

into the past. "I saw her first at a Family Men's Soirée at her parent's house. I often attend such events. It gives me an opportunity to get off in a corner with a patroness to discuss what I might have in stock to interest her, or for her to tell me what she's looking for. Marool was at the time about four, but her expression was merciless, like a hungry animal watching prey. Her eyes were without humanity. I saw her several times after that, as she grew older, and I thought each time that her eyes were like viper's eyes.

"After she ran off to join the Wasters, I saw her in their company from time to time, and of course, after she returned from her so-called pilgrimage, I saw her at the Panhagion and at the theater, and I heard things from other Houses about Mantelby Consorts who disappeared or died without explanation."

D'Jevier set down her cup. "About these two boys who supposedly killed her . . ."

Madame said, "Bane and Dyre. I believe they were her sons. I can't say whether they knew she was their mother, though I rather think not. Mismothering was probably the least of her sins."

The two Hags were shocked into silence. Madame sipped, staring at them over the rim of her glass, thinking that she, too, might have been shocked if she had not had the opportunity of knowing Bane and Dyre and the man she thought was their father. "Whether she was or was not their mother, I believe their father is a man known to me as Thor Ashburn. Not a Family Man, no g' to his name, but not a supernume, either. He offered my investors a very large fee if I would take these two boys and train them. Left to my own decision, I would not have done so for any sum, but as you know, we cannot always do what we would prefer."

"Indeed," D'Jevier said thoughtfully.

Madame went on, "Over the years I've heard this and that about Marool. Consorts talk among themselves at the Temple and in the park. The talk comes back, and the Houses hear what's said. What was said about Mantelby identified her as a sadist, an accomplished torturer, a gloating killer. She's been seen in public every day or so for eighteen years, however, so if she bore these boys, it was while she was away, supposedly at Nehbe."

"Interesting," murmured Onsofruct. "Our Haggers tell us the man who made the terrible machines also lives near Nehbe."

Madame set down her glass. "The thing I can't figure out is that Thor Ashburn seems unconnected to any known family. Also, he and his sons share a family stink."

"Skunk-lung?"

"That's what it's called," Madame confirmed. "Though it doesn't come from the lung."

"But none of the settlers could have had it," D'Jevier remarked. "It would have been a disqualifying attribute for a colonial."

"I have a suspicion," murmured Madame, "that those who had it weren't settlers. At least, not from the second settlement."

"First settlement survivors?" breathed D'Jevier. "There were no survivors!"

"How do we know, for sure?" Madame raised her eyebrows as she refilled their glasses. "I've been puzzling over this a good deal since meeting Thor Ashburn. I hated the man instinctively, the way we hate snakes, without thinking about it, knowing they have not enough brain to be swayed by pity or reason. And yet, he is mankindly looking, not unhandsome, not badly built. He had to come from somewhere. So, I asked myself, how do we know there were no survivors? Our ancestors didn't see any, quite true, but then, our ancestors arrived over a period of twelve years, in ten large shiploads, a thousand to the ship. None of them knew all the others, not even the ones on their own ship.

"If someone from the first settlement had shown up in a bustling neighborhood and said he was from upriver or downriver, who would have known?"

Onsofruct mused, "According to the servants at Mantelby Mansion, the boys claimed to be sons of thunder."

"Thor was a god of thunder back on Old Earth," said Madame. "That's what Thor means, thunder. Thor is also the supremacist planet from which the schismatic group departed to become the first settlers here."

"You're forgetting something," said D'Jevier. "The first settlement had no women, and the second settlement was almost a hundred years later! They couldn't have lived that long."

Madame nodded. "They weren't supposed to have had women, no. But perhaps they did. Stolen women. Enslaved women. They simply didn't want it known."

Onsofruct cried, "So why haven't we ever seen them? Why didn't they make themselves known?"

"We haven't seen them because they didn't wish to be seen," said Madame. "They know what the Hags would do about enslaved women, and they do not want us to know they are here. They must have maintained a hidden community, somewhere. This planet is certainly rife with enough wilderness to hide a whole population if it wanted to stay hidden!"

After a long pause, Onsofruct said, "In addition to the two sons of thunder, there's a sailor lad missing, who seemingly went off with the Questioner herself, plus another of your young men. His name was Mouche."

Madame cried, "Mouche?" She looked quickly at D'Jevier, then back at Onsofruct. "Is he all right?"

"We assume so. You seem to care a good deal. Who is he?"

"He's . . . just Mouche. Well, I confess, a favorite of mine. We have favorites, though we shouldn't."

"What can you tell us about him?" asked Onsofruct.

Madame poured a splash more brandy and sat back in her chair, surprised to find that her hand trembled slightly. "Nothing evil at all. I bought Mouche when he was twelve, and I made the first overture, having seen the boy in the marketplace. The father came to the House first, talked to some of the students and to Simon, who's one of my old boys. Only when he was convinced the boy would be well treated did he consent, even though his need was great."

"And his mother?" Onsofruct set down her glass.

"I didn't meet the mother. She must be a good-looking woman to produce such a son."

Onsofruct remarked, "He's handsome, then?"

"Oh, remarkably, yes. Many of my students are extremely good looking, and none are plain. Appearance is what sells! But it isn't his appearance that made me like him so. Most young men, well, you can imagine, learning to be a Consort is for most of them an occasion for a good deal of lewdness and that excretory jocularity that men seem to find funny. It's something we work hard to control, since by and large women are offended by it. With Mouche it wasn't necessary. Mouche was never lewd. He went through a stage when he was about sixteen when he seemed distracted, which isn't uncommon, but then lately, it seemed that he was above his work, very sure and capable but able to do it without thinking about it. No, it was more than that! He was able to embue a relationship with romance without personalizing it. He was able to do what we try to get all the young men to do; focus on the ideal, treat the real as though it were the ideal. Mouche could do that."

"A treasure," murmured D'Jevier.

After a rather long pause, Madame said, "Yes. A treasure. When that woman took him from here, I wanted to kill her. If I'd had a proper weapon in my hand, I might have done so. I managed to warn him, before he left, to be as inconspicuous as possible. Now, hearing that she's dead but that he is, so far as anyone knows, unscathed, I breathe again in hope. I have not had many like Mouche."

Onsofruct asked, "Why did the Questioner take him? Or the sailor boy?"

"Most likely she needed strong young hands to fetch and carry. Do you know where they went?"

D'Jevier explained about the sneakway in the wall.

"We must go after her, of course," said Madame. "Until my students are back, I have little purpose to my life, and my students won't be back unless we find this Questioner, get her or it off planet, and return to our own lives. Assuming the volcanoes leave us any life."

"I suppose we must go in search of her," said D'Jevier,

almost unwillingly. "Otherwise . . . well, we'll have the Council of Worlds on our doorstep. If by some chance our world survives all this rumbling and rattling, I'd prefer that the Council of Worlds not involve themselves in our lives."

"We should go as soon as possible," said Madame. "I'll need a couple of days to take care of immediate business, but then I can leave the House to my assistant. It's threeday morning. I can be ready early fiveday. Say at dawn."

"Let us use the time to prepare well," Onsofruct suggested. "We will want provisions, and some strong Haggers, and such things as lights and ropes. We can get that together by early fiveday morning."

"Very well," said Madame, already assembling her kit in her mind. "I will meet you then, at Mantelby's."

45

The Camp of The Wilderneers

The light carriage that Ashes had used to pick up his sons was abandoned at the edge of the wild, not far from the place Marool's parents and sister had died. The horse behind the carriage was already saddled and there were two more light saddles in the boot. Shortly the three were riding through the forest, along the level top of one of the great lava tubes to the north of the Combers. It was not the first time they had ridden together, though it was the first time they had ridden here, and only Ashes knew the way to their destination.

The horses' shod feet struck the top of the buried lava tube like drumsticks striking a gong. Most often the sound was muted, but occasionally, as they crossed a particularly reverberant space, the earth shivered around them with deep bell sounds, an enormous tolling, as though for some creature long dying or just dead. Bane was not normally fanciful, but even he was struck with the similarity of the sound to that of the bells of the Panhagion, which tolled away the old year at the festival of the Tipping.

None of them were sorry when the stony way ended. They turned to the side for a brief time and picked up another stone-floored path, almost like a road, this one completely muffled so that the hooves made no more sound than on any paved surface. Bane, staring at his surroundings, such of them as he could see in the moonlight, thought the lava trail was extremely roadlike. The dirt at either side of it was pushed up, like a curb, as though something huge and wide had moved this way, displacing the earth as it went. Several places along this track Bane found large, oval pieces of something, like enormous fingernails.

They rode for some hours, dismounting as needed to relieve themselves and once to eat food from the saddlebags and drink from the flasks. When dawn came, Ashes turned aside from the trail he'd been following, hobbled the horses and let them browse while he slept, leaving it to Bane and Dyre whether they followed his example or not.

The boys were unusually quiet, somewhat awed by the silence of the forest. House Genevois had always been clattery with boys, and they had spent their childhood on the farm where there was constant cackling of poultry, the low or bleat of livestock, the chatter of people. Here was no sound at all. The night had been windless. They had crossed no streams. No bird had cried, no small beast called, no large beast threatened. Sleep eluded them, and they dropped into uncomfortable slumber only moments, so it seemed, before Ashes roused them again.

When they remounted, the silence was still unbroken, and even Ashes looked around himself with a certain wariness.

"Is it always this still?" asked Bane, in a throaty whisper.

Ashes shook his head, his eyes swiveling from point to point. "No. Usually there's animals making noises. I don't like this quiet. It could mean Joggiwagga about."

"What?" grunted Dyre. "What's Joggi whatsit?"

"Very big and nervous and dangerous," murmured Ashes.

"Did Joggy whatsit clear the road along here?" Bane asked. "Something big came along these tops. The dirt's all pushed back. And there's funny pieces of stuff."

Ashes swallowed, his nostrils pushed together, then said, "No. That wasn't Joggiwagga. Those things are scales, and they came off another . . . another thing entirely."

"Something big?"

"Big, yes."

"Never seen any really big wild thing," opined Dyre.

His father retorted, "You boys favored little things, didn't you? Well, the one that made this trail is a lot bigger than the little critters you hunted for fun while you were at Dutter's."

"How'd you know?" asked Bane, astonished. "Never told you!"

"You don't need to tell me anything, boy. I know everything there is to know about you from before you was planted to the breath you just took. I know all about your hunting trips."

"Ol' Dutter, he said even if we killed something, he wouldn't let us keep any hides."

"No. That furry thing you hunted—there was lots of them when we first landed, and we hunted 'em for fur, but the Timmys, they won't let you keep any part of an animal here. Well, except for the littlest ones, birds and fish and mousy things. The only way to keep hides from anything bigger than that is put 'em in a safe, put the safe in a metal-lined room, then send them off world as soon as may be, the way we used to. Dutter knew that. He wanted no trouble with Timmys."

"Like to see the Timmy could take something from me," muttered Bane. "Like to see 'em try."

Ashes didn't reply. They had come to the end of the network of level lava trails they'd been following for hours and were now climbing onto the flanks of the ancient calderas that stretched in an unbroken range stretching south from the shore of the Jellied Sea, and perhaps beneath it, for all anyone knew. The day wore itself out in ascents and descents, in long traverses across sliding scree, ending at evening on a shadowed ledge that darkened as the sun set.

"Can't go on until moonrise," said Ashes. "Can't see where to go. We'll build a little fire and have some food, catch some sleep."

Bane and Dyre were too tired to complain. They ate, dropped into sleep, only to be wakened again, this time for hours of careful, slow travel by landmarks only Ashes could see, until almost dawn.

"The way's tricky from here," Ashes remarked, dismounting and hobbling his horse once more. "We'll wait for full light."

Full light came. They rode. Darkness came. They stopped, until moonrise once more, then went on. Shortly before dawn, after a long climb, they drew up near the edge of a cliff that marked the rim of still another immense and ancient caldera. Early light bleached the eastern sky. Two moons threw silver reflections in a lake far below, and beyond the lake flickered the amber glows of a scatter of campfires.

"Our people," said Ashes. "Wilderneers." He moved restlessly on his saddle, then turned to the boys and told them to dismount.

When they were afoot, he brought them close, within arms' distance, and muttered, "Before we go down there, there's things you got to know."

"Yeah?" sneered Bane. "And what would that be?"

Ashes reached to his side, thrusting back his coat to let Bane get a good look at the whip coiled around his waist, the sharp end hanging at his side, then grasped him by the shoulder in a grip that made him cry out. "You want some more of what you had before, boy? I'm not one of your flowery fencing masters or your wet-eared boys or some woman you can smart-mouth to. I'm Ashes and Thunder, and you'll hark or you'll suffer." He gave Bane a shake and released him, glaring into his face. "Now the two of you. You listen.

"A long time ago, we came here, a bunch of us, from the planet Thor. We'd had a bit of a disagreement with our brethren there, and we decided to find ourselves a new place where we could do things right without having to explain every other move. . . .''

''What was the disagreement about?'' asked Bane, interested in all this.

For a moment Ashes looked angry, but then he breathed deeply and said, ''Women. How we were going to handle women. We said women had no right to refuse any man anything. Whatever man she belonged to, he owned her just like he owned a horse, and you didn't let a horse say it wasn't going to be bred or saddled. We took a few women just to prove the point, and we killed some families that got in the way, and the whole thing blew up into a sort of war.

''Well, we had hostages, and we said we'd let the hostages go if they'd let us go, and they said so leave. They wouldn't let us bring any women, but we figured we could pirate some from somewhere, once we got settled. So, we scouted a few places and decided on this one, then we met up at a transfer point, and we captured a colony ship with almost a thousand men aboard, people we could use as slaves, and we came here. The place suited us. We settled in, we planted crops, we built a couple of fortresses, we started building towns, we did some hunting, some trapping, we sold furs off planet—after we learned how to get 'em off planet—we brought in some recruits, we sold biologicals, Dingle and Farfaran and other such stuff, and after a score or so years, after most of the towns were built and most of the slaves were dead, we decided it was time to bring in some women.''

Dyre gaped. ''Why'ja wait so long?''

''Too much trouble to get them earlier. Our system is, women are for breeding, and that's it. You gotta keep 'em locked, you gotta keep 'em private. Letting other men see your women, that'd be shameful. So, before we brought women in, we had to make places to keep 'em, places they could stay out of the way, do their own work without being seen. Courtyards, like. Like there in House Genevois. That wharf behind there, we shipped furs and stuff down river from there. When the courtyard was empty, the Timmys used to come out into it, and I used to sit up there under the tower watching them dance.''

''Timmys? You saw Timmys? Our teacher said they didn't come till after the second settlement!''

''They were here almost as soon as we were, but I'm not talking about that. . . .'' He paused, as though he'd lost track of his tale.

''So?'' muttered Bane. ''So, you brought women.''

''We were getting ready to, getting the ship ready, deciding who'd go and who'd stay, and then one night, the Timmys came out of the walls in packs, like ants. It wasn't just Timmys, either; they had other kinds of bigger critters with 'em, and there we were, all of us, wrapped up like so many packages, being hauled off into these woods here. They hauled us partway and they floated us partway, and they swallowed us partway, and we ended up down in caves, over there, some days west, beyond the far side of this valley! They took us out of the caves and down into a kind of pond. And they threw us in the pond. And after a while, we crawled out again.''

''So,'' muttered Bane again, yawning.

Ashes said angrily, ''So, some of us came out pretty much like we was before and some of us didn't.''

The boys stared at him, waiting, but he seemed to find no words to go on with his story. Finally, Dyre ventured, ''What do you mean, not like before?''

Ashes chewed at his lip, eventually saying, ''Some of us was changed, that's what I mean. And some went on changing. When we go down there, where the camp is, you'll see some of us who don't look . . . well, who don't look like we do, but you'll know they're Wilderneers by the smell. Since that pond, we all smell the same. But you won't know by the shape, so be careful who you smart off to.''

Bane's forehead was creased. ''So what did you do about the women?''

''We never got any women,'' said Ashes. ''When we came out of that damned pond, there weren't enough of us left in shape to man the ship, and in the meantime a trader ship had set down and taken all the slaves away, not that there was many left. We came roarin' down on 'em, and when they saw us, they killed a good many of us, then they took off in both ships, theirs and ours! Left a notice on the door of the fortress saying they'd salvaged our ship, taken it as a prize!

"So, after that we had no way to get women. Not until the other settlers came. Then we took some women, but they weren't our women, so it wasn't any good."

"Settlers let you get away with that?"

"The settlers didn't know it was us. The settlers don't even know we're here. Some of us, we go to town when we like, we wander around, we know what's goin' on, they don't know who we are. The rest of us, well, the rest of us learned to stay hid. There's caves . . . caves that go on forever. After they took our ship, we stayed in caves for a long, long time."

"So it was you, doing the women raids," said Bane.

"Well, it was us to start with. Some of us looked . . . normal, so we dressed up like them, let them think it was one family going after women from another family. Before you knew it, it was one family going against another family, like we'd given 'em the idea. They never did know it was us started it."

"So, you took some women. . . ."

"Just enough to find out it wouldn't work anyhow. We couldn't breed 'em."

"Whattaya mean, you couldn't breed 'em?"

"They died. We'd get close to 'em, and they'd die. Every time."

"But there's us," Bane complained. "We had a mother!"

"That was later, and I tricked her," Ashes said. "It was something we planned, to get some daughters born to us who could be our kind of women, women of our own. But . . . she didn't have daughters. She had you two."

A long silence, during which Bane and Dyre thought their way through the implications of this.

"You mean we're the only ones?" Bane asked. "The only kids you've had in hundreds of years?"

"The only ones the Wilderneers ever had," said Ashes.

"But . . . if all that happened hundreds of years ago. How come . . . how come you're still here?"

"We don't die," said Ashes, staring at the sky. "Way we figure it, critters that come from that pond, we can get killed—like that trader ship killed some of us, but we don't just die."

"We? You mean us, too?"

Ashes shrugged. "I don't know. You had a regular woman as a mother. Maybe it only works if you've been in the pond. Maybe it doesn't work for sons, or daughters. We don't know. We want to find out."

Bane raised his voice. "So what are we, huh? Some kinda experiment? You gonna see if you can kill us?"

Ashes shrugged again. "You're my sons. For now. And when you go down there, you're their kinfolk. For now. So long as you don't do anything or say anything stupid."

"Like what?" demanded Bane

"Like anything but 'yes sir' and 'no sir' and 'kind of you to say so sir,' " Ashes growled.

The boys got wordlessly back on their horses and rode along the edge of the caldera until they reached a break in the rimwall, a path leading down. Ashes's lead horse took to the trail as though he knew it well, and after a moment's hesitation, the others followed. Clouds settled and they rode for a time in glowing, clinging mist. Clouds rose and they found themselves almost at the bottom, the lakes away to their right, glittering with moon trails.

Something tall, massive, and darker than the sky reared into being at the edge of the trail. Though the horses took no notice at first, both Bane and Dyre started in fright, pulling up on the reins, causing their mounts to rear. At this, there came a titter from between the stones at the side of the path where something poured out of one declivity into another.

"Hush," said Ashes, "it's only Bone and Boneless." He glanced upward toward the slow clap, clap of leathern wings. In a moment the winged one dropped onto the trail beside him, eyes glowing, sharp fangs glittering. A lean, gray-furred body leaned toward the boys, almost hungrily.

"Ashes and Thunder," the thing said from a fanged mouth. "Welcome home. You brought me dinner?"

"They're not for your dinner, Webwings." Ashes nodded. "These're my boys. This here's Bane, that's Dyre."

Barely able to speak, the brothers managed jerky nods in the newcomer's direction. He stared at them for a time with glowing eyes, then grasped Ashes's arm and swung himself onto the horse behind him, wings falling to either side of the mount, the ragged tips trailing along the ground. When Ashes clucked the horse into a trot, Bane and Dyre did likewise, though reluctantly. Having seen this little, they were not eager to see more. The trail led toward cook fires that burned on hearths of stone in what seemed to be a permanent encampment, a sprawling community of stone-and-wattle shacks, of roofless enclosures, of pits and holes, all set well apart, with firewood piled nearby, and everything concealed from above by copses of large trees.

Ashes drew up at the edge of the encampment. His winged acquaintance slipped off the horse and walked away behind a high earthen wall. Bane and Dyre shared a glance between themselves and at their father who watched the wall, waiting. From behind that concealment a huge, bony hook slashed down, flailing in a forceful arc that slammed it into the shivering soil, fragments of sod flying. Then came another hook at the end of a stout cable or a thick rope, flailing down, piercing deep. The cables tightened; there was a sound like a gasp or grunt, not quite organic, and a monstrous mound of flesh tugged itself into view, something like an elephantine caterpillar, a thing the size of a large carriage or small river boat, though longer than that, for it kept coming as the huge grapples at its front were set again and again so the body could heave itself forward. The immense, immobile weight hauling along the ground, accompanied by a barrage of grunts and gargles, thrust up the earth at either side, leaving a groove like a ditch.

Terrible as the thing was, it was not the size or the sound that horrified the boys so much as the sight of the almost human face between the hooks, a face with wide, slobbery lips and a hole for a nose and eyes that peered from deep pits of gray, granular flesh under a ruff of large, oval scales, like those Bane had seen along the way.

The horses jittered as the thing came nearer: hook, heave, hump, hook, heave, hump, gargling and spewing, stopping at last a hook's length away.

"Crawly, I'd like you to meet my boys," said Ashes, rather too loudly.

The thing wheezed in a breathless, bubbling voice, straining against the buried hooks. The cables had elbows, even a kind of wrists, being otherwise twisted sinew. Closer to, Bane could see that the hooks were hands that had become enlarged with the fingers fused into sharply angled, bone-tipped grapples.

"So here's the offspring," wheezed the monster. "Well, well. Very human-looking, aren't they? How do you do, young sprouts. Doing well, are you?"

"Say yessir, when someone speaks to you," snarled Ashes, striking Bane on the back.

"Yessir," bleated Bane and Dyre, as with one voice.

The creature grinned and drooled, raising the large, oval scales around its neck into a hideous ruff. Greenish goo oozed from between the erected scales, emitting a greatly amplified wave of the family stink.

Webwings came around the side of his monstrous friend, smiling maliciously at Bane and Dyre. "Not what you expected, eh, boys?"

Bane swallowed, trying to moisten a dry mouth. "Didn't . . . didn't expect anything." In the light of the fire he could see what looked like spiders moving about on the creature's wings, spinning back and forth, thread by thread, repairing the holes and tatters. When the spiders had finished, they scuttled into holes in what would have been armpits if Webwings had had arms. Bane felt an irresistible urge to scratch under his own arms, and only a glare from his father held him motionless. Dyre was not so fortunate. He scratched and was thunked across the back of the head for it.

"This is Strike," said Ashes, turning to the other side, where someone else had approached without their notice, a creature knobbed and heavy at the top, thin as a rail below, bearing a long bony beak like a curved pike, with opaque bloody beads of eyes peering from either side. It had arms like boneless vines twisting at its sides, and it tottered on clublike legs as it struggled to hold its great bony haft aloft.

And behind it came something tentacled and horned, moving on a carpet of fibers, and behind that came something squatty with a mouth like a furnace. "Mosslegs," said Ashes. "And Gobblemaw. Say howdy."

"How do you do, sirs," said Bane, shaking his brother with one hand. "Tell the sirs how do you do, brother."

Dyre managed a nod and a gush of wordless air.

There was also Foot (a tiny person with one huge extremity that flexed endlessly upon a separate patch of soil), and, each on its own plot, Ear (a tiny person with huge ear that quivered), and Tongue (a tiny person with huge tongue that wagged). There was Belly, too, wide as a swamp, legs and arms flung out like those on a skin rug, with a wide mouth at one end where some many-handed being called Shoveler was busy pushing the carcass of a very dead goat into it.

All had faces, though some were very small. Not all had mouths and tongues capable of speech. All had arms and legs, though some were rudimentary. Not all had means of locomotion. Among the speaking and walking were a dozen or so who appeared mankindly enough to pass in a crowd, creatures with names like Blade and Shatter and Brigand, Machinist and Mooly, and some of the mankindly ones wore clothes as Ashes did, though more were clad in thick hair or bristles or scales or feathers, or had skin that was warty or horned or embossed or folded. No two were enough alike to mistake one for the other, not even the manlike ones.

Soon Bane and Dyre were at the center of a gathering, a score of creatures all talking at once, producing a windy gibberish that babbled on until the one called Shatter thrust through the mob and drowned them out with a stentorian cry: "Good-looking girls there, Ash. So these're the daughters, eh?"

Ashes's lips thinned, his jaw tightened. "So, what you got, Shatter? You got some girls hid we don't know about?"

Bane shut his eyes, reminded of Dutter's farm, where the animals had made similar noises and the supernume farmhands had joshed at him in similar phrases, until they had learned not to. He had never suffered insults without retaliation. Here, the life around him was itself an insult, past retaliation, and the inability to voice or display his outrage left him feeling weak, as though from loss of blood. He would feel better later, he told himself, and then he would do whatever he had to do, and when he did it, this mockery, yes, mockery would be remembered, for Ashes had no right to do . . . whatever it was he had done.

"Boys're bettern nothin', I suppose!" Shatter brayed.

"That's right, Shat. Can't blame a man for trying."

The one called Mooly bent himself in laughter. "No, we can't blame old Ash for tryin'! Or us for watchin' him try!"

The gathering split asunder. Ashes rode out of it, the boys staying close behind him as he pointed his horse toward a shack under a towering tree at the far side of the camp. There they turned the horses into a corral made of dead branches with bits of vine twisted around them, and while Ashes busied himself with unsaddling the mounts, the boys went inside. There was little in the way of furniture. A table and a chair. A low dirt mound cushioned with boughs and sheepskins to make a couch or sleeping place. They settled themselves on this, leaning forward toward the coals of the fire, piling on a stick or two as though this tending of the fire were necessary and demanding, choosing an appearance of gravity rather than acknowledge to one another the depth of their confusion and disappointment. They had not sorted out how they felt, certainly they had not sorted out what, if anything, they would do about how they felt.

When Ashes came in, they were still bent beside the fire, side by side, cross-legged and silent.

He regarded them narrowly. "Well?"

The first thing they needed, so Bane had decided, was information. "What'd you bring us here for?"

"You're family," said Ashes, hanging his jacket on a peg set into a tent pole. "You'll want to be in on family business."

"Don't exactly see it that way," said Bane, carefully expressionless. "Don't see much great future here. Not exactly what you promised. No reason to have killed *her,* if this was all we did it for."

"No women here," Dyre added in sulky explanation. "No sex machines. No hot baths. No massage. I had a look at what they was roasting on the fires, walking over here, and it's not food, it's garbage. You promised us good stuff, all kinds of good stuff."

"You had your good stuff with Marool," said Ashes. "I promised you good things while you were with her, boys. I said, you get yourselves educated at House Genevois, and I'll situate you at Mantelby Mansion. Well, you got situated there, one way or t'other, and you got good stuff, too, don't say you didn't."

"A few days," grated Bane. "And why her? Why not somebody we didn't have to kill? Somebody we coulda stayed with?"

Ashes said angrily, "I told you why, boy. She needed killing and she's the only one couldn't smell you. That job's over and that future's gone a begging. You don't want the good life any more than the rest of us do, but before we get it, first we got to clear the way! So, you've done the first part and killed one that needed killing."

"We killed her cause you told us to!"

"Well, I'm your daddy. I got that right."

"I been wanting to ask you, how come she couldn't smell us?" asked Bane, eyes narrow.

"Dingle. She used it when she was a girl. Ruined her sense of smell."

"Well, then, we'll find us some other women used Dingle. She couldn'ta been the only one."

Ashes sat down in the only chair the tent afforded, a folding affair of rawhide and curved sticks. "Well, not the only one, no, but women who use Dingle are mostly the ones too ugly to dowry for. Or they're sterile. Or they're crazy. Or all three. Once in a great while there's one like Marool, but it's rare.''

''There was our mama,'' said Bane, watching his father narrowly. ''Could she smell you?''

Ashes was momentarily silent. ''Well, no. But her and Marool were the only ones I ever found.''

''But it just happened Marool was the one stole us away from you?''

''Right,'' said Ashes, busying himself with his boot-laces. ''We all three knew each other, me and Marool and your mama. And Marool was jealous of your mama having my babies. So, when your mama died, she stole you away. And she was goin' to have a daughter for me, but she didn't. But I found you, so it all turned out all right.''

''Maybe,'' muttered Bane. ''Maybe it did.''

''So what's the family business?'' asked Dyre.

''Why, boys, this whole world is our family business! It belongs to us! We was here first, and we're going to take it back!'' Ashes lay back in the chair and stared at his sons through the smoke of the fire. ''We're going to take it back, kill off all the timrats, kill off all the settler men, all those g'family men. We'll keep the women. Some of them, anyhow. Whichever ones we can fix like we did Marool. We're going to build a race of giants!''

''Is this all of you?'' Bane asked, gesturing to indicate the camp. ''All that's left?''

Ashes stared into the fire. ''No. There's others. Bigger. Meaner. Sometimes they come to the edge of the light and we talk. They're with us.''

''How come they don't live here?''

Ashes made a peculiar face, a kind of chewing, as though trying to swallow something that wouldn't go down. ''They . . . they got changed in the pond. Really changed. They're too big for camp, for one thing, and there's nothing . . . nothing much we can talk to them about now. They're like . . . only set on one thing.'' He got up, started to speak, then thought better of whatever he'd been going to say. ''Later,'' he admonished. ''We'll get into all that stuff later.''

Bane shook his head, showing his teeth. He wasn't going to let go. "So, how come you've waited all this time? It'd a been easier when there wasn't so many settlers, wouldn't it? It'd a been easier when they just first arrived. You shoulda done it then, killed the men, took the women, got your own daughters, like you planned. I mean, those, out there, they say you planned daughters, right?"

"We wanted daughters, sure, but I told you we couldn't do it back then!" snarled Ashes. "We tried that. Grabbed a few girls outa their houses, took 'em back in the hills, did 'em there. We'd just get half done with 'em, and they'd die! They'd turn blue, try to breathe, then they'd die. I told you, it's the smell of that pond! Like it smothered 'em. Took us a long time to figure out how to get around that. Mooly figured out about Dingle. You get on Dingle, it builds up a kind of . . . resistance to the smell. Dingle grows easy, but back then it only grew far back in the hills. We had to bring it near the cities, plant it there so we could get plenty of it, easy. Then we had to teach people to use it, Wasters and rebels and like that.

"But you get a woman on Dingle, she'll abort, sure as anything. So, then Mooly had to find some other drug to counteract that effect. That took a long time, boys. That took a long, long time. We tried this and we tried that, over the years. Got to be legendary, we did, for stealing women, but we kept at it.

"So we did that, all of it, nice and slow, and we've got you. You're the proof that it works. When we take over, we'll take our time, do it right. . . ."

"How you going to do that? Take over?"

Ashes leaned back in his chair, staring at the fire, looking at the boys, then past them, then back at the boys again. "Well, there's a time coming. We can feel it. Kind of like a call in the bones. The mountains are gonna blow! Then the cities'll fall, boys. Cities'll fall. People, they'll be out, running around in the streets. We'll be there, waiting. There's hot springs here and there, we'll fill them with Dingle. Kill this one, take that one and drop her in a Dingle pot, kill this one, take that one to the Dingle, slow and easy. These folks, they got nothing like an army. Nothing like police. Just those Haggers, here, there, everywhere. But Crawly, he's as good as a fortress. Webwings, he's our lookout. Ear, he can hear a moth drop a day's march away. Tongue, he can taste blood in the air. We'll manage."

"When you gonna do it?" asked Dyre.

Ashes looked out the one small window at the sky, pointed westward where four of the moons made a cluster low along the hills, with another one trailing close. "Soon, boy. My bones say soon. They're all gathering. Real soon."

"And when we take it over, everything, then we get what you promised, huh?" Bane asked.

"Then you get what was promised you and I get what was promised me, and we all get everything we want. And more."

46

The Second Expedition Sets Out

Onsofruct and D'Jevier, together with five sturdy Haggers, waited for Madame outside the gates of Mantelby Mansion rather early on fiveday morning. They heard the carriage wheels approaching from down the hill, then saw the equipage as it rounded the nearest curve and came quickly toward them. Madame was not alone. She was accompanied by one veiled man without cockade and a family man known to the Hags by the cockade as Calvy g'Valdet. He leapt from the carriage and bowed deeply.

''Revered Hag,'' he said. ''It seems the Hags and the Men of Business are similarly motivated.''

''How did you find out about this, Family Man?'' demanded Onsofruct, with a glare in Madame's direction.

''Do not blame Madame,'' said Calvy. ''The steward here is Bin g'Kiffle's son.''

''Of course,'' murmured D'Jevier. ''We should have remembered that.''

''There was a special meeting of the ECMOB, and after

a good bit of talk that achieved nothing, they decided to send me to represent the Men of Business."

"Why you, g'Valdet?" asked Onsofruct. "Are you now in good odor with your colleagues?"

"No, Ma'am," he said. "Slab g'Tupoar nominated me. He said that Myrphee was too fat, Sym was too small, Slab himself was too lazy. Estif's wife wouldn't let him, and Bin bitches about everything. He said he didn't much like me, but I got things done. And here I am."

"Well, if your intention is to find out what happened to the Questioner, your interest is no less justified than ours, though I am surprised at the company you keep."

"I have known Calvy for many years," said Madame. "In my opinion, we need him and my well-trusted Simon to assist us in this exploration."

Onsofruct said stiffly, "If you think it wise, we will not obstruct you. I suggest, however, that the Family Man and Simon replace two of our Haggers rather than increasing our total number."

"Is the number important?" asked Calvy.

"Not if you are both excellent swimmers," remarked D'Jevier, rather frostily. "Since Timmys are no doubt involved in this disappearance, we have cast about in memory and fable and find many references to subterranean waters—at least rivers, perhaps even lakes. We are carrying an inflatable boat that holds a maximum of eight."

Calvy laughed. "I hadn't thought of that! By all means, let us replace two of your Haggers."

There was a momentary hesitation among them, an unspoken acknowledgment that they had not agreed upon a leader for their expedition.

Onsofruct ran her fingers down the seams of her unaccustomed trousers and said, "Madame? D'Jevier and I have seldom been outside the Panhagion since we were children. Do you have experience of this kind of thing? If so, we would be pleased to follow you."

Madame was herself dressed appropriately for the occasion in heavy trousers and shirt, with stout boots on her feet. She regarded the Hags with some diffidence, saying, "I can't claim to expertise, though a small group of friends and I have gone on lengthy cave hikes during the summers, exploring some of the badlands west of Naibah. I may have picked up some useful skills. I know that Simon and Calvy have had similar experience."

D'Jevier nodded. "You are better equipped than we. How do you suggest that we proceed?"

Madame smiled. "By handling a question that arose during our trip here. Calvy and Simon have pointed out that it will be difficult for them to be useful if they keep their veils."

"We are unlikely to be able to see through them underground," said Calvy, making an apologetic gesture toward the Hags.

D'Jevier replied, "I have no objection to your removing your veils while on this expedition. It would be foolish to handicap you out of mere custom; Onsofruct and I have quite dependable self-control, and we promise not to assault you sexually."

Madame merely smiled at this.

Calvy said, "Inasmuch as Simon and I are already carrying all we can manage, let's proceed with all five of your Haggers. When and if we encounter water, we can decide then what baggage to leave behind, who will go on and who will return."

D'Jevier nodded her assent, then led them around the house to a side entrance that gave directly upon stairs leading to the cellars. The room below had already been cleared of its sadistic machines, except for piles of scrap, and Onsofruct wasted no time in finding and opening the sneakway door, bowing Madame to enter first.

Madame stepped into the sneakway, looked and sniffed in both directions, and came to much the same conclusion Mouche had come to earlier. "That way goes back up into the mansion. This way leads down. I think we may rely upon it that they went down, though we'll watch for their tracks to be sure."

"If you'll allow me," said Calvy, drawing Madame out and taking her place in the narrow way. "I have done some tracking, and I am armed, which you are not."

"Armed, Family Man?" asked D'Jevier, threateningly. "Our laws forbid Family Men carrying arms."

"A canister of chemical repellant, Ma'am. Useful for dissuading vicious dogs while walking on the streets. And a rather large knife, useful for opening shipping crates. Both are allowed within the regulations. I am also carrying a staff which I have been trained to use." He turned on the downward way and moved off with Madame and the Hags behind him, then Simon and the Haggers bringing up the rear.

Down they went, as Mouche, Ornery, and the Questioner had gone, making their slow way through the rooty tunnel until it intersected the stream. Because they had lighted their way throughout, they noticed no luminescence. Indeed, they had sent two Haggers back the way they had come, had inflated their boat and were well down the river before they turned out their lights and began to see the wonders of the world around them.

47

Round the Down Staircase

For Mouche and his companion, the drift-trip down the big river had seemed timeless. Both Mouche and Ornery had slept for long, lost periods of quiet and peace. Every now and then the boats had stopped at some sandy beached curve and let them go ashore to eat and drink and relieve themselves, and according to Questioner, who seemed to be keeping track, this happened several times each day for several days. They had eaten only a little food from their packs, for Questioner had reminded them they had no idea how long they would be on this journey and thus no idea how long their food would need to last.

"I think we could eat their food," Mouche had said, indicating the darkness where pairs of silver eyes shone briefly from time to time. "I've smelled it, and it smells wonderful."

"Do not worry over food," came the voice from the darkness. "You will not be allowed to starve. You must come to the Fauxi-dizalonz in good health. When we come to the sea, we will feed you."

"How long to the sea?" asked Ornery, somewhat fretfully.

"Long enough to get there," came the fading voice.

Sometimes they felt that their escorts went away, for a kind of vacancy occurred, as though some essential component of the environment had gone missing, though where anything could go in this dim world, they could only guess. There were folds and cracks in the tunnel walls, and the tunnel constantly changed direction, and any of these irregularities might hide a way in or out just as they concealed the roosting places of many small creatures that plunged out into the air or down into the river, luminous forms that approached and receded, glowing parasols of light, soaring cones, winged diamonds, both above and below, as though air or water made little difference to them.

Three long sleeps into the journey, they became aware of a hushing sound, like the roar of their own blood in their ears. This very gradually grew into a soft roaring that grew more thunderous with every passing breath. If they had not guessed what caused it, Questioner would have told them. The sound was quite unmistakable, she said, for she had heard waterfalls on a hundred planets and water always sounded like water. By the time the little boat thrust up onto a sandy shore and tipped them out, unfolding into a flat blade of rubbery flesh that slipped away under the water, the roaring was loud enough to make conversation difficult.

"Now what?" shouted Ornery, who had been content to sleep the time away, curled in the end of the boat, dreaming of far shores and strange sights. Sailors, so she had told Mouche, learned to sleep whenever and wherever they could.

"You cannot dive the falls; for you the stairs," cried the voice from the darkness. "We have put a light."

The familiar hugeness swelled out of the water, a shiny dark mound that turned its pale, spherical eye across them then receded toward the falls. Within moments, it was gone, the guides were gone, and they three were alone.

"Light?" suggested Questioner. "Where?"

They found it hidden behind several broken shards of lava tube, the pieces nested like pieces of a giant cup, curved up against the wall, a glowing crystal set within the arch, illuminating the top of the stairs to the left. After taking a few moments for comfort's sake and redistributing their packs, they stepped past the light and onto the stairs. Flowing Green had not said *endless* stairs, though there was no end in sight.

Questioner lit their way as they variously clomped or danced or leapt downward. Here and there the sidewall opened to admit both the roar of the waters and curtains of flung spray, from each of which they emerged deafened and wet through. Finally came a roaring window near the bottom of the falls, where Questioner leaned through to light a great cauldron of boiling foam leading to a short stretch of glassy river, and then to a lip of stone over which the water poured unbroken into darkness.

They paralleled the level stretch of river, finding more stairs beside the lip of the fall. The next opening was a long way down, far enough down that the roar of the basin was reduced to a soft rushing, and again Questioner leaned out to light the water. The smooth pour shone with greenish reflections, utterly silent. Within the glassy flow moved pallid shadows that twisted and spun within the cataract, moving with the water into some unguessed at basin below.

Mouche made a noise that was almost a moan. "I dreamed this," he said in a helpless voice. "I dreamed this!"

"Well, Mouche," said Questioner in a chilly, admonitory voice, "I am sure you believe so. It is all very mystic and dreamlike, and though I can be sensitive to the moods and impressions such places evoke, I try not to give way to them. When dream is most attractive, then is time to be alert and practical, for it is then we are most in danger." She gave him a keen and penetrating look.

Mouche swallowed painfully. He didn't want to be practical. Every step in this journey took him either nearer to his dream life or farther from it, into new and treacherous territory, and he could not tell the difference.

"I'm sure you're right," he said, gritting his teeth.

"Be assured, I am," said Questioner. "Let us expedite this climb. You, Mouche, come here upon my left side. I shall extrude two little steps there, see, one at the back, one at the side, one for each foot to stand upon while you lean forward upon my shoulder. And you, Ornery, do the same upon my right, if you will. In that way we may make better time, and certainly in a less fatiguing manner."

Though doubtful, they did as she ordered, after which a brief clicking and clanking preceded a seemingly effortless, level and continuous descent of the interminable stairs.

"How are you doing this?" asked Ornery, who had always been fascinated by machinery.

"Two-part rotary tread, two outside sections, one wider, central section, operating alternately, first center legs then side legs. The knees are double jointed, of course, and the only trick is to shift my ballast properly."

"How long can you do it?"

"Several planetary diameters, I should imagine. Do you think we'll be going that far?"

Ornery fell silent for a time, thinking it remarkable how quiet the mechanism was. There was only the slightest *chickety-click, chickety-click* as the treads placed themselves, only the tiniest hum as Questioner descended, obviously unhampered by the weight of both of them and their packs.

"I can see how that works on stairs, but does it work on irregular slopes?" Ornery asked.

"It adapts itself. I am very well designed."

They went down the stairs for what seemed half a day with the water, intermittently lit by Questioner's headlamp, still soundlessly falling at left or right, depending upon the spiral of the stair. Mouche leaned upon her shoulder and slept while Ornery, more or less alert, whispered occasional comments and questions into Questioner's ear.

"Someone said you were made with mankind brains inside. Is that true?"

"True. Yes. Three of them."

"Do you know whose they were?"

Questioner surprised herself by answering honestly, "Yes. I was recently given that information."

"Old people, I suppose."

"No. Three young women. Very young, one of them, only a girl, M'Tafa, her name was. Of an untouchable caste, on a planet you've never heard of and I wish I hadn't."

"Why?" begged Ornery, sensing no discomfort and willing to be distracted with a story.

"The untouchables are simply that. They may not let their shadows fall on other people. They may not touch anything the higher castes touch or use. If they do, the thing must be boiled before it can be used again. If the thing cannot be boiled, they kill the untouchable instead.

"The untouchables speak a language of their own in order that the words spoken by the higher castes cannot be sullied on their lips. This child, M'Tafa, was a filth carrier. She sat outside an uppercaste nursery, and whenever the babies soiled a diaper, M'Tafa carried it to the laundry where it would be boiled. Sometimes, when no one was looking, she would touch things, very quickly, and then watch to see if anyone boiled them. They never did, unless they knew M'Tafa had touched them.

"One day a pet animal knocked over a lamp in the nursery, and the baby's crib was in the way of the fire. M'Tafa could not call anyone, for they did not speak her language. She could not put out the fire, for she had nothing to do it with. She was not supposed to touch the baby. Very quickly, so that no one saw, she moved the baby out of its crib, out of the way of the fire.

"Of course, someone figured out what had happened, for M'Tafa was the only one there. They could not boil the baby, so they killed M'Tafa. She was buried alive for her crime."

"Oh, horrid," cried Ornery. "That's terrible. Does she remember? Is she still . . . like, alive inside you?"

"She is, yes."

"Were the other two like that?"

"More or less. Tiu was a young bride, married to an old man who lived only a few days after the wedding. When he died, custom dictated that a faithful wife could offer to die on the pyre with him. Tiu did not wish to die so. She scarcely knew the old man. But, if Tiu did not die on the pyre, she could claim an inheritance, and since the grown children of the old man did not want to divide the inheritance, she was tied to the pyre and burned alive."

Ornery gulped, beginning to be sorry she had asked. "And the last one?"

"Mathilla. A similar story. A young bride of thirteen or fourteen in a world where women are hidden away. She was sequestered virtually alone in a harem by her old husband who was often away. The grown son of the old husband came to visit. He had a daughter her age, and he took pity on her and taught her to read and gave her books to pass the time. And when the old man found out, he charged her with adultery, though there had been nothing between the little wife and the grown son but pity and gratitude. She was stoned to death, for such is the penalty for adultery. Her own father threw the first stone."

Ornery breathed deeply. "Do they remember dying?"

Questioner sighed deeply. "I sometimes think it is all they remember."

Ornery said, "Many of our baby girls die, but not like that. They die when they are born. That's why all women have to marry and have children, because they are so few. It's why I pretend to be a man, so I won't have to."

She fell silent, thinking about Mathilla and Tiu and M'tafa. She had never considered before that in other places, things could be far worse for women than they were on Newholme.

"Why did they pick brains with so much pain?" she asked.

Questioner hummed for a moment. "The technicians are long dead, so I can't ask them. I know they wanted brains that were healthy, young, with few memories, so people dying of disease wouldn't do. I know they had to make some advance preparation, so people dying suddenly in accidents wouldn't do. They preferred planets which were less advanced, technologically, where fewer questions would be asked. They may even have been motivated by pity, thinking that, in a way, they were saving those three. And then, of course, they didn't expect that I would ever know enough to bring them into memory.''

Ornery thought about this, lazily, which led her to another thought. ''We met those two Earthers you brought with you. Why did you bring those particular ones?''

''They are dancers. I felt we might need dancers.''

''What for? You haven't needed them, have you?''

''We are not yet finished with our visit though, are we?''

They went on a bit farther, and Questioner said, ''Hark?''

Ornery listened for the sound of water, hearing instead the sound of voices. Someone or something was approaching from farther down the stairs.

Questioner unburdened herself, wakening Mouche, who shook himself sleepily, adjusting his pack and brushing wrinkles from his clothing. The voices came nearer. Questioner turned up her light.

They appeared quite suddenly around the turn of the stairs below, half a dozen Timmys, slim and graceful in their flowing membranes, plus a plump and furry bright violet creature a bit larger than they.

''Oh,'' cried Mouche in a tone of great pleasure. ''There you are!''

The furry creature separated itself from its friends or colleagues and dashed up the stairs to fling itself on Mouche, huge hands holding to his shoulders, back legs braced against his body, both tail and body hair fluffed wide in the pure and glowing color Mouche well remembered.

The being put one hand on Mouche's lips and said clearly, ''Mouche, Mouche.'' Then, looking around, ''Duster?''

Tears filled Mouche's eyes, part grief, part delight that

his friend had remembered. "Dead," he said. "Those two boys killed him."

"Jongau," said the creature in a tone of anger. "Very bad jongau." He climbed sadly down, head bowed, then approached Ornery. "You are the sailor. Good! And you are Questioner?"

"Yes," Questioner agreed with a regal nod. "And you are?"

"He's my friend," cried Mouche. "From when I was a boy. But he never talked, not then!"

"True," said the creature, returning Ornery's bow. "I did not talk to you then, but I was a friend. Also I am the last of the Corojumi, the last choreographer."

"Choreographer," said Questioner, intrigued. "A choreographer?"

"Once one of many, many, many. Now, only one."

"What happened to the others?" Ornery asked.

"The jongau killed them. And took their skins. And took the skins afar, to some other place, where we could not retrieve them. And so my friends could not come to the Fauxi-dizalonz. They could not be reborn. And now, I am the only Corojum, one alone."

"What's a choreographer?" Ornery whispered to Questioner.

"A designer of dances," Questioner answered. "One who creates the steps and gestures and meanings of dance, though sometimes they copy former choreographers . . ."

"Which is what we want to do," cried the Corojum in an agonized voice. "That is what we must do! We must copy the former dance!"

"But you have nothing to copy," offered Questioner.

"Exactly."

Mouche opened his mouth, "But . . ."

"Hush," said Questioner, raising her hands. "I can feel the questions bubbling up on your lips, but I feel that poised halfway down an interminable stair is not the right time or place. We must have a settled time in which to pursue matters uninterruptedly before we agitate ourselves with hasty questions and half answers."

The Corojum nodded. "Oh, yes, that is wise. Far better

to take time, better even to show than to say. Far better to illustrate than merely explain. Always in the dance, this is so. Come then.'' He turned toward the stairs and started down. ''It is only a little way now.''

They followed him. His colleagues, the Timmys, had already disappeared, and they did not reappear, even when Questioner's group emerged at last onto an open and level space. The Corojum ran ahead into darkness, beckoning them. ''Come. With less light you will see better.''

Questioner dimmed herself. After a moment, they did see better, and with the seeing came hearing, too, the soft shush of waves on a sloping beach. Before them was the subsurface sea, lighted with a hundred dancing colors and shades, wavelets of luminous peridot and emerald, sapphire and aquamarine, effulgent ripples running toward their feet across a flat beach of black sand to make a citron-colored froth at their toes. Along the beach to their left, a great curved tower went up into the luminous sky, disappearing at the height. Beyond it was another, larger than the largest buildings on Newholme, higher than the tallest, crystalline in structure, reaching upward like a great column.

''I saw these columns being built,'' said Questioner. ''I saw a record of this world when these pillars were the cores of little volcanoes.''

''True,'' offered the Corojum. ''First a plain here, then a thousand tiny firemountains, then their cores left behind, then the sea covering the plain with silt, then the plain rising again, then the roof pouring out from other firemountains. So Kaorugi told us, Kaorugi, the builder. It was Kaorugi who sent tunnelers to drill the holes to let the rain through to lick away the soft stone, Kaorugi who sent the closers to seal the holes up again before the land sank beneath the surface seas. It was Kaorugi who built the stairs and made the places for water to run deep into the world and out again, Kaorugi who created the first boat to sail this sea, but then, you know about the boats or you would not have brought sailors with you.''

''Bofusdiaga and the Corojumi sailed the ship,'' said Questioner. ''According to my informants.''

"We Corojumi guided the ship, yes. And Bofusdiaga told us how to make the journey. But Bofusdiaga was already too large for ships, Bofusdiaga is now too large to move, and besides, it is usually busy elsewhere, and there is only one Corojum, so we must sail as best we can."

The Corojum ran from them to the edge of the sea, put his huge hands to his mouth and called into the distance.

Watching this, Mouche asked Questioner, "Where did the waterfall stop?"

"Back there, somewhere," said Questioner. "I imagine in some kind of enclosed cave from which it siphons up or flows out into this sea. If there was, indeed, a designer of this place, it no doubt preferred to keep the noise and dense mists away from this shore. For visibility's sake, if nothing else."

"Are we under the ocean?" asked Ornery, apprehensively. "I mean, the Jellied Sea?"

"I think not," Questioner answered. "My judgment is that the first tunnel brought us under the badlands west of Sendoph, that the first small stream brought us farther west. The river then changed our direction, taking us north or northwest—which would be more or less toward the Jellied Sea—until we came to the fall, from which the stair twisted upon itself going mostly down. Now we are north and west of the place we began, looking westward across this sea, and above us are the badlands. This ocean is self-contained, with its own atmosphere, like a submarine vehicle."

"But the water's been running down into here," objected Ornery. "Wouldn't it fill it up?"

Questioner shrugged massively. "Kaorugi has no doubt taken that into account. Possibly it runs past furnaces of the deep which turn it into high-pressure steam and thrust it up somewhere else," said Questioner. "We need not worry how it happens since it is evident it does. Otherwise, we would all have drowned by now."

Far out on the luminous waves, a shadow appeared.

"A ship," cried Ornery. "A sailing ship."

Though of unfamiliar appearance, it was a sailing ship,

with a curly prow and two short masts that held reefed sails. It was being towed by their old acquaintance, Joggiwagga, whose moon-eye preceded the craft. On the deck, along the rail, stood a dozen Timmys.

Mouche stared, searching. They did not include Flowing Green, and he felt a surge of relief. For his Hagion to be here with him would have been too much.

"Why can't Joggiwagga just tow us where we need to go?" asked Ornery.

"Forbidden," cried the Corojum. "His place is not there. His place is here and outside."

"But our place is there?" cried Mouche.

"There, or nowhere, my friend. Together we will live or we will all die, as is the way of worlds. Together all creatures must live, changing together, else the world dies. All creation dances together, is this not so?"

"Usually," replied Questioner. "Is there a way I can get on that ship, or must I fire up the gravitics?"

"There is a way."

The ship stopped at the edge of deeper water, unrolling a silvery tongue that extended across the shallows and up onto the beach, stiffening into a ramp. "Welcome," said the ship. "Please watch your footing."

The tongue was as rigid as a gangway, and when they had come aboard, it rolled up behind them. The Corojum showed them where to put their packs, and the Timmys invited them to a table set with food and drink.

Mouche watched them as in a reverie, and Questioner watched him watching the Timmys. She thought the boy was in the grip of dreamtime. It wasn't sexual. She was sure of that. It was something else entirely, the lure of the marvelous and mysterious, the siren call of the unknown. Or perhaps the Timmy who had tended him as a child had had green hair.

After they had eaten and drunk and the Timmys had cleared away all evidence of the meal, the Corojum summoned Timmys, Ornery, and Mouche to work together in setting the sails.

"If it's alive," whispered Ornery, "why doesn't it set its own sails?"

"It's not alive like that," whispered one of the Timmys. "It's just alive enough to utter a few courtesies and keep itself mended."

Slowly, after several tries, the sails were swung into the desired position, and the ship turned slowly with the wind, which endlessly blew, so the Corojum said, down the stairs behind them.

"It is so, for so Kaorugi designed it."

"How far do we have to go?" asked Ornery, tightening a very organic-looking rope around a cleat that had obviously grown into place where it was.

"Until we get there," murmured Questioner. "Is that not so?"

"That is so," replied the Corojum. "That is always so."

48

Westward the Wilderneers

By Bane's count, four or five days had passed since the death of Marool and their arrival in the camp. That morning Ashes told him and his brother to pack up and ready themselves for a journey.

"Where to?" Bane demanded.

"I told you about that time the Timmys took us? That pond kind of place they took us to?"

"Underground, you said."

"No, not under. Just down in a deep valley, well, an old volcano. Anyhow, ever since then, some of us have kept watch on that place. Now, the mountains are getting ready to blow, and when that happens, we need all of us to be ready to take over, so it's time to fetch all our friends."

"Prob'ly dead by now," said Dyre. "That was a long time ago."

"They're not dead," asserted Ashes. "I told you we don't die! And you'd best shut that backtalk, boy. Best remember what I can do if I need to keep you in line."

He patted his waist, where the whip hung, its tip twitching hungrily toward them, the tip opening like a little mouth, a living thing.

Bane turned his eyes from the whip. "What d'you need us for?"

"Company. I like the company of my sons," said Ashes, laughing at them. "Besides, you're safer with me than staying here. The Shoveler might decide to feed you to Belly. Or Crawly might get hungry and forget you're part of the family. Or Mooly might decide to find out how well you can fight, and you don't want to fight Mooly."

"I'm not ascared of him!" asserted Dyre.

"More fool you, then," said his father. "You haven't been in the pond like we have. You may not have our ability to heal. Mooly's got a skin like steel plates and he's fast. Faster than anybody here. Including me."

"So, it's just us going?"

Ashes's face went blank, as though the question had derailed him. His features sagged, like wax, half melted. Bane looked at Dyre, gritting his teeth, readying himself to do something . . . anything. Dyre's mouth was open, and he shivered as though frightened. Then, gradually, sense seeped back into Ashes's eyes, his facial bones acquired rigidity, and he spoke as though nothing had happened. "It's just us, starting out. Who else decides to go is their business. Us sons of thunder are into independent action."

When they left, several other of the Wilderneers said they'd be coming along, soon, and midway through the morning, Bane spotted Webwings, high in the air above them, flying far faster than they were riding. He cleared his throat tentatively.

"Well, what you got in your craw?" his father asked.

"Webwings, he's up there. Those . . . those spiders on him, Webwings. Where did he get them?"

"They aren't spiders, they're part of him," said Ashes, patting his hip. "Just the way this whip is part of me, and Crawly's hooks are part of him. We came out of the pond that way."

"How come . . . how come some of you are so big?"

"Weren't big, not then. Some of us got bigger. Crawly wasn't any bigger than you to start with. Foot wasn't all that big, just one foot larger than the other. Belly wasn't, he just had a pot on him. Ear wasn't all that big, he could still get around, only he kind of held his head to one side. It's just those parts went on growing and growing while the rest of them shrunk down."

"Why is that?"

Ashes pinched his lips together. "Well, Belly always did think more about his next meal than anything else. And Tongue was a talker."

"And Foot?"

"None of us can figure Foot. It wasn't he liked dancing or anything. Gobblemaw was sort of like Belly. Mosslegs, we can't figure. Webwings we can't figure."

"When you all escaped from the pond place, what did the Timmys and those other things do?"

"Do? They didn't do anything. They tried! Tried to push us back in, gibbering and jabbering. Some of them used our language, too, 'Go back through, go back through,' but we'd had enough. We smashed a few and beat a few and got ourselves out of there. They didn't come after us, just perched all over the place, staring and chattering. Timmys. Joggiwaggas. Tunnelers. All kinds. Well, we gathered our people up, even the strange-looking ones, and we took them all up out of there, oh, that was some climb. We didn't want to go by the road, take too long, so we went straight up, pulling and heaving, carrying the ones that couldn't move on their own. Some of us decided to stay there, to keep watch, but the rest of us went back. . . ."

The last few words trailed off dreamily, as though Ashes were drifting into somewhere else. Bane and Dyre exchanged looks again, wondering, not speaking until Ashes began to talk again, as though he hadn't stopped.

". . . went back eastward, to the towns, and by the time we got ourselves sorted out, that trader ship had already landed. Some of us, the ones who could move easiest, we tried to stop them, but they had weapons on their ship, and some of us got killed before they took off in both ships."

Dyre was still digging at the problem that bothered him and Bane the most. "The Timmys didn't even try to stop you leaving?"

"No," Ashes snorted. "They pushed us in one side, and we swam out the other."

"Was it deep? Did they try to drown you?"

"Wasn't deep and they didn't try to drown us."

"So what did they take you there for?"

Long, dreamy silence, unbroken until Dyre asked the question again.

Ashes snorted. "Boy, if I knew that, I'd know a lot more than anybody else!"

Since Ashes immediately drifted into a reverie again, and since he seemed to have trouble dealing with the questions, Dyre gave up asking for a time.

They had gone a good bit farther on when Bane, who happened to be looking up to judge the position of the sun in the sky, saw Webwings approaching. "See there," he cried, pointing.

They pulled up the horses and waited. Webwings was searching the ground beneath him, possibly looking for them. Ashes took off his hat and waved it. The flying figure folded its wings and dropped, coming to rest on a large rock near the trail.

"I've got to go get the others," said Webwings. "Crawly and Strike and all the rest of us."

"Crawly and Strike should be coming," said Ashes, again in that dreamy voice. "They said so."

Webwings jittered, peering closely at Ashes's face. "Some of 'em went north to intercept the road. Movin's easier there. We've all got to get there in time. Time's running out. Got to get there." Webwings's voice had the same dreamy quality as Ashes's.

"We told our brothers we'd come get 'em," Ashes asserted. "Before we did anything about women or taking over. They'll all want to be there. Hughy Huge. Old Pete."

Webwings stared at the sky. "I saw Pete. In the mouth of that cave where we left him. He's still there. Grown to fit. Can't get out, I shouldn't think, at least not far."

"Good old Pete. We'll get him out. Crawly'll get him out. How 'bout Gorge George? An' Titanic Tom?"

"I caught sight of most of 'em."

"How are they all? Good to see them again."

"They're moving." He snorted and flapped his wings, sending the spiders fleeing to his armpits as he said distractedly, "Eager Eyes, you remember Eag, he can look down into the place, and he saw a whole bunch of Timmys and Joggiwagga and Tunnelers bringing some strange people there, just the way they did us. And one of the people is a blue person. You know what that's about?"

"That's got to be that Questioner's people," muttered Bane. "I heard all about them at Mantelby's."

Ashes stared at the sky, smiling slightly.

"What's a Questioner?" demanded Webwings.

Bane slid off his horse to shake his shirt and trousers loose from his sweaty body. "Seven or eight days ago, maybe more, this Questioner thing came down in a shuttle, and they brought it to Mantelby Mansion to stay. And the servants said that's why all the Timmys had to go, and why we ended up there, doing what Timmys had been doing, because this Questioner was there and she shouldn't catch on we even had Timmys. And she—they all called it she—had this one blue-skin with her, along with a bunch of other kinds."

"Oh," said Webwings dreamily, as though he had lost interest.

Ashes switched his attention from the sky to his fellow Wilderneer. "What do you think it means, Web?"

Webwings shook his head. "Don't ask me. I'm just telling you what Eager saw . . . down at the pond."

"What would they want with a blue person?" Ashes muttered.

"What did they want with us?" Webwings responded.

"Things keep changing around," Ashes complained. "I wish everthing would settle for a few years, let us make some plans."

The flyer shifted from foot to foot. "You know, Ash, seeing that pond, I got to thinking, you remember Foot . . . before?"

"Before when?"

"Before that pond. You ever know about his shoe collection?"

"Shoe collection?"

"We could never figure him getting that way, you know. Or me, but him especially. But lately, I've been remembering. Back on Thor, after he'd done it to some bitch, you know, he'd take her shoes. . . ."

"A fetishist?" asked Bane. "We learned about fetishists at House Genevois."

"So what's one of those?" his father asked.

"Somebody that gets off on a certain thing, like shoes, or gloves, or women's underwear, or even parts of flesh. . . ."

Ashes turned on Webwings, giggling like a schoolboy. "So what'd you collect? Dead birds? Girly feathers?"

"Forget it," said the other, sharply. "I just thought it might explain things."

"What did Pete collect?" Ashes went on. "I mean . . ."

"I said forget it," Webwings said, launching himself upward. "I'll tell 'em you're on the way." He spiraled high and then flew back the way he had come, toward the camp.

"What was he talking about?" asked Bane.

"Oh, he probably was talking about some of us, from Thor," Ashes said, once more in that dreamy, half-hypnotized tone. "Half of us, almost. The way they came out of that pond. They didn't want to come back to the towns, looking like that. They wanted to stay there. Well. So they stayed."

"You said they came to the edge of the camp, sometimes?"

"Not the ones that stayed by the pond, no. The ones that come to the camp are more like Crawly than anything. People like Rogger the Rock. And Black Cliff. And Hughy Huge. Back on Thor, they were muscle men, always on the body machines. Big guys, strong as bulls, and that pond made 'em more so than ever. And they've grown since. Oh, I tell you, they're just mountains of muscle. They don't talk much anymore, they just roll over everything, like it wasn't even there. That's why we built camp where we did, down in that hot pot, so they can't get down into it and roll over us all.''

''Why?'' asked Bane. ''Why would they roll over you?''

''Oh, they still get mad, sometimes. When we take the towns, we'll use 'em all. Talk 'em up. Use real short words. . . .''

They sat silent for a long moment. Bane asked, ''So. We goin' on, or what?''

Ashes merely sat, staring at the sky, indecisively musing aloud, as though he had forgotten they were there.

''Web could be right. I did know about Foot's shoes, back on Thor. I just hadn't thought of it for a few hundred years. And Tongue, well, he had some dirty habits, too. And it makes me remember when we were in that pond . . . the thing was . . . Well, you ever see one of those joke mirrors, the ones that're all curvy, make you look like you had wobbly legs? In that pond, it was like looking into one of those mirrors. Being outside, looking in. Looking at what I was, moving a little, making this bigger, that smaller, you know how you do. And when I came out, I was what I am now because that's what I always thought I was. Even the whip, I'd always had one, not a real one, but in my mind. They used to say that about me, old Ash, he can take the skin off. Old Ash, he can turn you raw. Well, I could.'' He giggled, very lightly, a strange, quavery sound. ''I did. All of us did what was natural to us. You can't do that, what can you do, huh?''

Dyre started to answer, but Bane caught him, keeping him quiet, letting Ashes talk. He'd already said more than they'd heard him say before, and over the last few days, Bane had decided he needed to know everything there was to know about all this.

Ashes kicked his horse into motion, saying, ''But those bastards on Thor, when this one or that one got skinned or tromped on or rolled over, they weren't man enough to take it or fight it, either one. Had to run to daddy this or uncle that and complain about us. We weren't *ord*erly enough. We used up the *wo*men, we didn't accept the *dis*cipline. Discipline, hah!'' He giggled again, that high, quavering giggle. ''They had one thing right, though, we did go through the women. It was getting hard to keep 'em in supply.''

He turned toward his sons, his face alight with malice. ''Trouble was, the good ones were stupid and the bad ones were rotten. Like Marool. If they're bad enough to be interesting, they're not good enough to use. Not fit to live, right?''

This time Dyre spoke before Bane could stop him. ''What did Pete grow into?''

''Pete? Old Petey. He came out of that pond considerably enlarged, and last time I saw him, sitting in the mouth of that cave, he had a piggy as long as old Crawly. He just sat there, looking at it, keeping it from getting sunburned. If it's grown into the mountain, it must be sizeable by now.'' Abruptly, he kneed his horse onto the trail, riding in the direction Webwings had come. ''Be good to see old Pete again!''

Behind him, Bane looked at his brother in terrible surmise, fighting down the urge to feel himself to make sure he was still the same size he had been that morning.

''I know one thing,'' mumbled Dyre. ''I know I don't want to go near that pond.''

With some difficulty, Bane summoned up his usual jeering manner. ''Don't want a big piggy, huh?''

Dyre moved onto the path, following his father, head hanging. Bane rode up beside him, reaching out to touch him, only to have his hand shaken off.

''Look, we need to decide something,'' Bane whispered, reaching across to rein Dyre's horse, letting some distance grow between them and Ashes's receding figure. ''I don't like all this much. He's talking funny. He's riding west for no reason at all, so far as I can see. And another thing, Webwings . . .''

''He flew back to camp.''

''Well, he said he was going to, but not long ago, I looked up, and there he was, headed west again. And he said the others were headed this way, too. Like all of them headed off like this, no reason, just going. Like . . . well, like some of those Old Earth creatures we learned about, going off on migrations, no reason, just going because their insides told them to, maybe right over the cliff into the ocean! I'm getting the idea all this sons of thunder business may not be what we're really after, you know?"

"How you gonna get away from him?" asked Dyre, nodding at the figure ahead of them. "Him and his whip."

Bane shrugged. "He keeps drifting off. Maybe we can get him to get shut of us. Just let us go. That Questioner thing came down in a shuttle, and the shuttle's still there, outside Sendoph. If this world is going to fall apart, like everybody says, I'd just as soon get a ride to someplace else."

"You can't fly a shuttle." Dyre laughed derisively. "You can't even fly a kite."

"The shuttle's got a crew, crotchbrain. Maybe we could get a few of the . . . the people at the camp to help us. If any of them stayed there. Maybe Mooly. Some of the halfway normal-looking ones. We take the shuttle, and we fly it to the ship, then we take the ship."

"Yeah, but the way he talks, the way we smell, I mean, what's the point? If we can't get any women?"

"We had women," Bane declared. "Stupid! At House Genevois, we had women. Not as many as pretty boy Mouche, but some. And they didn't die, either. So Madame knows how to handle the smell bit. All we have to do is grab her and take her somewhere and make her tell us. We can do that before we leave."

They heard a call, looked up to see that Ashes had stopped and was glaring back at them, beckoning.

"Later," said Bane, spurring his horse. "You keep your mouth shut. But later . . . we'll talk about it some more."

49

Sailing the Pillared Sea

On the ship, the Timmys retreated to an open-sided cabin at the rear of the deck while the Corojum explained the skills of the underground sailor. There were neither compass nor stars. Everything was either black or luminescent, and the only landmarks were the great pillars that loomed, dark and featureless, from the wavering yellow-green sea into the vaulted blue-green sky.

"Except," said the Corojum, pointing with a huge bony finger, "for the luminous lichen that grows on each face in signs that Kaorugi has set there."

"It's like blazing a trail," Ornery whispered to Mouche. "I read about that, something people used to do in forests, before they had locators. You'd chop a chip out of the tree, leaving a white blaze that you could see on your way back."

"Except these trees have about a hundred different blazes," muttered Mouche. This kind of sailing had never entered into his fantasy, among a forest of pillars on luminous water with a steady breeze blowing from behind them. Still, he knew the ropes and the knots, he could feel the sense of the simple rigging.

"Now," said the Corojum in a pedagogical manner, "you must understand that this journey we are about to make is the journey of Quaggima."

"Quaggima!" exclaimed the Questioner, turning from her position at the railing. "Quaggima?"

The Corojum quashed her with an imperative gesture. "Please, you must not interrupt, or we will not be in time. This is the story of Quaggima." His voice soared in a brief phrase, trilling at the end. "That is, 'Quaggida, stronger one sings.' Correct? You learned song as young beings."

"Yes," murmured Mouche. "Ornery and I, I guess we did. Not just those words, but yes."

"It is the Timmys' duty to teach the songs and dances of being to all creatures. For that reason they came to your first ones and all of your people since, no matter how you treated them or killed them or prevented their dancing. Now, at the beginning of the voyage, we sing first line to remind us of the sign, then we look for that sign. Quaggida is winged mouth, or mouth that sings." He leaned on the railing of the ship and pointed to one of the row of pillars they were approaching. After a moment's concentration, they could see that it bore a winged and fanged circle.

"See long teeth in circle, for Quaggida has teeth of fire. See bright bar to left? That means we must come so close as this, to see the sign, then turn to just pass it on the left! Quickly, be ready to change sails."

Obligingly, Mouche and Ornery were ready, and at Corojum's word, they set the sails to take them just past the left side of the pillar. Mouche, thinking it out, decided that changing sails at a certain distance from the pillar was important, as it set the direction for the next tack, though it was imprecise at best. The Timmys looked up but made no effort to help them. Evidently this voyage was to be tutorial in nature.

"As you learn the way, do not forget the pass sign,"

murmured the Corojum. "You must come this close to pillar, read sign, then pass the pillar on the correct side."

"So the pass sign is on the left, and we pass it on the left," muttered Ornery, concentrating on the approaching pillar.

They passed it sedately, not with any great speed. The wind was enough to move them, but not enough to speed them through the glowing water.

"Next line," demanded the Corojum.

"Somewhere among the dimmer galaxies," said the Questioner, promptly.

"Sign is spiral of galaxy," said the Corojum, a frown in his voice. "But song must be sung, not spoken."

"Sorry," said Questioner. "Just as an item of interest, how do you know galaxies are spiral?"

"Not all are," answered the Corojum, "but Kaorugi learned that many are. Please, interruptions are very bad idea."

"Sorry," she said again, lifting her eyebrows and grinning covertly at herself.

Mouche and Ornery finally saw a cluster of dim dots which, when they came closer yet, became the image of a central disc and several spiraling arms. The pass bar was again to the left.

"Change sail now," demanded the Corojum, then, as they were passing the pillar on the left, it said imperatively, "Next line."

This time, as though to forestall the Questioner, the Timmys burst into impassioned song.

". . . Doree a Quaggima t'im umdoror/Au, Corojumi, tim d'dom z'na t'tapor—" The song cut off, as though with a knife.

"Which is to say," asserted the Corojum, ". . . Luring the weaker-one that strong-one will seize!/Oh, Corojumi, weaker-one comes without awareness. . . .' Sign is same as Quaggida, but without teeth. Winged circle, for mouth that sings, and beneath, egg shape to show this is weaker or smaller one."

They seemed to go a very long way before the next pillar came into sight before them, a little to their right.

"Pass bar to the right," cried Mouche.

"So, go to right," murmured the Corojum.

Nothing more was said until they had passed the pillar on the right, at which point the Timmys burst into song once more.

"Bofusdiaga! Embai t'im umd'dol/zan'ahsal diza didom. . . ."

Again the Corojum translated. ". . . Bofusdiaga! From deep dark strong one flings/fiery loops that make a snare. . . ."

"Next sign is a loop," said the Corojum. "Like a noose."

They passed pillars that bore other signs, wave forms, squares, triangles, four yellow circles with green dots in the center. "The Eiger," said the Corojum, pointing this one out to them. "Four eyes, the Eiger, but that is someone else's voyage."

Finally, the loop came into view, a sign like a hangman's noose. As they passed it, the Timmys sang sadly:

". . . ersh tim' elol lai . . ."

"For weaker one's bright wings," said Corojum.

"So the last sign for that verse will be wings again, right?" asked Mouche. "With an egg, to show it's what you call the weaker one."

"Correct," said the Corojum, hugging Mouche's leg. "You learn quickly."

"Why am I hungry?" asked Mouche.

"Because it is half a day since we had food," answered the Corojum. "Next pillar we will stop. Six verses to the song, each at least half a day's sail, even in the old days, when there were many to set the sails and sing the song, time was the same."

"How far . . ." Mouche started to ask.

"Hush," said Ornery, grinning. "It's as far as it takes."

"I merely wondered," Mouche said between his teeth, "whether we might not be traveling around and around in here, like in a maze, before we get out. How do we know this is the most direct route?"

"Oh, it is not," cried the Corojum. "No, no. Why would anyone come to sea of Kaorugi to take direct route?

Dance voyages are for thinking, for planning, for learning. During voyage, we recalled the reason for dance. Also on this voyage, when there were many Corojumi, we talked of dance, remembering it in all its details. We decided who would dance which part, and who would make singing and music and when it would start. We spoke of moons and their power, and when that power approached at last, we were ready to go down into chasm, where dance must be done.''

They went wordlessly on, until the next pillar was reached, at which point they lowered the sails, and lay rocking slowly to and fro while the Timmys brought them large, shiny leaves spread with an assortment of fruits and breads, traditional, so said the Corojum, to this voyage alone.

The Questioner left the railing, found what looked to be a hatch cover, and sat down upon it.

''Come,'' she said to the Corojum. ''I have withheld my own questions, we all have. But now, while we have our lunch, surely questions can be asked and answered. The dance must be done, you say, but you are the only one left, and you do not remember the dance.''

''Only a tiny piece,'' said Corojum sadly. ''I remember the Timmys assembling. I remember a tiny, early part of the dance, and then standing upon the rim of the abyss singing. Some Timmys remember some, some Joggiwagga, some others. And Bofusdiaga remembers only the song, for Bofusdiaga left it all to us!''

''Then let us start with what we have,'' said Questioner, beckoning Mouche and Ornery to sit beside her. ''Now. Tell us about the dance.''

The Corojum said, ''The dance. So, long ago the Quaggima was caught, you know, the song says.''

''I saw her,'' said Questioner. ''Lying on an outer planet. I thought she was dead.''

''Not dead.'' The Corojumi shook his head sadly. ''Not dead, but very . . . wounded. Maimed? These Quaggida, when they mate, they lure weaker-one with their song, they capture them, but while mating, they almost kill weaker-ones. That one is left on the far-off mating place, all alone, while the egg grows inside.

"Then, when the egg has grown too big for Quaggima to keep it warm, Quaggima searches for womb fires. A warm place, you know? It is instinct. No one taught Quaggima, Quaggima merely knows. So, here in this world, closer to sun, were womb fires. Timmys, sing verse of falling!"

Their voices came from the aft deck:

> *"Quaggima it calls:*
> *Out of starfield coming, fire womb seeking*
> *Fire it finds, rock wallowing, fume reeking*
> *Oh, Corojumi, opener of space*
> *Bofusdiaga, burrower of walls*
> *It has need of birthing place*
> *Wheeoo, it falls."*

The Corojum nodded. "Quaggima did not really call us by our names. Kaorugi heard Quaggima calling: 'Oh, opener of space. Oh, burrower of walls.' In our language, openers of space are Corojumi—for this is a dancing matter—and burrower of walls is Bofusdiaga, so we used those names in our song. It was Kaorugi who heard the calling, and Kaorugi said to us, you Corojumi, you are openers of space. And you, great Bofusdiaga, you are a burrower of walls, so you will be openers and burrowers for Quaggima as well. So, we opened space, and Quaggima fell."

"Here?" asked Questioner, wanting to be quite sure. "To this planet?"

"Here. Inward, toward sun, intercepting us."

"How did Kaorugi know what Quaggima said?"

"Kaorugi perceives meaning, over much, long time. Yes. Timmys, sing next verse!"

> *"Quaggima it cries:*
> *I plant one living egg where womb fires are.*
> *See how starflesh suffers! see wings char!*
> *Bofusdiaga, singer of the sun,*

Oh, Corojumi, dancers of bright skies
It has done and I have done
I cannot rise."

Corojum nodded. "We did not know how big was Quaggima. We made too small a place. When Quaggima fell, it made far deeper chasm. All Quaggima's wings were torn and burned. Egg was laid there, beneath Quaggima's body, where stone is hot and steams rise, and egg sank down, into stone. What Quaggima said was true, it could not rise. It did not have wings to fly, like a bird-thing, only wings to soar, like a kite. And Kaorugi perceived it and felt pity and great interest and told us to care for Quaggima. Timmys, next to last verse!"

"Quaggima despairs
Driven against desire to fall and spawn
Now loving death and longing to be gone
Oh, Bofusdiaga, death defying!
Oh, blessed Corojumi, who repair!
The Quaggima is dying,
Take it in care."

"Kaorugi said, 'We do not know who Quaggima means when it sings about mender and death defier, we do not know where such creatures are or if they are listening, but *we* are here and *we* are listening, so we will become mender and death defier! We will stop pain, we will repair, and my creatures shall be death defier and caretaker to Quaggima.' And it has been so, for Kaorugi said it. Kaorugi said, 'You, my offshoot, Bofusdiaga, you be breaker of shackles and limitations. You be singer of sun, maker of mirrors, who will not allow stone walls to keep out the light. And you, you Corojumi, you create the dance, you repair the broken, you focus bright skies upon Quaggima.' "

"Very commendable behavior," commented the Questioner. "Does Kaorugi always say 'we'?"

"When Kaorugi means self and parts of self. We are

all parts of Kaorugi and do Kaorugi's will. When Kaorugi says we, Kaorugi means all."

"I understand. And what happened then?"

The Corojum whispered, "So we made Quaggima sleep to forget pain, and we mended its wings. But we were like Quaggima, z'na t'tapor, as you say 'unaware,' for egg of Quaggi grew with each wax of each moon. It sucked in substance of our world, and its shell got bigger and bigger. And then, as moons came all in a line, pulling, and egg rocked inside world, from inside egg we heard creature calling, 'Quaggima, Quaggima, crack egg and let me out!' And Quaggima began to hearken!

"But Kaorugi was there, everywhere, listening, and he cried, 'A great miscalculation! When creature breaks the egg, it breaks world, and all here nearabout, all our life and being that is Dosha will die along with Quaggima!'

"Timmys! Final verse, the one we sing at the chasm!"

> *"Quaggida destroys*
> *its life and ours. It lies beside the nest*
> *where its child and our doom are coalesced.*
> *Oh, Corojumi, bring deliverance,*
> *Oh, great Bofusdiaga, who alloys*
> *all life, grant it within this dance. . . ."*

"Yes, yes," said the Corojum. "Do you see? Her child is our doom, for when Niasa breaks egg, Niasa breaks world. Everything shatters. All Dosha dies."

"Aha!" exclaimed Questioner.

"So, what was to be done?" The Corojum scowled, posed, gestured broadly in a forbidding movement. "We say Quaggima must not wake to break egg. We say it must sleep. This was not an evil thing to say. The creature in egg . . ."

"Niasa?" asked Mouche.

"Little Niasa, yes, for we gave it a little name. Little Summer Snake, we called it, for it was laid in summer and so does our own little summer snake writhe within shell. Kaorugi says Little Niasa can go on growing in egg forever and ever if need be. There is no limit to its size so long as it has fires to feed on. Then, when world grows cold, after we are gone, then it can hatch. This did not distress Quaggima—she is called Big Summer Snake—for we had soothed Quaggima's pain and given good dreams and much good food and drink with our mirrors. . . ."

"Mirrors?"

"And lenses, for it eats sunlight, and Bofusdiaga sings to sun, making mirrors we use to send sunlight down into chasm. So, then, Kaorugi said, we must dance Quaggima to sleep. . . ."

"We is who?" interrupted Questioner.

"We Corojumi and Timmys and Joggiwagga and Tunnelers and Eiger birds, and everyone that moves!"

"I get the picture."

"And Corojumi said do this thing, and that thing, and the Timmys or Joggiwagga did it, and we all sang, and when Quaggima stirred, Corojumi said no, that doesn't work, and when Quaggima was relaxed and happy we said yes, that will do, and we put dance together, tiny bit at a time. And because Niasa was not yet grown very great, dance was enough."

"And you remembered it?" asked Ornery.

"We Corojumi remembered it. It was our job to remember it. And when came next time of many moons, we remembered it, and all Dosha danced it, and we improved it for Quaggima's pleasure. And each time many moons happened, we improved it more, over and over again. And then came your people, those jongau."

"The men from Thor," said Questioner. "I don't think they were our people. I don't think they fit our definition of human, even."

"They came, whatever people they were. And they hunted us Corojumi, and they took skins away. And soon there were fewer, and then only a few, and then none but me, and those young jongau would have killed even me, but for Mouchidi! And all pieces of dance were gone but mine!"

"Each of you remembered only a small part?"

"True."

"You said, they took the skins away, so they couldn't come to Fauxi-dizalonz. What have the skins to do with it?"

The Corojum threw up his hands. "You have all your thoughts in one place, in here," he knocked his head with one large fist. "We people of this world, Timmys, Corojumi, Tunnelers, Joggiwagga, all of us, we keep our memories all over us, in net, under skin. And when we are old, and our parts are worn, we go into Fauxi-dizalonz, and everything is refocused and straightened and made new again. Without skins, what was there to mend? Bofusdiaga tried with jongau, but it was no good."

"The jongau?"

"Your people who you say are not your people. Jong is like we say, throw away, trash. Them. Bofusdiaga thought, well, maybe they have eaten memories of Corojumi, why else would they want hides? So Bofusdiaga sent Timmys and Joggiwagga and all to bring those persons to Fauxi-dizalonz, and our people went to their town at night, and we tied them and brought them, and pushed them in the Fauxi-dizalonz, and the jong swam through and came out other side, gau!"

"Gau?" asked Questioner.

"Unmended and bent and too dreadful to live, and we told them, go back, go back, be remade as you were—for Fauxi-dizalonz will repair, you know—but the jongau would not and they smelled, so bad we could not come near them. And some of the Timmys went into Fauxi-dizalonz, to see if they had left anything there about the dance, but the jong had left only ugly memories and pains and horrors that Bofusdiaga took much time and care to filter out. Our peoples do not keep such things."

"Why can't you just reinvent the dance?" asked Mouche.

"First dance, perhaps, for it was simple and Quaggima was small. Even second, or third. But this is many times one hundred dance, more complicated than you can imagine, and with something . . . essential (is that word?) about it we cannot remember!" He sighed. "We will talk to Bofusdiaga. Bofusdiaga will consult Kaorugi. . . ."

"When we have completed the voyage," said Questioner quietly.

"Yes. When we have completed voyage."

50

The Abduction of Dancers

Ellin and Bao had arrived in the small salon just in time to see the protocol officer's blue legs being dragged away through an opening in the wall. Without thinking, Bao had thrown himself forward, trying to catch hold of the abductee, but before Bao could get near, he himself was grabbed by a dozen hands, lowered not ungently to the floor, and there tied and gagged. The last sight Bao had of Ellin was of her being similarly treated. The creatures committing the abduction were sylphlike, mankindlike in form, small but energetic, strong, and very set on doing what they were doing as expeditiously as possible.

Thereafter a transportation occurred through such complete darkness and in such complete silence that very little of it was perceptible to either Bao or Ellin. After a time, still in darkness, they were assured in whispers that no one was going to injure them in the slightest, their gags were removed, their arms were untied (though their legs were kept secured) and they were allowed to sit side by side, more or less comfortably, in a conveyance, type indeterminate, that was jerkily and noisily taking them somewhere, presumably away from Mantelby's.

The moment Bao's arms were freed he reached out to Ellin, who clung to him, partly in terror and partly in feverish excitement. "Where are we going?" she cried, almost hysterically, with a laugh on top of a sob. "Bao? That is you, isn't it?"

"Me, yes," he said, then called into the darkness, "Who's here?"

"Tim-tim are here," said someone in the dark. "You people say Timmys."

Ellin and Bao peered in the direction of the voice, making out a pale shadow against the black. The longer they looked, the brighter it became, an effulgence, an aura of light.

The voice spoke again from the darkness. "Bofusdiaga has sent a legger for you. We are taking you quick as may be to the sea, where is a swimmer waiting, then into a tunneler who will take you down to the Fauxi-dizalonz where you may help us recover the dance."

This brought so many questions to Ellin's mind that she couldn't settle on which to ask first. Bao saved her the trouble.

"What dance?" he asked.

"If we knew what dance, we would not need to recover it," the voice replied with some asperity. "This is not the time to ask questions about the dance. When we arrive, you may ask all the questions you need. Now is time to ascertain whether you are comfortable. Are you in need of food or drink or excretory privacy?"

The almost hysterical laughter bubbled in Ellin's throat, and she swallowed it, half choking herself in the process. "Thank you, but no. I'm not hungry or thirsty. Not yet, at any rate."

"Where's the other people you were dragging off?" demanded Bao. "Where are Questioner's people?"

"In another tunneler, going by a slightly quicker route. They are not hurt."

Since the Timmys would not answer questions about

the purpose of the trip, and since there was nothing at all to look at except a dimmish glow that the Timmys were either emitting or crouched within, Ellin sank back onto the rubbery surface with Bao's arms about her, and the two of them whispered together comfortingly, keeping, so Bao said, their spirits in good form.

"It is being important not to be getting in a state," he avowed. "We must be keeping our wits about us."

"Will Questioner come looking for us?"

"I am not doubting she will. She will be making a terrible uproar over this abducting, believe me."

"These . . . these people don't seem to care. Something in their voices . . . They sound extremely touchy, almost desperate, but not hostile. Not at all. Is it the volcanoes that have them so upset?"

"What has us upset," said a voice from the darkness, "is that mountains are falling. Great Gaman, most beautiful of caverns, is no more. What has us upset is *Niasa* will be hatched, I think, even if it means we die, all of us."

The voice began to sing in a language neither Ellin nor Bao had ever heard before, full of *ororees* and *imimees* and *wagawagas*. The song was unmistakably a lament, long drifting phrases in a minor key, with many repetitions that seemed to go nowhere, reminding Ellin of some twentieth-century ballet music by a man named . . . what had it been, Grass? Gless? After a time the warmth, the music, and the jiggle-jog of the floor beneath them created a cocoon of nursery-like peace around them and they fell asleep.

When they wakened much later there was light. Dimly glowing stones had been set here and there to cast a pale greenish light on the surroundings. When they sat up, they found their legs had been untied and they could make out the glowing forms of their captors, much brighter than before, sitting at some distance from them having, so Ellin muttered resentfully to herself, a picnic.

"I'm thirsty," said Ellin plaintively, running her tongue around her dry mouth.

Immediately, one of the Timmys rose and brought them

cups full of liquid. "Mir-juice," said the Timmy. "Not too sweet."

Ellin tasted it doubtfully. It was tart, cool, with a satisfying flavor somewhere between fruit and spice. By the time she had finished it, the Timmy was back with small loaves of bread. "We brought these for you," it said. "We took them from the pantry at Mantelby Mansion."

Ellin put one of the little loaves to her nose, then bit into it. It was one of the sweet breakfast breads Ellin had most enjoyed since being at the mansion. "Can't we eat your food?" she asked, somewhat tremulously.

The Timmy smiled a three-cornered smile, its eyes crinkling, its lips open to display bright yellow mouth tissues. "Assuredly. But, we thought when people are snatched up and carried off, when they are tied up and put in the belly of a legger and then are in the belly of a swimmer, and it is dark and things are most unfamiliar, then it is probably comforting to have familiar food."

Only then did Ellin and Bao realize they had indeed been moved into some new conveyance, though it felt and smelled exactly like the former one. The jogging motion had given way to a recurrent warping of their space, first to one side, then the other, like the swimming motion of a fish or snake.

Bao stood up and stretched, bracing himself against the sideways warping. "So, we are having familiar food. What are you bringing specially for me?"

Another Timmy handed over a neatly wrapped sandwich. Ham and cheese. "You are watching us," said Bao. "All the time we are being here, you are watching."

"That is true," agreed the Timmy. "Mostly we watched the other ones, for they are most different. But then, we saw you dancing, and we said, oh, they are dancers, we must bring them, too, and we asked Bofusdiaga, and the word came, yes, bring them. So, we took some things to make you comfortable, and if you had not come in upon us when you did, we would have come for you very soon anyway."

"That makes me feel so special," said Ellin, only slightly sarcastically.

The Timmy was alert to the tone. ''We will not hurt you. We do not hurt people. Oh, the Fauxi-dizalonz showed those other ones they were gau, but that was their own fault. Being gau is always the creature's fault if it will not go through and through to get fixed.''

''What other ones?'' asked Bao.

''Now they call themselves Wilderneers,'' said the Timmy, with an exasperated little shake of its head. ''They were the first mankind ones who came. But they were all . . . all one kind and all jong. Jong, that means . . . like something we sweep and throw away. We did not know they were jong until they went in the Fauxi-dizalonz. Then Bofusdiaga cried out, and we all came running to see. Fauxi-dizalonz turned an evil color, and they came out like evil monsters, and we told them, 'Go back through, take up all the disguises you have left there and fix yourselves,' but they would not.''

''Disguises?'' asked Ellin. ''You mean, masks?''

''Disguises,'' said the Timmy, coming very close and looking her in the eye. ''In your language, which is not always sensible. We say, what you wear out here,'' he tapped her arm, her shoulder, her cheek, ''is a guise (that is your word) for what is in there,'' and he peered into her eyes, as though trying to see her brain. ''If it does not match your insides, it is a dis-guise (that is your word, meaning a bad-guise), and you go through the Fauxi-dizalonz and get the outside to express the inside. Then back through to change the inside, perhaps, and sometimes back and forth several times, working it out.''

''Do your outsides look like your insides?'' she asked.

The Timmy hunkered down and considered this. ''Before mankind came, Timmys were shaped differently. When mankind came, Bofusdiaga thought we would be more . . . what is mankind words . . . acceptable, to look like you. So, some insides also shifted, to make it work.''

''Were your outsides looking like your insides before?'' queried Bao.

''Always, pretty much. First came life without any insides, just moving, eating, excreting, moving some more, no thought about it, no worries, just live or get eaten, building bigger and bigger. Then, the big thing grows a little bit of insides, enough to say to itself, 'Do not grow that way, the fire is too hot.' So, once it says that, it must have outsides ready to grow where it says! You see?"

"When you say 'insides,' " asked Ellin, "you mean brain?"

"We mean the thinkables. The person inside who talks with the person outside. The unbodied observer of that which acts. I suppose yes, brain, but you people, you have four brains, maybe five, all mixed up. You know?"

"I am not knowing this," said Bao. "What five brains?"

"First very little brain for some little something swimming around that does not do much. This brain makes you jump if someone bites you. Then you have brain for some cold thing that moves better and thinks a tiny bit. This brain says run, hide, that thing is dangerous. Then you have brain for some warm thing that runs and leaps and thinks. This brain says, build nest here, not there, or eggs will drown. Then you have bigger brain that thinks much and is aware. This is ape brain. We know about ape brain because the Hags talk of it. This brain says: me powerful; oh, child, dead, I grieve; alas, I love, I want. Then comes mankind brain, brain that talks, brain that puts ape thoughts into words, brain that uses and misuses many words! Only the last brain is what you call human, which is what we call dosha, which means fullness, capable of self-judgment and correction."

"All that!" exclaimed Ellin.

"Too much," agreed the Timmy. "Because your brains are not a good fit. They are like some too small boxes in another too big box. They rattle. Outside, you look like one person, inside you are five things, not all persons. So, if you go in Fauxi-dizalonz, you come out like your insides, with lizard tail and ape arms and your inside minds say, oh, look, this is who I am, and you think about that with brain five, then you go back in Fauxi-dizalonz and put the pieces back, but put them back in good order, so they work together and do not rattle."

Ellin had listened to this with increasing horror. "But,

but,'' she cried, ''I know who I am already. I know who my grandfather and my mother were, or I would know, if I looked them up, but . . .''

''Pff,'' said the Timmy. ''You mankinds with your fathers and mothers. This is one of first things we thought strange, you all the time talking my father this, my mother that. What does fathers and mothers have to do with who you are? Your planet is your mother; time is your father. Your insides know this! All life outside you is your kinfolk. Even we dosha are your kin, born of another planet but with same father as you. Starflame makes your materials, and live-planet assembles them, and time designs what you are, not your fathers and mothers. Pff. You could be genetic assemblage; Bofusdiaga could make you without fathers or mothers; and you would still be persons! But you could not have material without stars, or life without planet, or intelligence without time and be any way at all. It is your stars and your world and long time gives you legs to dance and brains to plan and voices to sing.''

''My mother gave me my ability to dance,'' said Ellin angrily.

''Pff,'' said the Timmy. ''And who gave her? Ah? Her mother passed it to her, and her mother passed it to her, and so back to the ooze. Planet and time gave dancing. Squirrels in trees dance. Horses dance in meadows. Birds dance in air. Snakes dance in the dust. Your mother did not invent it, she only inherited abilities to do it. So, she inherited well, but she did not do it herself.''

''You're saying my mother gave me nothing?'' Ellin was outraged, almost shrieking.

''What your mother can give you, maybe, is recipe for chicken soup. Apple pie. Maybe she invented that.''

''What are you meaning, chicken soup . . .'' choked Bao.

The Timmy cocked his head far to the side, stretching his neck, a very unmankindlike gesture. ''We hear Hags talk of chicken soup. Any kind of soup. This one recipe from this mother and that one from other mother, but even so, soups taste much alike. Timmy have recipes also.

Many good things. You ask Mouche. We made great good smells and flavors for Mouche.''

''Mouche the gardener?'' cried Bao.

''Mouchidi, the one the Corojum has sent for.''

After that, Ellin was too angry and Bao was too confused or bemused to ask any more questions, and very soon the swimmer began to swim much faster, with a great rushing-splashing noise along its sides, far too much noise to talk at all. Bao and Ellin settled into a comfortable hollow, stuffed bits of Ellin's bread into their ears, and let the rocking movement slowly lull them back to sleep.

51

Madame Meets A Messenger

Madame and the two Hags had chosen to sit in the rear of the inflatable boat. Simon and Calvy and the three remaining Haggers sat two on each side and one in front. They were so busy listening to the silence that they did not speak at all, and they floated on the small river for what seemed to them some considerable time before the tunnel narrowed, the water began to rush, and they found themselves plunging through the same narrow throat of stone the prior expedition had traversed, into the same larger river and across it, where the boat ricocheted violently off the tunnel wall.

"I suppose we're sure everyone went this way," murmured D'Jevier, as the Haggers and Calvy g'Valdet tried to paddle the boat back into the center of the stream.

"We saw their tracks on the sand. We saw the impressions made by at least two boats," muttered Calvy, fighting his desire to curse at the Haggers, who persisted in paddling against one another's efforts so that the clumsy boat spun lazily around as the current caught it.

"Let me," said Madame, moving to the place across the boat from Calvy and taking the oar from the Hagger there. "Watch me," she said to him. "It is necessary to coordinate the strokes or we go nowhere."

"Now where did you pick that up?" said Calvy in an interested tone.

"My friends and I do a bit of wilderness walking," said Madame, concentrating on her paddling. "And canoeing."

Among Simon, Madame, and Calvy, they managed to turn the boat so that it faced downstream and keep it there with only occasional dips of the paddles. When Madame thought the Haggers had the idea, she gave up her paddle and returned to the company of the Hags.

"Have you met the Questioner?" Calvy asked over his shoulder.

"We have," said Onsofruct. "A very civil contraption."

"Civil on the outside, but she wasn't fooled," said D'Jevier. "She knew something. Maybe everything. I thought we might sidetrack her onto the threat posed by the volcanoes, but she made it clear she knew what we were up to."

"You mean the Timmys?" Calvy asked.

"Oh, definitely the Timmys," D'Jevier acknowledged. "She had these two young Earthers with her, very open-faced and so milky-lipped that one might think them moments from mama's breast, but they turned out to be quite perceptive. I should have expected that. She'd scarcely have brought them, otherwise."

"How do you read all this, Madame?" Calvy asked over his shoulder. "This current journey of ours?"

Madame said, "How can we read it? The Timmys took the Questioner's people, her Earther aides went after them, then Questioner and two pressed men became third in line. Why the Timmys took the first ones . . ." She shrugged invisibly. "Who knows?"

"I've been doing some research," Calvy persisted. "Our records since we've been on Newholme show that episodes of vulcanism increase during lunar conjunctions. Multiple conjunctions are usually accompanied by some very big quakes. If the Timmys were here before we were (and I think we have to accept that they were), then they've evolved under conditions of periodic vulcanism and presumably would know how to deal with it . . . unless this time is really different from any former time.''

''As to that,'' said Onsofruct, ''we don't know about all possible former times. We've only been here a few hundred years.''

Calvy said, ''We don't know, but the planet does. There's a gravelly cliff west of Naibah that sheds a few feet of itself every time we have a quake. Each of the falls has time to weather and change color before it gets covered by the next layer. When you drill into the deposit, you get a nicely striped core, one you can read like tree rings. So, I had a few of my supernumes take some really deep core samples, as deep as we can get with the equipment we have.''

''And?'' queried D'Jevier. ''What did you find?''

''We got back about five thousand years. If we had better equipment, we could go deeper and probably read up to hundreds of thousands, but during those five thousand years, at least, we find thick deposits every seven or eight hundred years, but the gravel that's falling now is already thicker than the thickest previous layer.''

''You didn't tell us that?'' said D'Jevier. ''You didn't say a word about it.''

''My people finished up the report last night,'' Calvy responded mildly. ''I've not had a chance to tell anyone. It does make me wonder whether we colonists have destroyed or weakened some vital link in this planet's ecology.''

''But we haven't!'' Onsofruct objected.

Calvy gave her a grin over his shoulder, saying, ''Well, that's true to form. If we have, we could hardly admit it to ourselves if we had, could we? Or to anyone else?''

''But to allege such a thing . . .'' Her voice trailed away.

''It's only an inference, Ma'am.'' He paused in his paddling, then said firmly, ''Still, it can't be discounted without some proof to the contrary. How do we know what the first settlers did? Why were they wiped out, as we presume they were? Was it because they had committed some grave offense?''

Onsofruct opened her mouth to retort, more out of habitual response to any male criticism than from real conviction of the innocence of the first settlers. Her words were stopped by a sound they all heard in the same instant: a grating sound, quite distant, but coming nearer and growing louder.

They fell silent. Calvy, Simon, and the Haggers dipped their paddles, pushing the boat along a little faster than the water, then faster yet, as though to escape.

''Shhh,'' said Madame, leaning forward. ''If it already knows we're here, we can't outrun it. If it doesn't know, paddling may attract it.''

''It?'' demanded Simon, glancing at her over his shoulder, the whites of his eyes gleaming.

''The sound-maker. Let us go softly.''

The sound came from downriver, getting louder with each moment until it reached a screaming crescendo and abruptly stopped. The reverberations died away. Silence returned. The river curved slightly; they floated around the bend and abruptly bumped into a weir set across the river.

''What in the name of seven devils?'' murmured Calvy.

D'Jevier turned on a light and examined the weir. Not rock. Something else. Something smooth and rubbery that gave slightly when she pressed it with her fist. To their right a pebbly beach had been deposited along a shelving recess in the tunnel wall, and it showed the mark of two boats and footprints that led back toward crevices in the tunnel wall.

''They were here,'' said Onsofrunct. ''There's the treadmark of the Questioner, and the footprints of two people.''

They paddled the boat to shore, got out and pulled it up onto the pebbles where they stood, shining their lights on a patch of finer sand.

''Not only two people,'' said Simon. ''Other things, too.''

''Timmys?'' asked Onsofruct.

''That size, at least,'' said Madame. She turned her light

onto the small area around them. A rocky wall, a few fallen chunks of that wall, no openings that they could see—that they could . . . see.

"That wasn't there before," whispered one Hagger to another, pointing.

They all looked. An opening. Too small to worry about. They looked away, looked back. Perhaps not that small. Looked away, looked back.

"It's opening," said D'Jevier in a shocked voice. "The rock is opening!"

It was opening slowly, a vertical slit, perhaps as high as their boat was wide. It made a grating sound as it went on opening, wider and wider, displaying a gleaming orb inside which swiveled in their direction. An eye, with a vertical pupil. And another slit opening, a much wider horizontal one, below. A mouth.

From which, after some time—while they all froze in place, scarcely breathing—came a voice like rocks grinding together.

"I am sent by Bofusdiaga, burrower of walls, singer of the sun, death defier, savior of Quaggima. I am sent by him who alloys and thereby preserves. I have come to take you to the Fauxi-dizalonz."

Onsofruct sagged. Calvy and Madame caught her as she crumpled to the ground.

The mouth opened again. "Terror is inappropriate. Proper emotion is gratitude. I am tunneler. My way is much less tiring than the way of the Pillared Sea. Besides, many of your people are already there."

D'Jevier cleared her throat several times, managing to get the words out on the third try. "We're searching for . . . ah, some others who have come this way. . . ."

"First group, eight strange people belonging to Questioner. They are already at Fauxi-dizalonz arguing with one another. Second group, two dancers, they are now in swimmer, arguing with Timmys about mothers and fathers. Soon they will be at Fauxi-dizalonz. Third group: Mouchidi, Ornery, and the Questioner, they are far ahead on the Pillared Sea, experiencing the Quaggima voyage, and arguing with the Corojum."

"Mouche!" cried Madame. "Mouche also?"

"So I have said. You are fifth group. If we go same way, would not catch them in time."

"Who's the fourth group?" demanded Calvy.

"The jongau." The messenger spat the words in a hail of gravel. "Many jongau. Large and small, all horrid, they are going on the surface, and they are getting near to the sacred place."

"The jongau," said Madame. "Being?"

"That Ashes. Those sons of Ashes. All those bent ones. They will be there, too, and I have come to take you where you can meet them."

The voice made Madame think of walking on scree, a gravelly crunch, rattle, and slide. Was this irritation? Or mere impatience? "We are grateful," she said loudly.

The mouth turned up its corners, dislodging small boulders in the process. "At least you are not arguing! Mankind is a very arguing species! Bring your belongings," it said, then opened its mouth to display two complicated, bellowslike structures on either side and between them, access to a dry, sandy-floored space.

"I think it means we should go in," said Calvy, a slight tremor in his voice. "I presume it knows we are easily crushed."

The mouth waited. "After you," said Simon politely, needing two tries to get it out.

Madame pressed her lips tightly together, took a deep breath, lifted her pack from the boat and walked into the creature's mouth. After a long moment, D'Jevier and Onsofruct did likewise.

Simon looked after them, doubtfully.

"This is why women rule this world," Calvy observed. "We men can't make up our minds."

"I'm going, I'm going," said Simon, taking up his pack. "What about the Haggers?"

The Haggers were out in the river, having already waded some distance along the edge in the direction they had come.

Calvy called, "Farewell. Don't forget to turn off into the little stream when you get there."

They splashed more rapidly away, without replying. Calvy picked up his own pack and one of theirs; Simon took another; together they stepped into the mouth of Bofusdiaga's messenger.

52

Leggers, Tunnelers, and Assorted Traffic

Ashes rode westward like a man possessed by a dream, waking occasionally into a fit of anger, then falling into his reverie once more. His sons trailed behind him, lagging as much as they could without stirring him into a rage, whispering together so he would not hear them, for whenever he heard them he demanded to know what they were saying, what they were thinking, what insurgency they were planning.

"You'll do what I tell you," he said, not once but a dozen times when he came to himself. "You know what's good for you, you'll do what I tell you."

"He's got to have somebody to boss around," whispered Bane. "If we'd been girls, like he planned, he'd have been just the same with them, made them do whatever he wanted. He'd have hitched them up to Mooly, prob'ly. Or one of those others."

"I can't figure why Marool took us away from our mama," said Dyre, who'd been puzzling over this for the better part of a day. "He said she was jealous, but she didn't seem jealous over men. She had plenty of men. Why'd he want her dead? Specially, since she couldn't smell him. Seems like he'd have rather kidnapped her, brought her out here to keep around. She wasn't old. Maybe she'd have had a daughter for him."

"Other thing," mused Bane. "He never said how our mama died, did he?"

"Never said what her name was, nothin'."

"Somethin' else. There's this pond he talks about. So, you go in there, you can't die, right? So, how come when our mama was sick or hurt or whatever, he didn't take her there and fix her?"

Dyre looked crafty. "Maybe he hated her. Maybe he just as soon she died."

"That don't make sense! He wanted children, and he went to all that trouble, why would he let her die?"

"Maybe he couldn't tell her what to do, so he decided he didn't want to bother."

"Maybe Marool was her," said Bane, not thinking what he said, his unconscious prompting him to a truth he immediately recognized and wanted to unsay.

Dyre said nothing. He pretended not to have heard. He did not want to have heard because . . . well, because. They'd killed her, was why. And they'd done . . . lots of other things. And if she had been, well then, Ashes had lied to them. But if she had been, then why hadn't she known? Why hadn't they known? Why had they grown up in that place near Nehbe, and at Dutter's farm? She hadn't kept them by her, and she should have. If it was so. Which it probably wasn't.

Bane did not repeat himself. What he had said did not bear repeating. Not that it was wrong. Ashes had told them sons of thunder couldn't do wrong so long as they did what they wanted to. Whatever they wanted to do was right. It's just that he should have been told. If what he had said was right, he should have been told. Ashes said people back there on Thor, they killed off a lot of people who didn't believe what they did: mothers, fathers, kids, made no difference. So, it wasn't wrong to have killed her. It was just . . . Well, it was the way it happened. There could have been a better way than that.

Late in the afternoon, as the three rode abreast along a wider stretch of the trail, Ashes pointed off into the west at a certain high, ragged line of mountain.

"That's the edge of the chasm," he said.

"How deep?" grunted Bane.

"Well, there's a shallow crater and a deep one. The deep one's maybe five, ten kilometers to the bottom," said Ashes. "Before the pond, we used to have a member of our brotherhood named Maq Bunnari, Bunny the Book, we used to call him because he was always reading. He read everything, he knew anything there was to know about anything. So, just before we left Thor, Bunny was in charge of looking around for a place for us to go. There wasn't a lot of choices in the nearby sectors, but one of them was this place, so Bunny got the geological report, and according to him, the chasm was an 'anomalous feature.' Seems like that the chasm was a two-mouthed volcano to start with, pretty much dead, so the two domes fell in and that made two pot-shaped valleys, right? So, just like it was aiming for the bull's eye, a meteor fell right into the southern valley, and it punched a pretty big hole. The report said there was a hell of a big, deep cone-shaped hole down inside that mountain.

"Well, Bunny, he read this and he said there shouldn't be a hole that deep because most of the stuff that blows out of a meteor hole falls right back in. Bunny said if there was this big hole, something besides a meteor did it, and before we settled here, maybe we ought to find out who or what it was. Well, we didn't have time for that, but Bunny wouldn't shut up about it. One night after we'd been here a while, Mooly and Bone, they got aggravated at him calling them stupid for not finding out what made the hole, and one night they beat him up so bad he died."

Ashes barked laughter. "Bunny was right, dead right, it turned out. When those Timmys and their friends took us to the pond, we saw all kinds of things carrying gravel out of that hole and smoothing down the sides. They'd cut them a twisty road back and forth, too, so they could get to the bottom.''

''Can we get to the bottom?''

''Oh, we could probl'y get down there all right, they probl'y wouldn't care, but it'd be a waste of time. It's so deep, standing up on that ridge, you can't see the bottom.''

''Webwings saw the bottom. He said those Questioner's people was there.''

''Webwings only flew to the pond, and that's in the other crater, the shallow one. See, when the meteor fell, it broke the wall between the two, so you got this crater shaped like an eight, and back and forth around the top half you've got this road that goes down to the pond, then you go through the gap to the other crater, and you wind back and forth down to the bottom of that.''

''You been there lately?'' asked Bane.

Ashes shrugged, shaking his head. ''No reason to go. Web flies down to the pond sometimes, partway, anyhow. He says it's real busy down there, lots of critters coming and going. Up until now, I figure, with all that busy going on, no reason for me to get in the middle of it.''

''Where's . . . where's your old friends? The ones that stayed there.''

''Oh, some of 'em in the raggedy edge, up there. See, that's all volcanic up there, full of gas bubble caves. Nice and smooth and round inside, good shelter. That's where old Pete put himself, into a long chain of bubble caves, about halfway down to the pond. Some of the others, they're between here and there. Hughy Huge, he's along the road we're coming to. And Roger the Rock, he's some way ahead.''

''How much longer to get there?''

''Not so far, now. Down at the bottom of this hill we come to the road. From here on, we can go right straight there.''

''Who built the road?'' Bane asked. ''Timmys?''

''Damfino,'' grunted Ashes. ''I suppose it's Timmys or some of the bigger things. Stands to reason they had to have someplace to put all that gravel they dug outta that hole, and roads use up a lot of gravel. When they captured us and carried us in that time, it wasn't on any road, but when we came away from there, we climbed up to the rim and there it was. Some of our folks, they'll be along it, too. You keep an eye out."

Bane kept an eye out. His frustration and confusion had risen as the day had worn on. His own plan of escape, to capture the shuttle, now seemed to him the only sensible thing to do, if he could get away from Ashes. But then, he thought, of course he could get away from Ashes because Ashes had told him how. Ashes wouldn't die, not the way people did, but he could be killed. And if Ashes could put them up to killing their mother, then there couldn't be anything wrong with killing their father, could there? It'd be no trick at all.

Bane did not mention this to Dyre. He hadn't decided yet whether he needed to involve Dyre.

They came to the road just before dark, a level, straight, hard-packed and gravel-surfaced highway on which six horses could have ridden abreast. It cut through forests and hills, across valleys, leading onward and upward like the flight of an arrow to the ragged line of mountain Ashes had pointed out earlier. Ashes went only a little way along it before leaving it, dismounting, and leading his horse away. Following his example, Dyre stopped by the road, unsaddling his horse and dropping his pack.

"We'll sleep off here," called Ashes, from a grove some distance away. "Away from the road."

"Looks like a good place here," offered Dyre.

"Not far enough from the road," barked his father. "Down where I said."

Grumbling, Dyre picked up the saddle and the pack and took them farther down the hill. They made camp, warmed their food, ate it in silence, and rolled into their blankets. Three moons came up, almost in a line, with two more close behind. The world was bathed in half-light. Bane and Dyre fell exhaustedly asleep.

Away along the road something roared. The ground trembled. Bane sat up. Ashes was snoring. Bane poked Dyre, who sat up as well, clutching the blanket around his shoulders. The earth trembled again, and again, and constantly as the roaring grew louder. In the moonlight they saw something galloping toward them, huge and many-legged, rumbling like a string of freight carts on a cobbled street, continuing this horrid thumping as it rushed past and off into the west, toward the chasm.

"What was that?" cried Dyre, trembling.

"Legger," mumbled Ashes from under his blankets. "Sort of like the kind that carried us off, that time before. They go by here all the time. Go to sleep."

They lay back down. After a time they slept, to be roused again and again by the sound of leggers going past, in both directions, to and from the chasm, and once by the sound of something more ponderous than leggers, rolling. That time Ashes awoke and, telling them not to move from where they were, went up to the road. They heard him shouting, then the heavy rolling stopped.

"Ashes," said a thick, gurgling voice, like rocks rolling around in thick syrup.

"Where you going, Hughy Huge?" Ashes asked.

"Roll 'em over," gargled the voice. "Roll 'em over."

"Who told you?"

"Wings." The thing breathed, like a wind, heaving. "Wings said it was time to roll 'em over. Wings, he's comin' along. The rest of 'em, they're comin' along. S'long Ash."

The rolling started again, at first slowly, then faster.

"Who was that?" asked Bane, when Ashes returned.

"Hughy Huge," mumbled Ashes.

Bane judged it a good time for a sensitive question. "I thought Web said he was going back to camp."

"Oh, that's just Web," said Ashes. "Just Web. He's here. Of course he is. We have to . . . we have to be here."

"Why?" whispered Bane. "Why do we have to be here?"

Ashes sat down by the fire, stirred up some glowing coals and put a few sticks on them, blowing into the embers until they burst into flame, talking sleepily, half to himself.

"Some of us . . . we didn't like what that pond done to us. Some of us didn't know what to think. Web, one day he's mad, the next day he likes being able to fly, next day he's mad again. Lately, he's been mad more of the time. It's like he's bored. Web was always smart, like Bunny. Him and Bunny was close. Since Bunny's been gone, Web's kinda . . . like I said, bored. I think he just wants to make something happen."

Bane said offhandedly, making little of it, "How come nobody knows about you all? Back there, in town, they think Wilderneers are just a story."

Ashes ruminated a long time on this. "Well, we hid. One here, one there. After that time when they killed us, we hid. This whole world it's just full of places to hide. . . ."

"But the camp's right out in the open."

"Lately," Ashes agreed. "Haven't been there but a little while. A couple years. Most of us're still hid. Me 'n Mooly, we started the camp. It's a place to get together. Him and me, we go around, talk to this one and that one, bring 'em into camp, so we'll be ready, when the time comes. . . ."

"Look, you Wilderneers got a plan about the cities, right?"

Ashes nodded, like a man in a trance, not taking his eyes from the fire.

Still distantly, as though it were unimportant: "So, if you're here when the cities fall, the plan won't work, right? So why're you here?"

Ashes nodded again, distantly. "There's time. World's not going to blow up yet."

"How do you know?"

Ashes shrugged again, yawning, staring sleepily at the fire.

Bane turned away, outwardly calm, inwardly seething. The Wilderneers had a plan, but nothing came of the plan. They found themselves a new planet, but they had done nothing with it. They planned to get themselves some women, but nothing happened. Hundreds of years and nothing had changed with them, except that they'd grown bigger and stranger. They—or more properly, Ashes—had succeeded only once at reproduction. Their town was a shabby collection of huts and hovels, not fit to live in. Their food was offal. Some of them had only one emotion, and that was a kind of unfocused belligerence. Ashes and

Webwings had retained some quality of irritability, but aside from being irritated, what did either of them do?

Bane surprised himself at these thoughts, at the words he used to form them, words he had never had until he went to House Genevois, words he had learned from the conversation mistress but had rejected using in favor of the rude and impoverished blatting of his fosterage. He used them now, nonetheless. Well, Madame herself had said words were tools. A tool was a tool. A man didn't need to carry a tool. He could pick it up when he liked and put it down when he liked.

Still seething, Bane curled into his blankets once more, peering through slitted lids at his father's firelit face, brooding over the coals. What was he thinking? Was he thinking? He, Bane, wasn't at all sure Ashes could think, not straight. So, maybe . . . maybe he'd better concentrate on this business of getting away.

He remembered something Madame had said: "There is a class of person who cannot lead and will not be led. Such persons go their own way, uncorrupted by insight, unmitigated by experience. They do what they do, and usually they die of it, but they would rather die than cooperate with anyone else."

Bane had always made a point of ostentatiously not listening during Madame's lectures, so it surprised him how much of what she said he remembered. He remembered that bit, because it had made him think of Ashes at the time, wondering if he was one who couldn't lead and wouldn't be led. Now he was sure: nobody could lead that batch of weirds, anyhow. And none of them would be led. So if all of them were getting together, now, it meant something big was happening, something maybe they had no control over at all!

Brooding on this, Bane fell asleep. Ashes, too, returned to his blankets. The fire burned down to dying embers once more. They were not wakened by the quakes that came in the early hours, snapping the ground beneath them, but gently, like a laundress shaking out sheets. They were not wakened by certain other things that came quietly and stood looking at them for a time before going forward on business of their own, though when Bane and Dyre and Ashes woke in the morning, they saw the sinuous tracks of those beings all around them.

"What?" Dyre asked, pointing to the deep depressions.

Ashes yawned, shook himself, and said in an uninterested voice, "Joggiwagga, maybe. Something like that. On their way to the chasm."

"Why are we going there?" Bane demanded. "All kinds of things are going there, and they're all bigger than us."

"I guess that's why," said Ashes, moving about his morning tasks almost unconsciously. "Something going on. You can't gain ground without knowing what's going on, boys."

"I thought you was gonna take the cities," Dyre cried petulantly. "You can't take the cities if you're here and they're there. What if they fall down while you're gone? You can't get anywhere doin' that."

The whip was out and moving before Bane could take a breath; it moved of itself, without Ashes using his hands, like a prehensile tail, an autonomous appendage, snaking out from the front of Ashes's jacket, cracking with that all too familiar electrical sound, leaving Dyre writhing on the ground, spittle running down his chin, eyes unfocused.

"You," snarled Ashes. "You keep your mouth shut. I told you, and I won't tell you again. You do what you're told. And what you're told is, we're going to that chasm to see what's going on. We're gonna talk to old Pete. Talk to some of the others."

He picked up his saddle and threw it onto his horse, still growling to himself. "Talk to some of them. That's what. Talk to them and find out what's going on."

Bane lifted his brother from the ground, muttering, "You don't have good sense, you know that?"

Dyre cried, "I heard you say the same thing about the cities, about his plan."

"At night, when he was sleepy. And in a tone of voice like it wasn't important. Not pushing it up his nose! That's bound to jerk him up! Keep it shut, brother. I'll figure it out. You just keep it shut and come along."

53

The Farther Shore

On the third day of their voyage, while Questioner brooded on deck and all except the Corojum slept, the ship finished its voyage and was hauled ashore. The Corojum alone had been on watch as they passed the last two pillars, and he alone had sung the last lines, in his own language, while two of the Timmys manned the sails. When the keel of the ship grated on the bottom, the Corojum wakened the others, the Timmys gathered at the rail, the ship extruded its gangway, and they disembarked. The ship turned, of itself, and sailed out beyond the nearest pillars where, said the Corojum, it would come to no harm.

"Now what?" asked Mouche, wiping the sleep from the corners of his eyes.

"Tunneler," said the Corojum. "The Fauxi-dizalonz isn't far from here, and we could walk, but most everyone is there by now. There's just us left, and some of the jongau and some people from Sendoph."

"People from Sendoph?" asked Questioner. "Who might that be?"

"Two Hags," the Corojum said. "And Madame from House Genevois. And Simon, and a Man of Business."

"Madame?" cried Mouche. "Did she come after me?"

"Whether she did or not, how do you know all these things?" demanded Questioner.

Corojum looked surprised. "Swoopers and swivelers come through the walls, up out of the sea, through the air, like moths. They carry messages."

"Luminous things. Like flying kites or diamonds?" asked Mouche.

"Like that. How could we all work together if we did not know what was going on? The Man of Business is not a bad one. Calvy is a good mankind, and so is Simon, more or less."

"How do you know so much about them?" asked Questioner. "Do you spend a lot of time watching them?"

"The Timmys do. At first, we needed badly to understand *them,* those first ones. Then, after we took them to the Fauxi-dizalonz, we thought we *did* understand them. They were jong, gau, useless. Then you new ones came and we weren't sure. In some ways, your culture is like our own. You have supernumes, we have Timmys. You have actors and musicians, we have Corojumi. Had Corojumi. You have Hags, we have Bofusdiaga. You have Hagions, we have Kaorugi."

"The Hags are like Bofusdiaga?" Questioner regarded him with delight. "That is a new idea."

"Bofusdiaga balances things to keep all the parts functioning. The Hags balance things to keep all the parts functioning. We do not have anything like the Men of Business, though. It seems to us odd to churn one's needs in that way. Buy everything, churn it around, increase the price, then sell it back to people who made it. To us it seems sensible to make what everyone needs and let everyone use what he needs, but then we do not have five brains inside, rattling away. The ape brain you all have is very acquisitive, so our way would not work for you."

"How do you know it is the ape brain?" asked Mouche, yawning.

"I think you give five apes five bananas, biggest ape will take them all," said the Corojum. "Unless other four gang up on it, or, unless it is mother with child. So say the Hags."

"When will we finish this journey?" asked Ornery. "Can you tell me?"

"When we are finished," said the Corojum.

"When we come from underground," said Questioner, "I hope I will be able to reach my ship. I have not been able, up until now."

The Corojum did not meet her eyes. "Maybe that is Kaorugi. Maybe Kaorugi does not want you talking."

Questioner fixed him with a stare, but before she could say anything, the Corojum cried, "And here is our tunneler. This is as you say, last lap. It will not be long."

54

Assembly At The Fauxi-dizalonz

The tunneler bearing Questioner, Mouche, Ornery, and the Corojum traveled with a muffled roar interspersed with periods of almost silence that Questioner interpreted as movement through something more yielding than rock. Soil, perhaps. Or even predrilled tunnels. These relatively silent periods grew more frequent as they progressed, and the last part of their journey was accomplished in relative quiet. The tunneler stopped moving; the mouth end gaped large; and from the complicated structures beside the creature's mouth, its voice said, "We have arrived near the Fauxi-dizalonz. Others will be coming soon. Some are already here."

Almost drowsily, as though they had been long hypnotized by the motion and the sound, the three followed the Corojum out of the creature's mouth to find themselves on a high, wide ledge with sky and air everywhere but behind them. There the mouths of highly polished tunnels gaped, explaining the silence of their arrival. These ways had been cut long since, and among them were several smooth-walled caves, in one of which the Corojum suggested Mouche and Ornery deposit the packs before coming to stand beside itself and Questioner at the rim of the world.

They stood at the top of a sheer cliff that swooped in an unbroken wall to the bottom of the caldera where the jewel-green disk of a largish lake shone brightly in the morning sun.

"The Fauxi-dizalonz," said the Corojum, pointing at the lake below. "Your people are there, and I will collect them for you."

"Don't hurry on my account," said Questioner, moving a little back from the rim. "I'm really most concerned about Ellin and Bao, the two dancers. Have you done anything to them?"

The Corojum shook his head. "After what happened with the jongau, Bofusdiaga is reluctant to try it again. When you come, Bofusdiaga thinks we may arrive at a better way."

"One would hope," she murmured.

The Corojum went to the rim of the ledge, whistled, and was answered from the air. Within moments, a huge, four-eyed bird dropped from the sky, plucked up the Corojum in its talons, and plunged toward the distant pond.

"An interesting mode of travel," Questioner began, interrupted by a slithering *shush* that proved to be another tunneler, emerging from another portal onto the same ledge. When it opened its mouth, five disheveled persons staggered out: Madame, the two Hags, Calvy, and Simon.

"Madame, Simon!" cried Mouche, delightedly, then, "Revered Hag," with a deep bow to D'Jevier.

D'Jevier turned very pale.

Madame cried, "Mouche! What has happened to you? Who did that to your face?"

"Bane," said Mouche. "I can put on my veils. . . ."

"Of course not," snapped D'Jevier. "Let me see." She came close and ran her fingers down the healing wound, turning to Madame to say, "We must get him to the med-machines."

"I'm afraid it will have to wait," said Questioner.

D'Jevier started to speak, but was distracted by the sudden and noisy departure of the tunneler, rattling itself away in one of the bores.

"Come," said Questioner. "I have not met the gentlemen. Would someone introduce us?"

"Calvy g'Valdet," Calvy murmured. "And Madame's assistant, Simon. I'm sorry, but I'm afraid we don't know the correct form of address."

"At the moment we are being informal. Please call me Questioner. I do weary from all the unearned reverence I'm subjected to."

"Hardly unearned," murmured Calvy with a bow. "Your reputation is unsullied, certainly a matter for reverence."

Questioner laughed, a truly amused sound that seemed to draw all of them from their various reveries. "Come," she said. "Let us admire the view."

Accordingly, they turned their attention to their surroundings, though both Madame and D'Jevier found it difficult to take their eyes from Mouche's face.

At their right, a roadway opened upon the ledge, an avenue that stretched down and across the wilderness, straight as a rule.

"That doesn't appear on the orbital surveys," said Calvy. "None of this does!"

At right angles to this road, continuing the line of the ledge, a narrower way descended in a gentle slope eight-tenths of the way around the caldera before making a switchback that returned it to a point almost beneath them. The road continued in descending arcs, back and forth, back and forth, at last reaching the floor of the caldera, where it ran around the emerald lake and thence through a gap in the caldera wall to their left.

The ledge they were on also continued in that direction, making a sharp bend onto the wall of the twin caldera and giving them an unimpeded view down an abyssal cone. The road below wound back and forth on only the northern half of the cone. The southern half, from the rim down as far as they could see, gleamed blackly, smoothly, its surface interrupted by occasional vertical ridges, softly rounded, that ran convergently into the depths. The rim of this chasm sparkled as though set with gems. Questioner extended her sight to make out huge lenses and mirrors that reflected light down the black surface into the pit below.

"Well," said Madame to D'Jevier, turning her attention from this enigmatic vision. "We seem to have arrived, wherever this is. What's going on down there?" She pointed to the lake below, where a cluster of persons was being marshaled upward on the road.

"I see Ellin and Bao," announced Questioner. "My Old Earth aides, but I don't see the rest of my people."

"You do not sound concerned," said Calvy.

Questioner sighed. "I do not wish them ill, I simply don't mind if they're elsewhere. They are political appointees, presumably serving a kind of internship. Occasionally the committee gives me someone sensible, but that is not the general rule."

"What is that with your two aides?" asked D'Jevier. "That's not a Timmy."

"That is a Corojum," said Questioner. "According to it, the last Corojum, and he tells us the extinction of his ilk means our extinction as well."

"Now, then . . ." said Onsofruct angrily.

"Hush," said D'Jevier.

Onsofruct fell silent, fuming as D'Jevier said in a cautionary tone, "Let them tell us what's going on. It's sure somebody must, for we are at a loss."

"Do you know what's going on?" Onsofruct demanded of Questioner.

"More or less, yes. In a moment or two, Ellin and Bao will be here, and then we can put our heads together. Meantime, since we may be here for some time, let us look about this place with a view to occupancy."

Though unwilling to defer enlightenment, the eight of them scattered into the caves that backed the ledge, finding them already equipped for persons, with bedplaces piled with soft twigs and covered with blankets; a small, private cave set aside for a privy; water jars hung in the cool air, and flat trays of fruit and bread set nearby. Calvy, Simon, Ornery, and Mouche took possession of one cave, the three women settled themselves into another. When Ellin and Bao arrived, Bao joined the men and Ellin the women.

Questioner took no part in this bustle, instead continuing her examination of the abyss, noting now that the black, glossy surfaces seemed to quiver from time to time as though alive. Which, she thought, would explain a great deal. After a short recess of nibble, sip, lie down, and get up again, the Newholmians trickled out to join her at the rim of the ledge, where they were soon joined by Ellin and Bao. When they were all present, she gestured them to find a sitting place, studying them closely as they did so.

Mouche and Ornery, Ellin and Bao gravitated toward one another and sat to one side wearing faces that were almost copies of one another. Interested but wary and mostly uncommitted. Bao was perhaps a little more engaged in what was going on. Ellin was refusing to become involved. Ornery was merely cautious, and Mouche . . . Mouche had the appearance of someone who had removed himself as far from the present as possible and was existing on another plane by will alone.

The Hags and Madame looked merely weary, the men no less so. Calvy maintained an alert expression, letting his eyes wander, seeing all that was to be seen. Simon hoarded his gaze, seeing only one thing at a time, not moving on until he'd dealt with it. They sat in silence. The air around them moved gently. Flying creatures glinted by, occasionally uttering calls that were not unlike bell sounds, their various pitches contributing to a slow and wandering melody. From below, Timmy voices rose in song, underlying the bell sounds, supporting them. From on high came another voice, and they looked up to see one of the large, four-eyed birds circling high above them.

"That's an Eiger," murmured D'Jevier, her head thrown back to display the long, vulnerable line of her throat. "The bird who sees all. It's singing what it sees to Bofusdiaga."

"You know this," said Questioner, "because your

nursemaid told you, when you were a baby. Your nursemaid who is now dead."

D'Jevier flushed, looked at her shoes and said nothing.

"Well," Questioner remarked. "Let us accept that all you Newholmians had nursemaids who told you of Eigers and Bofusdiaga and Corojumi and Timmys and Joggiwagga. And here we are, confronting them in reality. This has been an enlightening journey for all of us, I have no doubt. Are you ready to discuss what it means? Or would you prefer to continue in suspicious ignorance?"

"Madam." Calvy bowed, grinning at her. "I am sure I speak for everyone when I say we would be . . . gratified to know what it means."

Though D'Jevier's mouth pinched momentarily, holding in her immediate rebuke, she did not utter it. She could not in all honesty disagree, and though Calvy had no right to speak for the Hags, in this case he had represented them honestly.

55

The Tale Of Quaggima

"As I have pieced it together, we are here today because of something that happened a million years ago," said Questioner.

"Which could be said for anyone being anywhere," Calvy remarked, his troubled eyes belying his charming smile.

Questioner's pursed lips and down-the-nose stare apprised him of the impertinence of charm. "There is more than mere timeflow at work here. Our lives have intersected those of a very large, long-lived, star-roving race called the Quaggi. Except for Ellin and Bao, who have heard the name only in passing, you all know about the Quaggi."

Her listeners glanced covertly at one another.

"Come now," she coaxed them. "You heard about the Quaggi when you were children." She stared imperiously at D'Jevier. "When you heard many other interesting stories. . . ."

"Say that we know about the Quaggi," Calvy interrupted, to spare D'Jevier's obvious discomfort. "If we don't, we'll pretend we do."

"Ah," said Questioner. "Pretense. Well, that is something you Newholmians do well. I continue:

"A very long time ago, when this solar system was still quite young, a Quaggida entered the system. I am told by the Corojum that reproductive males sit out on the cold edges of solar systems, summoning, and that one or more females eventually respond to that call. I infer the female is unaware of the consequences, or, if aware, A: finds the lure irresistible, or B: is resigned to her fate.

"When the female arrived she was impregnated. In the process she was rather badly injured and her wings were so mutilated that she could no longer fly. The Quaggida left her there, one would imagine in considerable discomfort, and flew off to get started on the contemplative phase of his existence."

Madame made a breathy exclamation, then subsided under Questioner's admonitory gaze.

"This may have been an aberration. It may have happened only in a single case. Or, it may be that both the violation and the concurrent mutilation are required by the Quaggian ethos, or the Quaggian physiology. In any case, the Quaggima lies there on the cold planet, barely able to move, while the egg slowly develops. When it has grown too large for its location, the Quaggima struggles with her crippled wings to leave whatever mild gravity is holding her, and she falls toward the sun, timing this to intercept some moon or planet which is 'warm.' "

She paused for a moment, and was interrupted by Onsofruct, who said angrily, "What has all this got to do with us?"

Questioner held up an admonitory hand. "It has everything to do with you, because it happened here!"

"Here? Where we are?"

"It happened here, on a moonlet of the outermost planet, and when the egg was ripe, the Quaggima fell to this world. She fell into a caldera where she somehow laid the egg beneath her in the warm rock. She did not die. I infer that the last act the female Quaggi commits is not the penetration of a warm moon or planet to lay the egg, but the breaking of that egg when it is ready to hatch.

"When she fell here, however, life was already present: intelligent, self-aware life. It was not life arising by differentiation and selection, which we are more familiar with. The life here had developed around suboceanic vents and had grown by ramification and accumulation. It was and is, I should think, a fractal sort of creature which recapitulates in each part or group of parts the structure of the whole. In any case, most life on this world is one giant living thing that permeates the outer layer of this planet, a thing called Kaorugi, the Builder, one single being who is able to detach and reattach quasi-independent parts of itself. Though some of the detachable parts were very simple ones, created to be merely self-replicating food items for other parts, all the other detachable parts have some intelligence, and some are self-aware to the extent that they have their own cultures and systems of artistic expression. The Timmys, for example. The Joggiwagga. The Corojumi."

"The Timmys," whispered Mouche.

"Indeed. The Timmys, who, according to Bao and Ellin, were shaped differently prior to mankind's arrival, and who were reshaped as erect bipeds only after mankind arrived on this world. They were made to look like mankind so that mankind would accept their presence. The entire life system, Kaorugi, is everywhere within the crust of this world, in the caves, in the tunnels, in and beneath the oceans, upon the surface, making up forests, pastures, and wildernesses. Since the separate animate parts are all parts of Kaorugi, there is no predator–prey food chain; strong does not eat weak; large sentient things do not live on small sentient ones; all things take their nourishment from sun, air, water, and the flying, sprouting, or swimming things, the self-reproducing, unconscious lifeforms Kaorugi has designed to serve as nourishment and habitat for its roaming parts. These unconscious parts are prolific and were created to have no sense of fear or pain.

"On this world, nature is not raw and violent. The green

or violet or blue hair of the Timmys, the bright fur of the Corojumi serve the same function as leaves on plants, to draw energy from the sun. On this world, everything lives for the purpose of everything, and when a part wears out, it returns to that pond we see in the caldera, a place or organ called the Fauxi-dizalonz, and is there reconstituted."

"You're describing Eden," said D'Jevier, wonderingly.

Questioner nodded. "One might say, Eden, yes. Obviously, there is none of the inevitable agony and terror that a food chain implies. Accidents, however, can happen even in Eden, and the intelligent, nonfood creatures of this world have an aversive reaction to being maimed or mangled, just as we do, though they may fear it less, for they know if they are rendered nonfunctional they can be returned to the Fauxi-dizalonz to be healed or remade.

"When Kaorugi became aware of the Quaggi—before the fall—Kaorugi recognized pain and responded to it with what we might call pity or empathy or perhaps only curiosity. The Quaggi called upon certain Quaggian deities by their attributes. Kaorugi had parts with those attributes, so Kaorugi deputized them to make a place for Quaggima and ease her suffering. It is this sympathetic effort that is memorialized in the song you all heard as children.

"In that song and others, Bofusdiaga is called the death defier, the burrower of walls, the singer of the sun. We know this crater next to us was prepared for Quaggima, but Quaggima's falling created a much larger hole, displacing a great mass of rock that promptly fell on top of her. She was buried, shut off from the sunlight that nourishes her. Now we see that the stones have been removed. Now we see holes burrowed through the rim of this caldera where great lenses and mirrors are set to focus and reflect sunlight upon her."

"She's still here?" cried Ellin. "Where?"

"There," said Questioner, gesturing. "She is there, stretched up from the abyss, covering half that great crevasse, her wings exposed to the light."

"There?" asked Calvy in an awed tone, pointing at the black, shining surface of the pit. "Those are her wings?"

"I believe so. Those convergent ribs are no doubt the stiffeners with which the sails are controlled. Bone, perhaps, or carbon fiber. When, or if, we get to the bottom, we will find her body and her brain and the rest of her. I have no very clear idea as to her anatomy, though I expect something serpentine."

"She's huge," murmured Madame.

"Her wings are huge, but I would guess they are quite fragile," Questioner explained. "They are actually stellar sails. When she flew, she sailed on the radiation winds between the stars, her wings spread over kilometers of space. By the time she fell here, her wings were so tattered as to be virtually useless.

"In the songs, however, Corojumi are called, among other things, those who repair. I infer, therefore, that the Corojumi have repaired her, possibly using the liquid substance of the Fauxi-dizalonz, which repairs all life on this world. The Corojumi were also choreographers, and we know that when the Quaggima was restless, the Corojumi designed dances that soothed her."

"Where?" cried Ellin. "Where could you dance? Where are her eyes to see the dancers? Her ears to hear the music? She'd have to observe it, wouldn't she?"

Questioner patted the air, saying, "Patience, Ellin. We will no doubt learn where the dance was done, and how."

"I am still waiting to find out what this all has to do with us," grated Onsofruct.

"Use your perceptions, woman!" snarled Questioner. "When the egg was laid, it was small. Over long time, however, it has grown! Had it not been soothed into sleep, it would have hatched long since! But, at some point when the creature within stirred very strongly, Kaorugi realized the hatching of the egg would mean the destruction of the world!"

"Destruction?" cried Calvy, incredulously.

Questioner nodded. "I've been running some simulations, just to see how the thing could be managed. One implication is inescapable. The Quaggi cannot escape planetary gravity using star-sails. I don't know the size or weight of the egg, but it has to be propelled out of the gravity well with the hatchling still folded safely inside, and it is possible that only nuclear force would provide sufficient propulsive power. We will, I imagine, find some kind of device within or around the egg, developing as part of it, that will propel the hatchling away from this world's gravity, with consequent destruction to a great part of this world. According to the Brotherhood of Interstellar Trade, the adult Quaggi extrude metal, which they draw from their surroundings. I imagine that the egg itself, or the thing inside the egg, or the Quaggima itself, has been mining this planet for fuel since it arrived here."

"You're sure of this?" asked Madame.

"Of course I'm not sure! Nonetheless, I can come up with no other reasonable inference."

"Destruction," Calvy said again, as though unfamiliar with the word. "Destruction of the whole world?"

Questioner replied, "The substance of the world will no doubt survive, as may some elementary lifeforms, but *the* life, the totality which is Kaorugi, is another matter. The explosion, with the resultant pouring of dust into the atmosphere, is likely to cut off the sunlight. Much of Kaorugi now draws its life from the sun and will die if sunlight is lost.

"Once Kaorugi realized the destructive capabilities of the Quaggi egg, it did everything possible to keep both the Quaggima and the developing hatchling quiescent. Evidently the hatchling can continue developing in the egg for a very long time, if necessary, and keeping it there was the purpose of the dances we have heard about. On another planet, one without moons, it might stay quiescent for eons. Here, however, as the egg went on growing, the tug of the moons became greater, the dance grew more and more complex."

"So?" demanded Simon, wonderingly.

"So, no one of the Corojumi could remember it all. They remembered it corporately, and they recreated and augmented the dance whenever it was needed."

"I can guess where you're going with this," said Calvy, staring at the pond below, where the Corojum stood in the midst of a great crowd of Timmys, a violet light shining among the other colors of the slender beings. "You said this was the last Corojum. The first settlers must have what? Killed them for their hides?"

"They did. What makes this most unfortunate is that all detachable, quasi-independent creatures on this world carry their neural and cortical networks inside their skin. Soon, there were no more Corojumi. The system managed to muddle through for the last several hundred years because there hasn't been a six-moon conjunction in at least that long.

"Now, however, a conjunction approaches. There is one Corojum left, but it doesn't remember enough of the dance to recreate it. Kaorugi can make more Corojumi, of course, perhaps it has done so, but they will not know anything about the dance. Without the dance, the Quaggi in the egg is going to wake the Quaggima, she'll crack the egg, which will set off whatever the propulsive force is, the hatchling will be burst out into space, and it's likely good-bye Dosha."

"Dosha?"

"We call it Newholme. They call it Dosha, which means *fitting,* or *proper,* or, in some contexts, *ours.*

Calvy started to speak, but Questioner raised her hand. "Two final bits of information that should be kept in mind. First, Kaorugi interpenetrates the crust of the planet. It feels the pain of the Quaggima, it realizes what will happen if she wakes and the egg hatches. It does not bear that pain and apprehension motionlessly. It writhes. It heaves. The mountains tremble and the caverns fall. Kaorugi itself is the source of much of the recent geological activity.

"Second, the Timmys, Joggiwagga, Eigers, and so forth are capable of independent movement and also independent thought. When these independent parts first realized the dance information was being lost, they went to the two cities, along with some large leggers and tunnelers and whatnot, and captured all the first settlers who had killed the Corojumi and dragged them to the Fauxi-dizalonz in the hope they might be holding some of the information. Their reasoning was that mankind ate animals—

the first settlers had brought livestock with them—therefore they may have digested the Corojumi and somehow absorbed the information.''

''So that's what happened to the first settlers!'' cried Calvy. ''They drowned in this Fauxi whatsit?''

Questioner shook her head. ''No. Fauxi-dizalonz isn't water, it's a living thing. The settlers went in the pond and they crawled out again. Unfortunately, they went in as jong, which means trash, and they came out as jongau, which means bent trash, trash cubed, something that is unworkable and useless. The implications of that occurrence are extremely interesting.''

''The man known as Thor Ashburn must have been one of their descendents,'' said Madame. ''But . . . there was nothing physically abnormal about him. Except his smell!''

''You're sure?'' asked Questioner in her turn.

Madame stared sightlessly into space. ''No. Of course I'm not sure. I never saw him unclothed. The boys were his sons, and I am sure they were physically normal, except for smelling like their father.''

Questioner said, ''He and the boys would be no danger to us, I don't imagine, but there are no doubt many others of his ilk.''

''All or most of whom—so said our tunneler—are on their way here,'' said Madame.

''Why?'' demanded Mouche. ''What're they coming for?''

''I don't know,'' said Questioner. ''Curiosity? Or maybe they're frightened. The recent tremors are enough to have frightened anyone.''

''And the tremors come from Kaorugi,'' mused Simon. ''In response to the pain of Quaggima. . . .''

''Which is in response to the movement inside the egg,'' said Madame.

''Which is in response to the tug of the moons,'' said D'Jevier.

''Which nobody can do anything at all about,'' concluded Calvy.

''Not unless we can recover the dance,'' said Questioner. "Which is an issue I have decided to consider separately from the ethical concerns posed in doing so. . . ."

"Ethical concerns?" cried Calvy. "At a time like this you're worried about ethical concerns?"

"I was created to worry about ethical concerns! Under Haraldson's edicts, we would have no right to interfere with the hatching. The Quaggi came here after a local population had arisen, however, so the rights of the local population should take precedence over the Quaggi's rights. They, it, Kaorugi, had already interfered with the Quaggi before mankind entered the scene, but that issue is Kaorugi's ethical concern, not ours. I don't blame it for what it did, and in my opinion it also acted rationally, though mistakenly, when it abducted my people."

"But taking your people wasn't rational!" cried Ellin. "What would any of us from off planet know about their dance?"

Questioner laughed wryly, shaking her head. "Persons, beings are often unable to see things they can't recognize, things they have no search-image for. Kaorugi is not accustomed to sexual reproduction. On this planet, creatures are budded or assembled in the Fauxi-dizalonz, and Kaorugi designs them and grows them as it needs them. All information on this planet is held by parts of Kaorugi. When Kaorugi needs information, it accesses the part that has it. From Kaorugi's point of view, it was rational to assume that if some of its information is missing, we must have it. Where else could it have gone?"

"Even if the Corojumi are gone," said Mouche, "the Timmys who performed in the dance should remember it. Why doesn't Kaorugi gather up the Timmys who danced and give their information to some new Corojumi?"

"Right. Quite right, Mouche," said Questioner, nodding her approval. "I asked the Corojum that same question during our voyage. The Timmys, however, weren't shaped as they are until mankind came. They retain the memories but not the shape. If that weren't enough, it seems your second wave of settlers had not only forbidden dancing but had killed and burned many of the Timmys who went on doing it. As a result, much of the Timmy information was lost.''

D'Jevier blanched. Onsofruct moved uncomfortably. Calvy nodded, mouth twisted. ''This time we really did it, didn't we?''

Questioner shrugged. ''Certainly someone did. Kaorugi is intelligent but not at all imaginative, because it has never had to be. Conflict acting on intelligence creates imagination. Faced with conflict, creatures are forced to imagine what will happen, where the next threat will come from. If there has never been conflict, imagination never develops. Wits arise in answer to danger, to pain, to tragedy. No one ever got smarter eating easy apples.

''Kaorugi, therefore, could not imagine beings who would willingly destroy the common good for personal gain, something mankind is very good at. Kaorugi knew nothing of individually acquisitive creatures, and it didn't learn until too late. The point I am trying to make quite clear is that all of us here must admit that it is, in fact, too late for any simple solution. We and Kaorugi must try something else.''

''It could kill the Quaggima,'' said Onsofruct. ''That's what it could do!''

They all stared at her. The Questioner arranged her face, keeping her expression disinterested. ''It couldn't, as a matter of fact. It does not kill.''

''Well then, you can! You've got a ship out there. It has weapons!''

''Onsy!'' said D'Jevier, warningly.

''Well, she could!''

''I'm not at all sure I could,'' Questioner said calmly. ''But aside from the fact I'm still unable to contact my ship, how would you kill it?''

''Blow her to hell!''

Questioner replied, ''Blowing her, as you say, to hell, would certainly destroy the egg, and if you destroy the egg, you'll set off the propulsive system and probably blow the planet apart. Which is rather what we're trying to avoid.''

"So no matter what we do, it's going to happen sooner or later anyhow," cried Onsofruct.

"The operative word is later," cried Calvy.

Questioner nodded. "I'm sure a century or so could make a big difference to everyone involved, including Kaorugi. Given even a few tendays, there are many things we could do, but we have only a day or so to do something else. Something wonderful and imaginative and expert that will give us breathing time."

She turned, gesturing to Ellin and Bao. "And here are my wonderful and imaginative experts. How shall we set about recovering the dance?"

Ellin gasped, turning quite pale as she said, "You're joking? You've got to be!" She looked around herself in a panic, reaching out for Bao.

"Oh, how faulty an expecting!" asserted Bao, giving Ellin a supportive arm and a sympathetic look. "We are being out of our depths here."

"No false modesty, hysterics, or avoidance rituals, please," Questioner murmured. "It's a simple question well within your field of expertise. My data banks tell me that recovery of old dances is something done all the time among dancers on Old Earth. Simply tell us how they would do it."

Ellin gritted her teeth and took several labored breaths before saying, "I'm sorry, Questioner. You took me by surprise, but you're quite right. There's no time for . . . whatever.

"Um. If I had to recover an old dance on Old Earth, I'd find all contemporary accounts of the performance. I'd look for letters written by cast members or observers, interviews given by them. I'd look for critical reviews, either printed or broadcast. I'd look at impressions noted by audience members or notes made at the time by dance aficionados. If the ballet had a name indicating a traditional or well-known story, like, oh, *Romeo and Juliet* or *Homage to Dorothy,* I'd find the story."

"Designs of costumes or even bills for costumes are useful," offered Bao. "Costume often defines character, and character defines movement. Same is being true for scenery. The music is being a good place to start, also musicians themselves. Then, one is doing what Mouche said. Surely not *all* Timmys who danced are being dead! So I would be talking to the ones left. They are describing the steps and movements they were doing, as well as those other people were doing.''

''If we still *have* some of the Timmys who danced,'' said Ellin. ''They aren't all dead, are they?''

''Not quite all, no,'' said Questioner, with a significant look at the Hags. ''The governing powers were not quite that efficient.''

Bao went on, ''If we have story, we can start with plot. Who are characters? What is represented, what is emotion? What is done? Surely this much Kaorugi knows!''

''According to the Corojum,'' said Questioner, ''Kaorugi knows only that the dance soothed the Quaggima and let it sleep.''

With her brow furrowed in concentration, Ellin offered, ''It might be plotless, Bao. Just movement for movement's sake. Kind of like hypnosis, or wall patterns. I always kept my walls on patterns because they were soothing. And if there's no story line, it's very difficult to figure out what went on.''

''Assume for the moment there was a story,'' said Questioner.

''Well then, I'd look for representations of the work of the solo dancers, verbal or pictorial, to see how they moved, how they worked, what their style was . . .''

''Style?'' asked Calvy. ''I don't see—''

Ellin interrupted him, ''We know the Timmys danced. Well, they were shaped differently. What could that shape do? What kinds of jumps, positions, movements? How did the choreographers work? Did they work out lengthy series of steps and teach the series, already set, or did they allow the dancer a share in developing the vision? On Old Earth, we'd ask the patrons of the ballet, as well, but I guess that doesn't apply here.''

''The music,'' said Bao. ''Again, I am emphasizing importance of music.''

"How many people are we talking about here?" asked Calvy. "How many dancers? Musicians? Scene setters?"

Ellin, who had, despite herself, become interested in the problem, shook her head firmly. "The numbers aren't that critical. Even in a large ballet, you wouldn't need everyone in order to learn what they did. A lot of ballet is ensemble work. One dancer in an ensemble could reconstruct the whole ensemble, or large chunks of it, because she would move as everyone else does, or groups would move in repetitive sequence. It wouldn't matter if there were twelve or two hundred, they might all be doing the same steps. The same is true for small groups: in a pas de deux, for example, either dancer could remember what the other one did. . . ."

Bao objected, "Except, there were being in twentieth century, so-called modern dances in which every person was doing something completely different from everyone else. Movements and groupings were being more sculptural. . . ."

"But if these were very small dancers, doing something to soothe a very large being, they'd have to move en masse to be perceived, wouldn't they?" Ellin asked plaintively. "I keep getting this twentieth-century, Old Earth flash of Busby Berkeley musicals. Hundreds of dancers parading around. Or carnival processions! Or even pageants! Something with hundreds, thousands of participants, all jingling and jiggling, headdresses bobbing, skirts swirling. . . . Looking at the size of the wings on that creature in the pit, I wonder if it could even perceive individual dancers."

"Postpone that concern," said Questioner. "For now, merely find out everything you can, without worrying about how we'll use it. We have no newspapers or reviews; we have no notes; we do, however, have some persons, creatures, who saw the dance or did the dance or provided music for it."

"I must be very stupid, but I can't understand why Kaorugi doesn't remember," cried Ellin, frustrated.

Questioner pondered. "Let me simplify. Imagine that your brain is spread out everywhere under your skin.

Imagine that you could detach your arm and send it off to pick strawberries, and imagine the brain under the skin had sensors to see and smell and taste with. Imagine your arm can remember what it is supposed to do, and can record what happens. When the arm comes back, once it is reattached, you would remember picking the berries. If your arm never came back, however, you would remember sending the arm, but not what happened to it. Kaorugi can remember deputizing its parts, but it can't remember what they do until and unless they return."

"And Kaorugi can't extrapolate the missing parts?" Madame said, shaking her head.

Questioner said, "Madame, I don't know all the implications of Kaorugi's mind. I think the dance was a subfunction that was left up to the Timmys and the Corojumi, a constantly changing detail Kaorugi never incorporated into its core. The Timmys and the Corojum are, after all, virtually independent. The system had plenty of redundancy until we came along, but this planet hasn't had a history of traumas and mass deaths. We brought the habits of murder with us, which meant the redundancy level just wasn't high enough."

"Ridiculous," muttered Onsofruct.

Questioner said patiently, "It does us no good to ponder and fret over what we don't have, let's start with what we do. We will go down to the Fauxi-dizalonz and find out what the one Corojum remembers. We will find out what the remaining Timmys remember and whatever else exists that might retain any memory of the dance. And by the way, what are the members of my entourage doing down there?"

Ellin shook her head in confusion. "Were they down there? We didn't see them."

"The Corojum said they were there," Questioner averred.

Bao stood up, took Ellin by one hand, and pulled her erect. "We'll see when we get there."

Mouche was standing at the rim, examining the crowd of persons below. His Goddess was not there, which gave him a sense of relief. On the voyage he had managed not to look at her, it, too closely, and just now he had carefully refused to listen to Questioner's exposition, knowing he wouldn't like the implications of it. He could not accept that Flowing Green was a part. His mystical dream required that she, it, be a singular creature woven of starlight and shadow, magic and romance. She was a perilous eidolon, a symbol of marvel and mystery. Instinctively, he kept a respectful distance to separate his Hagion from reality. Since she, it, was not by the Fauxi-dizalonz, nothing prevented his going with the others.

The road began its descent into the caldera from the north end of the ledge, and they went along it only a little way before cutting downward on a steep narrow track interrupted by rocky stairs. The road had a much gentler slope, but it went so far around the caldera before each switchback that it would have taken them half a day to traverse it. Even as it was, Questioner thought, setting her climbing legs on slow, a careful journey would take them some time.

Madame, the Hags, and Questioner were at the end of the procession. Madame stared after Mouche, worried by his manner. Something there. Something strange. When he came back, she'd have to try and find out what. She turned a troubled face toward the Questioner, who was watching her closely.

"You're worried about the boy?" Questioner asked.

"I am, yes."

"Mouche?" asked D'Jevier. "What's wrong with him?"

"He is enchanted," said Questioner.

"By them?" D'Jevier looked downward. "The Timmys?"

"One of them, I should think," said Madame. "Though how it happened . . ."

"He watched them," said Questioner. "At their dances, while he was at your establishment, Madame."

"Impossible!"

"Nothing is impossible when it comes to youthful mischief, as we all know," Onsofruct drawled in a muffled voice.

Questioner said firmly, "Since we are more or less alone, just we four . . . women, I think it's time for you to tell me the truth about Newholme."

D'Jevier refused to be cowed. "By all the Hagions," she erupted, planting her feet firmly on the trail and turning on her interlocutor. "Don't play games with us, Questioner. You know the truth! You know we lied about the Timmys. You've probably had that one figured out since shortly after you got here. I don't know what made us think we could hide it."

"I know some of the truth about that, yes," said Questioner. "But I am speaking now of the truth of Mouche and Madame. I mean the other truth."

The three women looked at one another. Onsofruct sighed. "What about Mouche and Madame?"

"This Consort business. This business of men going about in veils."

The two sisters exchanged a glance, and Onsofruct shrugged. "There's no point in not telling you. It's not unethical."

Questioner said, "You may be right, though I doubt Haraldson would have approved. It's part of the Newholmian pattern, and I need to know about all of it."

Onsofruct sat on a boulder at the edge of the path, removed her boot, and dumped gravel out of it, saying: "Tell her about the woman raids, D'Jevier. That's where the whole thing started."

D'Jevier did so, concluding, "The men who took them made no bones about their intentions. They'd been promised wives with the second ship, and they weren't going to wait. They had stolen women, they would steal more, and they intended to keep them all under lock and key to prevent their running away.

"Well, Honored Questioner, 'keeping women under lock and key' or 'stopping their running away' sounded like the worst sort of patriarchal repression to our foremothers, some of whom, as required by the Settlement Act, were cultural historians."

Onsofruct interrupted, "The women knew that if we got entrenched in a patriarchal system, no matter how useful it might be for a generation or two, there'd be no simple way to stop it sixty or seventy years later. Once a male dominance system got started, it would take centuries before their daughters and granddaughters could achieve equality."

Onsofruct got to her feet and started down the path again, Questioner close behind. "The women used the fortress in Sendoph. It was unfinished, but it had strong walls that were easy to defend, and our ancestresses had control of medical care, tools, weapons, and women. That gave them what they needed to enforce the newly written dower laws. Our foremothers knew that when women had to be paid for, they were more highly valued, so we told the men they'd either pay and pay well for a woman's reproductive life, or they would do without.

"Well, you know about the dower laws. Women have a contractual right to be well supported during their entire lifetimes—there is no divorce in an economic sense—and in return the women agree to contribute their reproductive capabilities to their husbands' lineage for a specified number of years. If a woman has talents or skills, the contract may include some contribution toward the business. The marriage contract can guarantee support, but no contract can guarantee affection or pleasure. Our people thought women should be entitled to those as well. After a dutiful childbearing, women had a right to the same pleasures men have always achieved through having mistresses."

"You gave them Consorts," said Questioner.

"Exactly. Someone to offer intellectual stimulation, to make conversation, to create romance, to cuddle and cosset, to make love to them. Men of Business are too busy with the game of business—which most men seem to enjoy more than anything else—to have time for pleasuring a wife."

Questioner asked, "And you're satisfied with the system?"

Onsofruct said, "Almost everyone is satisfied because we tried very hard to give everyone what they wanted. What men most wanted was clear title to their children's paternal genetics, so we gave it to them. What women most wanted was to lead productive and companionate lives. We gave them that by giving them broadly educated companions, Consorts who read, who enjoy the arts. Whenever you see art or hear music or enjoy culture upon Newholme, you may thank women and their Consorts, for they are the ones who keep it going."

"It wouldn't work if you had as many women as men," said Questioner.

Onsofruct and D'Jevier plodded on, blank-faced.

Madame said, "Our system works for us. It's coercive, yes, but no more so than every other system. We know Haraldson's edicts say people shouldn't be coerced in matters of reproduction, but you know as well as we do they've always been coerced, women particularly. Here, we tried to balance things."

"I give you credit for good intentions," said Questioner in a preoccupied tone. "I will report you, of course, but chances are the Council of Worlds will agree with you. Your system works. And it probably makes no difference, for you're sufficiently at risk over the business of the Timmys that the matter of coercion takes second place."

"You're going to report the Timmys, too." Onsofruct sighed.

"You'd expect me to, wouldn't you?" asked Questioner. "Though it's an interesting question whether they are, in fact, indigenes. I'm not sure detachable parts can be considered an indigenous race. And since there's only one of Kaorugi, it isn't exactly a race. It's more of a biota. Haraldson's edicts cover destruction of biotas, but killing the Timmys didn't kill the biota. The hearings on the question should be interesting, no?"

"Oh, certainly, certainly." Madame threw up her hands, as though throwing the subject to the winds. Then, looking down the hill, she remarked, "Let's catch up to your assistants and the men."

They went on at somewhat greater speed, Madame with a clear conscience, the two Hags somewhat troubled, and Questioner quite certain she knew what each of the others was thinking.

56

A Gathering Of Monsters

Though Ashes and his sons kept to the high road, their progress was slowed by the traffic in Newholmian leggers and tunnelers along with various of Ashes's kindred who rolled, heaved, crawled, slunk, poured, bounced, and otherwise ambulated along in the same direction. By the time half the morning had worn away, Dyre and Bane were dizzy with the variety they had observed and half paralyzed by the monstrousness of the movers and shakers—for so Ashes called them.

"Movers and shakers, boys," he crowed. "That's us, the movers and the shakers."

"When they all get there, what are they going to do?" asked Bane, keeping his voice in the even, careless register that Ashes seemed able to hear without growing angry.

"Like Hugh said, roll 'em over." Ashes chuckled.

Bane started to ask why, then desisted. Ashes wouldn't know why. Yesterday it had occurred to Bane that Ashes had never known why, and probably neither had any of the first settlers. They had been discontented with life on Earth, so they'd moved to Thor. They'd been discontented with the rules on Thor, so they'd broken the rules. They'd been discontented with the punishment received for that, so they'd moved. They had been discontented without women, so they'd tried stealing some. They'd continued discontented with the results of that; they would always be discontented, and probably they would never know why. During the night just past, he had dreamed of Madame's voice going on and on about angry men, discontented men, men who went off like bombs.

"What're you thinkin'?" asked Dyre.

"I was thinkin' about Madame."

"Old horny corsets? What about the old bitch?"

"I was thinkin', she was right about some things."

Dyre sniggered under his breath. "You're goin' soft in the head."

Bane took a deep breath. "I was just rememberin' she said that thing about men being angry. Ashes there, he's angry."

"I'm angry," snarled Dyre. "All those people saying we stink. It's enough to make you good and angry."

"I mean besides that. Got to be something more than that to make Ashes so ferocious."

"Hellfire, you know," said Dyre. "He's mad at those people on Thor who got in his way, and he's mad at the Timmys for what they did to him, and he's mad at the women for dyin' on him, and he's mad at Marool for doin' . . . whatever she did."

"And he's mad at you and me because we're not girls," concluded Bane. "And if we was girls, he'd be mad at us for something else."

"You are getting soft," muttered Dyre, pulling his horse back to conclude the conversation.

Bane said softly, between his teeth, "I'm just thinking I'm not set on dying just yet. And the way he's going, he's going to get himself killed and everybody else who happens to be standing too close."

Dyre pretended not to hear and they rode silently for a time. A legger came up behind them, abated its speed, and seemed content to follow. Nonetheless, Dyre kicked his horse into a trot and came up beside Bane, throwing suspicious glances over his shoulder. Bane ignored him, though Dyre had been right, of course. Bane did get mad at people saying he smelled. But then, they'd been at Madame's, and she'd stopped the way he and Dyre smelled, and nobody at House Genevois had ever mentioned it, not even Mouche, but they'd still felt mad. Like being mad was a sort of habit. He thought about this for a time, then tried again to involve his brother.

"All right, look. Who's on our side? There's Hughy Huge. And there's those crawlers we saw this morning, like Crawly, back at the camp, only bigger. And there's that one we heard about, the one that's grown into the mountain. And there's the ear and the eye and all, who're probably coming along. And there's Bone and Mooly, and the rest. So there's muscle ones, and mouth ones, and belly ones, and other kinds of ones. There's all kinds of body parts, all kinds but one. There's no brain one. Don't that make you wonder?"

"Wonder what?" snarled Dyre.

"Oh, shit, forget it." Bane frowned to himself and shut his mouth tightly, drawing his horse away from his brother's. Maybe there was something wrong with him. Maybe he was sick. Maybe he'd caught this sickness at House Genevois. He'd never had thoughts like this before. He'd always been pretty much like Ashes, mad at everybody, getting his pleasure out of hurting them, screwing them up. So now Ashes was really going to screw something up, and then what?

As though to accentuate this thought, the earth moved beneath him, the horse stopped, legs braced wide, white showing at the edges of its eyes, nostrils flaring. The tremor went on and on, then faded. Ahead of them, the road danced then stilled. Behind them the legger emitted a confused noise, for it had been knocked off the road and now lay on its side, all its legs kicking without being able to right itself. Suddenly the legs came loose in pairs connected by saddle-shaped bits, and a few of these pieces began galloping away down the road, making the horses shy away. Then the tubular body split into cylindrical sections that wheeled onto the road and began rolling westward, spinning like tires, while the abandoned legs assembled themselves into pairs of pairs and spun after them like four-spoked wheels.

Only a squarish part was left behind, one that immediately began a shrill screaming, ''Weeeple, weeeple, weeeple!''

The rearmost set of legs skidded to a stop, turned, sped back, separated itself to attach one leg pair at each end of the remaining part, then galloped off after the rest, the screamer still keening, ''Weeeple, weeeple!''

Another tremor began, a long, slow shaking that seemed to go on endlessly. The horses refused to move. Cursing, Ashes dismounted and sat on a quivering rock at the side of the road, the reins loose in his hands.

''Did you see that?'' Bane asked.

''See what,'' his father growled.

''D'ja see that thing come apart?''

''They all come apart. Joggiwagga comes apart into snakes and balloony parts. Leggers come apart into tubes and legs and voice boxes. Tunnelers are just legger tubes with a driller section added on in front. Swimmers are just tunnelers with fins added on.''

''How about Timmys?''

''Funny about them. They don't seem to fit together real well, and they don't come apart into smaller things.''

''How do you know all that?'' Bane asked.

''Been watchin' 'em. Long time.'' Ashes yawned, his face suddenly becoming vacant and unlike himself. Bane stared at him, wondering why he looked so mushy, as though his nose and chin were sinking into his face. ''You feelin' all right?''

''Why?'' snapped Ashes, suddenly himself. ''Something the matter with you?''

Bane shook his head slowly, making his voice sound uninterested again. ''You were yawning and looked a little sleepy, that's all. I thought maybe you hadn't slept real well.''

''Slept fine.'' Ashes got back on his horse and rode on

without a backward glance. Bane kicked his mount, as did Dyre, and they followed after.

"You were right," whispered Dyre. "He looked funny. Like somebody melted him."

"Like I said," muttered Bane. "I think we'd better be careful not to stand too close."

57

Quaggima And The Chasm

When Questioner and the women came to the shores of the Fauxi-dizalonz, they saw Questioner's entourage disconsolately huddled in the mouth of a nearby cave. Simon and Calvy were with the four young people, all concentrated upon the Corojum, who was tightly pressed against what appeared to be a curved rock wall. The new arrivals joined the others in time to hear the Corojum say loudly, "Bofusdiaga says your people won't help, so probably none of you will help."

"What people?" demanded Mouche.

"Your people. Bofusdiaga wanted to talk to them, but they became frightened and silly. Bofusdiaga is annoyed."

Questioner stepped forward and pulled the Corojum gently away from his attachment, earning a scowl from the Corojum and a tremor in the ground beneath them.

"Corojum, what's going on? We haven't killed any of you, like the settlers did. Bao and Ellin and I have only been here a few days, along with the members of my entourage. Why would Bofusdiaga be annoyed with us?''

''Because they won't be sensible. All they will do is talk about how they have been wronged. Those jongau, they were also wronged. Bofusdiaga says creatures who think only of how they are wronged cannot help with the dance and everything is lost.''

Questioner rubbed her head. ''If you had asked me, Corojum, I could have told you that those people in the cave would be of no help. They are young, rebellious, and not at all useful. At that age, many young people spend a great deal of time thinking they have been wronged.''

Corojum snorted. ''So. Bofusdiaga says past wrongs cannot be righted because past wrongs are past and time only runs one way. Bofusdiaga says all you independent creatures suffer great wrongs sometime in past, which is normal, but you stay always living in past so you can continue wronged forever! Forever miserable, forever tragical! Bofusdiaga says so long as you go on chewing yesterday's pains, you cannot eat today's pleasures, so it is no help!''

''This is Bofusdiaga, not Kaorugi?'' Questioner persisted.

Corojum leaned against the stone, faced the group, held up his hands for silence, and said with an attitude of sorely tried patience: ''Before Quaggima, in this place was only Kaorugi and this world that Kaorugi came into and made Kaorugi's own. Kaorugi, only! Itself! Solo! One living thing and its parts! You are also living things with parts. You say fingers to do work; Kaorugi says Timmys. You say arms; Kaorugi says Joggiwagga. You say eyes; Kaorugi says Eiger. You say conscious activity; Kaorugi says Bofusdiaga. You say creativity; Kaorugi says Corojumi. You understand?''

Questioner nodded, intrigued, as the Corojum went on: ''Only difference is, Kaorugi's parts know themselves and act by themselves. Well! After Kaorugi heard Quaggima calling, here was this world and Kaorugi and its parts, but also there was Quaggima coming toward it, Quaggima who evoked many new ideas: stars and galaxies and sex and other peoples, outside. Kaorugi had never thought of other people, and now Kaorugi had to think about that and other new things, and it was very difficult! So, Kaorugi takes a part of itself, the Bofusdiaga part, and Kaorugi says to itself, Bofusdiaga, 'You do this work here, you, Bofusdiaga, you go on being part that builds, alloys, puts together and takes apart! You take charge of the Fauxidizalonz, for I am going down deep to think!' And since then, Kaorugi has gone down deep all over, under cities, under oceans, under mountains, and Kaorugi is thinking, all the time thinking deep thoughts, and Kaorugi is not finished thinking yet."

The ten visitors looked at one another for support, at the sky, as though for inspiration, up at the ledge, as though for direction, finding no help.

"What is problem?" demanded the Corojum.

Calvy asked, "Where is Bofusdiaga?"

The Corojum stared at him incredulously, gesturing widely. "Here. This is Bofusdiaga. Bofusdiaga is all around us, anywhere inside this valley and in next valley, where Quaggima is, and I think spills over a little even farther."

"What if we want to talk to Kaorugi itself?" asked the Questioner.

Corojum's fur stood on end, both head and hands waved in negation. "Oh, no, no. Kaorugi would be very angry. Kaorugi does not want to be distracted and has made self unavailable."

"Rather like the male Quaggi in that respect," muttered Questioner, fidgeting, feeling inadequate. She could not recall ever before feeling inadequate and could not understand why she did so now, as though something very important was going on that she was not seeing! She took a deep breath.

"Corojum, Bofusdiaga is quite correct about the people in the cave. Most of them are very young and given to rebelling against their fathers and mothers. Do you understand the word mother?"

"Kaorugi understands; Bofusdiaga understands. So, I understand. Quaggima is nest keeper, child hatcher. Mankinds have also nest keepers and child hatchers also, called mothers. Other sex is called fathers."

Questioner said, "Well, the mothers and fathers of these children have grown tired of them, so they sent them to me, hoping this will help them grow up, which it sometimes does. For the moment we can forget them. They are not part of this. We, the rest of us, are not feeling wronged."

She said this with a swift glance at the others which they uniformly interpreted as a directive to give up any such feelings on the instant and not make a liar of her.

Mouche said, pleadingly, "We are really interested in helping, Corojum. Can't we please get on with it?"

Corojum stared at them, looking from face to face, letting his eyes rest finally on Mouche, who held out his hands pleadingly. "I will ask Bofusdiaga."

The Corojum went to the rock wall, leaned against it, and stared at the sky, his eyes moving, his body moving, various muscle groups knotting and relaxing, all in accompaniment to the communication, which was lengthy. Those closest could see that it had opened a seam along its side which had actually attached to the stone.

Finally, just as Questioner was running out of patience, Corojum pulled away from the rock and said, "Bofusdiaga says all right for now. Bofusdiaga will forget those others and cooperate with you. We have asked for all Timmys who danced to come here; some are here already. Every other creature who saw dance is coming, also. Some Joggiwagga, some Eiger, some others. . . ."

"Then I think we'd better get started, because we're running out of time!"

In the brief pause that followed, Questioner went to the cave and told the captives there to get themselves onto the high rim to wait for her, and if they wanted to avoid being eaten by the monsters, to do it without any talk whatsoever. Casting resentful glances behind them, they went, the last of them departing just before Corojum returned leading an assortment of creatures.

Questioner instructed the group: "Each of you take one of the portable data heads and record everything. Ask about the site, first. Where did they dance, where from, where to. Then ask about what they did, what they saw done by others. Corojum says when you are finished with the Timmys, they will translate for the others.''

So they began with the Timmys, their initial diffidence giving way to assurance as afternoon wore away toward evening. Questioner moved from place to place, feeding the data head information into the larger accumulator she carried in a compartment on her person.

''What is that thing, anyhow?'' asked Calvy, alert to the possibility of profit.

''An IDIOT SAVANT,'' she murmured. ''An Improved Deductive Imager Of Theoretical Scenarios And Variations, Ambassadorial, Non-Terrestrial. It was invented by HoTA—the same department that designed me—for use by Council of Worlds diplomats. It has a data bank that includes most of what we know about intelligent races; it takes everything that is observed, fact by fact, and extrapolates a logical scenario that includes all observed realities. Then it does variations on the scenario. It helps me understand both mankind and nonmankind races.''

Sundown neared. Ellin gaped with weariness; Mouche slumped; Madame, impossibly erect and Eiger eyed, continued her slow accumulation of data, as did Simon. Calvy and Bao gave up for a time to take a nap in a cave. D'Jevier and Onsofruct worked methodically, occasionally rising to take a few steps, roll their heads about and wave their arms, restoring circulation. Bao returned from his nap and bantered with Ornery and with the last few Timmys who were translating for the Joggiwagga and the Eigers.

''Is your IDIOT SAVANT coming up with anything?'' Calvy asked.

''Not so far,'' Questioner admitted. Actually, a three-dimensional moving construct of the supposed dance had emerged, but it meant nothing to her at all.

During all of this, the ground shivered and subsided, shivered and subsided. They were all overcome with weariness, cold, and hunger by the time the last few interviews were concluded.

Evening brought dark and a chilly wind accompanied

by stronger tremors, wave after wave, like a rising surf that brought falling rocks and a hail of gravel. Corojum told them to take refuge in a nearby cave, where the Timmys brought firewood and cooked up roots and greens, producing the same savory smells that had delighted Mouche at House Genevois.

D'Jevier and Onsofruct sat a little apart from the others. D'Jevier murmured, "Where's the green-haired one? The one that enchanted Mouche."

"I haven't seen it. And why do you care. What is it with you and this Mouche?"

D'Jevier flushed and did not answer.

"You've been going to House Genevois!" said Onsofruct, in whispered outrage. "You've been . . ."

D'Jevier shrugged. "Someone has to play the part of patroness during their training. It's our system. We're responsible for it."

"At your age!"

"I'm not dead yet, Onsy. And I like Mouche. Sometimes, talking with him—and mostly we just talked—you'd swear there was a sage inside that young head. Something's affected him strangely and wonderfully, and I don't think it was Madame, or not entirely, at any rate. What that other boy did to his face was inexcusable."

"Spoiled it for you?" sniped Onsofruct.

"No," snapped D'Jevier. "Nothing could."

Onsofruct merely shook her head, more annoyed than amused. D'Jevier was younger than she, but not that much younger. If anyone was entitled to a little fun, it should be she! She said as much.

D'Jevier responded, "Well, cousin, the pleasures are there. Do not blame me if you would rather feel hard-used than enjoy them."

When they had eaten, Questioner summoned them all together, including the Corojum.

"Corojum," she said in a measured, respectful voice, "during our questioning of the Timmys, they have spoken of fitting together. Please tell us how the Timmys can join together."

"Not so well, now that they are shaped like mankinds,"

he said, as though puzzled. "All Kaorugi's parts have seams that open and join together, seam to seam. Some are like tunnelers, end to end, or like Joggiwagga, making a circle around a middle piece. Timmys used to be shaped to make big things."

"So a lot of them all together, they could become a rather massive shape."

Corojum nodded. "They must keep airways open, but yes, they can make big assemblies with legs to move them and arms on the sides."

Questioner turned to Ellin. "That would explain the lack of grace, would it not?"

She turned back to Corojum. "And Joggiwagga. Do they get very large?"

"Some Joggiwagga are very large, you would say huge, to do heavy things, like raising up very large stones to mark the rising of the moons."

"Have we learned anything?" asked Madame in a weary voice.

Questioner replied. "One of our basic problems was how such small creatures, relatively speaking, as the Timmys could be observed in the dance. We have learned they used to be shaped differently and could mass together. We have also learned that the dance, as described by the Timmys, moved repetitively, in a quickening tempo. And, we have learned that the dance was done in the chasm, yonder, where the Quaggima is. All of this is more than we knew before."

"We have also learned there were no costumes or sets," said Ellin dispiritedly, "which makes it unlike any dance I was ever involved with. Even minimalist ballet had something by way of setting or lighting."

"We have learned something of the music," said Bao. "Singing by Timmys and drumming by Joggiwaggas, little ones and very big ones, on great singing stones set in the chasm. Some singing was by Bofusdiaga itself. Bofusdiaga is remembering the singing, which could be good clue if there were being words. It is being unfortunate there were no words."

"We have to go down there," said Ellin. "We have to

see it, her. We can't work on the dance at all until we see and feel where it is to be performed.''

''This is important?'' asked D'Jevier.

''Oh, Ma'am, yes,'' cried Ellin. ''I remember the first time I encountered a raked stage! I had always danced on a flat stage, with the audience tilted up and away for good views of it, but I was transferred to another History House where they had a raked stage, higher at the back, slanted toward the audience, and, oh, the whole time I felt as though I would fall into their laps! It is also more laborious, for much of the time one is running uphill or plunging down!''

''Also, partnering,'' said Bao. ''With raked stage, partner is being upstage above, or downstage below, and every motion is being changed longer or shorter depending on location.''

''I see,'' murmured D'Jevier. ''Well, then, those of you who know something about dancing should go. I can't imagine the rest of us would be of any help.''

Corojum, summoned, received this intention fatalistically, saying only, ''You have little time.''

''Corojum, we know that,'' cried Mouche. ''Believe me, we're doing everything we can as fast as we can!''

As though to underline this comment, the ground beneath them shook once more, and stones plummeted from above to splash into the Fauxi-dizalonz. Corojum looked up alertly as several Timmys came flashing into the firelight, hair wild and eyes wide.

''They come,'' called one. ''The jongau! The bent ones! Dozens and dozens!''

''Where?'' asked Questioner. ''On the road?''

''On the road, off the road, rolling, hopping, squirming, flowing, along the road.''

''When will they get here?'' Questioner demanded.

Corojum said soberly, ''Now is dark, only the one little moon rising will make them slow down, but they will come soon, for Bofusdiaga calls to them.''

''Why?'' cried Ornery. ''Why just now? Don't we have enough to worry about without them?''

''The bent ones are not finished,'' said the Corojum.

"They wouldn't go back through the Fauxi-dizalonz and get finished, so they're only part done. Part-done things do not last well. They lose cohesion, and their substance longs for the Fauxi-dizalonz, whence it came. If they do not come now, they will disintegrate."

"Interesting," said Questioner. "Since they caused this mess, why don't you just let them disintegrate?"

"Because Bofusdiaga does not waste material. Bofusdiaga alloys, changes, refines. You will see, very soon."

"Then we must not delay," Questioner said. "Let us go to the chasm."

The Corojum fussed, "It is dark in the chasm. . . ."

"Never mind that. I can light the place adequately. Let us go now, before we are overtaken by events."

They went, Questioner and the four young people, accompanied by a small horde of Timmys trotting and Joggiwagga writhing and Eigers flying overhead and Corojum riding in the crook of Questioner's arm. When they had gone a little way down into the chasm, a huge mooing sound began in the chasm below them, much akin to that mooing Questioner had heard in the recording.

Mouche and Ornery both sagged, stricken with such sadness they could barely move. It was the feeling each had felt before, Mouche on the bridge, Ornery in the tunnel, a terrible melancholy, an aching terror, as of something despairing over aeons of time.

Questioner turned on her lights. The area around them leapt into visibility. Across the chasm, the coal-dark drapery of Quaggima's wings quivered against the rock wall, as though in response to the sound coming from below. As Questioner had understood the intent of the cry she had heard recorded, so she understood the plaint of this one, a fractious whine: "Oh, I am in pain, I am without ease, time drags, living drags, can no one help me, can no one help me. I want out, I want out, I want out." The plaint had an odd reverberation, an almost instantaneous echo, as though spoken slightly out of sync by more than one voice.

With the light, the voice stilled. Mouche took a deep

breath and staggered to Ornery, helping her up. Ornery put an arm around him, and they supported one another.

"She is very restless," said the Corojum, pointing to the movement in the wings, now clearly discernable to them all. "The egg has been moving under her and she has been getting worse for days and days."

"Sticking to this track will take too long," said Questioner to the Corojum. "If we have as little time as you say, we must get there more rapidly."

Corojum whistled. They looked up just in time to see the talons of the Eigers that snatched them from the trail and plunged with them into the depths of the chasm, Questioner and the Corojum held by one great bird, each of the others borne singly, along with a cloud of Timmys who flung themselves into the air, circling and soaring on flaps of skin that joined their arms and legs, like larger versions of the swoopers in the tunnel. Even stranger were the several Joggiwagga that flattened themselves into spiked disks that sailed downward, like spinning plates.

The Questioner's light surrounded them as they circled, slowing as they neared the bottom. There they were deposited gently one by one on the circular floor, smooth as glass, black and glossy.

"Obsidian," observed Questioner, brushing herself off, dislodging a few fluffs of down in the process. "Now, where is she?"

Corojum gestured, head down, bowing to something behind Questioner. She turned and stared into an immense, faceted eye the size of a building. Several more such eyes were arranged symmetrically below three tall, flickering antennae that rose like feathery trees. Below the eyes was what could be a mouth, complicated and surrounded by ramified angular structures that twitched restlessly. Below that, laid sideways along the floor, partially enclosed in the glassy floor, was the long, striated, dully gleaming body of the Quaggima, twitching, vibrating, waves of motion rippling down it from the head, away into the darkness.

Though the creature gave no evidence of seeing them, they all bowed. Questioner abated her light, dimming it to a softer, rosier glow, and muttering commands to her troops.

"Mouche, pace off the length of the body. Take a data head and get every inch of her recorded. Ornery, take another data head and go bit by bit over the upper body and head; be sure to get good, clear views. Ellin and Bao, I'd like to test for a reaction, so would you two do something in the way of a pas de deux? I'll give you some music and atmosphere—anything you'd prefer?"

The two dancers looked at one another. "Debussy," said Bao. " 'La Mer.' "

Questioner flipped mentally through her catalogues, found the appropriate references, and began to emit the music, along with shifting watery lights that poured like a tidal flow across the dark glass beneath her. . . .

From within which, something watched her. She bent over and beamed her light down, disclosing another faceted eye above a shifting, shadowy depth of moving wings, and beyond the wings, far down, far, far down, another eye. . . .

"This is the egg!" she said to Corojum, without moving or interrupting the music.

"Of course it's the egg," said Corojum. "What did you think it was?"

"When the wing moves, I can see far down past it, far, far down. There's more than one in there."

"She told Kaorugi, always they have at least twins," said Corojum. "One male, one female. Each Quaggima mates only once. If they are not to go extinct, she must produce at least two offspring. Sometimes they have four."

"Are the ones in the egg aware?"

"They are more aware than she is. Long ago, before the egg grew so big, she was awake all the time. She used to cry until the whole world sorrowed, so Kaorugi talked more with her, and when she could talk with someone, she was not sorrowful, but when the egg got bigger, she began to be agitated again, and talking with Bofusdiaga was not enough. That's when the dancers put her to sleep. Sometimes, like now, when the moons pull and pull, her children move and she feels them moving. What wakes her most is when they cry like they were doing. She hears that!''

"That crying wasn't from the Quaggima? It was from the egg?''

"From the egg, yes, though it is like her crying. And if Quaggima wakes up and hears them crying to get out, she will break the egg for them and so die. And so will we, Corojum and Timmys and Joggiwagga, Bofusdiaga and Kaorugi, all, dead. And you, too.''

"Maybe Kaorugi shouldn't have healed her.''

"It is Kaorugi's nature to heal. So Kaorugi says, it is the nature of all life to heal, no matter where it arises. Creatures that do not heal are not natural to this universe, they come from outside. This one wanted to die at first, but after Kaorugi made her well again, she did not want to die. She was then, as you mankinds say, on a dilemma. So she said to Bofusdiaga, let me sleep, let me not think about it.''

"And since then she's been asleep.''

"More like how do you people say it, hypnotized, dreaming. What is word? Entranced. I think she sees you as a dream, but she is watching Bao and Ellin.''

Indeed, the glittering eyes did seem fixed on the dancers, and the antennae turned toward Questioner, hearing the music. Drawn by the sound, the Timmys also began to dance, forming a moving backdrop for the two Old Earthers.

The egg shivered, the world moved. Reeling and teetering, Ellin and Bao went gamely on with their extemporaneous performance. Beneath them, the eyes moved to follow their steps.

"How would she break the egg?'' Questioner asked the Corojum.

"Down at her far end, there is a kind of tail that is very heavy and stiff. And from there going deep, deep down to the end of the egg are capsules, like a . . . a . . . string of beads, bigger the farther down they go. Bofusdiaga says they hold heavy metals. The egg puts out roots, says Bofusdiaga, and it brings the metals bit by bit out of the world, atom by atom. And when she is ready to break the egg, she hits those capsules with her tail, and the first one drops into the next, breaking it, and so on, each bigger and bigger, going down and then something in the last one mixes with it, and it goes up, all at once, like a volcano exploding.''

''And?''

''And she is blown to pieces, but the baby Quaggi are in the shell, and the shell is in a rock tube, and the way it is shaped, it gets exploded far out into space, and then they fly.''

Mouche came trudging back into the circle of light. ''About four hundred eighty meters, Questioner. Maybe a little longer. It's a long, tapering body. The surface is much rougher down at that end, and it was hard to keep my footing. She has a kind of tail or stinger down there that seems to pain her and it quivers.'' He turned to stare into the faceted eyes, trying to penetrate their mystery. Something in this utterly strange place was familiar to him. Something was happening here that he had experienced before.

''A tiny body for all that wingspan,'' murmured Questioner. ''This pit is at least five kilometers deep, the wings are folded in half, with both of them opened out it would have a twenty-kilometer wingspan. . . .''

Corojum remarked, ''She is bigger than when she fell. She told Kaorugi she could grow bigger yet, but the mate doesn't want them to grow bigger. That's why they do as they do. They do not have to ruin the wings; they do it because they want to.''

''The rapist mentality,'' remarked Questioner. ''Seems always present. Tell, me, Corojum, when is the six-moon conjunction, exactly?''

Corojum stared at the sky. ''Now, on other side of Dosha, four moons are almost aligned, they will draw apart, then tomorrow they draw together again with two more. By noon they will be joined in line with the sun. They will stay in line only a short time, but oceans will rise, egg will be shaken more than ever, Quaggima will wake, all will be over.''

"That soon?" breathed Mouche.

Questioner said, "If we had a few days, I can think of several solutions to this fix we're in. There are probably drugs that would keep Quaggima asleep. Certainly we could lift her out into space, given a little time, and also we can lift the eggs, though it would take the cooperation of Kaorugi and the tunnelers to cut them loose from below. But one day simply isn't long enough, even if I could reach the ship, which I can't!"

She seemed furious at this, and Mouche said sympathetically. "I'm sure they'll fix whatever went wrong on the ship, Questioner."

"And I am as sure they won't," she snapped. "Not unless they let the Gablians do it."

Corojum puffed out his fur and sighed.

"I must think," said Questioner. "I must go up above and spend a little time in total concentration."

Mouche was crouched beneath the great faceted eyes of Quaggima, intent upon Questioner's IDIOT SAVANT.

"Mouche," Questioner said impatiently, "let's go."

"Give me a moment," he begged. "Can you leave me this SAVANT thing, Questioner? It almost seems to make sense. . . ."

"We'll wait with him," called Ellin, stopping her whirling motion and drawing Bao with her to Mouche's side.

"Stay if you like," Questioner murmured. "Come when you're ready. Corojum, let us go up."

The Eiger took them up, away, Questioner and Corojum, leaving the four young people crouched before the Quaggima, intent on the glow of the screens and the dance of glittering motes within it. Beside them stood four Eigers, each with its multiple eyes fixed on one of them, ready to carry.

The wing beats of the Eiger bearing the Questioner faded upward in the chasm. Mouche exclaimed.

"What is it?" breathed Ellin. "What are you thinking, Mouche?"

He drew breath between his teeth. "It should make sense. I have this feeling that I know what's going on.

The movements they described, the music they used . . . Did either of you get a better description of the music than I did?''

Ellin and Bao handed over their own data heads. Mouche linked the three together and fed this new information into the larger device, directing it to extrapolate.

It did so, building and refining, variation after variation. Long sliding sequences. Slow advances and retreats. Turns, twists, then long sliding sequences again. And again.

''It reminds me of something,'' said Bao. ''I just can't tell what.''

Mouche stood up, taking a deep breath. ''It reminds me of something, too,'' he said. ''It's just . . . it shouldn't make sense. I mean, it doesn't make sense.''

They watched the stage go on with its improvisations, heard the drumming settle into a definite rhythm. Mouche and Bao stared at one another in dawning realization. Ellin and Ornery looked at one another in confusion.

''It shouldn't make sense. But it does,'' said Mouche. ''Oh, yes, it does. No wonder I thought I knew. . . . The feeling. The yearning. . . . I wish I could ask someone. . . .''

''There is someone. . . .'' said a small voice.

They turned toward a shiver of silver, a flare of green.

''Flowing Green,'' said Mouche, unable to breathe. ''Where . . . where have you been?''

The silver eyes tilted. ''Waiting for you, Mouchidi. Waiting for a little quiet. Oh, so much noise and confusion! So many persons. So many jongau! And poor Mouchidi, wounded so.'' She moved toward them, lilting. ''Now is a little peaceful time, so listen to my words! I dreamed you would come here. I dreamed we would go to the Fauxi-dizalonz together. I dreamed the world would continue. They all think you will be of no help. They all think I am strange, not well made, to think such things, but Bofusdiaga made me for you, Mouchidi. Bofusdiaga made you for me, too, a little.''

''Made you?'' whispered Mouche.

''Made me from some of your own self and some of

Bofusdiaga's own self. Made you a little bit like me. I knew to come here, to tell you of the dancers."

"You know what the dancers were doing here?"

"I know what you mankinds call it."

"What do we call it?" cried Ellin.

"You call it making love," said Flowing Green.

58

The Jongau And A Matter Of Gender

High above the chasm, Ashes and his sons arrived at the end of the straight road and moved out onto the ledge that looked down to the Fauxi-dizalonz. Behind and around them were the remains of the settlers from Thor, the jongau, the bent ones. Emerging from bubble caves here and there around the circumference of the caldera, others edged out, softly gleaming in the pallid moonlight, casting dark shadows behind them. Some of those farthest down struck the stone with whatever parts of themselves were available—heads, toes, tentacles—and these blows resolved into a cadenced drumming upon the walls. Those high on the ledge stepped in time with the cadence, turning with lumbering precision to move downward on the long, gentle road that switched back and forth as it descended into the caldera, at first only a few, then more and more as each new monster reached the ledge and marched across it, over the lip and down.

Here were Crawly and his cousins, four beats to a flail,

twelve beats to a drag, flail-two-three-four—drag-two-three-four—down-six-seven-eight—below-ten-eleven-twelve. Here was Strike, four beats to a foot step, *rye-ut ut ut, lay-uft uft uft, rye-ut ut ut, lay-uft uft uft*. Here was Belly, dragged behind the Shoveler and Gobblemaw, like a harrow behind a team of oxen, four bars to the belch; *hup plod plod plod, hup plod plod plod, hup plod plod plod, squawwweeough.*

"Old Pete," murmured Ashes, who was marching along quite erect, arms swinging at his sides. "He's a little way down yet. Crawly'll drag him out."

"What do we do when we get to the bottom?" Bane asked.

"Gonna roll 'em oh-ver," said Ashes. "Hup hup hup roll 'em, hup hup hup over."

Hughy Huge came down like a gingerly cannon ball, Ear clinging to one side, Tongue to the other, *blather, rumble, blather, rumble*. Foot hopped, *bingety spop, bingety spop*, and Mosslegs swished, *slooush, slooush*, all in time, all in perfect time.

"You learn to march like this on Thor?" Bane asked.

"Drill-two-three-four, this is what a drill's for," said Ashes, keeping time.

Boneless oozed over the lip of the ledge, splooshing in cadence. Bone clattered behind him, *brack-bruck brack-bruck.*

"There's old Craw-lee. He tooka short cut," chanted Ashes.

There was Crawly indeed, flopped on the roadway outside a cave, flailing his claws into the pale flesh that blocked it, heave-two-three-four, heave-two-three-four.

"Pete, he's coming out, huh," breathed Ashes, still keeping time. "Pete he's coming out, huh!"

Pete had come out, or his body had, though his appendage was still emerging, foot by foot, a gigantic sausage, a titanic pizzle, white as alabaster, smooth as marble, throbbing with discontent. Crawly turned and clasped Pete's figure with his hind legs, dragging Pete along behind while Crawly himself proceeded down the road, flail-two-three-four, heave-two-three-four.

The moon had risen high enough to show all this nightmare vision to Madame, the two Hags, the two Men of Business, and to Questioner, who arrived just as the last of Pete popped out of his cave and came thumping down the road in Crawly's wake. Corojum summoned several Joggiwagga and a great number of tunnelers and leggers who assembled themselves into levees that reached from the foot of the road to the Fauxi-dizalonz.

"Can the pond hold them all?" whispered Madame. "And what in heaven's name are they?"

"Creatures by that Old Earth artist, Hieronymus Bosch," murmured D'Jevier. " 'The Garden of Earthly Delights'!"

"More likely Kaorugi's joke," said Onsofruct. "Surely Bosch never meant his paintings to be taken literally."

"She's right, though," said Calvy, unexpectedly. "I've seen them in a book, and that's what they look like."

Madame asked once again, "Will the pond hold them all? And what will they be when they come out?"

"And why have they all come at once?" demanded Calvy. "Is this an invasion?"

"They came," said the Corojum, "because they have to. They aren't as stable as finished persons. When Bofusdiaga makes someone, he builds in the call. When it starts to come apart, it has to come back and get fixed. Bofusdiaga does not like losing material."

"Penis-man," murmured Simon, in awe. "Look at that thing!"

"I'd prefer not," said Onsofruct frostily. "Quite indecent. And what is that flaccid sack? A stomach?"

"Belly boy," said Calvy. "I don't think the pond can hold them all."

"It will," said Corojum. "A little at a time. Though it will overflow when they liquefy, and we will need to move up to higher ground." He moved off toward the steeper trail, and the others trailed along behind him. When they had gone up thirty meters or so, they stopped on a conveniently spacious ledge and merely watched.

"There's Thor Ashburn," said Madame, from Questioner's side. "And the boys, Bane and Dyre. What will become of them?"

"We'll make the young ones go through twice," murmured Corojum. "Even if they fight us. We want no more jongau."

"Look," cried D'Jevier. "An Eiger, coming out of the chasm!"

"It's carrying Bao," said Madame.

The Eiger circled for a time, as though uncertain where to put its burden. Then Bao saw the group on the ledge, called out, and the great bird turned, swooped, and dropped Bao gently at their feet.

"Questioner," said Bao breathlessly. "Oh, Questioner. . . ."

"Look," she said. "Look at the monsters."

"No time for monsters," he said. "Questioner, you must listen."

"What is it?" asked Madame, turning toward him. "Have you come up with something."

Bao flushed. "I . . . that is we, yes. We think."

"What is it?" asked Calvy.

"I am showing you on the IDIOT SAVANT," said Bao. "I cannot describe it."

Wordlessly, Bao set up the device, and the screen came alive with the image of the Quaggima, with glittering points and blots of light. "The lights are being the Timmys," said Bao. "And the Joggiwagga."

They watched for a time as the sparks and blotches moved slowly around the Quaggima, repetitively, back and forth, back and forth, then quickly another motion, then back and forth. . . .

"Are you not seeing it, Madame?" begged Bao. "Mouche was being sure you would be seeing it."

"I don't see anything," said Madame. "What am I supposed to see?"

Bao approached Simon and murmured something. He, in turn, murmured to Madame, and she stared at the screen with a shocked expression. "Oh, by all the Hagions. . . ."

"What?" demanded Questioner. "What did he say?"

"He said the . . . that is, the dancers . . . they're making love to it," said Madame.

"To the Quaggima?" Questioner turned to Simon. "Is that what he said?"

"He said *stroke, stroke, tweak,* Questioner."

"He said what?"

Madame threw up her hands. "Never mind what he said! I believe he's right! Only . . ." She looked puzzled. "Of course, the anatomy is all wrong. How in heaven's name would we . . ."

"Give me a moment," cried Questioner, turning her attention momentarily to her data banks. "I see! If the Timmys amassed to do this . . . ritual, well, now that we can see it, Corojum can tell these current Timmys what to do. . . ."

"No," said the Corojum, in mixed anger and sadness. "It would take many, many Corojumi to tell them what to do. And much rehearsal, also."

D'Jevier cried, "But if the Fauxi-dizalonz can make anything . . ."

Corojum said, "Can disassemble quickly. Can put together in new shape with new information much more slowly. Making things right takes time. A few little things take as long as one very big thing. To make many, many Timmys would take a long time."

Questioner said, "So we won't try for Timmys. It can make one big thing."

"Where is pattern?" cried Corojum.

"Mouche is a Consort," Questioner responded. "He is trained to do this kind of thing. And you, Simon, you were also trained. And you, Calvy, from what I am told. And there are those monsters moving down the road, including one . . . one organ that might be useful."

"You're saying you expect the Fauxi-dizalonz to create a Consort for this Quaggima?" cried D'Jevier.

"Why not?" snapped Questioner. "You should approve of that." She turned to the Corojum. "It would work, wouldn't it? If Bofusdiaga will cooperate."

Corojum dithered. "Is this something my friend Mouche would want?"

"Bofusdiaga can put him back the way he was, can't he?"

"Creatures are never exactly the same," whispered Corojum. "Maybe he will not be willing?"

"Does he have to be willing?" muttered Onsofruct. "Consorts are sold into duty all the time, are they not? I'm sure they're not always willing."

"Onsy, I'm ashamed of you," cried D'Jevier.

"I will talk to Bofusdiaga," said the Corojum, plodding away with his head down and his fur lying flat, the picture of dejection.

"We can't do this," cried Madame. "It's unconscionable."

The world shook. From the chasm opposite they heard the great mooing, a plaint of such enormity that they covered their ears and grimaced with pain. Stones plunged past them. The procession of monsters stopped their descent and held on. Whenever the sounds of the stones stopped, the muttered cadence of the monsters was heard: *hup, hup, hup, hup*. Finally, after long, terrorized moments, the tremors subsided.

"Perhaps you find it more conscionable to die," Questioner said to Madame. "I think you will find yourself in the minority."

Another tremor struck, then a milder one, then one milder yet.

"The moons are separating on the backside of this world," said Questioner. "We will now have a time of peace before the end. Which may, or may not, be long enough!"

The monsters had resumed their progress downward. The observers stood in silence, watching, waiting until the Corojum came into sight once more, trudging toward them along the edge of the Fauxi-dizalonz.

"Bofusdiaga says yes, he can do it," said Corojum. "He will take all material from those coming down road; he will filter out bad stuff; he will hold rest of it in readiness. Then you have Mouche and Simon and Calvy go in, and Bofusdiaga will make a big one body to do the will of the little one's minds."

"Me?" cried Calvy, in outrage. "Me!"

"Bofusdiaga needs more brain stuff than one person," said the Corojum.

"So it's fortunate you're here, Family Man," said D'Jevier. "You and Simon and Mouche, and that other one, what's his name? Ornery."

"Not Ornery," said Questioner. "She's a girl."

"A what?" cried Onsofruct. "A girl? What is she doing in sailor's garb? She's not allowed to do that!"

"Allowed or not, she's been doing it."

"By all the Hagions," muttered Onsofruct. "We're losing our grip upon this world."

"Let's get beyond this crisis," pled D'Jevier. "Then we can decide what needs doing about our grip upon this world."

"Mouche comes," said the Corojum. "With Ellin and Ornery."

Mouche did indeed come with Ellin and Ornery, all of them Eiger borne. He was softly lowered before the others.

"He told you?" Mouche panted.

Madame nodded sadly. "Yes, Mouche. We understand that we must make a partner for the Quaggima."

"The Fauxi-dizalonz is going to make it," said Questioner.

"Out of Timmys?" asked Mouche in a distant, detached voice. "As before?"

"Evidently there's insufficient time," said Questioner, giving him a sharp look. Where had she seen that expression before? "The Fauxi-dizalonz doesn't work that way. It can make one large thing in the same time it can make a few small things. We have the pattern, however, and if you'll look up the hill, you'll see our raw material."

Mouche's eyes focused on the descending monsters, and his jaw sagged. "What are they?" he demanded.

Madame explained. Ellin caught her first glimpse of old Pete and turned aside, flushing.

The two Hags approached, trailed by a disconsolate Calvy and Simon.

"Mouche," murmured D'Jevier, wiping tears, "we appreciate your sacrifice."

"It was nothing," said Mouche, slightly puzzled. "I figured it out at the same time as Fl . . ." He caught himself. ". . . Bao. He figured it out as much as me."

"Still, many would have concealed the truth because of the implications."

"I am glad to be of service, Ma'am," he said, still puzzled, made more so by Calvy and Simon's faces as they turned away and departed, without speaking, arms around one another's shoulders as though for mutual support.

The women turned away as well, D'Jevier saying to her sister, "You see, Onsy. He is one of a kind. A marvel."

"I don't know what's so marvelous," said Mouche.

Madame replied, "Neither Calvy nor Simon have your sense of duty, Mouche. They are not really willing to go into the Fauxi-dizalonz to be made into a Consort for the Quaggima."

"A *Consort* for the Quaggima!" shouted Mouche, his voice reaching all the retreating persons. "Are you crazy?"

Calvy and Simon turned as one, staring, mouths slightly open.

D'Jevier turned, white-faced. "I thought you understood."

Questioner held up her hand imperiously. "We know the Quaggi anatomy is quite different, Mouche. But if the Fauxi-dizalonz can make and remake, to order, so to speak, we can simply use you trained people—you, Mouche and Simon and Calvy—to create a male for the Quaggima."

Mouche smiled, his face serene once more. "You didn't explain it to them, Bao."

"Explaining what?" yelped Bao. "I myself am not understanding. . . ."

Mouche said in that same, distant voice, "Actually, considering the size, the anatomy isn't that different. All the pertinent parts have their mankindly parallels. And I'm sure the Fauxi-dizalonz could probably come up with a Consort of some size. And I'm sure that would be quite appropriate . . . if the Quaggima were female."

"But I saw her . . . him . . . it. . . ." said Questioner. "Out on that moon. And I saw him. . . ."

"You saw one Quaggi violate another Quaggi," said Mouche. "You assumed it was the male assaulting the female. In fact, it was a female who did the assaulting. She laid an egg in him. We ran an analysis from the data, and the egg was actually imbedded under the skin next to the male organs. That's how they do it. The females are bigger and stronger. They lay eggs in the males, and the males are the brooders. We got the sex wrong."

D'Jevier cried, "That's silly. Even Bofusdiaga says . . ."

"Bofusdiaga has no experience of heterosexual creatures," said Ellin, crisply. "After mankind came, Bofusdiaga made the assumption it was female, because in mankind and their livestock it is the females who have the eggs."

Ornery said, "It's the female that sits out there on the far moon and sings her siren song, and it's that song that excites the male and makes him follow it. Later, when the egg is ready to hatch, the young ones call in almost that same voice."

Madame said, "I know that some creatures respond sexually to scent and some to appearance, but you're saying this one responds to sound?"

"It's true," said Mouche. "When the creatures in the egg call, the sound stirs the same excitement as the mating call did, and the Quaggima gets so excited, he thrashes around and breaks the shell of the first bomblet or whatever it is, and that sets the hatching sequence off. It ends with some kind of explosion. . . ."

"Nuclear," murmured Questioner. "A shaped, nuclear charge."

Mouche went on, "What Bofusdiaga and all have been doing with their dance is relieving his sexual arousal. That's all."

"But why didn't someone realize . . ." Madame murmured.

"What did this world know about sexual arousal?" snarled Questioner, suddenly very much aware of much she had overlooked. "Nothing! And, seemingly, neither do I. After all my instructions to you about not jumping to conclusions—"

"Forgive me for interrupting," said Mouche in the same serene but distant tone he had used since coming from the chasm. "We have every reason to believe this can be managed, but first the four of us need a little rest and something to eat and drink and some quiet conversation." He took Ellin by the hand and tugged her away, up the steep slope toward several tall stones that held between them a patch of moonlit quiet and private space. Bao and Ornery followed them.

"I must be forgiven, also," said Corojum, "But I am lost in all your talk. What is sexual arousal? What do you mean, Quaggima is not mother. She is child hatcher!"

Questioner replied, "On our home planet, Corojum, back when we had animals, sometimes the male was the child caregiver or hatcher. A bird called the rhea, for example. The seahorse and the stickleback, which are kinds of sea creatures. It just happens that the Quaggi is a race in which the males are the caregivers."

"Males are choosing to be this?"

"They are not choosing," Madame said in an annoyed voice. "They can't help doing it, any more than a pregnant woman can help doing it. If the egg is attached, then the Quaggi can't get rid of it. It has to bear it, even against its own will."

"Could we separate it?" asked Onsofruct. "Could the tunnelers separate it?"

"Do we have the right to interfere with another race's mode of reproduction?" Questioner asked.

"But the hatching will kill him," said Calvy. "It's already crippled him and kept him bound here for an eternity."

"Evidently, that's the way things are done among the Quaggi," said Questioner.

"Does that make it right?" cried Simon. "Just because that's the way they evolved? It's a reasoning, feeling being! It was impregnated against its will!"

D'Jevier laughed, almost hysterically. "Oh, read your

history, Simon. Read your history. Some philosophers would no doubt argue that the hatchling, being innocent, has more right to life than the father! Historically, in similar cases, women were expected to sacrifice themselves!"

Onsofruct cried, "Then why should not this male creature die for its child as women have often done? It has already had a long life."

"Aside from the ethics of the situation, he shouldn't die for his child because we'll all die with him," said Madame with asperity. "Revered Hag, this is not philosophy, this is reality. Will you please keep in mind what's going on!"

"I need maintenance," snarled Questioner, more or less to herself. "This is ridiculous. How could I have made such a stupid error. Well, let us start again! Instead of Mouche, Calvy, and Simon, we will use you, Madame. And the two Hags."

Madame and D'Jevier were shocked into silence. Not so Onsofruct, who cried, "Well, if you think we females are going to make a partner for it, forget it! I for one, am not going to do it. Let us have another Miscalculation. Let the world blow itself to Kingdom Come. I don't care."

59

Into The Fauxi-Dizalonz

Following Onsofruct's outburst, the people on the ledge regrouped themselves in a mood of general discontent and befuddlement, the Hags and Madame taking refuge behind several large rocks at the western end of the ledge, the two men finding refuge at the eastern end. They could look upward and see movement among the standing stones, where the young people had gone to talk, or downward, where the tunneler levees were so solidly implanted they might as well have been made of stone.

At the female end of the ledge, Onsofruct said for the tenth time, "I won't do it."

"You expected Mouche to do it," snapped D'Jevier.

"He is younger than we," said Onsofruct. "He is more adaptable. If he won't do, let the off-planet girl do it. That dancer. Let Questioner do it. She's female."

"If I were less bionic and more fleshy," said Questioner, from a midpoint on the ledge, "I would leap at the chance for such an experience. Oh, yes, I would go with you."

"You mistake me," grated Onsofruct. "I refuse to go at all."

"You are female. We need females. Why would you shirk your duty to your people?"

"I have never shirked my duty to my people."

"Your duty at times must have been unpleasant," said Questioner in a tone of barely repressed annoyance. "Keeping things as they are."

Silence stretched. None of the three asked what she meant.

She continued, "When Mouche told us of our mistake, I castigated myself for stupidity. Then I wondered what else about your world I might have missed, and of course, once I started looking for it, I saw the mold, the pattern, which should have shouted to me from the beginning."

"And what pattern is that?" asked D'Jevier.

Questioner came nearer, leaning against one of the stones. "I never have enough time, I seldom have skilled help, but I always have a surfeit of data. I know all that there is to know about life here and there, including on Old Earth. There, historically, various hierarchies were preoccupied with Cura Mulierum, the care of women. Of course, in order to care for women, it is first necessary to make both men and women believe that women cannot care for themselves."

"True," said Madame. "So I have read."

Questioner went on: "The care of women has always presented a problem for government or religion, for there were always leftover women who could not be conveniently disposed of."

"Widows, I suppose," said D'Jevier tonelessly. "Or women no one wants to marry. Or women who don't want to marry."

"Oh, all of those, yes," said Questioner. "Plus women who do marry and can't bear it, or prostitutes, or girls who have babies with no way to support them, or single mothers with large families, and wrinkled old crones hobbling about, muttering imprecations and getting in the way."

"Handling surplus population is a perpetual challenge,"

said Onsofruct. "Has it not been written that the poor are always with us?"

Questioner shook her head. "Handling surplus men isn't that difficult. Just start a lively war or find some new frontier—there's always dangerous work that needs doing. If that fails, one can create lethal rites of passage to kill off batches at a time. One needn't pretend, not with men. The gang chief or general simply talks them into a fury and sends them into battle, and then gives them a medal after they're maimed or dead. Or, the employer gets them to use up their lives in a factory and then tosses them aside with a memento and an inadequate pension. Team spirit does the rest."

"The same would apply to women," said Madame.

"Women are not such good team players, so society has to enforce its control by pretending it's for women's own good. Then, too, women do produce babies, which multiplies the problem."

Onsofruct said in a remote voice, "Purdah always worked well. It allowed troublesome women and girls to be disposed of without anyone knowing. If no one had ever seen your wife or daughters, who would wonder if they disappeared? And then there were nunneries, and witch hunts. I understand religion on Old Earth managed to remove a great many elderly women by claiming they were witches."

"The most efficient strategy was economic," said D'Jevier in that same remote, uncaring voice. "Pay them so little they can't get by, or don't hire them at all because women belong at home, and then throw them in jail when they turn to beggary, thievery, or prostitution because they and their children are hungry."

Questioner said, "How fortunate you are that the problem has never arisen here on Newholme."

"Fewer women than men are born," said Madame.

"So I have been told," said Questioner. "But the Hags and I know that isn't true."

The silence stretched. The Hags stared at one another, their faces very still and white.

Questioner rose. "I might have excused the slaughter

of the Timmys for various reasons, but doing away with half the female babies born on this planet I cannot excuse."

D'Jevier turned away.

Madame cried, "No! You wouldn't! Jevvy? You couldn't have?"

Silence. The Hags stared into the distance, saying nothing.

Madame demanded, "D'Jevier, tell me it isn't true!"

D'Jevier said, "Let us explain . . ."

"No," said Questioner. "Do not try to explain. I am, quite frankly, sick of explanations!"

After a lengthy silence, Onsofruct whispered, "What will you do?"

Questioner drew herself up. "Assuming we are left alive to do anything, Revered Hags, I will sterilize the race of mankind on this planet, as I have done elsewhere for less provocation."

She left them, going out onto the ledge, unwilling to listen to the pleadings that no doubt hung on their lips. It didn't matter what they said. She didn't care what they said. Within her, Mathilla, and M'Tafa, and Tiu didn't care what they said. It was simply more injustice. More repression and torture. It was unforgivable!

Ignoring the tumult at the other end of the ledge, Calvy and Simon were watching the descending monsters. The first of them, one of the great crawlers, had reached the Fauxi-dizalonz, bellowing as it plunged. Behind it, the next one pushed into the liquid, dissolving at the leading edge before the following edge had reached the pond, a pond which lapped at its shores like a living thing, its ripples spreading ever more widely.

The next one in the line was a spherical orb of muscles. "Roll 'em over," it cried. From one side Ear dangled, and from the other Tongue flapped, "Roll 'em over!"

It entered the pond like a cannon ball, with a great body-flopping splash that splatted down in a glistening layer that covered the monster like partially set aspic, dripping from his enormous form as he sank gradually into the goo. Tongue, dislodged by the splash, floated about on the surface, gargling ''Help, help, I'm drown-ding. . . .''

Flailing and dragging, Crawly came next, with Old Pete jouncing and throbbing behind him, and it was there that the procession stalled, for Crawly entered the pond so slowly that he dissolved while barely in, leaving no traction to move Old Pete. All the monsters came to a halt, still marching in place, voices calling the cadence: *hup, hup, hup*. Then from somewhere a great voice uttered, shivering the surrounding soil. Several leggers raced from a nearby cave, disassembled to get themselves into position, then reassembled to push Old Pete into the pond, little by little, to the accompaniment of shouted commands by their own voice boxes. ''Grab him by the balls! Catch him higher up! Push him in!''

When the last of Pete vanished in the goo, the leggers broke into their constituent parts and fled while the next rank of monsters, still hup-two-three-fouring, moved forward and into the increasingly turbid Fauxi-dizalonz, whose surface was spreading wider with each addition.

From their position on the ledge, Madame broke the silence. ''Up around the first curve, there's Bane and Dyre, and that's Thor Ashburn next to them.''

''Why is he naked?'' asked Onsofruct, distractedly. ''And what's that he's got wrapped around his waist?''

''It looks very much like a whip,'' murmured D'Jevier. ''Though it seems to be attached between his legs.''

Glad of the distraction, Madame focused on the distant figure. ''Well,'' she remarked, ''I would say it's a smaller version of Penis-man's appendage. One designed for inflicting punishment. How very interesting. Clothed, he showed no hint of it at all.''

''I believe you're right,'' said Questioner from her position at the center of the ledge. ''An interesting variant.''

''None of this makes sense,'' said Calvy, coming to stand beside Questioner. ''How is one to understand it?''

Questioner said, ''The Fauzi-dizalonz is like a mirror that reflects one's desires. When you go through the first time, you come out looking as your thoughts and desires would form you, looking like that thing which is most important to you. To that monster, the one you call Penis-man, being male and light-skinned was most important to him. He emerged pale and male and sat in that cave for centuries becoming ever paler and maler. Whatever the others are, they display what was important to them.''

Calvy said, ''If there had been women among them, no doubt some would have emerged as Breast-woman or Uterus-woman or Hair-woman.''

''Lips-woman, or Legs-woman,'' offered Simon. ''Mouth-woman, Nagger-woman . . .''

''Enough, Simon,'' said Madame, joining them from among the stones, D'Jevier trailing behind.

''But what's the Fauxi-dizalonz good for?'' begged D'Jevier. ''What's its purpose?''

Questioner said, ''I infer that when Kaorugi sends one of its parts out to do something, the part returns with information. The information may be so vital that it will suggest a change or improvement in general structure. In the Fauxi-dizalonz, the information can be evaluated and implemented and possibly spread around to other units.'' She fell silent, thinking. ''From what we've heard from the Corojum, I infer also that the Fauxi-dizalonz destroys information. If a part has experienced evil or felt great pain, Kaorugi takes that memory away. . . .''

''But these monsters didn't go back in the Fauxi-dizalonz? So what will Bofusdiaga do with them now?'' asked D'Jevier.

''They have been too long unfinished to send back through. Now they are only raw material,'' said Questioner, ''from which to assemble a partner for Quaggima. Using one or more of you ladies for motive power.''

Among a small grove of standing stones, the four young people were hunkered down knee to knee with Flowing Green.

''Long ago and long ago,'' whispered Flowing Green in a voice like wind through the trees, ''Kaorugi knew all living things, for there was only Kaorugi to know. Then came Quaggima. Oh, but it was strange when Quaggima came. Outside-ness came with Quaggima. Other-ness came with Quaggima. Separate life came with Quaggima. Kaorugi knew no outside, no other, no separateness from self until then.

"Kaorugi went deep, to think. Kaorugi makes all living things, but Kaorugi had never thought of making a thinking thing that was not part of itself. Only after Quaggima came, only after mankinds came and killed so many Timmys and Corojumi, only then did Kaorugi wonder if Kaorugi could make something that was not part of itself.

"Kaorugi told the last Corojum to take a pattern of this otherness, and Corojum took a pattern from you, Mouchidi. Corojum took a tiny bit of you, skin and blood, and Corojum bit you and put a tiny bit of Kaorugi into you. Inside you, the Kaorugi part grew. And the part Corojum took from you, Kaorugi used it when it made me. I am a strangeness, Mouchidi. Even Corojum says so, and Corojum is my friend. I am made of Kaorugi and made of you, a Timmy, yes, but a separate-part mankind creature also.

"So, now, if all is not to end or go back to long ago beginning and start over, we must create together, you and I and Kaorugi. Something that is not mankind alone. Not Timmy alone. Not even Kaorugi alone. And we must do it for sorrow of Quaggima, for pity of little ones in the egg, for delirious delight of it, for ecstacy of it, for love of it. . . ."

"We," said Ellin. "You mean you and Mouche?"

"Flowing Green and Mouche, yes, but Kaorugi says better if also Ellin and Bao and Ornery, if they can," said Flowing Green. "Because Ellin and Bao and Ornery are good pretenders, and to make what must be made, we cannot be only what we are, you see?"

"I don't see," said Ornery, stubbornly.

Flowing Green whispered a sigh. "On your machine, you saw what the dancers did, what they became, each part doing its own part, thousands of them. This was long in the design, long in the rehearsal. We have no time for design, no time for rehearsal, no time for the many to be choreographed into something huge. We must do it as one thing, first time! To become what we must become, we must imagine. That is the word? We must turn into something else. We must . . . join, lay aside, divest . . ."

"Metamorphose," suggested Bao. "Be turning into a new creature?"

"This is so. Questioner is right. It must be one thing. Male and female and neither. Joy and sorrow and neither. Pleasure and pain and neither. Bigger than we are, and wider and longer, a thing to be to Quaggima what Quaggima needs, and we must do it right, first time."

"Extemporaneously," offered Ellin.

"Yes," cried Flowing Green. "You are good pretenders! I have listened to you in the walls! You imagine. You dance, you are someone else. You are always being other people. You *want* to be other people. And Bao, when he dances, he is a woman person else. And Ornery is a man person else, not what she was born, and Mouche . . . oh, Mouche is all kinds of things to the women people he knows. Kaorugi is fascinated by you mankinds, that you are not content to be only the thing you are, so you are full of dreams. Well, this is a dream. In this dream we will really become another being. I am . . . accustomed to this, but mankinds are not. You dream it, you do not do it, but of all mankinds on this world, you four are the best mankinds to try to really do it. Not the Hags, too old, too set, like stone. Not the Questioner, she is not even all flesh that can be reshaped. Not the men, they are set, too, in maleness, only, not like Bao, or even Mouche. . . ."

"It is seeming to be a risk. . . ." murmured Bao. "We might fail, we might die. . . ."

"Ah," said Flowing Green. "Yes, we may fail, we may die, but if we do not do this, we will truly fail, we will truly die."

Mouche leaned forward and took Ellin's hands in his own, murmuring words of encouragement. She would do it. He knew it, and so did she, but she needed to be encouraged.

Bao turned to Ornery, taking her hands, saying in his woman's voice, "This is being wonderful. Think, Ornery, what an adventure!"

Ornery surprised herself by smiling into his eyes, feeling

herself respond to his excitement. "Yes," she said. "Oh, yes. What are we to do?"

"Now we wait," said Mouche. "Until it is time."

Questioner moved only a little distance from the women, and Madame followed her to lean plaintively against the rocky side of the caldera. "Questioner, I realize how angry you must be, but believe me, I didn't know. Most of the people on Newholme didn't know. What you accuse them of . . . it must have been done entirely by the Hags. You aren't suggesting that they, and I, go into that pond as a kind of punishment or reparation, are you? You'd have told us if there were some other way?"

"Punishment is not my business," said Questioner. "As I have said to others, it never works anyhow. Putting right is my business. Unfortunately, when things are put right, often the innocent suffer with the guilty. If there were some other way, I would try it. Even if I could reach my ship, which I've been unable to do since we first went underground, my crew could do nothing on this short notice, so the situation is simple. We will all be destroyed within the next few hours if something isn't done, so you women have the choice of self-destruction now, soon, or of living the remainder of your lives in some honor."

"Honor!"

"You will have saved the Quaggi and its egg. A not inconsiderable achievement."

"You will save the Quaggi," cried Madame, "but you will let us die?"

"I, Madame?" Questioner's eyebrows rose. "I would not think of such a thing. I will simply recommend that mankind not continue on Newholme past the lives of those now living. Even our earliest espousers of human rights limit them to life, liberty, and the pursuit of satisfactions. They do not guarantee posterity or immortality."

Madame turned away to hide her face. "How long do we have . . . before we must go into that place?"

"Until the last of these monsters have been absorbed. By then, it will be day. The moons collect near noon, so says the Corojum. All six of the larger ones will be more or less in line with the sun; there will be darkness at noon; we will have one dilly of an eclipse.''

Madame returned to the Hags to tell them brokenly what Questioner had said. They stood where they were, watching. There was nothing else they could do.

Slightly above them on the road, Ashes looked down on the observers and called his sons' attention to them.

''That's Mouche over in those rocks,'' said Bane, outraged. ''What's he doing here?''

''And there's that Questioner thing,'' said Dyre. ''And there's ol' Simon and Madame.''

''Who? two, three, four,'' muttered Ashes. ''Simon? two, three four.''

''Just somebody from House Genevois,'' muttered Bane, embarrassed to see Mouche looking up at Ashes's nakedness. ''Why'd you hafta take your clothes off?''

Ashes ignored him. Any clothing worn by the Wilderneers had been stripped away. The rags lay along the descending path. The sight of Mouche made up Bane's mind for him, and he edged away from Ashes, stepped over the edge of the path behind a large boulder, and waited there while the procession passed him by. He did not notice that Mouche and Ornery, Ellin and Bao had also slipped away to disappear along the boulder-strewn slope that led down to the pond.

Bane heard wings and looked up. Webwings dropped onto the concealing rock and perched there. ''What you waitin' for, boy?''

''I think all you folks should go in first,'' said Bane carefully. ''Cause you've already been in once. Then Dyre and me, because it'll be our first time.''

''Oh, we're gonna get all refurbished, we are. Been kind of shabby, lately. You noticed that? Kind of shabby. Kind of worn. But we'll come out lovely, we will.'' Webwings almost purred. ''Shiny. Like stars. Just lately, I've been thinkin' about it. All of us have. Hughy Huge. He told me he was gonna be a star.''

''That's right,'' said Bane. ''I'm sure of it.''

Webwings spread his wings, the spiders beneath them quivering in anticipation. He launched himself into the air, circling upward, then from the height fell like an arrow, making scarcely a splash as he slipped into the pond and was gone.

There were only a dozen or so monsters remaining. Below Bane, on the switchback path, Dyre was straggling along at Ashes's heels. Bane whistled softly. Dyre looked up, saw him, looked back at Ashes, then darted upward, off the path to make his way upward toward Bane. They watched as their father marched into the Fauxi-dizalonz without a backward glance, moving briskly forward until even the top of his head had disappeared.

The few Wilderneers who had been behind him finished their march, their voices growing weaker, their very substance seeming to lose definition. The tunneler levees had pulled back as the liquid level rose, and were finally removed altogether when the turbid pond filled the caldera to the very foot of the road. The surface was barely riffled, but the depths were full of dark shadows and stringy shapes that writhed like leeches. The shapes swam just under the surface until early light drove them into the depths. As the sun came higher, shining more directly into the caldera, the pond began to clear, and with torturous slowness it continued clearing until, when the sun was high, it shone at last with the bright, emerald green they had all seen at first.

The world began to move beneath them, a different movement than any they had felt heretofore, a pounding, like a heart beating far beneath them.

Across the caldera from where they stood a great slot opened in the rocky wall and from it came the great voice of Bofusdiaga, making the caldera shudder as it cried, "Now!"

Madame straggled toward the steep path, with the two Hags at her heels, like naughty children, plodding toward punishment.

The Questioner approached them. "Are you ready?" she asked.

"You're going down there with us?" asked Onsofruct angrily. "Can't you rely on our word? We have said we will do it. We will."

"Put it down to curiosity," Questioner said. "It is one of my tasks to gather information, and how this will be accomplished should be very informative."

They plodded slowly down the path to the point where it disappeared under the emerald surface, then simply stood, unmoving, staring into the depths.

"I'm frightened," said D'Jevier apologetically. "I'm scared silly."

"Don't stand here and exacerbate your fear," suggested Questioner. "Just take a deep breath and dive."

"No," said Mouche.

They turned. Mouche was close behind them, with Ornery, Ellin and Bao, and the Timmy with emerald hair.

"What do you mean, no?" asked Questioner, annoyed.

Mouche reached out to touch her shoulder, then moved to do the same to Madame. "I mean these women are unfitted for this task. Madame here would do it out of duty, but as she herself has taught us, duty is never enough. The Hags do it out of some other emotion. Whatever it is, it is inappropriate. You are all too much what you are. Too set into your identities. Timmy tells us you cannot do what is needed."

"And you can?"

He grinned at her. "Remember your lectures, Madame. You told us we had only to set our minds on our Hagions. So, I serve the Hagion by serving the Quaggima, by serving the creatures of this world. You told us we are all caught up in serving this through serving that. Nothing, you said, is ever quite clear or direct in this world, and love is the most unclear and indirect of all."

"And does love come into it?" whispered Madame.

"Flowing Green says it must, though she uses other words for it. Otherwise, our design will be faulty, our execution weak, our concepts flawed. To use your words again, Madame."

They did not know what to say, Questioner least of all, and Mouche gave them no time to come up with something apposite. He leapt past them, the others following, like creatures riding a wave of inevitability. In a moment they were gone, vanished, diving quickly, disappearing in the depths.

For one moment, nothing at all seemed to happen. The pond sparkled innocently in the sun, throwing bits of broken sunlight into their faces. Full of questions and expostulations, Calvy and Simon scrambled down from the ledge to join the others; the Corojum appeared out of nowhere; and from somewhere up the slope, Timmys began to sing a hymn to light.

The world shook again, and again, a stronger beat than before. Tunnelers emerged from various caves and began digging at one side of the Fauxi-dizalonz.

Questioner asked, "What are they doing?"

"Doing what must be done," said the Corojum. "And when that happens, you need to be away from here."

"Away?" asked Calvy. "Where?"

"Away from this place. High up, away from the falling rocks. Up on the road, maybe. All of you."

"I don't want to leave him," cried Simon. "Mouche, I mean. He's in . . . in there somewhere."

"Mouchidi isn't in there. You couldn't help him if he were, and you are in danger," said the Corojum. "Bofusdiaga says you are to go."

Calvy said, "I want to watch what happens in the other chasm."

"Have you no shame?" Onsofruct challenged him. "Here are persons making great sacrifice for our sakes, and all you think of is lechery!"

"Oh, it is more than lechery, Revered Hag," said Calvy, irrepressibly. "The road starts up there on the ledge, where Questioner's people are waiting. From up there, we can see down into the other side." He turned to the Corojum. "Can we wait up there?"

Corojum glared at him wordlessly. "Mankinds can be trivial. I have said so to Bofusdiaga, many times."

"Sorry," Simon murmured. "But I'm with Calvy. I intend to see what goes on."

"Corojum," cried Madame. "Was that Timmy the one who . . . who Mouche was much interested in?"

"Flowing Green," said Corojum. "Tim is . . . it is a

new kind of Timmy, made of Mouche's blood and Kaorugi's mind. Flowing Green has watched Mouchidi forever from the walls. And when he came to House Genevois, the Timmys opened the way into the walls, and they tempted him in, and he watched Flowing Green from there. Both, watching one another. All these last years of his life, his own tim has been setting tim's voice into him, setting tim's own dance into him, and he has some of tim's substance in him, too. Some of Kaorugi, inside Mouche.

"Together we have thought, perhaps Mouchidi will be the one. Now tim has lured him or taught him to do this thing, and he has convinced Ellin, and Bao has convinced Ornery. . . ."

"What is this thing?" demanded Questioner, almost angrily.

". . . to do this thing as Bofusdiaga did it," whispered the Corojum. "For they," he indicated the Hags with a jerk of his head, "no, they cannot."

Onsofruct burst into tears.

"We probably cannot," said D'Jevier, shuddering. "The Hagions know I'm not fit for martyrdom! I'm not pure enough, not resolute enough, not inspired enough. I haven't been pure since childhood, nor resolute except in duty, nor inspired recently at all. Except now and then by hope, I suppose. We are only weary old women, trying to do the best we can. Hush now, Onsy. Come, Madame, Calvy, Simon. Let us get out of the way of this great work and wait to see what happens."

60

Many Moons

Five moons were in the sky, two west of the sun, seeming to linger in place, and three coming from other directions, moving swiftly, ever closer. The world shook and shook again. Stones fell. Distant peaks shivered and danced. The sixth moon, said Questioner, was actually hidden in the sun's radiance and would shortly begin to obscure it. While the people held on, trying to anchor themselves on the high ledge, the tunnelers continued their frantic digging between the south end of the Fauxi-dizalonz and the opening into the Quaggima's crater. Soon it was apparent they were cutting a trench to join caldera to chasm, leaving only a narrow wall of soil and rock to hold the Fauxi-dizalonz in place.

Meantime, Timmys ran here and there, carrying, fetching, coming, going. As the moons crept closer to one another, Timmys poured by the hundreds down onto the track that led into Quaggima's crater, massing to either side of the space where the new trench would breach the wall.

"What is Bofusdiaga going to do?" asked Calvy. "Drain the pond into the other crater?"

"It looks very much like it," said Questioner. "Furthermore, it seems to be putting every resource it has into the job."

"Look," cried D'Jevier, pointing upward with a hand that shuddered with each pulse of the world. "Two moons across the sun!"

There were two, one on the leading side, the other on the following. From below the sun, a third moon climbed toward it.

"I saw those moons when this world was young," said Questioner to Calvy, in a didactic tone. "I obtained a recording of the birth of this system. All these moons make it a very complex and interesting system."

"At the moment," said Calvy, "I refuse to be interested. I would trade all of them gladly for a moonless night with no tides."

"Don't you think Mouche and his friends will be successful?"

Calvy contorted his face into a mocking grimace. "If you want the truth, Questioner, I don't know what success amounts to. My idea of success would be to be home, with Carezza and my children. Mouche seems to intend a great deal more than that, though I'm damned if I know what."

Beneath them, the thudding of the world built in volume and force. This was nothing like the tremors they had felt in the past. This was purposeful, powerful, a recurrent jar that allowed only a moment for the previous blow to reverberate into silence before striking again. As though stirred by the sound, the Fauxi-dizalonz began to boil, sending up fogs and fumes, spirals of mist, whirlwinds of foam, at first in random fashion, then gathering into one shadow that darkened beneath the waters. A being was growing there. Only one. And they could not see what it was like.

Within the green, an accumulation. Star-shaped, it spun slowly in the flow, a mindfulness at each point, each point a sense of awareness. Here. Now. I. Am. Here. Now. They. Are. Here. Now. We.

Reaching out, left and right, thought touched thought. We. I. We. I. Across, left and right, thought touched thought. We. I. You. We. I. You. Each linked to each, lines of association spreading to make a glowing star in a shining pentacle, and at the center, a smaller pentacle where something new began to grow.

At four of the points, persons fought to reclaim themselves, as drowning men gasp for air, and Flowing Green sang to them.

"Dissolve," it sang to Ellin. "Into the pattern, into the music, just dissolve. Skein away like melting sugar. Become one with the patterns on the wall, in peace, in quiet, as if you were in Mama One's lap once more. . . ."

"Dissolve," it said to Bao. "Leave all concerns behind. There is nothing here but pleasure. Let it all go, parents, expectations, worries, all are fading. Let them go. . . ."

"Dissolve," it said to Mouche. "Into the sea, Mouche. Into the liquid roaming, the cry of the waterkeens, into the slosh and swim of the sea. . . ."

"Dissolve," it said to Ornery. "Lay death away, lay pain away, your people are here, renewed, part of everything, and you will rejoin. . . ."

"Dissolve," it said to itself. "Become what you covet becoming, tim-tim. Be one with him, with them, with all. . . ."

They loosened. They gave up being. They joined and re-became, a new thing. A stronger thing. A thing that knew more than any one of them had supposed it was possible to know.

The new thing heard a calling. "Oh, I long, I long, I long. I am alone, alone, alone. Death comes on me, time runs away, pain awaits, fire awaits, and I am alone, alone, alone."

A certain mindfulness reminded: *Do not say don't be silly. Say, instead, of course, I know, I understand. Do not go too softly. Go strongly, as one who is perilous and brave.*

A certain mindfulness said: *Do not smell of this world, but of the vast sea, the spaces between the stars.*

A certain mindfulness said: *Do not dance as a woman would dance, as a man would dance, as legs would dance, but as wings would dance, as these two would dance if they were lovers making a promise that would echo among the galaxies.*

Do not be bound by gravity, for we will swim weightless within this liquid world. Do not be bound by breath, for we need not breathe, or by thought, for we need not think. Here is only sensation and the need for joy. . . .

The being began to form. Two points joining two others to make wings. One point to make a head containing eyes to perceive light and images. Organs to perceive and make audible signals. Organs to create and perceive heat. Organs to compute and calculate. Organs to encompass and caress.

"I know where it is," it said to Kaorugi. "I hear it calling. I feel its longing. I am ready to go."

"Not just yet," said Kaorugi. "You must grow. Add to yourself. Accumulate. Before you go, you must be larger, much larger."

"Where am I?" a certain mindfulness wondered, in momentary panic.

"Here, Mouchidi," whispered Flowing Green. "Don't worry."

"I don't know enough to do this."

"You don't. We do. And Kaorugi has figured it out. Seeing our shape, he is understanding what it is for."

"I am dancing . . ." Ellin thought.

"I am a woman, dancing . . ." Bao thought.

"I am having a great adventure," Ornery told herself.

"Let me go," thought Mouche. "I can't take me with me. I'll just have to let me go. . . ."

The form solidified, still growing. The wings began to toughen, their great spars folding and unfolding.

"Let me go." A fading thought.

"Mouche?" whispered Kaorugi. "Ellin Voy? Gandro Bao? Ornery Bastable?"

There was no reply.

"Flowing Green?"

Still no reply.

"Ready then," said Kaorugi to his tunnelers. "Now."

The tunnelers at the trench redoubled their efforts. In the Fauxi-dizalonz, the form became more definite, with edges and fringes. The thudding at the heart of the world came more rapidly.

Calvy, clinging to a boulder, shook his head angrily. Oh, to be so close and have this wonder hidden from him!

"Come," murmured Simon, dragging him from the edge. "Your curiosity will kill you, g'Valdet."

So quickly they could not follow it, the Fauxi-dizalonz rose of itself, making a single great fist of green that broke out the narrow dike of rock between it and the trench and poured furiously down that trench to the lip, tumbling over it into the chasm, eating the trench ever deeper as it flowed.

Deeper and deeper yet it cut, splitting the wall between caldera and chasm, all the Fauxi-dizalonz spilling into the abyss, an endlessly flowing green that poured silently, a cataract of purest emerald, down and down and down. Within the flow, an enormous and glassy shadow moved. Wings it had, or perhaps tentacles. A body it had and many eyes, for they peered upward for an instant before it plunged over the wall. They could not tell what it looked like, and even after it was gone, the emerald flow went on.

Below, the abyssal pounding slowed. The green rose around the Quaggima, totally submerging him except for the upper stretch of his wings. Beings of fire danced in the depths while music rained upon them from the walls of the abyss, for there the Timmys sang and the Joggiwagga beat upon stone pillars to make sounds like bells and blew into hollow stones to make flute and horn sounds while all around crouched a thousand other Joggiwagga, drumming on their own hides, stretched between their spikes. Behind and beneath it all sang the huge voice of Bofusdiaga, the mountains giving voice, the world making thunder.

The flow slowed, abated, finally ended. The trench ran dry. The Fauxi-dizalonz was an empty well, a deep and murky vacancy, all its contents plus the wellspring of its self drained away into the new lake that had accumulated within the chasm.

"I can't see anything," whispered Calvy, who had moved back to a rimstone that still rocked to the rhythms of the deep.

"I don't think we are supposed to," said Questioner, extending her stabilizers. "Shall I tell you what the Timmys are singing?"

Calvy looked incredulous. She smiled and said:

> "*Quaggima despairs,*
> *driven against desire to brood Her spawn,*
> *now loving death and longing to be gone.*
> *Oh, Bofusdiaga, pain defying,*
> *Oh, blessed Corojumi, who repair,*
> *This Quaggima is dying,*
> *Give him your care!*
>
> "*Quaggida destroys*
> *all life but Hers. He lies beside the nest*
> *where his child and our doom are coalesced.*
> *Oh, Corojumi, bring deliverance!*
> *Oh, great Bofusdiaga, who alloys*
> *all life, grant through this dance*
> *compensatory joys. . . .*"

"How do you know that is what they are singing?" asked D'Jevier. "It is not in our language."

"When we were afloat upon the Pillared Sea, they sang it upon the ship during the voyage of Quaggima, and Corojum had the kindness to translate it, though he left out the genders or mixed them up. You are not the first people to achieve compensating pleasures, Lady. Long before you came here, Bofusdiaga understood the need for them."

D'Jevier snapped, "Are you convinced that at least that part of our arrangement is a good one, then? That our Consorts and our systems are appropriate?"

"Ah, no," said Questioner. "On Newholme, I am convinced of very little."

The song went on, and the dance. The moons moved into line with the sun and a gloom descended, a palpable shade that seemed to war with the music, advancing upon it, being driven away only to advance again. The earth shook, the mountains skipped, distant peaks tumbled like children's blocks, and still the music went on, the liquid depths surging again and again, waves leaping high, only to fall into glassy calms that swirled and eddied and rose again.

When two moons moved from the face of the sun, the music softened. As other moons sailed out and away from their gathering, the music softened more. The world stopped rocking, and they breathed again. Bofusdiaga's voice fell silent, then those of the Timmys, and last the drumming of the Joggiwagga ceased, leaving only the great stone flutes and horns making sonorous harmonies over the misty depths.

During all this time, even during the worst of the tremors, the tunnelers had been repairing the trench, chewing up loads of stone and regurgitating them into the ditch, while leggers pounded them down with their many feet. Lit by the fiery light of midafternoon, only a rough scar on the stone marked where the ditch had been. All was silent. No Timmy spoke, no creature moved. Birdthings sat silent along the rim, like a fringe.

The watchers waited. Inside the nearest cave, the members of the entourage muttered among themselves. At last, as evening came, a green spring began to bubble up into the depths of the Fauxi-dizalonz, throwing emerald sparkles in all directions. The stone music faded into quiet. The birdthings flew. Fogs rose from the abyss of the Quaggima, thickly roiling upward to fall as cool rain. When the rain stopped, the abyss was flooded down its western side with a fierce and golden light that gave them a transitory look at every detail of the chasm. The great black wings lay quietly upon the walls, and at the bottom the obsidian gleam of the great egg shone beside the still form of the Quaggima. Nothing else.

The world turned. The abyss shifted out of the sunlight,

shadow streaming across its bottom and onto the eastern wall.

"Where are they?" whispered Simon. "Madame, where's Mouche?"

She shook her head. Nothing so small as a mere person could be seen at this distance. But then, Mouche and his companions had not been that small when they had flowed away. She would have asked the Corojum, but it had disappeared while they had watched the moons. Now there was nothing in the upper caldera but the sodden surface, a scar on the rock, the slowly filling pool of the Fauxidizalonz, and the trundling back and forth of the tunnelers and leggers who were smoothing the stone where the trench had been. Of that great being who had plunged over the edge into the chasm, there was no sign at all.

They sat without speaking until the sun had fallen well toward the west, at which point they were recovering sufficiently that Madame and Simon were beginning to murmur to one another their grief over Mouche, and the Hags, huddled with Calvy, were beginning to cast aggrieved glances at Questioner.

Seeing this, Questioner rose and said imperiously, "Now is not the time to discuss the future, if, indeed, it becomes a matter for discussion at all. I intend to have a closer look." She went toward the steep track, and the others straggled after her, for no reason except that it gave them something to do.

They had gone three-quarters of the way down when D'Jevier asked, "Madame, aren't those your boys?"

Madame searched the caldera, seeing two young men standing beside the rapidly filling pool.

"Bane and Dyre," murmured Madame. "They were never my boys, but I wondered where they'd got to. Now what are they doing?"

"Making up their minds to enter the pond," said Questioner, who had amplified her hearing. "Bane is telling his brother to jump, and his brother is saying he'll wait until the water gets higher."

A clutch of Timmys approached the two boys, backed

by a Joggiwagga. Those on the trail could see the argument that resulted, but they could hear none of it.

Questioner asked Calvy, "These boys killed Marool Mantelby. Leaving aside for the moment the fact that Marool was their mother and that she probably needed killing, what does your system of justice require?"

Calvy replied, "Strictly interpreted, our law would require blue-bodying. For both of them."

D'Jevier commented, "That's true. But when we wrote those laws we did not have access to a Fauxi-dizalonz."

She had no sooner spoken than the pond began to bubble and percolate, shimmering of its own motion rather than from the wind. A tongue of green licked out of it and wrapped around both Bane and Dyre, lapping them down into the depths. At once, several of the Timmys ran around the pond to the opposite side and waited there.

The persons from the ledge reached the level of the caldera floor before two squat, ugly gargoyles crawled from the pond to stare at one another in horror. Their stench could be detected even by those across the pond. The Timmys did not suffer it. Immediately, they pushed the two back into the pond while, across from their point of entry, other Timmys readied themselves.

Questioner and her associates drew closer to observe the eventual emergence of two undistinguished and indistinguishable young men who gagged and gasped upon the shore, but gave off no detectable odor. The pond glittered, made a strangled noise, and spat a mouthful of clothing onto the shore beside them.

Questioner approached the two, prodding Bane with one foot. "How are you, boy? Are you all in one piece?"

"I'm all right," said Bane. He gagged, rolled over, then crawled toward his sodden trousers. "I'm hungry. We haven't had a decent meal since we left . . . wherever it was. Where was it, Dyre?"

"House Genevois," said Dyre, trying to find the sleeves in his wet shirt. "Haven't had anything good to eat since then."

"And what are you doing here?" asked Questioner.

"Damfino," said Bane, staring about himself in wonder. "Hey, lookit all the Timmys with no clothes on!"

"Do you young men by any chance remember Marool Mantelby?" asked Calvy in an innocent voice.

"Or someone called Ashes?" asked Madame.

Bane and Dyre looked at one another, mystified, then back at the group. "Sorry, don't think we've met anybody like that."

Madame shrugged. D'Jevier shook her head. Onsofruct narrowed her nostrils and stared through slitted eyes. They were Bane and Dyre, truly, but they weren't the same young men.

"Blue-bodying?" D'Jevier asked Onsofruct.

"I see no point in it," said Onsofruct, turning to Calvy and Simon. "Do you?"

The two men shook their heads, then stopped, fixing their gaze toward the chasm. "Look," breathed Calvy, pointing down the almost invisible scar where the trench had been.

Laboring toward them over the lip of the chasm came four trudging figures. Ellin and Bao and Ornery and Mouche. Not exactly Mouche. Mouche with a billow of emerald hair that moved like seagrass. Mouche, smiling quietly. Mouche-timmy. Mouche-Flowing Green.

None of them spoke. The four approached, plodding wearily, yet with glowing faces.

"Now we are having time!" Bao called to Questioner. "Yes? Time for tunneling out the Quaggi egg? For lifting Quaggima?"

Mouche stopped where he was, leaning against the rock as if exhausted, but the other three came on to meet the group advancing toward them.

"Were you seeing dance, Questioner?" asked Bao with a wide grin. "We are being damn sexy."

"I'm afraid not," she replied. "No one up here did. We heard climactic music, we saw whirlwinds and surf."

"It was all very dramatic," said Calvy. "But not at all sexually explicit."

"Good." Ellin sighed. "At the time, I thought it was very beautiful, but I wouldn't have wanted it to be . . .

observed, or even recorded. Besides, in stories it's nicer when they leave a good deal to the imagination."

"Tell me," Madame whispered to her. "What actually happened?"

Ellin and Bao struggled to find words, glancing at one another. Finally, Ornery said, "The way I remember it is that first we sort of dissolved and then we sort of aggregated, and the thing we aggregated into was put together with all of Ellin's romantic notions and Bao's womanly beings and all the satisfactions I'd ever had, plus everything Kaorugi knew about the Quaggima, plus everything Mouche had learned about lovemaking, and then that being dived over the cliff, and we made love to the Quaggima. That kept it distracted while all the pulling and tugging was going on, and afterward, it went to sleep. That's all."

"And I'd have been embarrassed, really, except it wasn't me, or Mouche, or any of us," murmured Ellin. "It was something else entirely."

"What happened with Mouche?" asked Madame.

Ellin nodded. "That was a little surprising. When it was all finished, Kaorugi separated us out again, but not Mouche and Flowing Green. Flowing Green was always sort of part of him, so Kaorugi—or maybe Bofusdiaga, I'm not quite sure—left them together."

"How very strange," said Questioner.

Bao shrugged. "Being frank, Questioner, it is not seeming that strange to me. After all this doing and dancing and being, I am regarding gender things in a new light. Both are being much more capacious than I was ever thinking!"

"We owe you a debt of gratitude," said Questioner, meaning it sincerely.

Ellin shook herself and spoke again. "That's true. But you needn't owe us, Questioner. When we've had time to consider it, we may ask you a favor."

"So soon after such an experience? You recovered from it quickly."

"Well, we talked about it on the way up, while we were resting, and we figured *somebody* owes us a favor. It won't be inappropriate or greedy. You can count on that."

Bao said pleadingly, "We are not bothering you with it now, Questioner. Everything is being too upset and weird, and there are rocks still falling off mountains. And besides . . . besides . . ." His voice trailed away. Besides, he had been going to say, Flowing Green had changed everything when she had talked to them before the transformation. She had told them something wonderful, right there at the end—something they hadn't even had a chance to think about. Not yet.

"Well, if you want a favor, I can at least consider it," said Questioner. "You've been good and dutiful aides. You're deserving of some consideration. And what about Mouche?"

"You'll have to ask Mouche," said Ellin. "I don't feel all that different from before. Not yet. There were only five of us, but the memory is already fading. I know why the Timmys couldn't remember, all those thousands of them. But Mouche . . . I don't think he will forget. I think something different happened to Mouche."

"I shouldn't be surprised," muttered Questioner. "Though this planet has, on several occasions, surprised me." She turned to stare at the two Hags, who were standing a little distance away. "Unpleasantly," she added with a sniff.

Onsofruct caught Questioner's glance. Her eyes brimmed with tears, and she turned away to hide the tears that spilled down her cheeks. "It's going to happen, Jevvy. Our grandmothers made the wrong choice."

"No," said D'Jevier angrily. "They made the right choice. It just doesn't happen to fit into Haraldson's edicts."

"What?" demanded Calvy. "What are you talking about?"

"She's going to sterilize mankind on Newholme," murmured D'Jevier.

"Because of the Timmys?" Calvy cried, not waiting for an answer. "She's going to sterilize the people?" He turned to confront Questioner, saying accusingly, "Sterilize my children? That's a rotten way to repay Mouche and Ornery for their efforts on your behalf, Questioner.

Or all the people on this planet who never killed a single Timmy. No future for them, either?"

"What are you talking about?" cried Ornery. "She's going to do what?"

"The innocent suffer with the guilty," said Questioner, with a significant glance at the Hags. "And it is not because of the Timmys! Let them explain it to you." She moved ponderously up the hill away from them.

Behind her, D'Jevier burst into tears, to be comforted by Ellin, who stared after Questioner, wondering if she and Bao should stay or go after her. Bao put a hand on her shoulder, holding her in place. Well then, they would stay. They did not yet understand what exactly was happening, but they understood well enough that Mouche and Ornery along with the rest of Newholmian people were condemned to a fate that had sunk the others of their group deep in grief.

Away toward the chasm, Mouche looked up, noticed the unhappy group by the Fauxi-dizalonz and came slowly toward them.

"How can I tell him?" wept Madame. "Everything he's done for us, for us all, and now this. I can't tell him."

"It wouldn't make any difference to him, would it?" asked Ornery. "He never had any future, anyhow. Not in the way of children and a family."

"But this is different," Madame cried. "Different . . . when it's the whole world."

Ornery, watching Mouche's slow approach, was not at all sure that the difference was worth mentioning.

61

Love Cards Wild

Over the succeeding days, the Quaggi egg was tunneled away from the body of Kaorugi and also out of the body of Quaggima—a job for which Kaorugi created two large creatures with geo-surgical aptitudes. The blast capsules beneath the egg were also carefully disassembled and Questioner's ship—whose captain had claimed "parts failure" as an excuse for failing to respond during the gathering of the moons—proved capable under the Gablian commander of lifting Quaggima and the egg and the dangerous hatching mechanism from the planet's surface. Quaggima was deposited on one of the tiny moonlets orbiting Newholme, for a time of rehabilitation, but the egg was taken farther out, to be cracked when Quaggima was ready. According to Bofusdiaga, Quaggima intended to take his children under his wing, male and female both, to start a Quaggian rights movement, a movement that might seek an allegiance with the Council of Worlds, who would be asked to lend certain ships to the task of rescuing abused and dying Quaggi. During the enlightening intercourse that had taken place in the chasm, the Quaggima had acquired strong feelings about Quaggian sexuality.

These effort were still underway when Mouche paid a visit to House Genevois, where he found both Madame and D'Jevier, pale and shadow-faced, grieving the future loss of their people upon Newholme. Mouche hugged them both and told them to keep up their spirits, use their heads, the game wasn't over, there might be a card or two to play yet, burying them in so many hope-inducing cliches that they both laughed.

"Are you coming back to House Genevois, Mouche?" Madame asked. "I will understand if you choose not to do so."

"Questioner has offered to pay off my contract. As for what I will do, I am uncertain at the moment, but I think we would all agree, Madame, that I am an unlikely Consort." He shook out his shock of green hair, letting it flow like seagrass, grinning at her in a devilishly intimate manner.

"You are unlikely, Mouche. You're also unusually impertinent." She gave him a tearful smile.

The smile undid him. He had sworn to himself to say nothing, but these women needed a hint of hope. "Madame, I have set myself the task of changing Questioner's mind. If I fail, keep in your minds that Kaorugi does not want mankind departed from its world, and Kaorugi is capable of much we do not understand."

He dropped a kiss on each forehead and took himself off.

"You'll miss him," said D'Jevier.

"We both will," said Madame. "And I'm so glad the Fauxi-dizalonz fixed his face. But think, Jevvy, what he said!"

"About Kaorugi?"

"The last few nights, I've found myself dreaming about him—not sexually—and in the dream he was pointing into the distance and calling, 'There, there it is, Madame.' I was sure he was pointing to the Fauxi-dizalonz. And what he said just now. . . . Do you think Bofusdiaga would let us? Some of us? Even . . . all of us?''

''If we are to have no mankind future, you mean? Oh, yes, Madame. I've thought of that, too. Could we become? As Mouche has become? Do you suppose the Corojum would ask on our behalf?''

They thought about this, with emotions that ranged moment to moment from revulsion and apprehension to wonderment and hope.

Corojum, speaking, so he said, for Bofusdiaga, had suggested that Questioner transport a quantity of previously unknown Newholme botanicals to test the market among the populated worlds. One or another entity of Dosha seemed to be determined to maintain contact with the outside worlds, though whether this was Bofusdiaga or Kaorugi itself or some new, commercial subentity, Questioner wasn't sure.

Whichever, rather than attempting to deal with the cargo, the captain of *The Quest* ran true to form by tendering his resignation. ''My aunt is the delegate from Caphalonia!'' he said. ''She wouldn't have obtained an office for me on a *cargo* ship!''

''Quite right,'' Questioner had said. ''Beneath your dignity. There's a freighter arriving tomorrow. I'll send you home with my entourage.''

''But,'' said the captain.

''Not at all, not at all,'' Questioner boomed. ''Don't thank me. Glad to do it.''

The Gablian commander was immediately promoted to captain. Ornery had learned a good deal about cargo in her years as a sailor, and she offered to help the Gablian crew stow the bales and cartons.

Calvy had been so deeply depressed by the Questioner's decision to sterilize mankind upon Newholme that he went into a funk every time he saw his children. Trying to raise his spirits, his wife suggested a visit to the extraordinary caves west of Naibah, and Ellin and Bao were invited to go along.

Thus for a time everyone was busy and occupied except Questioner and Mouche. Mouche wasted no time in asking

Questioner to dine with him. He had an agenda, a very specific agenda, which he and Flowing Green had arrived at.

The two met in the side room of a cafe in Sendoph, where they enjoyed a very good early dinner, sipped a little not bad Newholmian wine, and agreed to spend the early evening playing a few hands of Gablian poker. As Mouche had arranged, the room was empty except for themselves, though the walls were no doubt full of eyes and ears, a hundred tattletales ready to run to Bofusdiaga at a moment's notice.

When Questioner arrived she was in a state, as she confessed to Mouche. A mood, Mouche thought of it. Despite the fact that all concerned had managed to avert a tragic outcome of the Quaggian Dilemma (thus far), Questioner had not come away from the episode feeling either satisfied or relieved. Indeed, if anything, she was more irritable and exasperated than before.

Mouche did not let it pass. "It is clear to me you are sad and irritable," he said, dealing them each five cards, the last one face up, "because the beings from whom you were made are in great pain and terror, and you know this even if you do not feel it."

"How do you know?" she demanded, regarding her exposed king of shovels with a scowl. "Did Ornery tell you?"

Mouche had a ten of love showing, and he made a face as he picked up the facedown cards and arranged them in his hand. "Not until later, but Flowing Green knew all about it. She saw you in your maintenance booth. She heard you talking to your inward persons. You have a deep pain there, but it need not remain."

"Is your Timmy recommending a cerebrectomy?" Questioner sneered.

Mouche gave her a look so patient as to be almost patronizing. "No, Flowing Green and I recommend only the removal of unpleasant memories and the substitution of some happy feelings. We can be at the Fauxi-dizalonz in an hour in your shuttle, and Bofusdiaga has already agreed that the parts of you needing surcease are organic parts that it can work with.''

''Why should I do that?'' she asked, astonished by this suggestion. ''I've done well enough so far.''

''You have,'' he agreed. ''But until just recently, you were unaware of the tragedy you carry inside you. Mathilla, M'Tafa, and Tiu cannot be freed of pain until you help them. Bofusdiaga can not only free them, he can also grant them happiness.''

She gritted her teeth. Learning of the three from an outside source had brought them into her memory banks by a route HoTA had never intended. All her baffles and wards had been outflanked and the lives and deaths of the three indwelling minds had been resurrected in herself.

''They are no longer severed from your consciousness,'' said Mouche, accurately reading her face. ''It is their anger and agony you feel on a daily basis, hour by hour.''

''I can bear it,'' she said through clenched teeth.

''Of course you can bear it,'' he said. ''The question is, why should anyone bear it? Bearing it does no one any good, least of all you. Like the jongau, you'll come to survive on hatred, and like the jongau, you'll disintegrate. I remember what Corojum said about living in the past. And I remember that when we spoke with Timmys who had themselves been killed by men and later resurrected in the Fauxi-dizalonz, none of them remembered the terror or horror. They knew about it, yes, but they did not feel it. So, when you have been in the Fauxi-dizalonz, you will know about your indwellers, but you will not feel their pain.''

She stared at him, examining him with all her senses. Nothing there now of the quivering boy who had accompanied her on the underground river. And the green hair was certainly unusual, as was his hybrid facial appearance. Slightly lofty. Like a minor angel. Though he sounded very little different from before, he thought quite differently, she could tell.

''It's not the same,'' she murmured.

''It *is* the same,'' he asserted. ''In recent time I have come to understand that, Questioner. Flowing Green has observed that the true story of any living thing has pain in it, and life has to be that way. Curiosity is a good goad, but pain is a better one. It is pain that moves us, that makes us learn how to cure, how to mend, how to improve, how to re-create. Inside all of us, even the happiest, are memories of pain. Ellin, Bao, Ornery . . . they all had hurt children inside them. We came to know one another's pain during our adventure in the chasm. Each of us cries that we are lost. We ask the darkened room, who are we? And we demand easy answers: I am my father's son. My mother's daughter. A child of this family, or that."

"That's the nature of mankind," she agreed.

"True, but Corojum had an answer that is equally true, and I like his better! We are made of the stuff of stars, given our lives by a living world, given our selves by time. We are brother to the trees and sister to the sun. We are of such glorious stuff we need not carry pain around like a label. Our duty, as living things, to be sure that pain is not our whole story, for we can choose to be otherwise. As Ellin says, we can choose to dance.

"The minds inside you suffer, Questioner. Let them have joy."

She frowned, turning her glass in her hands, not replying. Tactfully, Mouche turned his attention elsewhere, feeling movement behind the walls, a scurry, a coming and going. Every word he said was reported. Every motion he made. Still, thus far in his game he was content. He had played a card, and she would think about it. She would construct a dozen reasons why not, but before she left Newholme (if Bofusdiaga let anyone leave Newholme) she would go into the Fauxi-dizalonz. For the sake of those children, if not her own.

Now the next play. He laid his cards face down on the table before him, saying: "See how empty the streets are. The Timmys now have no need to hover over people, and many of them have gone back to doing whatever they did before mankind came. Do you include the fact that mankind killed many of them in your decisions about Newholme? Are their deaths one of the reasons that the mankind population will be sterilized?"

Questioner shook her head slowly, still mulling the matter of the suffering children inside herself. "It wasn't for that, Mouche. I could argue it, but the question of individuality would arise. The Timmys are, after all, only quasi-independent beings. They were made to look like people by Bofusdiaga, but in the past they were otherwise, and maybe in the future they will be stranger yet. If they are malleable beings, made as Bofusdiaga wills, then what was actually killed? They were distinctive only in the information they carried, but not even information was lost, for the dance has been regained. In any case, it won't be needed in the future."

"This is so," Mouche agreed.

"However," she went on relentlessly, "the killers didn't know the Timmys weren't individuals when they killed them. Their intent was genocidal. That's a point against mankind on Newholme."

Mouche nodded sympathetically. "True, Questioner. Though not all the people were involved even then, and none now living were. How about the culture, the dower laws, the supernumes, the men having to wear veils? Does that figure in your decision?"

She shook her head. "Blue-bodying is against the edicts, I should say, but corrective action would have been easy enough without extreme measures. On that ground alone I would have recommended that in order to comply strictly with Haraldson's edicts, the people here should establish another colony where their dissidents could go. The system is actually no more coercive than many other systems that are supposed to be voluntary. The men give up a little to get most of what they want, the women give up a little to get most of what they want. Neither sex is completely satisfied, but neither is completely dissatisfied."

"So you accept the system?"

She frowned. "As D'Jevier pointed out to me, the population is generally healthy, the lifespan is long, the average intelligence is rising. I would recommend corrective action, not punishment."

"Ah," murmured Mouche. "I'm glad of that."

Questioner gave him a very direct and imperious look. ''All this is purely argumentative, however, for my decision to sterilize this planet is based upon the fact that the Hags are doing away with half the girl babies born on this world. Believe me, that is all I need to decide as I have done.''

She kept her eyes on him, waiting for a reaction. She'd anticipated his being shocked by this, but he showed no evidence of surprise.

''Oh, is that so?'' he asked, raising his eyebrows only slightly.

''That's an odd reaction!''

''Well, Questy . . . may I call you Questy? Ma'am seems so . . . formal. As I've said a time or two, what Flowing Green knew, I know. And Flowing Green knew everything there was to know that could be found out listening and watching through holes in the wall. When did you learn of this?''

She said in an exasperated voice, ''I've known there was something out of line almost from the first. The actions of this alleged virus seemed entirely too dependent upon where one had one's children and what family one came from. Calvy has eight, four boys, four girls. Marool Mantelby was one of eight daughters. Both Marool's mother and Carezza bore their children at home. It became glaringly obvious that the Hags were keeping tight control on the woman supply in order to remain in power, and that some men like Calvy, who had figured it out, were letting them do it.''

''You think staying in power is why they do it?''

''That's usually the reason for arbitrary cruelty.''

''You think it's cruel?''

''Don't you?'' she cried, stung.

''Do you know what happens to the babies?''

''They do away with them! I said as much to the Hags, there at the Fauxi-dizalonz, and they didn't deny it. Not even when your friend Madame begged them to.''

He reached forward to lay his hand on her own, just for a moment, stroke. ''They didn't deny what you said, which is true. But they didn't understand what you *meant* by it. You meant by 'done away with' that the babies are killed."

"Of course," she cried. "What else?"

"Everything else! They're put in stasis and sent off planet, to newly settled worlds where women are in short supply and where every little girl will be very much valued and honored. As they are here. The Hags exact a good price for them, and the profits support old women here on Newholme who could be in great need otherwise."

Questioner found herself momentarily speechless. She had never considered any other outcome than death. She had assumed . . . she who had long ago learned never to assume. She sat for a long moment silent before whispering, "Why didn't they explain?"

"Because you were angry, and you told them not to attempt explanation."

"By all the follies of Flagia, why did I assume they killed the babies?"

"Because of your own suffering children who were killed," murmured Mouche. "You were angry on their behalf. Madame says when we focus on our anger, our vision begins to constrict. Soon we are caught up in fury, and we turn it upon everyone."

She complained, "But the Hags didn't have to choose that way of doing things. Surely there's a better solution!"

"If you can suggest one, I know they'd be happy to hear it. They aren't monsters, Questy. They're the descendants of the cultural historians on the second ship, and their ancestresses knew very well that surpluses breed contempt. Too many of anything reduces the honor in which it is held: too many men, too many women, too many children, too many people.

"The Hags saw their duty as taking care of women, and they did it. There's no female prostitution or slavery on Newholme. There are no poor elderly widows. There are no poor, unwed mothers. If I were calling the game, I'd call that a trump card." He took up the card from one side of his hand, the ten of love, and laid it face up on the table.

Questioner frowned at the table, spreading her own

hand, face up. Not a love card among them. Only shovels and clubs, labor and management. Duty and efficiency. Her life. "An artificial shortage surely isn't what Haraldson had in mind—"

Mouche interrupted her. "I know. I thought you'd say that. But I've been talking to Calvy. He's one of the few men on Newholme who actually reads the COW journals, including your reports. He told me to remind you about Beltran Four."

"Beltran Four!"

"Mmm."

"It's a very warlike planet."

"Many fewer men than women?"

"Yes. Because so many men are killed in the battles."

"And the warrior elite keep the battles going. For honor. For reputation. For rapine."

She said reluctantly, "Yes."

"And did you sterilize all mankind on Beltran Four? Because half their young men are slaughtered in battle?"

She frowned at him. "Calvy told you to ask me this."

"He did. He said he'd been following your career for some decades, reading your recommendations and the reports you'd made to COW. He said to ask you which was worse, slaughtering half the young men in battles, or selling half the girl babies to planets where they'll be appreciated? On Beltran Four, a male hierarchy guarantees that they will have their choice of women. On Newholme, a female hierarchy guarantees that women will have a choice of men. In both cases, the surplus is eliminated, but here, at least, no one dies."

He turned up the jack of love and laid it beside the ten. "Another point for Newholme, Questy?"

Questioner shifted uncomfortably. When she had assessed Beltran Four a quarter-century before, she had not recommended any punishment. What went on there was all too common. Though Haraldson had hated war, he had known it would happen. War was natural. Men being killed in war was natural. Why was this situation worse? She had no sooner thought the question than Mouche answered it.

"You're holding women to a higher standard than men," he said. "Madame used to tell us that this is traditional, for men have usually been the judges, and they put women either in the gutter or upon a pedestal. Men have traditionally forgiven one another, for they know and excuse their own failings, but they do not forgive women for falling off the pedestal."

She thought, of course, and of course. For a woman to be respected she must burn on a pyre like M'Tafa, be immured in solitude like Mathilla, submit to being buried alive like Tiu; for a woman to be respected, she must take the pain of life without demanding the joys, she must sacrifice herself, preferably without complaint. She may have no pleasure except what she is granted by father, or husband, or son. Damn Calvy!

"Are you finished with your argument?" she asked, her voice giving no indication of yielding.

"Not yet," he said, taking a deep breath, for there was more at stake here than she knew. "I have the Kaorugi card to play."

"Which is?"

"Will you agree that Kaorugi is a lifeform?"

"Kaorugi is a lifeform, certainly."

"And will you agree that Haraldson's edicts prohibit the torture or harassment of lifeforms?"

"I agree. I'm not intending to interfere with Kaorugi or any of its subparts. Quite the contrary."

"Ah, but Bofusdiaga says you are. All his life until Quaggima, Kaorugi was singular and alone. Then Quaggima came, and Kaorugi had a companion. He delighted in that companionship, strange though it was. Then mankind came, and Kaorugi had still other creatures to learn about and from. He learned new feelings: vanity, pride, ecstacy, disgust—a whole volume of emotions.

"Now Quaggima is gone. It's partly due to you that he's gone, you know; you helped take him away, and you've left Kaorugi, who is virtually immortal, with mankind only. If you sterilize the planet of all mankind, Kaorugi will be sentenced to solitary confinement. Kaorugi doesn't want that. So, if you take away mankind, you are torturing Kaorugi."

He turned up the queen of love, laying it next to the jack and ten. "The Kaorugi card."

"And that's why I should change my mind?" she cried. "I should evade my duty so Kaorugi can have some company and learn more about the universe?"

"Not only for that, also because Haraldson would not approve of your interfering with the lifeform on this planet," Mouche murmured. He hadn't said all he could have said about the lifeform on the planet. If Questioner insisted on sterilization and managed somehow to get off planet to do it, Bofusdiaga would not let mankind die. They would become something else, of course. Rather as Mouche had become, though without some of the elements that had made that becoming successful, assuming it was successful. It would not necessarily be a bad thing or bad in all cases, but still that part of Mouche that was purely mankind preferred that his people be allowed to choose what they would be.

"You seem to have innumerable arguments," she said in a grumpy voice.

"Not innumerable, no. I have played all my cards but two."

"Well, play them," she said impatiently. "Get on with it."

"This is one you should like, Questy. Now that your political appointees are out of your hair, not that they were ever any good to you, you should demand the liberty of choosing your own aides. Competent ones. People who will work with you."

"Competent aides," she murmured, intrigued despite herself. "I must admit, that has its attractions. Could I possibly have a competent ship's crew, as well?"

"We could work on that. Ornery might be just the person to assure it. We, that is Ellin and Bao and Ornery and I, would like to be your aides, Questy. We've held off discussing it with you, for there's been a lot to think about, but it's the only thing that makes sense. Ellin can't go back to History House, she's beyond that, and so is Bao.

Ornery needs wider seas than the ones she's been traveling, and I can't be a planetbound Consort now. I know too much. I've seen too much, felt too much. I can't do it even by serving my Hagion, for the Hagion I served is part of me, and that part of me isn't interested in an eternity of Consorthood on Newholme. . . ."

"An eternity?"

He bit his lip. He hadn't been going to mention that just yet. "So it seems. We've been through the Fauxi-dizalonz, Questy. We could still perish, far from here and unable to return, but if no accident catches up with us, and if we get back here to Newholme every few hundred years or so, we're in for a very long haul. It might be nice for you to have some friends who remember when you were only a youngster, two or three hundred years old."

She stared, open-mouthed, as he placed the king beside the queen.

"Besides," he said, "Kaorugi wants the four of us to go with you, for then, at intervals, when we return to the Fauxi-dizalonz, Kaorugi will experience the whole galaxy, or as much of it as we have seen in the interim."

"So you have it all figured out," she said helplessly.

"All four or five of us have figured it out. You offer me and Ornery and Ellin and Bao adventure and exploration, we, including Flowing Green, offer you comradeship—and another point of view, which is always valuable."

"I'm not sure my life is that adventurous. You may get the short end of the deal."

"Well then, even the score. Give us something we all want. Approve of Newholme, as it is. Let our friends and families alone. No sterilization."

"You're trying to suborn me."

He swallowed a sigh. Kaorugi preferred the presence of independent, alien creatures, but if Kaorugi could not have that, Kaorugi would have something else. Kaorugi did not like what it had learned of the sterilization order. Kaorugi felt, as had been foreseen, that justice was simply the last straw, but the Timmy part of Mouche would not let him speak of that. The Timmy part of him would not allow Kaorugi's contingency plans to be forestalled.

Well, if Questioner were to be moved, it had to be with eloquence. Or . . .

"I'm trying to convince you, Questioner. Why not just agree?"

"Because," she said angrily, "I was created for a purpose, and I feel my purpose is being undermined here."

Or . . .

He fingered the last card in his hand. The ace of love. "Is that really what you feel?"

She fumed. She wasn't sure what she felt. Sadness, certainly. And anger. She muttered, "You're probably right about my feelings, coming from what I know about the three children. The buffers were there for a reason, and I shouldn't have gone around them."

"It's not only the three children," Mouche murmured. "The council loads you down with work, then saddles you with incompetent people and still expects you to work miracles."

"While constantly cutting my budget," she said furiously. "They even interfere with my technical support. That's why I couldn't get in touch with the ship when I needed to! Parts failure! That idiot! Can you believe that?"

He did not believe it. Flowing Green knew there had been no failure of parts, only Bofusdiaga, determined to give them no alternative to solving the Quaggian dilemma. Not even Flowing Green knew the extent of what Bofusdiaga could do.

Focus, Mouche told himself. As Madame had always said, Focus!

"Part of it is that you work very hard, and no one really appreciates what you do," he said softly, moving his chair a bit closer to hers.

"I was designed for it," she sniffed. "But it is hard, yes. I'm human enough to feel that."

"Of course you feel it. You must get terribly annoyed."

"It's what I was created for," she said less forcefully. "But none of us like to feel our efforts are wasted. . . ."

"True. And even when we know our efforts aren't wasted, we like to be appreciated."

"Yes," she admitted, almost in a murmur. "It would be nice."

"I admire you so greatly," he said. "We all do."

"Really?" She laughed, rather sadly. "That's something new."

"You aren't admired by the members of the council?"

"By and large they treat me like a computer. It's understandable, I suppose."

"They disregard your humanity, because it makes them feel uncomfortable, I imagine." He put his hand on top of her own. "It probably surpasses their own. But we . . . I think of you as a friend. And I'm honoring myself when I give you that title."

"Oh, Mouche. Really." She felt herself flushing.

He shook out his mane of emerald hair and looked at her from under lowered lashes. "It's time that someone took care of you, Questioner. After all the care you take of humanity, it's only right that humanity do something for you in return."

"For me?"

He gave her a dangerous look as he reached out to run his hand along her neck, where several of her sensation circuits were placed near the skin.

"Ahhh," she said unwillingly. "Ahhh."

"I've researched you in these recent days, Questy," he whispered. "Flowing Green and I." He lowered his fingers, recently returned to their Consortly softness, stroking the line of her shoulder. Stroke. Stroke. Tweak.

"Mouche. For heaven's sake. . . ." She quivered with unfamiliar pleasure. "For heaven's sake. . . ."

"Oh Corojumi, grant deliverance . . ." he sang softly, with a purposeful stroke, laying the ace upon the table.

"Last card . . ." she gasped.

". . . grant Questy in this dance . . ."

"You stacked the deck," she whispered.

". . . compensatory joys," he sang, the green hair swirling high above his head as he and his Hagion smiled into her eyes.

"For the soirée, I think the mahogany satin," said Gertrude, the Wardrobe Mistress. "You look marvelous in it."

Genevieve demurred. "It's what I wore last time. I really look like a Nose in it."

"You know," said Gertrude, head cocked to one side, "you're growing into your nose. Last year, it seemed large, true, but this year, no. This year, it seems a proper part of your face. The art instructor, Master Vorbold, said you would be striking. He was positive it would happen, and I believe it has!"

The mirror agreed, but only if Genevieve stood tall, head carried imperially poised on her long neck, shoulders relaxed, face quiet. Then the face was fine, nose and all, just as it was in the family portraits. Her dark skin was unusual in Haven, but acceptable since it was inherited from Queen Stephanie.

"I'll bet your father's bringing the colonel back," whispered Carlotta, as they were having their hair done. "I'll bet the colonel has asked for your hand."

"No," said Genevieve, with a pang of regret. "Father wouldn't consider the colonel for me." Not in this play or any other.

"Why not?" demanded Barbara. "He's young, he's handsome, he looks healthy!"

Genevieve worked it out. "In the first place, he's a commoner, which means he's uncovenantal. And then, Father is looking for a son. He did not get one by birth, so he will try to get one by marriage. It is much more important that Father get on with the person than that I do, and the Colonel is not the kind of person Father would ever be comfortable with." She said it calmly, but heard it with a pang. What she had said was absolutely true. Now why was that? Why wasn't Father perfectly comfortable with his own equerry?

What was it about Aufors Leys that Father was *not* comfortable with? Not merely his being a commoner, for Father was quite comfortable with some commoners. It wasn't his appearance, which was heavenly, or his manners, which were impeccable. It had to be something, but she couldn't think what. Just something about him. His attitude perhaps. Yes. That was likely it, his attitude of being *real.* Aufors was more *real* than Father was. This idea was difficult to think out, but once having thought it, Genevieve could not unthink it. Aufors Leys was real, but like her father, Genevieve was probably not.

Everyone was ready for the soirée early. Father arrived early, also. He bowed, took her hand, and led her out through the open doors of the ballroom onto the terrace.

"Genevieve, Prince Yugh Delganor will be attending the soirée tonight, as my guest."

Yugh Delganor. She cast out a net of memory, seining for Delganor. A guest at Langmarsh House, not long before school started this year. A tall, thin man with dead eyes, hollow cheeks, and no conversation. As she had been taught, she had given him opportunities for conversation, but each had been a stone dropped into a bottomless well: no splash, no echo. He had been very well dressed. Middle aged. Perhaps older. Not bad looking, but vaguely repellant and utterly without animation. Genevieve had assigned him a walk-on role and had been glad when he had departed.

"I remember the name . . ." she murmured.

His lips thinned. "You should remember more than the name, girl! Yugh Delganor is the Lord Paramount's nephew, son of his younger brother."

"Ah," she murmured. "Prince Thumsort, is it?"

"No, no. Thumsort is the youngest of the three. Delganor's father and His Majesty, Marwell, Lord Paramount were twins. Since the untimely death of the Lord Paramount's son, Delganor is the heir presumptive. Thumsort comes third, since Delganor's sons have also perished."

"Couldn't the Lord Paramount have another son?"

"The Queen is past it, girl! She hasn't had the good sense to die and let him find another wife, and a son out of any other woman would not qualify. Why don't you know all this?"

She murmured, "I don't think you have ever told me of it, Father."

He sniffed. "I keep forgetting this school does not always teach you what may be most important to you. I hope at least you have guessed something of what this evening portends."

Something tore. A bit of that membrane that made a comforting translucency between herself and the outside world ripped away, leaving a hole. Reality showed through, only a glimpse—ominously dark—and her inner parts cramped in panic. She found voice to say, "Since you had not mentioned this matter before, no, I have no idea."

He frowned, displeased.

She sought to mend the veil that protected her, pulling it together between herself and the reality of his words. "Are you perhaps engaging in some enterprise with Prince Delganor?"

He glared, not at her but at the horizon, barely visible between the trees. "I have been summoned to Havenor, to attend upon the court. It could be a lengthy term of service. When I mentioned other responsibilities, the Lord Paramount kindly thought of your needs. The Lord Paramount does not invite all and everyone to reside in Havenor. He has waited to receive others' opinion of you, of your poise, your behavior, your appearance, the purity of your soul. Prince Delganor gave him an opinion. Aufors Leys has also done so. Delganor is coming tonight to extend the Lord Paramount's invitation for you to reside at court during my posting there."

"I don't understand . . ."

His face contorted in anger. "Of course you do! Do not be willfully stupid, Genevieve! You have been well reared, well educated. Your soul has been kept pure. You are suitable! And because you are suitable, the Prince has condescended to come here tonight in order to deliver the Lord Paramount's invitation. He may ask if you have any objection to leaving school. You will say no. He may ask if you have any matrimonial interest, since that might distract you from the duties of the court, and if he does, you will say you do not."

Stillness, and herself saying in a stranger's voice from a place of clarity. "I did not particularly like him, Father."

He barked, a single *ha,* unamused. "That is of no matter. There will be a good many at court you will not like, any more than I do. Nonetheless, we accommodate ourselves. Who knows? You may find a husband there."

"I am entitled to a decade more of my youth, Father. And I do not think I would like marrying a courtier."

"That, too, is of no matter. Your mother was young when we were wed, she did not much like marrying me, nor I her. It worked out well enough."

She closed her eyes against those words, remembering a face, hearing sounds of agony, smelling the metallic reek of blood. A woman's voice whispering, "Jenny, Jenny, oh, my darling girl . . ." Had it worked well enough, their marriage? Not for mother, she did not say. Mother died, she did not say. You killed her, she did not say, feeling the first fluttering of something other than panic, something foreign to her, a loose thread of fury, hanging there, tempting her to grasp it, let what would unravel!

She ignored the thread, saying softly, "My education is unfinished, and I will miss my friends here at school."

"That also is of no matter. The honor you are offered outshines any such concerns, and Mrs. Blessingham can no doubt recommend tutors at High Haven if you wish to continue your education." He turned on her, face hard. "Keep this in mind! This whole matter may be in the nature of a test, to see whether we, you and I, are the kind of people who will make difficulties! Believe me, Genevieve, if you think of doing such a thing, think again. Rejecting an invitation from the Lord Paramount, brought to you by no less personage than the Prince, would not be good for me, and if you are not thoughtful of my reputation, as you have a duty to be, it will not be good for you, either. Whatever the Prince proposes comes directly from the Lord Paramount, and I am sworn to serve the Lord Paramount."

"His invitation is actually your command, then." She was surprised at the calm in her voice. "You are saying that I have no choice."

"No honorable choice, no. Later on, well . . ." He barked laughter, as though at something he had just discovered. "Yugh Delganor may well marry again. It is not impossible he might find you attractive enough to consider you for . . . some very exalted position."

And there she was suddenly, at center stage. The lights were on her, the attention of whoever it was, out there in the darkness, the watchers, among whom she had hoped to stay, always, always. Now the action centered upon her and the plot lines knotted and wove and all other characters faded into shadow. She drew away from him, hearing the rustle of her gown on the tiles loud in the silence, feeling the evening air clammy on her bare shoulders while a greater coldness froze the pit of her stomach.

She whispered, "Does he have family?"

"He has family, yes. He's been married two or three times, but his wives died." He said it offhandedly, as though it didn't matter. "As I recall, his first wife died in childbirth and one of the others died of batfly fever the year it swept the lowlands. Such things happen. I must say, your attitude surprises me."

"Forgive me, Father," she said from that brightly lighted place where she stood, that cell in time where all seemed to converge. "It is only that I, too, am much surprised. You have never mentioned any of this to me. This invitation comes out of the blue in the hands of a man who was not even polite to me when he visited Langmarsh House. Perhaps he is above politeness."

This time her father laughed with genuine amusement. "Well said, daughter. Perhaps he is, indeed. Whether he is above it or not, I know you will be sensible enough not to insult him. He has received good report from Colonel Leys, who has confirmed Mrs. Blessingham's opinion of you. She has said you are poised and quiet and your purity of soul has been approved by the scrutator. The Colonel has seconded this judgment."

"The Colonel . . ." She shook her head, confused. She had not been quiet with the Colonel. He had not asked about her soul. Not at all!

"The Colonel will be going with us to Havenor," the Marshal said, misunderstanding. "When the Lord Paramount suggested the colonel give an opinion it was for good reason. Leys is my equerry, and he would be responsible for your safety and comfort at court. His making an assessment of your manner is appropriate." He turned away, as though finished with words.

She tried, unsuccessfully, to think of something that might delay this matter, or forestall it altogether, but before she could think of anything, he exclaimed:

"Ah, there he is!"

She turned her head toward the distant door where Nemesis stood, tall and dark and dressed all in black, his eyes staring in her direction like flawed marbles, blindly.

"Remember to whom you are speaking," her father concluded, tucking her arm firmly under his own and moving off to greet his guest.

Somehow she greeted, bowed, responded to words. Somehow she got out onto the terrace with the tall man, without noticing that her father ushered them there, shutting the doors behind them. She did not come to herself until Delganor had taken her hand in his and was saying, ". . . the Lord Paramount wishes me to convey his pleasure at the prospect of your attendance at the court, in Havenor."

The words reached her ears, but beyond her ears she felt her brain shudder and cramp at his voice. Beneath her glove, the skin of her hand crawled. She could not bear for him to press her hand again or say anything more. To put an end to it, she assented, withdrew her hand in order to make the full, dramatic curtsey, after which she remained bent, watching his heels as he retreated from her. He exchanged a few words with her father inside the door. She barely breathed, wishing she had dreamed what just happened. This had not been a play. She had not merely watched. She had been present, hideously present, and she would have given anything she owned or ever thought of attaining if she had been elsewhere throughout it all.

Genevieve's invitation to court had come about thusly:

The Marshal, who had been at Havenor on business, was bidden to an immediate audience with the Lord Paramount. Not stopping to put on court attire, he went upon the notice and was admitted into the small hearing chamber where the Lord Paramount spent part of each morning attending to the business of Haven. His Majesty sat on a low dais, in a gilded and padded chair beneath a baldachin hung behind and on either side with weighty purple velvet to shut out the draughts. The carpet around him was strewn with booklets, both talking book and view-cube, and a tottery stack of other such booklets occupied a small gilded table at his side. His crown was slightly tilted, for he habitually leaned his chin on his left hand, turning the pages with right, listening with his eyes half shut, like a dreaming tortoise. He was in this position when he received the Marshal, alone except for two members of the recently imported off-world security force—Aresians sworn to the Lord Paramount's service and protection—who stood on either side of the door, weapons at the ready and eyes scanning the room in ceaseless watchfulness.

The Marshal saw all this as he came through the door, particularly the guards—bulky men, and strong looking, as all Aresians were. The two of them traded him look for look, silently, without a hint of feeling: no animosity, no acceptance, just alertness. The taller one was dark haired with a beard so black that his smoothly shaven skin looked blue. The other resembled him, though he was lighter, a bit thinner. They were good men, both. He wouldn't mind commanding men like these.

"Your Majesty," murmured the Marshal, bending a knee.

"Marshal," said the Lord Paramount, without moving, the pages slowly turning. "You know that new minister, the one from Barfezi? Name of Gormus."

"Efiscapel Gormus, yes, your Majesty, I've met him."

"Don't like him."

"I'm sorry to hear that, sir."

"I don't know what it is about County Potcher in Barfezi! The place breeds these freethinkers like lice, and here's another of 'em, all full of schemes to connect to off-world, join the community of man, open our arms and our hearts. And our pockets, he doesn't say. And our private business, which is none of off-worlds' affair! Well, I don't like him. Don't like the influence he has on some of the other ministers. Decided I need a balancing weight." He looked up, his eyes fully open, piercing the Marshal with his stare. "I'm inviting you to come to court."

The Marshal paused before answering, for the words had been peculiarly freighted with meaning, and that meaning suddenly penetrated. "You mean, live here, sir?"

"Can't be here without living here, can you?"

"No, sir." He thought, furiously. What was he supposed to say now? He'd never thought of such a possibility. He was no courtier! But he could scarcely say so, at the moment.

"Ah . . . I am deeply honored, Your Majesty, and I will comply as soon as I can arrange the few . . . responsibilities I'll have to see to first. . . ."

The Lord Paramount's eyes had not left the Marshal's

face, but now they slid aside, like a snake from a rock. "Of course, of course, for the moment I'd forgotten. You have a family—what is it, a daughter? Delganor mentioned her to me just recently. He met her at your place in Langmarsh. As I recall, he spoke well of her." He breathed for a moment through his teeth, a little whistle, *whee-oo, whee-oo,* in and out. "If possible—though it may not be—she should be with you, of course. All the young women at court have assigned duties, and we'd need to be sure she could acquit herself in a covenantly manner. Let's have someone take a look at her again, just to confirm Delganor's impressions. By the way, what's her name?"

"Genevieve, sir."

The Lord Paramount's eyes were on the turning pages. "Of course. Genevieve. Well, I'm sure she's quiet and respectful, a dutiful daughter, covenantly, pure of soul, a proper candidate." The Lord Paramount looked up, piercingly.

The Marshal found himself feeling slightly queasy, almost sick, like a man hard pressed, unable to catch his breath. It was known that the Prince was seeking a wife, but it would be presumptuous to imagine Genevieve as a candidate for . . . well, what the Lord Paramount was obviously referring to.

He chose to evade the question. "That would be hard for a father to judge, sir."

The Lord Paramount gave him a sharp look. "Ah . . . you think so? Well, I have an idea. Since that equerry of yours would be looking after her here in Havenor, let him take a look at her. We old fellows, we can't judge women, and it's not our place, anyhow. Though Delganor does very well. Proper judge of livestock, Delganor. Gave me a marvelous stallion, just recently."

"As Your Majesty wishes," murmured the Marshal, backing away from the presence while trying not to show his discomfort. Why had he mentioned having responsibilities? Still . . . if the Lord Paramount had meant what he might have meant . . .

Behind him, in the small council chamber, silence fell. A servant crept through a side door and circled the throne, putting the scattered booklets into a basket and rearranging the pile at the Lord Paramount's side before creeping out once more. The Lord Paramount dropped the booklet from his lap onto the carpet and took the top one from the pile, leafing through it, marking the pages here and there. The Aresian mercenaries by the door continued their restless watch upon the room, raising their weapons briefly as the curtain behind the baldachin opened and Yugh Delganor slipped through to lean familiarly across the Lord Paramount's shoulder.

"So, do I invite the girl to join us all here at Havenor?"

The Lord Paramount smiled. "Give it a little time, Yugh. It isn't as though we're in a hurry, eh? Look at this animal, here. Like a sheep, only tiny. It's a kind of lapdog. I want one. Or several."

"As Your Majesty wishes."

"Ten of them, I think. That way I'll have replacements. They don't last long, pets. Such short lives. Better bring them in stasis. And look here, this admirable new type of rug weaving looms. I must have some of these."

Yugh Delganor scanned the booklet, bowing. "Your Majesty is no doubt correct."

"I'll have Krivel look at it. We may be non-technological, Yugh, but we have to keep up with things, ah?"

"Your Majesty can say nothing less than truth."

The Lord Paramount nodded, the pages flickering in his hands. "Let that young colonel look her over, the Marshal's daughter—look at this dinnerware! Quite marvelous—if you think she's all right and he's a suitable one to . . ."

"Oh, definitely. Very . . . puissant."

"Then he'll no doubt find her charming, despite the nose."

"She may have grown into it by now," the Prince interrupted.

"Despite the nose," repeated the Lord Paramount, an edge to his voice. This time Delganor did not interrupt him. "Then you can go down to her school or academy or whatever it is and invite her. If all goes well, we'll have you wed shortly. Your third wife, won't it be?"

"Fourth, Your Majesty."

"Pity. I remember your first wife. Charming girl. Look at this boiler arrangement, Delganor. Now that's innovative . . ."

The Prince did not reply. He merely bowed and departed, taking no notice of the Aresians who had measured his every movement and recorded his every word. The Prince was a source of much information to the intelligence people on Ares. They drew sustenance from every casual word uttered by the Prince. More than from the Lord Paramount, who spoke unequivocal nonsense most of the time.

After a time the lips of the guards curved in not-quite smiles at the slither of booklets spilling from the lap of the man on the throne, followed by a gentle but unmistakable snore.

"So, likely we'll be getting a new woman to flit about here for a while," said one, Ogberd by name, speaking barely above a whisper without moving his lips. "Destined for the Prince. Brother, it's interesting that they never stay long, do they?"

His brother, Lokdren, assented with an almost invisible nod. "Lady Marissa was the last young one, and none since she married Lord Tranquish. Lately I've felt like an attendant at a home for the aged, and by the Great Sportsman, it's a waste of time!"

"Shhh," hissed the other, with a quick glance at the throne, where the Lord Paramount had stirred slightly. "Aged or not, we are sworn to him, and as the universe knows, we Aresians never waver from our oath of service." His lips firmed as he said sententiously, "Faithful service is our pride. It says so in the Aresian security services prospectus."

The other actually did smile at this, a quick twitch of the lips, his eyes roving the room as they always did, taking note of every gentle movement of curtain, every shift of light, every sound that might presage a visitor. He stiffened slightly at a sound in the hallway outside the door, then relaxed at the familiar tramping of feet. Behind the two, the doors slid soundlessly open to admit the change of guard who eased into the places Ogberd and Lokdren silently vacated.

Outside in the corridor, Lokdren removed his helmet, wiped his brow, and continued the interrupted conversation, though softly. "I'm less concerned with what's in the prospectus than I am what's in our orders. We may be fulfilling the prospectus, but we're damned well not finding out what we came to find out!"

Ogberd's lips twitched. "We've learned a lot about rug weaving looms and chandeliers and wine-making equipment and miniature sheep, though, haven't we?"

Lokdren shook his head. "More than I care to know, frankly. Time is running out. Father's getting impatient. He sent another indignant message this morning. If we don't come up with something soon, he'll do something irrevocable."

"Do you care?" Ogberd shrugged.

His brother nodded back. "Haven's a nice enough little place. Some of the people are pleasant. I'd hate to see them in Father's hands, the mood he's in, put it that way. He won't stop at anything. I'm sure of it."

"Nonsense. Father's an honorable sportsman."

"Is he now? Are any of us? *Given the consequences if we don't find out?*"

"Given the consequences . . ." Ogberd sighed. "Damn. Well, I don't know. Given the consequences . . . I suppose even Father . . . well, I suppose even he could . . . do the unthinkable."

Lokdren thinned his lips and snarled. "Better start thinking about it, brother. Just so it won't be unthinkable, when it happens."